PERIL IN THE PARISH

PERIL IN
THE PARISH

Dorothy Cannell

SEVERN
HOUSE

First world edition published in Great Britain and the USA in 2022
by Severn House, an imprint of Canongate Books Ltd,
14 High Street, Edinburgh EH1 1TE.

Trade paperback edition first published in Great Britain and the USA in 2023
by Severn House, an imprint of Canongate Books Ltd.

severnhouse.com

British Library Cataloguing-in-Publication Data
A CIP catalogue record for this title is available from the British Library.

ISBN-13: 978-1-4483-0863-7 (cased)
ISBN-13: 978-1-4483-0992-4 (trade paper)
ISBN-13: 978-1-4483-0967-2 (e-book)

All Severn House titles are printed on acid-free paper.

MIX
Paper from
responsible sources
FSC FSC® C013056
www.fsc.org

Typeset by Palimpsest Book Production Ltd.,
Falkirk, Stirlingshire, Scotland.
Printed and bound in Great Britain by
TJ Books, Padstow, Cornwall.

To my friend Carole Brocksieck, for all the memories shared, the laughter and recalled wisdom of her mother Vera Barnes.

ACKNOWLEDGEMENTS

With thanks to John Burrows for his interest in the writing.

CAST OF CHARACTERS

Florence Norris: Housekeeper at Mullings, soon to marry George Bird.

George Bird: Proprietor of The Dog and Whistle pub, well liked in Dovecote Hatch.

Lord Edward (Ned) Stodmarsh: His family has lived at Mullings for generations. He is devoted to Florence because she had a great deal to do with bringing him up.

His maternal grandmother Mrs Tressler.

The Stranger: Shows up at the pub one foggy night with a tale of grief and evil.

Reverend Pimcrisp: Recently retired vicar of St Peter's Parrish.

Aiden Fielding: The new incumbent, more approachable than his predecessor.

Maude Fielding: His sister who has for many years kept house for him.

Sophie Dawson: Aged twenty-three, orphaned and brought up by an uncle, she arrives in Dovecote Hatch in hope of connecting with her mother's female cousin.

Henry Dawson: Sophie's uncle.

Agnes Younger: Now on her deathbed. For years she could only hobble about with difficulty following an accident.

Sally Barton: Takes a job as Sophie's maid and becomes her friend and protector.

Mr and Mrs Barton: Sally's parents. She is their only daughter, surrounded by a bevy of brothers.

Bernard Crawley: Bookkeeper at the estate agency where Sophie worked until coming to Dovecote Hatch.

Mrs Crawley: Views Sophie as a threat to her marriage and large family of young children.

Mrs Blount: Sophie's landlady prior to her embarking on a fresh start.

Nurse Newsome: Visiting nurse. Currently tending Agnes.

Una Smith: Her recently married daughter. A subject of gossip following her husband's abrupt departure from the village.

Bill Smith: Regarded by many as a bad lot.

Constable Trout: Usually spends much of his time helping children across the street and rescuing cats from trees.

Elsie Trout: His wife. A valued daily help at Mullings.

Inspector LeCrane: This is not his first professional visit to Dovecote Hatch.

Mrs MacDonald: Cook at Mullings and Florence's good friend.

Graham Lieland: Private secretary to Major Wainwright. A former airman badly burned in 1914-18 war.

Miss Gillybud: Viewed askance by devotees of Reverend Pimcrisp because of her lack of religious belief.

Mr Quigley: A Churchwarden, he is passionately interested in old rare books.

Lenore Quigley: His wife, a recluse.

Victoria Hobbs: Owns Hobbs Haberdashery with her nephew. She was a great admirer of Reverend Pimcrisp.

Gervaise Kaye: The Nephew. He does not like his aunt any more than she likes him.

Mercy Tenneson, young, beautiful and seeing a good deal of Lord Stodmarsh.

Dr Chester: Local GP

Mrs Chester: His wife. A former nurse.

Dick Saunders: The butcher's son. Helps out at The Dog and Whistle and is very taken with Sally Barton.

Alf Thatcher: Postman and George's closest friend.

Major Wainwright: Bluff and hearty, enjoys an evening at The Dog and Whistle.

Miss Milligan: Breeder of boxer dogs.

Lord Asprey: Reverend Pimcrisp's cousin and benefactor.

Mary Thomas: Worked with Sophie at estate agency.

Mr and Mrs Euwing: Agency owners.

Grumidge: Butler at Mullings.

Molly: His wife, head housemaid. Plan is for her to take over as housekeeper when Florence leaves to get married.

Winnie: Kitchen maid. Has a habit of interrupting conversations between Florence and Mrs MacDonald.

Dr Maitland: Uncle Henry's doctor.

Mr Kent: Uncle Henry's solicitor.

Mr and Mrs North: Verger and wife.

Fred Shilling: Grave digger.

Jeremiah Rudge: His predecessor, husband and father of Tim and Anne.

Rupert Trout: Schoolboy son of Constable and Elsie Trout.

Young Mrs Barton: One of Sally's sisters-in-law, is a waitress at the Spinning Wheel Café

ONE

'Twenty years ago, today I buried my sister,' said the stranger standing at the bar of the Dog and Whistle in the village of Dovecote Hatch.

'Sorry to hear that, sir.' The landlord, George Bird, known to his regulars as Birdie, was an affable, balding man of above six foot and expansive girth. He wore his fifty-odd years comfortably in the manner of a pair of well-stretched shoes. Having worked in pubs since he was a lad, several of them in the seedier neighbourhoods of London, he'd been made privy over time to a wide range of personal information. There'd been chilling disclosures from little old ladies you'd think wouldn't swat a fly and tales of domestic bliss coming from men who looked as though they'd just strangled someone for the amusement of it. All attentively heard out and engaged upon with genuine interest, but taken in his stride. Aware that often times it did to keep a container of salt at hand.

Ridiculous, therefore, the evocation – wrought from the words 'I buried my sister' – of a furtive figure hunched over a spade, a mound of earth to the side and a woman's corpse swathed as if for decency's sake in the gauze of time. George hoped this lapse hadn't shown on his face. He repeated his proffer of sympathy.

No answer from the stranger. His empty gaze suggested he'd retreated inside himself and closed the door. Was he even aware he'd spoken? George picked up a white cloth and needlessly buffed a glass, waiting as though he had all the time in the world to listen, which was in fact the case that evening.

'Such anniversaries can be hard. Help to talk about it?'

Still no response. Nothing stirring on that parchment-pale, hollowed-out face.

Could hear dust settle, thought George.

Only the two were present in what the locals still called the taproom despite this being 1933, not back in the seventeenth century when the pub had been a coaching inn. Although a stark way of putting it, George mused, the man's choice of phrase was common enough in referencing a funeral. Must be his intonation that had stirred up that grim image suggesting he'd spoken literally. The words had been uttered softly, almost in a whisper, accompanied by that blank-eyed stare and the palms of the hands pressed together.

As George polished another already gleaming glass he remembered an evening spent at the pictures a couple of months back with his increasingly successful artist godson Jim. The film they'd seen had included a grainy scene depicting a penitent in a Roman Catholic confessional. A man seeking absolution from the silhouette behind the grill. 'Father forgive me for my sins. I can't remember when I made my last confession. I'm the man the police have been searching for in connection with the disappearance of that young woman last seen walking on the heath . . .'

George refocused on the moment at hand. His offer of a different drink to replace the still untouched whisky brought not so much as a twitch of the stranger's lips. Well, like was often said, human nature's a funny old business. George had learned long ago that a customer, whether a regular or one coming through the door for the first time, could embark on a revelation and the next instant regret having spoken and clamp his or her mouth shut. That allowed, it was becoming ever more difficult to persuade himself there was nothing unduly odd about the stranger's behaviour, or to push back on the thought that here might be a man with something dire on his conscience.

The clock on a shelf behind the bar ticked into the silence. What within the course of ordinary life experience might hold the man in its grip? Embarrassment – warring with the need to confide in someone – anyone – the tender emotions that had come flooding back on this anniversary date? Understandable contrition he'd believed could only be eased by bringing the matter into the open? Remorse at not having dearly loved the departed as nature demanded of a brother? Regret at not having been present at the death? Shame at having rejoiced in receiving an inheritance?

George could readily sympathize with the guilt-ridden in the aftermath of death. He'd blamed himself long and sorrowfully for refusing to acknowledge until close to the end that his late wife wouldn't pull round from what the doctor had downplayed as woman's troubles – a difficult change. Aware of the truth as she must have been, but knowing her husband of twenty-five years wasn't ready to face it with her must have made those final months of her life the loneliest of journeys.

Buried my sister. Just a turn of phrase as George had acknowledged. Why, despite his efforts to resist the sinister did the words seem to linger dankly in the air as if disinterred after having also lain two decades in the grave? Why did the stranger's eyes, a dark brown, bring newly turned damp earth back to mind? Why did George feel a shivery pity for an unknown woman? Those who knew him would have been amazed that he was allowing his imagination to lead him down dark alleyways. He didn't think of himself as the sort to leap to unpleasant conclusions. The fact that his life had fairly recently been impacted by murder did not rear up as an excuse. Present happiness, his upcoming marriage to Florence Norris, housekeeper at Mullings, the great house of the district, the woman he had come to love in a way he'd have thought impossible on becoming a widower, had placed that encounter with evil squarely behind him.

He told himself his continued overreaction to the man's statement must result from its having been dropped into an otherwise hushed atmosphere. Blame the lack of background conversations, laughter and movement, drifts of cigarette and pipe smoke. for the notion that he might at any moment be made privy to something more dreadful than he'd heard from a dozen degenerates.

TWO

It was now nine o'clock on an evening in mid-March. Dovecote Hatch was set in hilly country and the village street inclined upward to where the Dog and Whistle was set at the top of a rise. Some twenty minutes earlier the cobweb mist that had dimmed the valley below for much of the afternoon had thickened into a rapidly rising fog. This had created a rare occurrence for such an hour at the Dog and Whistle, especially of a Friday when business was always particularly brisk.

The taproom had rapidly emptied of customers. Cut short was the usual talk about local life: Miss Milligan's new litter of boxer puppies; the progress Major Wainwright was making on the second volume of his memoirs with the invaluable assistance of his secretary; the unlikelihood that Miss Agnes Younger would last much longer following her second stroke in three months.

Even the staunchest of the regulars had not dallied in making for the door when the light from the streetlamp beyond the window blurred to a watery yellow smudge producing the palest of haloes. To a man and woman they'd the country person's respect for the grey deceiver. Home and hearth beckoned as they would not have done in a torrential storm or even a blizzard. There was something about a world blanketed in damp wool that did things to the inside of your head.

'Fuddles you up so's you don't know whether you be coming or going, or why it matters,' is how a farm worker had put it.

Even Alf Thatcher, the long-time postman who'd been heard to declare time out of mind, that he could get around the village blindfold, didn't give a downward glance at the two inches of bitter remaining in his glass.

'Call me superstitious, Birdie, but it don't do to thumb your nose at old Mother Nature. It's nothing for her to shift whole streets around, put trees where they shouldn't be and make steps that has always gone up go down instead. Show the old girl proper respect and mayhap she'll clear this one by morning. Doesn't feel like a stay out to me.'

Alf was George's closest friend in Dovecote Hatch and an all-round decent bloke. No surprise that he offered to walk a couple of elderly men, somewhat tottery on their feet, to their doors, before proceeding to his own home and wife Doris. Major Wainwright, gruff but courtly, had made a similar offer to two nervous women, leaving his pipe behind in the general haste. Undoubtedly, he would be irritated with himself for this lapse, but he would have a regiment of pipes waiting in formation at home.

Left to himself George had set about the business of clearing up, washing and drying glasses and tankards, emptying ashtrays and wiping off tables. For such a large man he moved lightly. In contrast to the muffled world outside, the taproom seemed even cheerier than usual.

A log fire burned ruby red in the hearth, scattering gleams upon the patina-mellowed plaster walls, the blackened oak ceiling beams and narrow latticed windows, and further burnishing the already bright horse brasses and copper utensils on the mantelpiece.

It was not, however, only his surroundings that warmed George's heart. At two o'clock the following afternoon he and Florence had an appointment with the vicar to set their wedding date – hopefully for the last Saturday in June. Their acquaintance with Mr Fielding was limited to having spoken with him briefly either going in or out of church on the past four Sundays. This narrow period wasn't because they'd never darkened the doors of St Peter's previously; it was because Reverend Fielding had only arrived as the replacement for the seventy-odd, long-time incumbent in mid-February.

That Mr Fielding was reasonably young, approaching forty at most, was viewed favourably by the majority of parishioners. That he was above average height and good looking in a rugged way did not in general go against him either. A couple of the ladies from the Altar Guild had expressed mild dissatisfaction with his beard, albeit a neatly trimmed one. What might be acceptable in another line of work was not in their view entirely suited to a man of the cloth. One would prefer one's vicar to display an entirely open face to the world so as not to give the likes of Miss Gillybud, an atheist and not one whit ashamed of it, the chance to suggest he had a weak chin to hide. Nonsense given those broad shoulders, but one could not expect the godless to refrain from venting their spite.

Mr Fielding's unmarried state had brought mixed emotions – hope on the part of mothers with marriageable daughters beyond their first youth and regret by others that there wasn't at long last to be a vicar's wife to organize the Mothers' Union and host teas on the vicarage lawn. There was, admittedly, a sister who'd come to keep house for him. It was to be hoped she'd apply herself selflessly to such activities.

It was with Miss Fielding that George had spoken when telephoning in regard to his and Florence's wish to set the wedding date. She had sounded a bit of a dragon, but might justly see that as her allotted role – guardian of her brother's calendar from unnecessary intrusions. It was of no matter to George if she breathed fire or had a beard like her brother. Such details did not interest him. He and Florence had not hastened into marriage; he had understood her wish to wait until Molly, the head housemaid at Mullings and now married to Grumidge the butler, was confident of being able to take over as housekeeper. Florence's loyalty to the Stodmarsh family ran deep.

The late Lord Edward Stodmarsh had treated her with great kindness, encouraging her from her days as a young kitchen maid to educate herself by making free of his library, reading whatever books caught her interest. Shortly after she'd returned to Mullings as a war widow and became housekeeper, he'd escorted her to see an early Bible, gifted, several years earlier, to St Peter's by Lord Asprey, Reverend Pimcrisp's cousin, and friend of Lord Stodmarsh. He had known she would not only delight in viewing it, but also learning its history from Mr Quigley, churchwarden and bibliophile.

Even more importantly for the bond was that Florence had been deeply involved in the upbringing of Lord and Lady Stodmarsh's grandson, also named Edward. Having come into the title at seventeen and now in his early twenties he remained devoted to her. Insisting she continue to call him Ned. This she did, although only in private. As a boy he had sulkily resented George for wishing to take Florence away from Mullings. Now he wanted the happiness of both and when told of the engagement proclaimed it was his dearest wish to walk her down the aisle without further delay.

Greatly appreciated by those of St Peter's parishioners, who found the pews hard on their 'rheumaticky' backs, liked to get home to their roast beef and Yorkshire pudding on time, or enjoy more courting time on their day off, was that Mr Fielding had so far kept his sermons short and to the point. His focus being on the blessings bestowed by the Almighty and the abundant opportunities provided each day for performance of good deeds, however small, instead of a hammering on and on about Sin and the Awful Price to be paid on Judgement Day by all but the few.

George and Florence shared the frequently voiced hope that Mr Fielding would in additional ways bring a breath of fresh air to disperse the odor of fire and brimstone the old gentleman had left behind him.

'Never could stomach that old plaster saint. Made one feel damned low,' Major Wainwright had rumbled over his tankard of ale that evening before the fog took everyone off home. 'Would come away from church thinking Dovecote Hatch could only be saved from becoming another Sodom or Gomorrah by constant vigilance against the snares of the devil. Always at your shoulder, ready to get his pitchfork into you for taking a seat at the bridge table or queuing up for sausages in the butcher's shop instead of subsisting on gruel.'

'Pity for him he wasn't an RC priest,' came a voice from the back. 'Just think how he'd have rubbed his hands at all he got to hear in the confessional.'

George wasn't so sure. Remembering his recent evening at the cinema with godson, Jim, he wondered if Pimcrisp, with the voice of a killer breathing through the grill, might not have passed out cold. It's one thing to battle evil with words, another to meeting face to face at your own possible physical peril.

'Sins of the flesh,' barked Miss Milligan, 'always his favourite rant from the pulpit. Impure thoughts and such like sanctimonious piffle. Comes from a nasty mind. Impure thoughts! Made me, a bred in the bone old maid, yearn just this Christmas time to be kissed breathless under the mistletoe by the first man through the door.'

'Ooh! You are a one, miss,' piped up young and pretty Sally Barton with a giggle. 'I wouldn't half have liked to hear the earful the old sour puss would have given you if he'd got wind of that.'

'Certainly made heaven sound the size of a telephone box that only God himself and a couple of his closest friends could squeeze into,' said the headmaster of the village school. 'But let's be charitable and suppose he was trying to do right according to his beliefs.'

'More like bloke was right round the bend,' wheezed an old codger.

There was that, thought George. He might have felt obliged to add something, however meagre, in defence of Pimcrisp, had he not remembered what Constable Trout had told him several years prior.

'Started noticing, Birdie, that some of the little lads and girls was avoiding me, some even scuttling round the corner when they saw me coming. Them the same ones that before'd run up to me to tell me their cat had a new litter of kittens, their mum had washed their toy rabbit and shrunk it, or it was their birthday next week. Couldn't figure out the change till I talked to our Rupert about it and he told me Pimcrisp been going on at Sunday school about stealing. How pinching a currant out of a bun at the baker's, let alone stealing a stick of liquorice from the sweetshop, could get you locked up till you were a hundred. And how a lot of policemen all over England believed the proper punishment for thievery was what they used to do poachers. Cut off one hand the first time and the other if they did it again.'

George wiped his hands on the cloth and reached for a fresh one.

Sally giggled again. 'I'd sit in the pew of a Sunday thinking he's enough to make you want to do something really naughty and get your name in the papers, just couldn't make up my mind if it'd be for stealing a pair of stockings or running off to go on the stage, like old sexton's daughter did way back.'

'Whoever told you that got the wrong end of the stick.' The

headmaster took the pint of bitter George handed him. 'Left home to go into service, like hundreds of other girls. Not a juicy enough story for those fuelled by Pimcrisp, to look for the worst and if it wasn't there to make it up.'

'Well, now he's gone, let's forget him,' said George's friend Alf Thatcher, peaceably. 'He can't do any more harm.'

'Trouble is he's not just left some of us the worse for moral wear, he's still sowing misery.' Major Wainwright scrubbed irritably at his moustache. 'There's that poor Miss Hobbs, my housekeeper's been telling me about the state she's got herself into the last weeks.'

This was the owner, along with her nephew, of Hobbs' Haberdashery four doors down from the pub. She lived above the shop, a confining life, added the major, which in his housekeeper's opinions might have contributed to the nervous breakdown she'd suffered following Mr Pimcrisp's departure. Someone brought up that she remained under the care of Dr Chester. There'd been talk of attempted suicide from an over-dose of sleeping pills, accompanied by a note stating she could not face life's continuance now that he who had held the devil at bay was gone.

'The poor dear,' said Mrs Saunders the butcher's wife. 'It's bad enough to be disappointed in love, but when you've let it be known you're expecting a proposal any day and the next thing you know your sister is engaged to the man in question, well that's a hard pill to swallow. And never the chance to get over it, as she might have done if she'd not had to see him again. So, I'm not surprised she turned odd one way or another.'

'Sad,' agreed Sally. 'Could've gone on pining for him year after year, even hoping he'd clutch her in his arms one day, and tell her he'd made a terrible mistake and wished he could turn back the clock and find himself married to her. His one true love. Or she'd feel wicked about it.'

'I had an aunt,' said a Mr Howard, 'that was left at the altar and the way it took her she turned into a kleptomaniac. You couldn't put your fork down without her getting it into her pocket. Better, I suppose, for Miss Hobbs to go batty about the devil and his clutches.'

'It's not like the rest of us are expecting the new vicar will turn services into jolly occasions like picnics or outings to fairgrounds,' said Mrs Saunders. 'I've no objection to a bit of tut-tutting from the pulpit. For those as needs it. My hubby, for all you'd think he'd be passed it at sixty, can still do with reminding of a Sunday to keep his mind on business when a pretty young woman comes into the shop.' She chucked comfortably, with a wink at Sally Barton. 'Particularly the fair-haired, well-rounded sort that looks as though butter wouldn't melt in their mouths.'

At which Sally, who fitted this description, gave one of her giggles.

It was about then that a growing awareness of the deepening fog brought about the uneasy stirring that erupted into the surge for hearth and home.

Ah, well, George mused, some half hour later, while continuing his solitary tidying of the taproom, it'd be nice if the new vicar proved to be a decent bloke of the sort to pour healing balm on troubled breasts. But as of the moment what counted most was Mr Fielding's ability to perform the marriage service without making a muddle of it. The Reverend Pimcrisp had become increasingly incoherent towards the end of his tenure. George, picturing Florence coming down the aisle towards him, wished the old man a healthful retirement on the estate of his cousin, Lord Asprey.

An idea glowed into being. He'd ask if the Bible presented to St Peter's by that benevolent nobleman could be on display following the service. It would mean a lot to Florence. A reminder of the day Lord Stodmarsh took her to see it and they returned to Mullings companionably discussing its history as recounted to them by Mr Quigley the churchwarden. Smiling, George placed Major Wainwright's pipe on a shelf behind the bar.

A moment later the street door opened and the stranger walked into the Dog and Whistle.

THREE

His age appeared to be in the late thirties to early forties. No hat or cap. Dark hair springing back from a high pale forehead, shaggy at the neck and sides suggesting it was weeks overdue for a cut. Not one of the well-to-do from the look of his coat. It was of the sort to be seen going up or down a working class street any day of the week. Rough-spun and of indifferent tailoring. It was also at least two sizes too large.

Other than to ask for a whisky he made no reply to George's greeting and accompanying observation that it was a nasty night to be out. It wasn't until he'd taken several sips from the glass set down in front of him that he uttered those words: 'Twenty years ago today I buried my sister.'

'Sorry to hear that, sir.'

Then the silence . . .

For George there had followed that excursion into the realm of melodrama. Hard upon a return to common sense came shame. His focus should have been otherwise. The man looked exhausted . . . worn out . . . done in, the shadows under his eyes intensifying his facial pallor. He could be ill – the oversized coat accounted for by a recent dramatic loss of weight.

'Here's to happier times,' he said, hoping his voice offered the right amount of sympathy; anything verging on hearty would sound false.

'Yes.' The stranger finally released his hands from their prayerful palming and sat tapping the whisky glass with two fingers.

'How about I get you something to eat on the house? No bother at all to fix you a ham or roast beef sandwich.'

The merest sideways twitch of the head.

'Staying around here, or just passing through?'

No response, other than an intensifying of the fixed stare.

The renewed silence thickened as if weaving itself out of

strands of fog drawn in through a gapped window frame. George waited before saying anything further. A belated thought came as he again unnecessarily polished a glass.

Did the man's appearance result not from fatigue or illness, but from his having fallen on hard times after losing his job? Weeks . . . months of never knowing where the next meal was coming from, or how long he could keep a roof over his head – if he wasn't without one already. Had the overly large coat been purchased second-hand when the previous one deteriorated to the point of making him look like a tramp?

Sadly such men were an all too familiar sight up and down England these days on account of vast numbers of the un-employed – stripped not only of flesh, but seemingly their life's blood. Fortunately there wasn't much of that around Dovecote Hatch where there had been, and still was, a need to replace farm workers and other manual laborers killed or injured in the Great War. Besides which the Stodmarsh family, now represented by the young Lord Stodmarsh, continued to take care of those in need as they had through the centuries. It was city people, in particular, former factory workers, as George understood it, who'd been driven by the droves into desperate poverty.

And here was a man on route to a nearby town where he'd heard there might be the possibility of a job. George put all ghoulish nonsense out of his head and decided to offer him a room for the night.

The stranger raised his head. The dark brown eyes bored holes in the parchment face.

'Was middle of the night with the wind a' blowing when we laid her in the ground.'

'Night?' George had the peculiar sensation that the words reverberated back at him from every nook and cranny of every room from cellar to attic, that the clock ticked at a fevered pace and a chill, damp wind slid down his back.

What came next did nothing to brighten the mood. 'Can still feel the spade in my hands, smell rain on the way, hear the groaning trees and my heart pounding for fear of being spotted before getting her safe underground.'

George poured himself a whiskey. Slow swallow before

raising the glass to his lips. There it was; despite all his attempts at holding hard to common sense he had from the start been right in bracing himself for something dark and dreadful. A log splintering apart in the grate contributed to the impact of the shattering revelation. That it was bound to a time twenty years in the past was of no matter. This man had come into the Dog and Whistle with a deranged need to unburden his soul. Having done so would he linger or vanish back into the night?

And yet . . . George floundered, should he cast off all compassion? Mr Pimcrisp would have believed so, that here was the wickedest of the wicked ripe for the burning. But what would be the thinking of Mr Fielding? Would he quote: 'All have sinned and fallen short of the glory of God'? More importantly what would Florence think – beyond wishing the man anywhere but alone with George on a foggy night? Had the man acted while in his right mind? If not, was it actual murder?

That overlarge coat! Again George's usually unlively imagination was off and running. Could its wearer have plucked it at random from a row of pegs prior to escaping from Broadmoor or some other asylum for the criminally insane? Might that pallor coupled with his being severely underweight plausibly be due to meagre portions of wretched food and lack of access to sunlight? Was he presently intent on celebrating his freedom by killing again?

Don't go down that road, George told himself. Maintain a calm interested manner. Do nothing to arouse rage. That's what Florence would do, but not merely out of self-preservation. She'd want to hear the whole story, to understand its beginning and end, and to strive for some words of kindness to ease the suffering of a fellow human being.

George watched the man finally down his heretofore untouched whisky.

'Had you and your sister never got along, or was there an unusually violent argument that day?'

The stranger was suddenly reinvigorated to startling effect. He jerked backward, had to grab for the edge of the bar to keep from falling.

'What drove you to it?'

'You think I killed her!' he exclaimed. If he wasn't completely bewildered he had to be one of England's finest actors. Released from its monotone his voice hinted at the cockney overlapping a country dialect.

'Well,' began George feeling some of the tension seep out of him, 'that's the way I was leaning.' With life returned to his face the man looked younger than he'd formerly appeared. 'What did happen . . . how did she die?'

A ragged breath. A tightening grip on the bar edge. 'She took her own life. Slashed her wrists. Ma had waked round about midnight feeling cold and gone down to refill her hot water bottle. She screamed up the stairs. Our dear one was lying in the old tin bath in the kitchen. Pa'd brought it in from the shed of a Friday night for her. Always had her bath of a Friday. Liked to wait till round nine o'clock after us three was up to bed. The water was red with blood.'

'Terrible.' How inadequate that sounded. 'How old was she?'

'Seventeen.'

'And you?'

'Thirteen.'

'A child.'

He caught George's eye. 'Not after that night I wasn't. Know it can't go down easy giving me the benefit, if I've got you to thinking I'm a wrong 'un, or out of my head. I could be lying about not killing her. Children's been known to do monstrous wicked things including murder. There were that eight-year-old girl in Scotland a few years back that cut her baby brother's throat and smeared her face with his blood saying as how she'd always wanted to have rosy cheeks.'

'Who'd forget?' George poured the man another whisky and one for himself. He was still readjusting his thinking.

The man picked up his glass and took a sip. 'Sorry to have put the wind up you. It's like this, see, I've been bracing meself for days to come and explain matters to you, and today I was blessed to get a lift in my parish priest's car. He's been a good friend to me and the wife; but soon as I started to tell you about it, with this being the anniversary, I was right back there in all that grief and horror. Out come the words in the wrong places. Front to back.'

George had rarely felt more at a loss. He fixed on the man

being a Roman Catholic with his own father confessor to hand. 'You wanted to talk to me?'

'That'd be the way of it.'

'Not just any happenstance person?'

'Had to be you is how I saw it.' The dark-brown eyes were now focused to the point of intensity.

'Why? You don't know me from Adam.'

'T'was because of the Mullings' murder being all over the newspapers and on the wireless a couple of years back. Hit you close, didn't it? Your godson being a suspect till the identity of the killer come out.'

Jim! It was he who'd been to see that film with George. The one with the fugitive and the priest.

'That said to me you knows what it's like to be afraid of an innocent person getting strung up for what he never done. And then – if once wasn't bad enough – friends of yours, Alf Thatcher – the postman and his wife, was drawn into the nastiness which followed another suspicious death.'

It was George's turn to be silent. What had happened at Mullings was now several years in the past, but a few months previously a wealthy man named Kenneth Tenneson had died as a result of falling down the staircase at his home Bogmire House, a grim looking edifice built of dark stone ensnared within a wildly overgrown garden. Just the sort of place, it had been long said, where a murder might be expected to take place. When Tenneson's will was read Doris Thatcher, seemingly unconnected to him, was revealed as the major beneficiary under his recently made will, raising questions as to whether his death had been accidental.

'You're right,' said George, 'I do understand how it is when someone is wrongfully suspected of a serious crime. But, dreadfully sorry as I am for your tragedy, I don't know how that can help you. Or what brings you here now. Unless . . .' He paused as the obvious hit him. 'You've reason to fear your sister's body is about to be discovered.'

The man became completely still. 'Can only thank God my parents are dead and saved from it. They was plain, decent folk, that never asked for much in life outside of family. Here's where you fit in should you be so good, Mr Bird, you've got the ear of Inspector LeCrane that was brought in by the local police to handle both cases. It were all over the radio and newspapers about him giving credit for solving the Mullings Murder to a Mrs Norris – as is housekeeper there.'

'So he did.'

'He'll be grateful to her and sorry for what you and your nephew went through and put himself out to sort things out, easy like.'

George eyed him thoughtfully. The Tenneson murder, unlike the earlier one at Mullings, hadn't received anything near national attention. So how had word of it reached the man if not from a local source? He'd mentioned Alf Thatcher. Knew him to be the village postman. Also he seemed to be linking Florence closely with George, a relationship that had been private until very recently.

'I did think first of going to Mrs Norris for help with the inspector. But that would've meant me showing up at Mullings and risking her being asked questions about who I was and why I'd come. Could've been awkward for her. Besides I was brought up to believe a woman is to be sheltered.'

George didn't interrupt to say experience had taught him women were capable of shouldering burdens that would fell many a strong man. That was true of his late wife and Florence.

'So when I heard you and her was getting married and how you're a decent bloke, not pushing and prying into people's business, but always ready to hear someone out, this seemed the best way – asking you to be my messenger to LeCrane.'

'It's clear to me,' said George, 'you've had to be in touch with someone living close by – if not in Dovecote Hatch itself.'

The dark eyes met his squarely. 'Wasn't trying to pull the wool over you about that. But I can't tell you who. Wouldn't be fair. What comes out down the road's different.'

'Or give me your name?'

'You'll know it 'fore too long.'

George knew when it was pointless to press further. 'Is this other person someone from your past?'

'There's them that knows what's owed.'

'You're local . . . born and bred.' It wasn't a question. Dovecote Hatch or a neighbouring village was in the man's voice pushing up against the cockney. He started to say more, but George continued. 'Making it more than likely your sister's body is buried close by? Weren't you worried in coming here of being recognized? But for the fog this place would have been packed.'

'I've been gone years, but I wasn't for taking unnecessary risks, I'd planned on waiting till after closing time and knocking on the side door.' Something of the shuttered look returned to the man's eyes. 'That night the parents and me thought her safe from ever being found. Leastways we made ourselves believe that would be the way of it.'

George refilled his other's glass.

'At first Ma was like one gone mad. Screaming and throwing herself about, thrusting Pa and me away when we tried to get to her. When she stilled it was horrible to see her wringing her poor arthritic hands. "Why? Why?", she kept crying. Whatever the trouble she could've come to me. I'd have seen her through.'

George's hand tightened on the cloth he was holding.

'Then suddenly she went still as if the life had drained out of her too – staring down at the knife . . . dark with blood . . . she'd picked it up off the floor. "Vicar won't let her be buried in the churchyard and then he'll give one of his fierce sermons about her, how she'll burn in hell for ever. I won't see her shamed like that, not my dear, good girl. We'll say she's gone away. Girls are always leaving – off to towns to find jobs where the money's better."'

George could see the images, hear the broken voice, hear the echoes of a mother's anguish. Had it crossed her mind her daughter might have discovered she was going to have a child?

'Pa lifted her out the bath. She was wearing her nightgown; she wouldn't have let herself be found with nothing on. Modest. Ma dried her and put her in a fresh one, while Pa and me dressed and decided how it would be done.'

'Why don't we go and sit by the fire, you look ready to drop.'

'Thank you, but I can't stay but a mite longer. We didn't know that night why she'd done it. Thought could've been she'd got her heart broken by the fellow she'd been walking out with the past few months – that he'd broken things off; he was in a different class and it wouldn't have done, but next morning I found the letters.'

'Explaining why she couldn't go on?'

'Weren't none of them from her. Wicked, unsigned ones they was, saying she was no better than Jezebel and such women in the Bible as caused good men to sin. Like I said, she was modest, shy, some might've said a bit prim. That's what made it so particular cruel. I never showed them to Ma or Pa; Pa wouldn't have rested till he found out who sent them and then there'd've been a murder, but I held on to them. They came to think her heart were broke over the lad.'

'Thinking they might be needed just in case your sister didn't continue to lie undisturbed?'

'Not that; like I said we didn't worry on that score. Not first we didn't for some time and then we got used to pushing it out of mind. It was that she'd left them letters for me to find. It was like a special trust. Must have put them under my pillow after I went to sleep – likely the last thing she did before getting into the bath and . . .'

'Don't put yourself through any more remembering,' said George quickly. He thought for a few moments before continuing. 'It seems to me you're unnecessarily prolonging anxiety by not going straight to Inspector LeCrane with your story. You'll find him a reasonable man, willing to hear you out without any backing from me; although I'd go with you if it would make you feel more confident.'

'Not the time,' came the reply. 'I have to think of the wife. She's had a difficult way of it lately. Our four-year-old son got hit by a car around Christmas time, only come out of hospital a fortnight ago, and then there's the baby keeping her up nights, and if that weren't enough her father that lived with us after her brother went out to Canada died early February. Ever so close they was. This is his coat I'm wearing.' The man rubbed the front of it. 'Says she couldn't bear to throw it out, that just seeing me in it brings him back. Twice the size of me he were. No, I can't fetch this trouble down on her, right now.' There was a gleam of tears in his eyes.

Sometimes listening was the best answer.

'She deserves the chance to look forward – to a better life

with me in a proper job again instead of just filling in for the window washer when he needs extra help. The place where I worked got into financial difficulties and closed down and it's not easy finding anything in my line.'

'So where does that bring us?' George asked.

The man dug into his coat pocket and pulled out an envelope and gave it to him. There was nothing written on the outside. 'Like I said, my sister left the truth for my hands to pick up. At the time I was too young to know what to do it with it. And there was Ma and Pa to be spared. When the time comes – and you'll know it – I'd be obliged if you'd take that to the Inspector LeCrane.'

The envelope was no bulkier than one from Godson Jim, whose letters always went into several pages; but it weighed heavy in George's hand.

'Inside's the anonymous letters sent to my sister, the one she left for me and one signed by me and Ma and Pa about what we did. Didn't I say you'd get to know all about it afore long? I'm hoping the inspector'll think it right to leave me and my family to get on with our lives in peace. What the police needs to do is hunt down the writer of those letters and bring him or her to justice.'

George hesitated. He could hand the envelope back, or commit himself to doing as asked. He got no further in his thoughts as the outside door opened revealing a rectangle of fog through which emerged a form with a face that to the stranger, from his startled gasp, must have seemed scarcely human. George's reaction was one of pity, not alarm. He recognized Graham Lieland, Major Wainwright's secretary, tragically disfigured by burns suffered when the plane he flew during the war caught on fire.

Mr Lieland's glance ignored the stranger. 'Good evening, Mr Bird,' he said in his cultured voice. 'I've come for the major's pipe that he left behind. It's his favourite and he'd like to take it with him when he leaves tomorrow on a visit to friends.'

'I have it here, sir.' George turned to lift the pipe from the shelf where he'd put it. When he again turned back to face the room, the envelope was on the bar and the stranger had vanished, as if he – not the secretary – were an apparition woven out of the fog.

FOUR

S ophie Dawson was not clairvoyant. She, therefore, had no psychic glimmering, no prickling of the spine, no inner stirring as of a veil lifting on the night George Bird had his encounter with the stranger at the Dog and Whistle. Nothing to alert her that inexorable forces were at work. Ones which were about to entwine her in an unfolding drama set in the small world that was Dovecote Hatch.

She had slept soundly on the Friday night. At eight o'clock the following morning she, occupant of a bed-sitting room on the upper floor of a narrow Victorian house that opened directly on to the pavement in Ilford, Essex, was almost ready to set off to her job as a typist at an estate agency. Working a half day on Saturdays was not something she minded. Unlike many twenty-three-year-olds she did not dream of an exciting life with lots of free time in which to do only as she pleased, instead she felt fortunate in having a roof over her head in a street which whilst dreary was not frequented by unsavory characters. Something she had feared might be the case given how little she could afford to pay in rent.

As it was she usually managed to set aside a few shillings a week for a rainy day. Ilford was close enough to London for her to have gone there on a Saturday afternoon to take a look at Westminster Abbey, the Houses of Parliament or visit one of the art museums, but she had always hesitated to spend the train fare. Miss Thomas, the young woman with whom she worked – smartly modern, with an engagement ring on her finger – clearly viewed her as depressingly frugal and hopelessly dull, knitting or reading away her evenings. Sophie, however, would have thought it self-centered to be discontented with her lot. Only occasionally did the thought creep in that she was started on the way to spinster-hood. A husband and family would be nice, but she did not see this as a likely possibility. Always shy she became embarrassingly stilted or mute in the presence of young men.

Slipping on her grey costume jacket over a white cotton blouse with a Peter Pan collar, she wasted no time sizing up her appearance in the wardrobe mirror. She had never thought herself anything out of the ordinary when it came to looks. In this she failed to do herself justice. She was of medium height and had what her landlady, Mrs Blount, called a proper figure with a bust, hips and small waist, in welcome contrast to the beanpole look that seemed to be all the fashion these days. With her oval face, hazel eyes and softly waving fair hair she was a pretty girl. Not startlingly so, to the point of beauty, according to Mrs Blount's opinion, but of the English rose sort. Mary Thomas would have thought much the same. Really the girl needed a shaking. If the girl had been plain there'd have been an excuse for never going to dances or parties where she would be bound to meet some young man eager to court her.

Sophie had moved in as one of Mrs Blount's 'lady lodgers' three years previously on leaving Oglesby, a village near Brighton. There, following the deaths of both parents from diphtheria when she was six, she had been brought up by an elderly uncle, her father's considerably older brother. Uncle Henry had provided her with a good education and seen that she was well-clothed. When she was ten he had agreed to her request for a cat, acknowledging it would be company for her, had taught her to play the piano and taken her with him to the library on Saturday afternoons. But it had never occurred to him that she might benefit from spending time with young people, particularly after she left school. It was in the aftermath of his death, following an extended illness, that she'd seen the advertisement in a national newspaper for a typist at an estate agency in Ilford.

There had been no possibility of remaining in her old home. It was heavily mortgaged and had to be sold. Uncle Henry had left no debts, beyond household bills, but as his solicitor explained to Sophie, the best she could hope for by way of a legacy would not amount to a hundred pounds. Mr Kent had been greatly distressed on imparting this news. He was one of Uncle's few friends as was Dr Maitland. Both were middle-aged men with daughters of their own and they could not have treated her more kindly, commending her devotion as a niece, her sweet nature, her serenity and courage in facing such an uncertain future.

Regrettably, this praise, coupled by gestures of affection, an arm around her shoulders, a clasping of her hands, had made her a little uncomfortable. She was unused to compliments and Uncle Henry had never been demonstrative; but that did not excuse her ingratitude. That wretched shyness of hers! So foolish when she had always previously been at ease with Mr Kent and Dr Maitland. Had appreciated that they seemed to enjoy talking to her about their lives including mundane trials and tribulations. To which she had responded with reminders of how much good they did and how well people thought of them. What made her reaction to their present kindness worse was that both men had urged her not to feel compelled to leave Oglesby, offering – independent of each other – to help her find a house or cottage to lease and promising help with expenditures.

Sophie had assured them of her wish to make a fresh start. She would have the hundred pounds and a means of supporting herself. This optimistic belief came from having taught herself to type. She had put up a note in the village shop inquiring if anyone had an old typewriter they no longer used. A few days later a middle-aged woman had arrived with one, announcing she was the vicar's sister, and the machine had been donated at a charity function. Upon handing it over she had cut short Sophie's expressions of gratitude by proffering the suggestion that when not clattering away on the keys, as would be required on a regular and rigorous basis, she might give thought to attending church once in a while.

The move to even a medium-sized town hadn't appealed to Sophie. Her preference would have been somewhere small; but the one remaining relative she knew of, a female cousin of her mother living in a country village, had returned a cool reply to her letter written on Uncle Henry's death. Sophie's hope had been an invitation to visit for a week or so, providing the opportunity to look around for work, even if it meant going into service. She knew, without knowing how she knew, that there was a great house in the district with lots of staff wearing smart uniforms. Perhaps Cousin Agnes thought she was angling to be taken in for an extended stay and been made very uncomfortable. The idea brought a painful flush to Sophie's face.

In the end the only job she was offered was the one at the estate agency in Ilford. Once settled at Mrs Blount's she had sent Cousin Agnes a brief, but cheerful letter, focused on how much she enjoyed the proximity to London. When saying goodbye to Mr Kent and Dr Maitland she had promised to stay in touch. Something she should have done, but had put off, thinking she'd wait until she was sufficiently settled to have something interesting to write about; but when the weeks in Ilford stretched into months it began to seem too late.

It had been the same with starting to go to church; she had meant to do so when still in Oglesby; she knew she should, in the hope that a belief in God would turn her into a warmer hearted person. It might also be a way of feeling closer in memory to her parents. She had a vivid memory of them taking her at night to a Christmas service. A place that smelled like mouldy potatoes, too many people and candlelight trying to be bigger than the dark.

Uncle Henry did not hold with church, but when it became clear he was not long for this world, someone must have requested the vicar go round and see him. Sophie suspected this was Dr Maitland's wife who was of an organizing bent. Admittance only occurred because Sophie refused to throw a jug of water over the man to get him out of the damned house; but she could tell from the muffled tone of Uncle Henry's grumbling that he was not averse to having him come again. The visits continued a couple of times a week for over a month. These were heartening interludes in that bleak stretch of time. The vicar's amused acceptance when informed religion was a load of Tommy rot, his moving his chair closer to Uncle Henry's so he could listen attentively to some wandering tale that stalled during moments of dozing, his coming up with anecdotes connected to Uncle's interest in geography and maps. Strange, how somehow, despite being such a recent entry into their lives, his comings and goings helped settle life back into its known shape.

He also made time to talk with Sophie when he was there. Thoughtful enquiries as to whether she was getting enough sleep, finding time to play the piano, or how the cardigan she was knitting progressed. No urging her to pray. His eyes were kind, but not probing; on departing his handshake was brief and firm. Such ordinary moments, but afterwards the sound of his voice flowed into her thoughts, smoothing and resettling them. There also followed moments of happiness she could not sensibly define. Whatever the cause it couldn't be because she was developing romantic feelings for him. He had to be over thirty, with a beard that seemed to put him in an even older generation.

She was offered no other jobs other than the one at the estate agency in Ilford. This wasn't surprising since she didn't have a certificate for her typing or know shorthand. The pay she was offered took into account this lack, but was sufficient for her to live at Mrs Blount's rather than a seedier neighbourhood. Mary Thomas, who answered the telephone, did the filing and went on errands, made the same as she did, but had the advantage of living with her parents who did not expect anything from her wages. Sophie suspected her employers, a married couple named Euwing, also paid Mr Crawley, the bookkeeper, as little as they could. Though appearing to be in his fifties he had a young family to support. The poor man had holes in the fingers of his gloves and his shoes always needed resoling.

That Saturday morning Sophie heard the doorbell ring as she was getting her well-worn navy coat and slightly newer hat out of the wardrobe. She had put these on and turned off the gas fire when footsteps pounded up the stairs. Within moments Mrs Blount thrust open the door and burst into the room. She was a stout woman with fallen arches, not usually given to speed; this along with her agitated expression informed Sophie that something was wrong.

'What is it?' Anxiety surged although it was unlikely to have anything to do with her personally. Being on your own in the world had the benefit of precluding news that a loved one had met with a terrible accident or sudden death. And even had there been such a person any information in that regard would not have caused her landlady to look on the point of collapse. Could it be Mrs Blount's dog had got out and been hit by a car? She hoped not; it was a dear little creature.

'There's a woman out on the step, Miss Dawson, she's got five children with her, all of them little, the youngest in a push-chair. At first I took her for a beggar, she's that shabby, but she says she's here to have it out with you about carrying on with her husband.' Mrs Blount's face was red as a beetroot and there was a good deal of puffing between words.

Sophie stared back at her in bewilderment.

'I wouldn't have thought it of you, Miss Dawson, really I wouldn't. I took you for a lady, or I'd never have had you here.'

'She must have come to the wrong house.'

Such would have been Uncle Henry's explanation. Make sense where you can out of folly, had been one of his dictums. He most certainly would not have accorded Sophie the right to collapse on the bed or otherwise make a display of herself had there been a dozen such women at the door. Sophie's upbringing might not have suited Mary Thomas or other modern young women, but it stood her in good stead now.

'Wrong house won't wash, Miss Dawson.' Mrs Blount's substantial bosom heaved. 'She asked for you by name.'

'But I don't know any men in a personal way, let alone married ones.'

'Well, I'll have to take that with a pinch salt, won't I? You'd better go down and sort it out before she starts peeling the bell. I closed the door on her. I wasn't letting her and those children into the hall. They've all got runny noses and look like they haven't had a good wash from the neck up, let alone a bath, in weeks. What Miss Willis and Miss Irving will have to say if they find out about this I dread to think.' These were Mrs Blount's other lodgers, elderly maiden ladies both away for the weekend, the former spending the weekend with family, the latter gone to stay with an old school friend.

Sophie hurried out on to the landing. Mrs Blount's voice followed her down the stairs. 'I'm glad my husband isn't alive to see this day, he'd have been mortified. If the apoplexy hadn't taken him when it did this would be the moment.'

She shivered as she reached to open the front door. Despite wearing her coat and hat, she felt chilled. The narrow, darkly papered hall was always cold in winter, but it wasn't that. She couldn't think who the woman standing outside could be, but whoever she was surely had to be looking for another Miss Dawson. And yet there was a sense of the past weaving into the present, something disguised by not being understood, catching up with her.

Last night's fog had dissipated, but a gust of damp wind assailed her along with a rasping voice vibrating with rage as she opened the door. She drew it to behind her without closing it. Despite all that was going on in her head she remained aware it wouldn't do to upset Mrs Blount further by having to ring to be let back in.

'If you hadn't come down, I'd have started pounding on the door till the whole house shook.' The woman's eyes blazed in a face contorted out of any recognizable shape.

As Mrs Blount had said she was shabbily dressed. Her gloveless hands were clenched into fists, her coat was too thin, the headscarf inadequate to keep her from getting an earache. The five children were more warmly, if grubbily, dressed; but Mrs Blount had also been right about the runny noses and need of a good wash. The oldest, a dark-haired boy, looked to be eight or nine, the others descended in steps and were all fair-headed. The one in the pushchair, an infant of around two, wore a pixie hood big enough to fit one of the older ones. Whether it was a girl or boy was uncertain. It let out a wail and despite her distress and bewilderment Sophie's heart went out to the poor little thing. The others stood peering vacantly at her, except for the oldest, who eyed her nastily. One a couple of years younger, another boy, sat down and was scratching at the pavement with a stub of chalk.

'I'm sorry.' She spoke as levelly as possible. The woman looked to be fifty but likely wasn't that old given the ages of the children. 'I've no idea who you are.'

'Don't give me that, you bloody little tart! Unless my Bernard's not the only lovesick fool you've got your claws into? Well, that'd be one in the eye for him!' A mirthless laugh revealed several missing teeth. 'Serve him right if he has to wait his turn at the end of a mile-long queue. But maybe not . . . Have them all in bed at the same time, do you?'

Sophie thought this might be the moment when Uncle Henry would have collapsed on the nearest bed. Surely such things didn't really go on even amongst people whose morals weren't all they should be. The thought of anyone overhearing was horrible, but fortunately there wasn't a soul within range.

'But I don't know a Bernard!' Sophie protested, then instantly realized this wasn't so; she did know a man with that Christian name although she hadn't once called him by it, never thought of him as such. 'Oh, surely you can't mean Mr Crawley? I've never had anything to do with him outside of work.' Again she caught herself. What had seemed insignificant reared to mind. 'Except for last night; I was at the stop waiting for my bus. He was doing the same and told me he'd heard some in front him say the buses were all running at least thirty minutes late because of the fog. He suggested we go into a café behind us to get out of the damp and warm ourselves up with a cup of tea.'

The child in the pushchair wailed again.

'Shut up, Em'ly,' chorused a couple of the others.

'Last night! Tell me something I didn't know.' Spittle flew, barely missing Sophie. 'I saw the two of you through the café window looking ever so cozy, you brazen whatsit. I was watching from around the corner outside the estate agency when the two of you finished work. I'd got a neighbour to watch this lot for me. Not like I didn't know funny business has been going on for months now, him washing his hair twice a week instead of once a fortnight, combing it ever so careful before leaving in the morning.'

Em'ly in the pushchair began kicking her heels. The boy with the chalk threw it at her and got a cuff round the ear from the oldest. Sophie started to speak, to say she'd thought Mr Crawley had decided to spruce himself up in order to better pass muster with his employers, but she was cut off.

'The primping was only the start. He began talking about you in his sleep, mumbling on about you being his beautiful Sophie and how he couldn't go on without having you in his arms.'

'Oh, surely not?'

'Was like bleeding poetry. I kept waiting for it to rhyme. When I laid into him he'd get all stuttery and white-faced saying the only Sophie he knew was Miss Dawson that did the typing. And there was nothing improper for me to worry about. Said you were too far above him to have any ideas in that direction.'

'There was nothing, Mrs Crawley. Nothing at all. Last night in the café he never said a word out of place. He talked about how his mother had insisted he wear a chest poultice in winter because of how badly he'd suffered from catarrh and how relieved he was that her prayers had been answered and he'd outgrown it. It was his lumbago he worried about now, in case the doctor insisted he take days off work, which would run him the risk of getting the sack.'

'You must think I'm daft!' Mrs Crawley gave the pushchair a jerk and Sophie thought for a second she was going to slam it into her.

'He said he thought Mr and Mrs Euwing might leap at the chance to take on someone younger that they could pay less and get to work even longer hours. He's bound to worry about you and the little ones.'

'Oh, let's have a chuckle, you smug bitch! A funny way he's got of showing it. Expecting me to listen to him moaning on about how bad his days are, as if mine are filled with nothing better to do than sit looking out the window to see what the neighbours are doing.'

'That must be difficult for you, but I do think Mr Crawley has reason for concern when it comes to Mr and Mrs Euwing's penny pinching.' Sophie still managed to keep her voice even, but in cowardly fashion she wanted only to escape. 'They let the typist before me go because she asked for a half-crown a week rise.'

'He should have had it out with them years ago, let them know how lucky they was to have him at their beck and call, but there we are! He never did have the guts to stand up for himself.' Mrs Crawley sounded as if she was winding down. Several of the children looked at her as if taking this as a signal she was done and would take them home.

Imagining herself the wronged wife made it unlikely she had been sleeping well. That coupled with a never-ending round of scrubbing and scrimping would send many a woman over the edge. Sophie wondered what more she could say to relieve her mind, but Mrs Crawley was back to talking.

'Weak as watered-down milk has always been Bernard. Never dawned on me he had it in him to pull the dirty. Mr Prim and Proper he was when he married me. Didn't know what he was born for, like they say of old maids. Took me to figure out what went where and show him the ropes and even then he couldn't get it right.'

Sophie could no longer bring Uncle Henry to mind; he had vanished into a realm where nothing approaching such disclosures would have been possible without bringing on the end of the world. Her lips moved as if jerked by strings.

'How did you find out where I lived?'

'Got on the bus you took last night. With it being foggy Bernard didn't notice me get on. Likely he wouldn't have known me from a bottle of milk if it'd been a bright sunny morning. Not with his eyes blinded by you.' Mrs Crawley's voice had gone flat; she could have been reciting a poem she didn't know and had no interest in learning. 'I sat four rows behind you, not knowing the point of it really, just being glad to be sat down. And when you got off I did. I'd meant to have it out before you went indoors, but I knew I didn't have it left in me, that it'd have to wait. I thought about those women in the Bible that got stoned to death for what you've been doing, but then I said to myself, If she wants him let her have him and she can bloody well take what goes with him – his children.'

What followed, though over in a flash, wasn't blurred. Not even around the edges; it was vividly, exactingly revealed – second by second – at every stage. Sophie's was the image that remained immobile as if caught by accident in a photograph. Mrs Crawley reached down a hand and hauled up the boy who had been sitting chalking the pavement. Next, Sophie felt her arm gripped by digging fingers. 'Albert,' to the oldest, 'you take hold of that pushchair and get your sister through that door. The rest of you follow and no lagging. You've got a new ma from today on and mind you make her life a living hell.'

FIVE

Friday had been a routinely busy day at Mullings for its housekeeper Florence Norris. After breakfast she'd consulted with Grumidge, the butler, about the spring cleaning due to start the first week in April, talked over the upcoming dinner party in honor of the new vicar and his sister with Mrs MacDonald, the cook, and asked Elsie Trout if her twelve-year-old son would like to give the gardeners a hand with the weeding. Elsie, wife of Dovecote Hatch's police constable, had recently started helping out in the kitchen several days a week and Rupert was a nice lad deserving of some pocket money. The afternoon passed with working on the weekly accounts and mending the lace edge of a tablecloth. Following the evening meal she'd sat over a pot of tea with Mrs MacDonald and Molly, the head housemaid and married to Grumidge. That Molly didn't look her usual rosy self had concerned her, but this was explained away by the onset of a headache due to the heaviness of the weather.

Florence had gone to bed at eleven, settling pleasurably down to read a chapter of *Precious Bane* lent to her by young Mercy Tenneson, with whom His Lordship had been spending an appreciable amount of time over the last several months. Dear Ned! He and Mercy were entirely right for each other if they would come to realize it instead of quarrelling over this, that and nothing. After turning off the light she prayed for Agnes Younger, near to death in the village, and Mrs Newsome, the village nurse, who had her hands full, not only in caring for this patient but with her daughter's situation with her brand new husband. Or, as Mrs MacDonald – who had a lively turn of mind – put it: The Tale of The Absconding Bridegroom. Then, as always before falling asleep, Florence thanked God that George Bird had come into her life.

Four o'clock in the morning found her rigidly staring out of her bedroom window. She had wakened from a dream in which

she was standing at the church altar, looking up at George. He
was about to place the ring on her finger. A jolting sound . . .
and she was turning to look down the aisle. The arched oak
door stood open, framing a figure that shaped itself into a man
– Graham Lieland, Major Wainwright's secretary with his ruined
face, the result of horrific burns suffered from a fighter plane
crash during the war. Pity seized her. Now he was lifting his
hands, peeling away the skin – the raw looking ridges and
glossy whiteness of skin that no longer looked human . . . only
it wasn't skin, but the rotting gauze of a shroud. And as it fell
away she saw the face of her husband, Robert, who had died
on the battlefield in Flanders, been buried there . . . become
one more tombstone amongst so many.

The window overlooked the kitchen garden. The fog had
thinned back to the mist which had prevailed for most of the
previous day, but even with the lamplight behind her there was
nothing of the here and now to claim her attention. Her gaze
was fixed on the distant past.

She saw the uncertain fourteen-year-old kitchen maid she
had been on arriving at Mullings. Saw her handed a basket of
vegetables by a gardener and turn to take it inside to Mrs
Longbrow, the housekeeper of that era. Saw, ten years later, the
young woman who had emerged from that twig of a girl, sitting
on a log in a rare moment of free time, her face alive with
happiness. This Florence loved living at Mullings, Lord and
Lady Stodmarsh had developed affection for her, but at that
moment she was thinking of Robert Norris, the eldest son of
the family who managed Farn Deane, the home farm of the
estate, as their forebears had done for the past four hundred
years. Their wedding was a week away. All that was loveliest
lay ahead. War did not yet loom on the horizon. She and Robert
would grow old together, their love enriched by labours shared,
children reared . . .

Florence stepped away from the window and sat down on
the bed. Robert's photograph was on the dressing table, his face
warmed to false life by the lamp set next to it. So young, yet
it was a man who looked back at her, not a boy. She had known
when he went off to war that he would not come back. She had
not believed in a loving God at that moment, but she had not

allowed Robert's parents or two brothers to sense her absence of hope. Perhaps she might have felt differently had there been a child, but the longed for baby hadn't come; disappointment had grown to sorrow that in its turn ebbed into acceptance. If she had told anyone of that sense of inevitability – the certainty that Robert was lost to her and all who loved him, undoubtedly she would have been told that wasn't a premonition. Merely the instinct to brace for the worst if it came.

She had kept herself busy to the point of exhaustion after he left, attending to the housework and cooking at the farmhouse, taking over the portion that previously had been the province of her now ailing mother-in-law, seeing to that dear woman's care. Searching for socks to darn, mending shirts that were ready for the rag bag, polishing boots that would be muddied in an hour. When a few months later the telegram had come, she had invited the white-faced delivery boy into the kitchen for a cup of tea and encouraged him to sit until he felt better.

Florence had stayed on at Farn Deane until Robert's younger brother, Tom, married in 1921. It was at this turning point that Mrs Longbrow came one afternoon to say that she had decided to retire as housekeeper and had suggested to Lord and Lady Stodmarsh that Florence take over the position. They were eager for her do so. On her part there had been no hesitancy in accepting. She had kept up her friendship with Mrs MacDonald, the long-time cook, and had always got along well with the other members of the staff.

There had been grief at Mullings during her absence. The Stodmarsh's elder son and his wife had been killed in a motoring accident leaving a then two-year-old son. Florence's heart had gone out to the child, but she had not anticipated having anything beyond the peripheral to do with his care. Shortly after taking up her new duties, however, she found herself drawn into his upbringing. Young Master Ned soon started trotting in search of her every chance he got and when his nanny was proved to be unfit and had to be dismissed, and he became upset at the prospect of another, Lord and Lady Stodmarsh asked Florence to have him with her whenever she could manage it.

Her Ladyship, whose health was poor, particularly wished for this, never evincing resentment as the bond between her only grandchild and the housekeeper deepened over the years. Florence had never made the mistake of thinking of him as the son she might have had. What they had was more than enough to bring her to the point of realizing her life was full and she could remember Robert without searing pain. This had been the situation for several years before she had met George Bird. What began as a friendship became imperceptibly something more. They had not hurried into marriage even after realizing they loved each other.

Ned had still been a school boy at that time. Lady Stodmarsh died, followed a couple of years later by her husband. At seventeen he'd inherited a title, along with the responsibilities that came with it – managing the estate and even more importantly seeing to the welfare of not only his tenants, but the villagers in general. That his maternal grandmother, Mrs Tressler, had left her own comfortable home to come to Mullings had been of great consolation to him. She had, however, required Florence's assistance in finding her feet as mistress of an establishment in a place with which she was largely unacquainted.

Inserted into that time frame had been murder, with its aftermath of suspicion, dread and notoriety. Another period of healing had been required before Florence had been at the point where she could begin training Molly to take over from her as housekeeper.

George had not only understood her loyalty to all at Mullings – Mrs Tressler whom she had come to deeply like, the staff and especially to the boy she'd helped bring up – he had supported her in postponing their marriage, but the time had now come for them to begin their life together as husband and wife.

Realizing she was cold, Florence drew the bedclothes up around her shoulders. The dream scene in the church was still with her, would not recede, obliterating the pleasure she had felt all week at the prospect of the meeting she and George were to have that afternoon with the vicar. They had reason to feel sentimental about being married at St Peter's. Their first encounter had occurred on coming out of church one Sunday morning shortly after his arrival in Dovecote Hatch. She was wearing an old black coat and must have looked what she was: a widow past her first youth.

She had heard that the Dog and Whistle had a new owner, and as he matched the description she'd been given, of a tall and otherwise large, balding man, she had gone up to him to wish him welcome. He was standing still, oblivious to her approach because he was looking at Miss Agnes Younger not far ahead, hobbling her way with the help of two sticks along the verge. It was her habit not to impede the way of those walking at a normal pace.

Florence had forgone her words of welcome to the newcomer, had not even introduced herself. She had seen his concern, the frown – close to a wince, when Agnes paused to secure her balance. She addressed him in a lowered voice, although there wasn't anyone else close by. There'd been fewer congregants than usual due to a particularly nasty influenza going around. Mr Quigley, the churchwarden, had a particularly bad case of it, Nurse Newsome had said it was touch and go with him, and most who had attended had not lingered. On occasion, Reverend Pimcrisp chased after someone he had noticed fidgeting and looking shifty with it in the pew. But not that day; he was looking under the weather himself. His sermon had been shorter and less bellowing than usual.

'You're wondering why no one walks alongside her, ready to assist if she should stumble. It must seem unchristian, but Agnes Younger is a fiercely independent woman.'

'Doesn't take being pitied?' He also kept his voice down.

'She has a reputation for routing any overtures she views as interfering. Possibly she feels that the more strongly because she wasn't born that way. She was a capable busy woman, keeping house for her brother until his death. The accident, a fall from a ladder while she was picking apples, happened shortly afterwards.'

'How long ago?' They were walking now, he shortening his lengthy stride to match hers, but still keeping an eye out for Agnes's progress.

'Fifteen, maybe more.'

'Any family here abouts?'

'None. She had a female cousin on her mother's side who'd

occasionally come and stay for a few days when the brother was alive. She came for his funeral, but never afterwards. It would be in character for Miss Younger to cut the tie with her out of that loathing of anyone feeling sorry for her. What made the situation especially sad was that she had become engaged to be married a few months before her brother died. That was broken off.'

'By him?'

'No, her.'

Florence knew this man she'd just met had reached a decision before he answered. 'I'll go after her, keeping several paces back, stopping when getting too close to look around me. Hopefully she'll put that down to my being new to the area.'

'She might if she turned around to see who was behind, but she can't do that without risking a fall. The only way she wouldn't suspect what you're about is if she heard you talking to someone, expressing interest in who lives in this house or that, admiring a particularly well laid out garden and asking if the owner kept an allotment. It would also help to be headed for somewhere, such as Coldwind Common. It's about a half mile from where she lives, so you could continue on your way after she reaches her home. It's called Orchard House, because it is surrounded by orchards.'

'Apple?'

'Mostly cherry and plum. It's about ten minutes from here, a few turns off Vicarage Lane which is to our right beyond the graveyard.'

'Have you time to walk with me?'

They had reached the lychgate with Miss Younger a dozen or so steps ahead of them before they had finally introduced themselves. Doing so had come as an afterthought. It had seemed to Florence that this was one conversation among many that had gone before, that he was with someone she already knew well. He hadn't taken her for a gossiping woman, as he might well have done. He had seen into her heart and she his.

It had been very much the same with Robert one Sunday when his mother had invited her to tea. Previously she had only seen and exchanged words with him in passing, but within minutes of his coming into the sitting room at Farn Deane that afternoon she'd felt as though she'd come home. There was one difference. Fast upon that realization with Robert had come the breathtaking delight of being in love with him and the resulting emptiness whenever they were apart. The recognition that her regard for George ran deeper than friendship did not happen until several months after that first meeting and her happiness on discovering that he returned her feelings was of a more serene kind.

But that had not meant her love for him was less than it had been for Robert, or that he was not as essential to her life. She'd no doubt of that during their courtship or when she had agreed to marry George; but now had come the disturbing dream. The sound of Robert's voice had been around and within her.

'I didn't die. I've come back to you.'

When she had looked for George to see his reaction the place where he had been was empty and she had felt relieved. She could not have looked into his eyes. Robert's hands were reaching for her. It was at that moment she had wakened.

Now seeing the book, *Precious Bane*, on the bedside table she strove to convince herself that reading it before falling asleep had triggered the dream. Its narrator and heroine Prue Sarn's disfiguring harelip must have called forth Graham Lieland's face ravaged by war wounds; the same war in which Robert had died. But she couldn't fully accept this sensible explanation. Her mind twisted and turned. Impossible to rid herself of the fear that the dream had been lying in wait, ready to appear on the night before she and George were to go to talk with the new vicar about setting their wedding date.

SIX

Sophie stood on the pavement outside Mrs Blount's house staring after Mrs Crawley's retreating back. She could have caught up with her easily, without having to run, but what would that have accomplished beyond an emotional escalation of what had already passed between them? Had there been a policeman in sight Sophie might have approached him and begged his assistance in persuading Mrs Crawley to turn back and collect her children from Mrs Blount's house; but no uniformed figure was to be seen. This was perhaps just as well. Sophie would have wilted under the questions put to her. Even more importantly she had no wish to make trouble for Mrs Crawley with the law. Though still in shock over the woman's accusations she felt sad for her.

Beneath the rage had been weariness, that of someone too drained by day-to-day drudgery, too spent of optimism to unbend her mind to the idea that Sophie wasn't carrying on with her husband – had no interest in him beyond that of co-worker. Impossible to make her see that what Mr Crawley was experiencing wasn't real, but instead the fantasies of a middle-aged man for a very young woman and that he would soon return to his senses. Sophie could think herself into Mrs Crawley's mind and heart. How awful to be told by one's husband that he was in love with someone else, especially when there were all those little ones involved. Only the utmost misery could have brought any mother to act as she had done, ignoring her children's distress and confusion at being left with a stranger. What must be going through her mind now? And there was that other question – how was Mrs Blount dealing with the assault on her senses of having five children, including one in a pushchair thrust through the front door into her hall?

Shivering with cold and nerves Sophie hurried inside to discover how bad was the state of affairs. It could have been worse, anything can always be worse; the ceiling was still in place and the staircase hadn't shifted notably. But Mrs Blount could not be expected to look on the bright side. The apple-red face of Em'ly, in the pushchair, clashed with her pink pixie hood. Her howls would have dented steel, but had no visible impact on her three brothers and one sister. The dark-haired, oldest boy was standing on the bottom stair with Mrs Blount's prized Royal something China vase on his head. The girl, of about three, sat on the floor spreading the spilled daffodils and water from the vase around her and the remaining two, the boy who'd chalked the pavement and another, looking close enough in size to be his twin, were scuffling next to the hall tree. The morning's post that was always placed on the table against the staircase wall to be collected by the tenants was scattered on the floor.

As for Mrs Blount, she could have been Lot's wife, turned to a pillar of salt, until her mouth started working and finally ejected a moan, followed by a series of frantic exclamations.

'Miss Dawson! Tell me what have I done to deserve this? When Jesus said, "let the little children come up to me", I never uttered peep on the subject. Maybe he missed out as an only child, but I was the oldest of twelve and, as I told my husband at the start of our marriage, I was done wanting my own, let alone anyone else's underfoot. So you figure it out – do I have to stick my head in the gas oven, or do you get this lot out of here?'

What sounded like a thunder bolt followed. The eldest boy had bowed his head, perhaps thinking he was in some sort of church, given the reference to Jesus, dislodging the vase, shards of which joined the puddle of already spilled daffodils. Em'ly was startled into silence and the scufflers into stillness. The girl, sitting poking at the daffodils, looked up inquiringly. Sophie braced for Mrs Blount to faint or go into hysterics, but mercifully neither disruption occurred.

'Well, I suppose that's something, Miss Dawson,' heaved the lady, 'at least now I can hear your explanation of this outrage. And make it the short version, or we'll have one of them piddling on the floor, if that there little missy sitting in slop from the daffodils hasn't done so already. Naturally I'll expect you to replace that vase. It was a wedding present from my dear mother-in-law and real bone china.'

'Of course.' Sophie looked around at their small listeners. They like this she thought – hearing me being put in my place, getting a ticking off. It reduces me to being one of them. I can't blame them. The only person to blame is Mr Crawley. Unless somehow . . . without intending it I gave him the wrong idea – behaved in a way that suggested I was flirting with him? She managed to steady her voice. 'I'm sorry, Mrs Blount, but I must wait to explain the situation until I get back from taking these children to their father.'

'So it wasn't a case of that woman showing up looking for another Miss Dawson. She was right about you carrying on with her husband.' A suggestion of disappointment at being proved right lined this onslaught. Mrs Blount had shown over the past years that she'd liked Sophie. Had grown as fond of her as she would allow herself to be of any lodger. 'Oh, the wickedness! And me telling people how lucky I was to have you for one of my ladies! That you wasn't the flighty sort. Enjoying your knitting of an evening. Always so quiet and neat in your ways. Talk about being taken in! If that poor creature had dumped her brood on you in any house but this I'd buy her a decent coat. Let you have it good and proper she did, is what I got from one of those two.' Mrs Blount pointed at the twins. 'Said if you wanted her husband, you could have him and take what went with him.'

'That's what she told me. But I don't . . . want him . . . it's all a mistake.'

'And where, if I may inquire, is he at this minute? Waiting for you in some fancy hotel bedroom?'

'No.' Sophie took hold of the pushchair. She was past feeling insulted and well past praying this was a nightmare from which she could awaken. 'I'm very sorry you're upset, Mrs Blount, you have every right to be. I promise you'll have the full story when I return. Come along children, we're leaving.'

Mrs Blount, having expended more energy at the start of one morning than in a month of Sundays, remembered her age, her poor feet and that she generally liked to be considered a good sort. Not given to gush, not overly pally with the neighbours, but ready enough to do a good turn without too many questions asked. She sank depleted on to a chair set against the wall.

'I suppose the neighbours were out gawking.'

'No. There was no one anywhere close, not even walking by.'

'Ah, but you wouldn't be able to count the noses pressed up to windows. Smell a good story a mile off can them round here.' Mrs Blount sighed. 'Better have them pull down their coat sleeves and turn up their collars. You don't want them dying from pneumonia on the way. Would slow you down getting into his arms.' Despite that sting in the tail she asked quite mildly where Sophie would find Mr Crawley.

'He'll be at the estate agency; he's the bookkeeper and like me goes in on Saturday mornings.' With this Sophie wheeled the pushchair out the door with the other four children trailing silently behind her. On the pavement she manoeuvred to face them.

'My name's Sophie. Will you tell me yours?' She could hear the wheedling in her voice – knew it would confirm their belief that she was the last person in the world to be trusted, but she had to say something to show she wasn't hostile to them.

Nudging at the edge of her mind was the realization that she also was about to be cast adrift from her known world. On her return Mrs Blount would certainly demand she pack her bags and find other lodgings. But this was no time for self-pity. They were blameless. She was a grown woman at the core of their distress. Without realizing it at the time she must have done something to bring this predicament about. Wouldn't a worldlier girl have turned down Mr Crawley's suggestion that they go into the café last night and sit out the rain, knowing that doing so was utterly inappropriate?

'Why you want our names?' It was the oldest boy speaking. The dark hair was shaggy. He was thin-faced, with a sallow complexion, narrow eyes and the arrogant slouch of a Dickensian street urchin living off his wits. 'We're nothing to you. And good thing too! And don't you go blaming Ma for tossing us in the middle of things! What was she supposed to do – sit home putting her hair in curlers? Or drinking tea with her pinky stuck out?' He mimicked the gesture.

'Oh, no! Don't think I criticize her. I'm sorry for her!'

'Well, don't be, Miss Toffee nose!

There was no moment of inspiration for Sophie. If the right words of response existed they were not within reach of someone who had been brought up by Uncle Henry, for whom children, other than herself, did not exist. And even she had not always seemed quite real to him. She was alone with herself and so came out sounding stupidly, stiltedly, inept. 'I'm sure your mother is a lovely person and already terribly anxious to have you back with her.'

'If I was the king I'd chop you head off.' This made him sound more of a child, but the curl of his lip belonged on the face of a seasoned cynic.

'So's we could kick it down the road!' One of the twins piped in.

'Be our new ball it would,' added the other. 'The one we got for Christmas went flat.'

Sophie's eyes stung. Not for herself, but for them. Would they all, apart from little Em'ly toddler, carry this memory with them for the rest of their lives? 'I don't blame you for feeling bloodthirsty,' she said, 'but as I told the lady in the house, there's been a mistake and the best thing is to get you all to your father as quickly as possible.'

'And isn't he going to be tickled pink!' the oldest boy jeered. 'He don't care diddle for us. That ball he give us cost all of sixpence. He's been shelling out the lolly on you, taking you to dance halls . . .'

Finally, Sophie had the sense not to answer. Turning the pushchair around her, she set off on the short walk to the bus stop. Within moments the little girl sat down on the pavement and from her mutinous expression made clear she wasn't going to budge. That problem was solved when the oldest boy said, 'Up you go, Dolly,' and hoisted her on to his shoulders.

At the corner they turned on to a much busier street. The twins dodged ahead causing her to panic that they'd step out into traffic, or would disappear into the throng of pedestrians, which they promptly did. Moments later she spotted them swinging on a lamp post. There was only a small queue at the stop and a bus, the right one, was drawing up to it. They'd miss it if the twins dawdled in joining them. Fortunately they came running and Dolly was set down on her feet. Sophie had just taken Em'ly out of the pushchair when a man, one she recognized as living three doors down from Mrs Blount, came to her aid, collapsing it and stowing it on board. The three boys and Dolly shoved themselves higgledy-piggledy on to an empty seat. Popping over the back of it like jack-in-the-boxes.

Sophie with Em'ly in her arms took the one behind. There was a flustered moment when the conductor approached and she realized she didn't have her handbag with her, but she remembered the purse in her coat pocket and quickly dug out change for the fares, dropping a precious half-crown in her haste. Em'ly struggled to get off her lap and when Sophie tightened her hold screamed in rage. Silence returned when the oldest boy leaned over the back of his seat and shoved a fuzz-coated sweet into her mouth; a respite, but what if the bus jolted and she choked on it?

'You've got your hands full, there, lass,' said a motherly looking woman with a northern accent, seated alone, directly across the aisle.

'She don't need nobody feeling sorry for 'er, do she, Sam? And she in't our ma.' It was one of the twins who popped over the seat this time.

'Well, I didn't think she could be, at least not of you bigger ones, much too young for that. Minding them for a friend, are you?' She smiled kindly at Sophie, who was cut off from answering by the oldest boy, whose name she now knew to be Sam.

'Her's our dad's fancy piece.'

'What did he say?'

Sam repeated it.

Sophie's face burned; she could feel everyone on the bus staring at her, except for the north country woman who, the smile wiped off her face, looked out the window. But within moments she turned around, leaned close and whispered, 'You poor, sad lass. You're not the first and you won't be the last to be led astray by promises of a good time. My sister got mixed up with a married man when she was a girl, lucky for her Dad put a stop to it short shrift. He wasn't angry at her – more like disappointed. You won't want to disappoint your parents, will you now?'

Don't answer, look straight ahead. That was Uncle's Henry's voice in her head; had he been there in person he'd have ordered the woman to mind her own business or he'd pull the communication cord to stop the bus. That it was trains that had them not buses was immaterial. It would have got the point across. Uncle Henry always got his point across. 'My parents are both dead,' said Sophie.

'What a bleeding shame,' scoffed Sam.

Gasps from one of the closest seated passengers.

'Now then, young man, that's not the way to talk.' The north country woman's voice remained kindly. 'Not even with every right to be upset, though why in the circumstances you're with this young woman, I can't imagine.' She looked at Sophie. 'My sister wasn't a bad girl, and you don't look one either. Perhaps if you talked to a clergyman, he could help sort things out. Someone kind and not too judgmental, maybe not so far up in age he can't remember what it's like to be young and foolish, that's what you need.'

Over the past five years, Sophie had not allowed herself to think often of the one clergyman she'd known. But suddenly he was there; she could see his square face, the neat beard, thick brown hair, a shade darker than his eyes. Thoughtful eyes – lively when amused. She could hear his deep voice. The voice that had soothed her when Uncle Henry was dying. It strengthened her now. He had believed in God, something she was still not sure she did. And, yet, couldn't she imagine him saying God could be counted upon to take care of all, shoulder life's burdens, smooth the way out of her present difficulty, if she would but lean on Him. She knew, without wondering how she knew, that he would advise her not to explain the true situation to the north country woman, but not to snub her with silence for being concerned.

'Thank you for trying to help,' she said.

'Think on what I've suggested, lass.'

The bus stop came into view. Em'ly had gone off to sleep, she felt heavier that way, and getting out into the aisle was made even more awkward by the other children, pitching into them from behind. This along with the bus lurching and swaying to a halt and the surging up of other passengers eager to get off, it was a miracle Sophie was able to count all children as present and apparently un-maimed when they finally made it on to the pavement; the conductor retrieved the pushchair and handed it over. Sophie was then elbowed aside by the three boys. Between them, with what seemed a minimum of elbowing and shoving for them, they got the groggily awakened Em'ly into it. 'Up you go, Dolly!' Sam hoisted the girl of about three on to his shoulders and wandered over with her to look in a baker's bow window.

'Cream buns,' he proclaimed with all the flair and flourish of a magician producing them out of a top hat. The twins drew in next to him. Dolly, back on his shoulders, shrieked and clapped her hands, resulting in a wobble, but a deft grasp of both ankles secured her back in place.

'How 'bout getting us some?' Sam poked Sophie's arm.

'They'll get all over you.' She could picture it, the clownishly smeared faces, sticky hair, and hands – just as her responsibility was about to end; not that Mr Crawley could reasonably complain. 'Wouldn't raisin ones do?'

This produced a look of pure contempt from Sam.

She didn't attempt further persuasion. Not because she was depleted, unequal to intensifying the children's dislike of her, or didn't want to delay a moment longer than necessary in getting them to their father, now just moments away. She didn't tell herself they couldn't look more in need of soap and water than they did now. Or that they'd lick the cream off their faces faster than it could spread. She had witnessed a moment of joyful hope and seeing it die left her not just sorry or sad, but something closer to grief.

'Cream buns it is.' She angled the pushchair towards the bakery door. One of the twins opened and held it for her. A scramble followed, but none of the children breathed a word; they stood like toy soldiers behind her while she waited behind the two people ahead of her to be served. Outside she handed each of the twins a paper bag. One contained a dozen sausage rolls. No one thanked her. She didn't notice. The delighted grins were enough.

'Why'd you get six buns? There's only five of us.' Sam, Dolly still on his shoulders, looked perplexed for the first time since Sophie had set eyes on him. 'Want one for yourself?'

'I thought it might be nice to take one home to your mother.'

'You won't get round 'er that way, if that's your game. And why all them sausage rolls?'

'In case you're still hungry when the buns are gone.'

'Dad don't like sausage rolls.' The sneer was back in his voice, though sounding somewhat half-hearted.

'Doesn't he?' The Euwing Estate Agency stood right across the street and suddenly Mr Crawley loomed large. She hadn't allowed herself to focus on the unpleasantness of confronting him, the horrible awkwardness of it; her focus had been fixed on handing over the children and walking away, but would he allow her a brisk getaway? As of this morning she had thought of him, when she'd thought of him at all, as a meek and pain-fully shy man – his manner of speech halting, his eyes uncertain. Now, inescapably, about to face him, her heart pounded. She'd have to ask Mary to fetch him outside; the thought of the scene created if she went in with the children was appalling.

She got them across the street; there was a lull in the traffic and a man helped her off the pavement with the pushchair. Em'ly woke with a grizzle; Dolly slithered down Sam's back and made a grab for a cream bun, being held teasingly aloft by the twin who'd had charge of them. A middle-aged couple was studying the property listings in the agency window. Please, don't let them go inside! And oh, don't let this be one of the rare Saturday mornings when Mr and Mrs Euwing weren't occupied elsewhere, with buyers or sellers!

The middle-aged couple noticed the children encroaching with their cream buns and hurried off. 'Well, get on with it.' Sam reached for the pushchair. 'Can't wait to see Dad's mug when you tell 'im to leave you alone and bugger back 'ome to Mum. Course that's if'– his narrow, dark eyes bored into hers – 'you 'aven't bin stringing us along and it's all bin lies about you not wanting him more'n a smack in the face.'

He wants to believe me, she thought, he wants to be able to finish his cream bun without there being a nasty taste left in his mouth. She watched him move with the other children a little further down the street before opening the agency door and, leaning in from the step with little above a whisper, managing to get Mary Thomas's attention.

That pretty young lady with the curly dark hair was seated at the front desk, looking the epitome of efficiency as she leafed through a fashion magazine.

'Mary!'

'Goodness! You made me jump! Why on earth are you lurking out there? So you're late for once, the Euwings haven't sprung a surprise appearance.'

'I need you to . . .'

'You're all of a dither. Don't tell me – I know, you were delayed by a tall, handsome stranger, with a deeply mysterious voice, asking directions to somewhere or other, and time fell away as you gazed into each other's eyes.'

'Mary. Stop talking and listen to me. Get Mr Crawley and tell him to put on his coat and come outside – the reason I'm late is I have his children with me. All five of them.'

Sophie had the door closed before another word could be said, let alone a question raised. The children hadn't budged; they were eating the sausage rolls.

'He'll be out in a minute or so,' she called to them, but they didn't come nearer and only Sam looked at her. How would Mr Crawley be receiving the news of what awaited him? The minute passed, was supplanted by another and another . . . surely he'd have his coat on by now. Her heart began to beat off the seconds . . . what if he didn't come? What if he'd fainted? You only heard of women fainting from fright. But it must happen to men too.

'He's hid under his desk,' jeered Sam, suddenly at her side, 'the bleeding coward.'

SEVEN

At five that morning Florence had dressed and otherwise readied herself for the day. The looking glass on her dressing table did not betray her. It revealed as always the dignified housekeeper. Tall and slim, garbed in navy blue, with her brown hair drawn back into a heavy coil at the back of her neck. But in the aftermath of her disturbing dream questions lingered. Had some hidden part of her wondered if she was being disloyal to Robert in remarrying? If her life with George could equal what she had known of happiness all those years ago? Were her earlier explanations of what had prompted the dream incidental to this being the day when she and George were to talk with the vicar about setting the wedding date?

He had been devoted to his late wife; still had a photograph of her set out as she did of Robert, but she'd never wondered if she would be in any degree second best to him. It was vital that she meet him when he came for her at Mullings, so they could set off for the vicarage together, without a sign of worry on her face. But it would be there, under the skin, that inkling that Robert had come back to life for her, and she wasn't sure she could let him slip back into the past without a struggle. And George, dearest George, deserved so much better than less than her whole heart.

At ten minutes to six, a half hour beyond her usual time, she went down the back staircase past the butler's pantry, where Grumidge was lining up silver serving dishes in readiness for breakfast to be borne aloft. She greeted Annie, one of the kitchen maids, who was going into the scullery with a bucket and mop, before entering the kitchen where she found Mrs MacDonald, who had once confided to Florence she would like the inscription on her tombstone to state: Cook at Mullings. And the dates of her tenure.

She was a white-haired woman in her sixties, whose considerable bulk did not prevent her from moving nimbly between stove and sink. A Scotswoman who'd never set foot in Scotland and did not know one tartan from another, but was nonetheless fiercely proud of her heritage. It did, however, as she was known to lament, carry a heavy burden. From childhood on she had been the recipient of 'the sight'. That this claimed burden, as she chose to call it, had never been born out in any situation that sent shivers down the back, did nothing to diminish her dour belief that she was amongst those gifted with the power to part the veil between present and future and behold the shape of lurking menace.

The previous morning she had been voluble on the subject of the Absconding Bridegroom, whom she had declared would prove to be a fly-by-night without ever having set eyes on him. That she might have been influenced in this prediction by hearing he was a commercial traveller with flashy good looks, glossy black hair, possibly dyed, and a pencil thin moustache, she refused to concede. The man had disappeared from the face of Dovecote within three months of marrying Una Newsome, daughter of the village nurse, who in addition to that upset had her plate full tending Agnes Younger in her final days.

She now set an earthenware teapot on the deal table that took up a sizeable rectangle of flagstone floor. 'On the bright side,' she now said, speaking as if interrupting herself mid-thought, obviously gloomy, 'the fog's lifted, like didn't seem it would in a fortnight as of last night. Meaning the doctor can drive over in a nip soon as needed.'

Despite the sad subject Florence was grateful for being caught up in conversation. It put a distance between her and what she needed to think of as that foolishness. 'Perhaps, Nurse Newsome's daughter will lend her a hand. I've heard she's done so in the past, taking the night watch and this that and the other. It may help her to be kept busy, although she does have her job at the haberdashery.'

'Poor young woman,' Mrs MacDonald said with a sigh. 'Well, not so young at that, must be in her mid-thirties. I imagine she'd given up hope of landing a man till that creature showed up.'

Covering a bowl of bread dough with a muslin cloth she now set it on the hob by the fireplace to prove.

'You're looking whey, my dear,' she said. 'Had a bad night?'

'I woke too early and couldn't settle to go back to sleep.'

'Bridal nerves?' Despite her few vagaries – in addition to believing herself a prophetess of doom, she had an enthusiasm for red knickers and hats with too many feathers – Mrs MacDonald was an astute woman.

Florence sat in a chair at the expanse of scrubbed table and reached for the teapot. She was tempted to confide in this old friend about the dream, but to spread her worry like butter on someone else's bread wasn't in her. She managed a smile. 'Be a bit silly at my age.'

'Well, I dun know about that.' Mrs MacDonald sat down alongside her and filled both their cups. 'It's a big shift after all these years being set here at Mullings. It's a good change you're making, your George is one in a million, but change it is and that can't never come easy. Could be he's up betimes these days fretting about putting a foot wrong when it comes to your happiness. Where you're going to live for starters. Can't fault him for that. Common sense to iron out the wrinkles before you put the sheets on the bed.' She coughed as if a gulp of tea had gone down the wrong way. 'In a general way of speaking, that is. It's the foolish creatures like Una Newsome, as was, that leap into marriage without the thought they give to buying a bar of soap.'

'I count myself very fortunate.'

'You'll be wanting this afternoon with the vicar to go without a hiccup – like not forgetting what you've agreed on for the ceremony. Always does to take into account the altar ladies; they can turn quite nasty if you change from yellow roses to pink at the last moment. Now you and I know you'd take anything of the sort in your stride, but men aren't used to coping with trifles, so I'd have George say as little as possible. Awful to have a Christmas carol pounded out instead of the wedding march.'

Mrs MacDonald did not speak from experience. The 'Mrs' was a courtesy title; as a young woman she'd never had a follower, or ever felt regret over her single state, but she had a romantic streak, besides being deeply fond of Florence. No doubt about it, she would miss her old friend deeply when she left Mullings, but to dwell on that would be selfish.

Florence would have liked to change the subject but couldn't dredge up the words; the dream was filtering back; she was at the altar being drawn away from George to go to Robert. She stirred her tea and Mrs MacDonald continued. 'Speaking of the new vicar, Alf Thatcher was telling me when he brought the post ten minutes gone that Mr Fielding spent a few months here about twenty years ago. Winter time it was. It was the sister that told him. He'd just left his public school, Rugby I think it was, and had been having a go round with his father about not wanting to go into the army, as was family tradition, because he'd got his heart set on the Church. So what does Pa decide but to give him a taste that'd proper put him off the notion by sending him to spend a month or so with Reverend Pimcrisp?'

'Really? How did that come about?'

'Seems the Fieldings are acquainted with Lord Asprey as you'll remember is a cousin of the Reverend Pimcrisp.'

'And very proud of the connection.' Florence refilled her cup. 'His one worldly vanity, it might be said; though he was disappointed when His Lordship presented St Peter's with an early edition of the King James Bible instead of a stained glass window, with the upside down crucifixion of St Peter, for the north transept.'

'Well, it's easy to see Pa's thinking, isn't it?' Mrs MacDonald was back to the new vicar. 'Send the lad off to a godforsaken country vicarage at a time of year when the wind was guaranteed to howl down the chimneys, and let him nurse his colds and chilblains in the company of a man who'd gone daft in the head thinking of naught but whether God or the Devil is boss. That should make him see the wisdom of turning soldier. But didn't work out as hoped, maybe because the lad brought a friend with him and the two of them thoroughly enjoyed themselves spending most days tramping around the countryside and getting to know the locals.'

Florence strove to be interested. 'Really? I hadn't heard any of that. George, of course, wasn't living here then, but I don't think anyone has told him or he'd have mentioned it to me.'

'Alf said Miss Fielding didn't say how her brother got on with Mr Pimcrisp, but however that went he returned home still keen as mustard on going into the Church. And what I say is he was likely born to it; from what I hear he's spent more time visiting the sick in the weeks he's been here than Pimcrisp did in all his years on the job. In and out of Miss Younger's and her glad to see him from what young Sally Barton, that's been helping her out for some time, told Elsie Trout.'

Here was Florence's chance to change the subject. 'I was thinking about Miss Younger when I woke and couldn't get back to sleep. I must go and see her today.'

Mrs MacDonald said there could be no more competent and caring nurse than Nurse Newsome especially when the end is near. 'And it'll be good if Una can pitch in at night. They're very close – mother and daughter, like it's nice to see, which makes it even odder Nurse Newsome not knowing a thing about the marriage till it was right on top of her. The whole thing's like some mystery out of a penny dreadful. Take for instance him doing his flit on a Sunday. Said it was because his poor old mum had been taken bad, and he had to hop to it and get to her.'

Florence's curiosity was stirred. 'What's odd about that?'

'Well, that's just what I said yesterday when Elsie brought it up, but she pointed out the Newsomes aren't on the telephone, so Bill Smith could only have heard about his mother's illness by post. Let's say he got the letter on Saturday, why – if he was that worried his mother might be about to breathe her last – did he wait a day before setting off for her bedside? Like Elsie said, anyone could call themselves Bill Smith, there's more of them than grains of sand in that desert the Hebrews had to cross to get to the Promised Land, so who's to say he isn't a bank robber or murdered his real wife.'

'What about his job? Is it local?'

'Commercial traveller.' Mrs MacDonald's indicated all that was to be said about that. 'Polishes and scouring powders, open the door to one of them and you risk getting your throat cut is what I've always said.'

Florence smiled, the dream receding as her interest increased. Elsie's years of marriage to the village policeman had sharpened her interest in life's mysteries big and small. 'It's a thought,' she acknowledged, 'but there could be all sorts of reasons for the delay. If the letter came by the last post on Saturday Una might have begged him not to start out till morning, especially if the weather was bad.'

'It wasn't, though.' Mrs MacDonald got up to put the kettle back on. 'That was the day Mr Fielding arrived and I remember Annie saying to me as she stood peeling potatoes that it was nice of him to bring decent weather with him, and the next moment she'd sliced her thumb with that old knife I'd told her time out of mind never to use. And a nasty cut it was too, with her carrying on something awful. The only howling storm that Sunday was her.'

'Perhaps he wasn't feeling well, a bad cold or something of the sort, or maybe he wasn't particularly fond of his mother and begrudged going.' Florence got up from the table, taking her cup and saucer over to the sink.

Whatever the story end it was probably fabricated melodrama, her heart went out to Una whom she only knew by sight, a woman suspected of being abandoned did not receive the kind of sympathy accorded a widow. Pity, yes, but of the kind that heaped humiliation on pain. Mrs MacDonald was a kind woman, but there were many of the other kind, only too gleeful to rub salt in the wound when feigning commiseration.

And I having been blessed for a second time by being truly loved should be ashamed of myself, Florence thought.

'I'll go to Agnes Younger's this morning, and take along a basket of food,' she said, 'and see if there's any way I can be of help to Nurse Newsome. Perhaps she could take a rest while I sit with Miss Younger for an hour or so.' Her thoughts slid back to the Sunday when she'd first met George and how they'd kept as discreet a distance as possible when following Agnes home. They had done the same thing on several future occasions until she stopped coming to church, the effort likely becoming too much.

'Your paying a visit will be just the ticket, my dear.' Mrs MacDonald beamed at her. 'I've a nice steak and ale pie to put in a basket for you, along with an egg custard that maybe Miss Younger could get down her if she isn't only able to take liquids. There's a thought, I'll add a jar of mutton broth and a bottle of elderberry wine. When will you go?'

'Around ten.'

'Good thing there's only a net curtain mist out there after last night's fog. Like Alf Thatcher said it's not often Mother Nature gets done being huffy this quick.'

Florence set off a little before that hour, taking the pathway through the woods that led from the rear grounds of Mullings to the top of the village street, with the green to the left over-looking the valley below. At its far end of the green Ned – to those closest to him; Lord Stodmarsh to most others – stood in what appeared to be an intense conversation with Mercy Tenneson, whose guardian had died towards the end of last year from a fall down his staircase. She was eighteen and beautiful in a dark, and according to some middle-aged matrons, untamed way. These persons thought it regrettable that His Lordship's grandmother, Mrs Tressler, had taken an interest in the girl, inviting her to spend Christmas and New Year at a family house in the Scottish Highlands and subsequently inviting her to lunch-eons and dinners at Mullings. That this generosity sprang from an awareness of a budding romance between the two young people did not sit well with socially prominent mothers of marriageable daughters. Miss Tenneson's background was questionable.

How galling, as a devoted mama, to be faced with the possi-bility of such a young woman being raised to the level of being the first lady of the district, when dear Belinda, Marianne, or Caroline were so much better fitted to that exalted role! That Miss Tenneson was captivated by the title and lifestyle that went with it, rather than the young man himself, stood out a mile. His Lordship was of quite ordinary appearance; a young man of only middle height, wiry build and reddish brown hair, not some tall, dark and handsome Galahad. If one did not know differently he might at first glance have been the butcher's boy.

Florence, knowing of this talk, sighed as she looked across the green to beloved Ned and the girl he said put him in mind of Cathy in *Wuthering Heights*. How difficult to be at the centre of such avid speculation, although what Una Newsome was experiencing was worse. The village had decided Bill Smith was a thoroughly bad lot and nothing he did, or she said, to suggest otherwise would do him an ounce of good. Florence thought Mercy a perfect match for Ned. A spoiled debutante would bore him in a week, as had been proved when he had briefly believed himself in love with Lamorna Blake from The Manor at Small Middlington. Given time this would become the general view and Mercy would be declared the most delightful girl in the world and His Lordship blessed to have won her heart.

On reaching the Dog and Whistle only a few doors down the village street Florence was tempted to knock on the side door. George was almost certain to be in and the urge to see him was strong.

She had begun to think she should tell him about the dream; not to do so would seem a betrayal. Or was she making a mountain out of a molehill? Her feet slowed, then quickened to take her onward, past Hobbs' Haberdashery, the Saunders Butcher's Shop and Payson's Greengrocery. It didn't take her more than five minutes to reach the church and turn on to Vicarage Lane, which housed only the two-hundred-year old grey stone house and, around a short bend, the sexton's cottage with a rear gate opening into the churchyard.

Talk about living with death ever at your elbow, was a common observation. The current occupant, Frank Shilling, was a cheerful man. Excessively so it was said by some, being frequently roused to raucous song of the music hall sort, when he had a grave to dig. There were those who harkened wistfully back to the days of his predecessor, old Jeremiah Rudge, who'd rarely spoken beyond an affirmative, or negative, grunt. Most certainly he'd never warbled. Silent as the grave, could well and truly be said of old Jeremiah.

The house on the corner of Vicarage Lane was home to Gervaise Kaye, who along with his aunt Miss Victoria Hobbs, was owner of the haberdashery a few doors down from the Dog and Whistle. He was known to have a fine tenor voice, making it a crying shame he refused to sing in the church choir. Frank's vocal outpourings possibly, if not probably, offended his ears if he happened to be home during the day.

Mr Harold Quigley, churchwarden, two doors down, might well have objected on religious grounds to Frank's choice of anthem. More likely, according to Sally Barton, it was the noise itself that outraged him. Sally, who did for Mr and Mrs Quigley, claimed that if and when he was in his study – which was most of the time, pouring over his collection of silly old books – you so much as dropped a duster over, he'd run around in circles clasping his head and bleating like a sheep.

What Mrs Quigley thought on the subject would have aroused no one's curiosity. She was a recluse, rarely venturing out in daylight and never without a dark veil, and as such had faded from general interest years ago.

Miss Gillybud, whose house was a little further along Silkwood Way, may have had her ears spared Fred's 'concerts', but it was doubtful if she would have minded the bawdiest of ballads wafting her way. She was an unabashed non-believer, but one people found hard to dislike, being only stirred to spoken anger when witnessing the repellent, such as one child being cruel to another or someone mistreating an animal.

Florence had always admired this enclave of Dovecote Hatch, the houses – better perhaps described as roomy cottages – possessed sizeable front gardens with the occasional tree and a good deal of shrubbery, and back gates that opened on to Coldwind Common. She spotted Frank in the churchyard with a wheelbarrow talking to another man; Florence couldn't tell who it was until he turned. Given his distance from her, coupled with the netting of mist, the horror of his face wasn't visible. What she saw was a tall, slim, straight-backed man with brown hair. He could have been handsome, might well have been so once, as Agnes Younger might have been pretty in the days when she was upright and vigorous. Looks shouldn't matter, but they did – personally and wretchedly to the onlooker. Were there times when Graham Lieland and Agnes Younger wished they had died when catastrophe stripped them of their known selves? Would Robert, given the choice, have preferred death to returning home to Farn Deane as someone unrecognizable on the outside and inwardly an entirely different person from the man she and his family had known and loved?

Silkwood Way curved into Old Beech Road. At its end Florence turned right and was shortly picking her way down the drive hemmed in by tangled overgrowth from the surrounding orchards, leading to Agnes Younger's house. Or it might better be described as a fair sized cottage, which might once have been charming with its pinkish brick and green roof, but now its windows, where not meshed in briar, were clouded with the dirt of years and its front door was almost bare of paint. Florence set down her basket, before reaching for the rusted knocker. It fell with a dull thud. Within moments the door opened with a creak, almost a moan, that seemed to speak of the decades of pain and loneliness within that cut her to the core effectively blocking out all thoughts of self. This was as it needed to be, because filling the opening was George.

EIGHT

Once when the Euwing Estate Agency had been particularly busy Mary Thomas had said she couldn't think because of the thoughts racing around in her head. Sophie had laughed, they'd both laughed at the nonsense of it, but now she couldn't have described what had being going on for the past several minutes more clearly. Her mind had emptied of all but an awareness of the children now immobile on the pavement a few yards distant and the agency door. It hadn't opened on Mr Crawley coming out to face his responsibilities. She'd had a general idea of what she would say to him, all rather muddled because of the extreme awkwardness of the situation, added to which there was no knowing how he would respond. Now she had lost the thread. The words had unravelled into incoherence. It was as though she were falling asleep on snow-covered ground, sinking into futility, lulled into the belief that she had come as far as she could go and the world must go on without her.

She heard a raised voice. Uncle Henry ordering her to pull herself together and display some maturity. One of his admonitions to her from the time she was eight, or thereabouts. No, not Uncle Henry; it was Sam. She felt his hand on her arm. 'In't going to faint is you?'

'No.' Sophie came back to herself. 'Thank you for being concerned.'

'Wasn't. Just don't want you keeling over and a p'liceman coming ups asking questions that'll have us stuck here jawing about what's none of his business. Ma will already be working herself up thinking you've done us in.'

'Oh, surely not!' But wasn't it certain that Mrs Crawley after her grand gesture was frantic with panic and remorse? She had to be, anything else would be completely unnatural. No mother, however ill-used and angry, could be sat down with a cup of tea and a biscuit having placed her children in the clutches of a conniving, husband stealing woman . . . or at least believing that to be the case. Sophie looked at Sam. 'I'll go back in.'

'If you don't I will. Like I said he's hid himself.'

Sophie pictured Mr Crawley jammed into the stationery cupboard. Or had he slipped out the back way? She was suddenly sure the latter was the case and so took in a breath of relief when the door opened and he descended the step, his threadbare coat buttoned up to the neck, twisting his hat in his hands.

He was a man of medium height and build, but this morning he looked small, shrunk deep in a coat insufficient to the weather. His hair was the colour and texture of Vaseline. He was in his entirety a colourless man. His pale eyes were watering; they frequently did because of his susceptibility to colds. He'd suffered from them since childhood. They'd worried his mother, it was why she'd always insisted he wrap up warm, had tucked two hot water bottles into his bed at night, had him drink egg and milk or hot lemon with honey. He'd told Sophie on several occasions how wonderful his mother had been and how he had only married after her death. And she had listened, as she'd always done to the confidings of Uncle Henry's friends, his solicitor Mr Kent and Dr Maitland, in regard to their home situations. Out of kindness or because her own life was lacking in interest?

He stood blinking, not seeming to notice when his hat slipped through his twitching fingers.

Sam was still at Sophie's shoulder.

'Be a man, Pa, turn off the water spout, tears won't cut it,' he jeered.

Now close up, Sophie could see that this morning Mr Crawley's moist eyes came not from a cold, but from crying. That's what had kept him from coming out sooner. She felt a rush of anger. His children waiting out here in the cold! He shouldn't have had a thought for himself once Mary told him the situation, even the little she knew of it. She looked achingly towards the younger children. Em'ly in her pushchair, the others huddled down on the pavement. Dolly appearing asleep.

Sam's voice rose to a thin shout. 'You better get us home, you've broke Ma's heart, you have, got her in a state she don't know what she's doing.'

Mr Crawley didn't respond. His gaze, one of pitiful appeal, was exclusively on Sophie. She started to speak, but he was ahead of her. 'You've no need to worry, my dearest, about any of that. The wife has family that'll take her and the kids; live in the country they do. Always going on about how she'd rather be there.' His mouth worked itself into a smile. 'What matters is that you and I are meant to be together, that we love each other . . .'

'Mr Crawley!' Sophie had rarely, if ever in her life, spoken so sharply. 'This foolishness is all in your imagination. I have absolutely no romantic feelings towards you. Take your children home this minute, or I'll fetch a policeman. I just saw one around that corner.' She pointed to their left. 'He won't have gone far.'

There had been no such sighting; she was counting on the threat to bring out Mr Crawley's usual timidity. Instead, the smile that had hovered tentatively at the corners of his mouth widened and his eyes took on a glow.

'I know she's made you feel guilty, but you see the sort of women she is, using her children to tear us apart. That should tell you what've I've had to put with over the years. You can't let yourself feel sorry for her. Think of it! The prospect of starting our new lives together!'

'There is no prospect!' Sophie knew she should not stand there going back and forth with him. But if she walked away, what would he do about the children? Abandon them in order to follow her?

'Australia! We could make a wonderful life there. Mother always wanted to emigrate. It would be taking her blessing with us.'

'She don't want you, Pa!' Sam yelled. 'First I thought like Ma did, she'd led you on. I worked her up in m'mind as rotten to the core. She didn't look like it; wasn't painted up to the nines, still I wasn't going to be taken in, and then I got to wondering why someone that was young and pretty would look twice your way. The more we was with her more stupid it seemed. Told the others she in't a bad sort at all. It's you, only you, that's rotten. What if Ma goes and sticks her head in the oven before we gets 'ome? Thought of that, 'ave you?'

Sophie didn't hear what if anything Mr Crawley responded. Her heart hammered. If she hadn't been close to fainting before she was now, but she couldn't be that much of a coward. Forcing a steadying breath, she clutched Sam's arm. 'I'll take you all home. You just have to tell me where you live.'

'No, no, my dearest!' Mr Crawley snuffled. 'You can't let that woman get her clutches into you.'

'That woman is your wife!'

'Bleedin' hell he's crying again.' Sam's disgusted voice was interrupted by a delighted outcry from the other children. Turning sharply Sophie saw them charge, pushchair and all, towards the opposite corner. Mrs Crawley was hastening towards them; next moment she was hunched down, arms around them as far as they could reach.

Sophie didn't give Mr Crawley the chance to open his mouth. She was already backing away, bumping into a woman with a shopping basket. 'If you follow me, I'll scream,' she said.

'Well, I like that!' exclaimed the woman.

Without an apology, Sophie took an opening in the traffic as impetus, raced across the road and zigzagged left, down an alleyway between two shops and on to a side street. No sound of pursuit, but she kept up a quick pace until she had rounded a couple more corners. Time to think when everything made a little more sense. Boarding a bus as it pulled up at a stop, she was about to drop on to a seat, when the thought seized her that Mr Crawley might have got on at the stop outside the estate agent's. A nervous glance round proved this fear groundless. There were few passengers besides herself and he was not amongst them. He wouldn't have gone upstairs if he wanted to spot her getting on. By the time she disembarked and walked the short distance to her lodgings she had pulled herself together and conceived a plan of action. It was not ideal; there was one particular negative, but she wasn't going to dwell on that. If it didn't work out, she would have time to reassess her situation. Her immediate undertaking would be to face a justifiably outraged landlady.

The doughty Mrs Blount must have been at the front room window, because the door opened as Sophie approached it. Though her face was no longer puce and she wasn't panting like a volcano about to erupt, her gaze did not suggest that the offer of a cup of tea was forthcoming. 'Well . . .' She ushered Sophie into the hall, now restored to its natural state, prior to the onslaught of the children. 'Didn't sweep you into his arms and carry you off to parts unknown then?'

Sophie almost responded, 'Obviously not.' The impetus to be rude was alien to her nature, but she was drained, frayed and anxious to be alone.

'He's the last man on earth . . .'

'Clearly he didn't see it that way. Took back his children, I hope, or did you have to drop them off at the police station?'

'He wasn't receptive, looked right through them, but then his wife came along and gathered them up. They may be home by now; I don't know how far away they live. I'm so very sorry, Mrs Blount, for all you've been put through. And now, if you'll excuse me, I'll go upstairs and pack.'

'A good thing your rent's paid up till the end of the month. Good for you, I mean.' Mrs Blount's voice lost a fraction of its bite. 'Starting over you'll need every spare penny.'

Was it a reminder that additional recompense was owing? Sophie couldn't blame her. 'You must let me know the value of that vase that got broken. I know there's no replacing it from a sentimental point of view, but I hope you can find another just like it.'

'Never mind that. My late husband's sister gave it to me. Said she'd paid the earth for it, then come to find out she'd got it off the market; if she paid five bob for it that was generous.' A pause with some puffing to it and a rise in colour. 'Went round things in my mind while you were gone. First, I thought, who'd have believed it of Miss Dawson! Her and a married man! Well, like they say, still waters do run deep. Then I got to thinking what if you'd been telling the truth about having no idea he was keen on you. And so I've come to feel,' she concluded magnanimously, 'that in all Christian charity I should hear your side of the story.'

Sophie didn't want to talk about Mr Crawley ever again, but she offered up no resistance when Mrs Blount led her into the front room and indicated she should seat herself in an armchair. It was not a welcoming room. She had only been in it once before; that was three years ago when she had come in hope of renting the bedsitting room. She had felt then that it resented any intrusion into its virtuous gloom, in the manner of a querulous invalid who desires only to be left in silence. A gouty invalid. The chairs and occasional tables had gouty legs. Mottled wallpaper mimicked a mottled face. The veining of the marble fireplace suggested veiny hands.

At this moment she would have liked to sag back in the chair. It, however, encouraged no such liberties. Even to have rested her elbows on its arms would have been an affront. But, despite the lack of a fire in the grate, Mrs Blount appeared to be warming up, either because she was curious to know more about the sorry saga, or because sympathy was stirring beneath her mountainous bosom.

She even went so far as to open a glass-doored cabinet and produce a bottle of brandy. Pouring some into a glass she handed it to Sophie, then with a larger measure for herself, she sat down in a facing chair.

'Drink that down. It'll steady your nerves.'

'Thank you.' Sophie took a dutiful sip; she hated brandy. Dr Maitland had insisted she drink some on the day Uncle Henry had died and when Mr Kent had arrived shortly afterwards, he'd pressed another glass on her. Kindly meant, of course. One couldn't refuse kindness, especially when offered so affectionately by two men she'd known much of her life. And now Mrs Blount was doing her best to be supportive.

'So what's this man like?' the lady enquired. 'Attractive, or just full of himself.'

'Neither. He's colourless. The sort who fades into his nondescript clothes, washes out into the background, with a personality to match. Maybe I should have guessed that just by listening to him about his colds and his mother that I could be giving him the idea I was interested in him in a personal sort of way.'

'Well, Miss Dawson, that can be the way of it when you go feeling sorry for a man.' Mrs Blount swallowed down a second brandy, set down the glass and sighed windily. 'I got myself in a similar pickle some years back.'

'You did?' Sophie strove to sound interested and in other circumstances she would have been deeply, but now the fear that Mr Crawley might follow her here, edged further into her mind. Returning on the bus she'd convinced herself he wouldn't risk doing so for fear of creating a scene that would certainly rile her beleaguered landlady into summoning the police. Now she was no longer convinced.

'I can tell you're surprised,' Mrs Blount was saying. 'There was this man, a neighbour a couple of doors down that lost his wife. And her only forty! About my age at the time. Terribly sudden it was, dropped dead while hanging out the Monday wash. Some sort of seizure or stroke. Luckily no children; less for the husband to cope with, but even so the loneliness had to be awful, coming home from work to an empty house. No hot meal on the table. "Might as well be dead himself," said Mr Blount, so I asked him what he thought about me cooking some extra of what we were having for our dinner and taking a plate over to the poor fellow two or three times a week. And do you know what he said?'

'What?'

'That it was just like me always being so thoughtful when most stopped bothering once the excitement of the funeral was over.'

'What a good husband.'

'No woman had better. He even offered to do the delivery, but I wouldn't have it. He always enjoyed reading the evening paper after we'd eaten and then having an hour's snooze and well deserved, always working so hard to give us a decent life. Well, the first time I went along the man – I won't sully my lips saying his name – kept me on the step, but the next evening he invited me to step inside. I didn't stop above a couple of minutes that time, but then it got to be a little longer. He seemed so grateful for a bit of company and with Mr Blount reading his paper and having his snooze it didn't seem right to rush off home. Not when his was empty most of the time.'

Mrs Blount's voice flowed on. Evenly when describing the man's admiration for her macaroni cheese, yes, he'd been very fond of anything with cheese, so one evening she took him a Welsh rarebit. Rising when he began praising her other charms. Sophie tried to stay focused; it really was good of Mrs Blount to confide her tale of Man at his Worst, but she was on pins and needles to be able to leave this house. It wouldn't take her half an hour to pack her suitcase.

'It was just little compliments at first. About how much I seemed to get done in a day. But then it was that I was so full of life it was a joy to be around me; I should've taken exception to that, but there, like I've said I was sorry for him and that evening he'd been particularly pleased with my cheese and spinach pudding. Everyone said he'd been devoted to his wife. A thin, scrimpy creature she was, but some men like that sort of figure . . .'

Again Sophie lost the thread. On reviewing her plan of escape, if she got to make it without Mr Crawley's reemergence, uncertainty loomed. Was she selfishly imposing herself on someone whom she'd never met, even if only asking for help in securing a job?

'Turned out he wasn't. Well, Miss Dawson, I didn't much like it when he said she hadn't been much of a cook. Seemed a bit disloyal, with her not in the ground long enough to stir up daisies, but I suppose I'd got into the way of making excuses for him. He had a way of looking at me as if I'd slipped down from heaven, especially when we were having a sherry together. I wouldn't have accepted anything stronger.' Mrs Blount set down her thrice emptied brandy glass on the table beside her chair. 'Sherry always seems so respectable. It's the clergymen's drink, so I've heard.'

'Is it?' Sophie wondered vaguely if the only clergyman she had herself known drank sherry. Cups of tea, that she knew about; he had drunk at least two every time he came to spend an hour or so with Uncle Henry.

'Yes, I was taken in . . . led astray. One evening he turned on the gramophone and suggested we waltz around the room. That was too much. I told him I wasn't that kind of woman and made for the door. He laughed. The most horrible laugh! Then he said the words that are seared in here.' Mrs Blount pressed a hand in the general region of the heart. 'They make me flame with mortification to this day. "Oh, come on you lovely bit of cuddle. Don't pretend you've been coming over for the pleasure of hearing me praise your left overs. If you only knew how sick I am of cheese"!'

Sophie forgot her own problems. 'Oh, Mrs Blount what a brutal thing to say, when you'd sincerely endeavoured to be a good neighbour in every sense of the word.'

'There was worse! He said my husband couldn't be much of a man if I was happy to leave him of an evening for greener pastures. I never told Mr Blount that; it would've broken him. I never said a word to him of any of it. Best to pull a veil. But the next time he talked about how England was going downhill fast, I agreed that truer words were never spoken. I'll admit to you, Miss Dawson, there were times when I wondered if I was at fault for not spotting what he was sooner. That glass of sherry has haunted me over the years. But, there now, he was a fiend. A spawn of the abyss! Whether that's the case with this man you're dealing with, I won't hazard a guess. Maybe he needs to see his doctor and take some tablets that'll put him right as rain. But we can't count on that happy outcome, now can we, Miss Dawson?'

'Absolutely not.' Sophie rose from her chair.

Mrs Blount did likewise. 'I wish I could let you stay on; you've been a good lodger, and I hope in sharing that dreadful episode in my life I've let you know I'm prepared to take you at your word that you did not, at least intentionally, do anything to bring this trouble upon yourself. But I can't risk another scene like the one this morning, it could be he who shows up at the door next time.' Her complexion again showed a propensity to puce. A gasp escaped her. 'This past half hour and that thought didn't enter my mind, but now that it has . . .'

You can't get rid of me fast enough, thought Sophie with a rush of relief.

'If he's a true mental case' – Mrs Blount picked up the glass of brandy Sophie had barely touched and swallowed it down – 'there's no telling what he might do if he finds you here! The commotion he'd create! Whatever would Miss Willis and Miss Irving have to say about that? They've lodged with me longer than you have, Miss Dawson, and both so used to my ways! To have them walk out! To have to look for new occupants for their rooms . . .'

Sophie wasn't sure if she'd responded to any of this. It didn't matter, Mrs Blount wouldn't have heard a word anyway. At last! she thought on reaching the top of the stairs. Moments later she had two suitcases out from under the bed, placed on it and opened up. Into one she piled her clothing, sponge bag and other daily essentials. Leaving a couple of cardigans on the bed. She then raced around the room, gathering up her personal possessions to go in the other. Books, some she'd had since childhood, her maternal grandmother's walnut writing case, Uncle Henry's desk clock, her tortoiseshell dressing table set, the pincushion that had belonged to her mother, the photos in their silver frames, one of her parents and the other of Uncle Henry. She used the cardigans for wrapping the fragile items.

From the writing case she had taken a couple of sheets of writing paper, two envelopes and postage stamps and put these in her handbag. These for the two letters she must write and send before catching the train. One of apology to Mr and Mrs Euwing, saying she had appreciated working for them, but circumstances forced her to leave their employment. There'd have to be more, of course. A fabricated summons from an ailing relative. The second to Mary, along the same lines as to reasons, coupled with the request that she say nothing to the Euwings about her showing up that morning saying she had Mr Crawley's children outside. However agog with curiosity Mary might continue to be, she wouldn't spill a bean.

Anything else? Sophie's eyes were searching the room for any overlooked items when Mrs Blount came puffing into the room.

'All done?'

'I think so . . . yes.' The room indeed now had the impersonal look it had worn when she had first seen it.

'Here you are then.' Mrs Blount handed her a grease-proof-paper-wrapped package and a small Thermos. 'Tea and cheese and tomato sandwiches to keep you going till you can get yourself a proper meal.'

'How very thoughtful.'

'Set your mind to where you'll go?'

'I have a relative, a cousin of my mother's; I'm not going to land myself on her, but she lives in a small place and I'm hoping she may be able to advise me about where to find a job.'

'Well, you're young and healthy . . .' Mrs Blount's voice

trailed away, she was looking at her wristwatch. 'I do hope you'll let me know how things turn out so as to put my mind at ease.'

'Of course I will.' It was a relief to be parting on terms that would have seemed impossible earlier in the morning.

'Those suitcases don't look like they'll be too much for you to carry. Hopefully you won't have too much walking to do. I went next door and asked to use their phone so I could ring for a taxi. I said you'd tell the driver where you want to go, but thought it would probably be the station; they said he'd be here in ten minutes' – Mrs Blount glanced again at her watch – 'which only gives us a few ticks to get you downstairs and out the door. There, that sounds like him now.'

A breathless rush and Sophie found herself out on the pavement, saw her luggage stowed into the back of the vehicle and herself seated behind the driver endeavouring to gather her scattered wits. Better that way; no room for any of the likely emotions, regret, anxiety as to what lay ahead, or relief that Mr Crawley was gone from her life. Never to return.

NINE

The stranger's visit to the Dog and Whistle had resulted in a restless night for George Bird. He had jolted awake every hour so to replay the episode in his mind. Had he been a fool to swallow the man's story about his sister's death. Had such a person even existed, let alone been secretly buried at dead of night, out of a desire to shield her memory from the shame of suicide. Or had he merely been a man, forced by the fog to halt his journey, wherever it was to take him, and pull the leg of a village pub keeper. George would doze and surface again to a further drumming of questions. What did the envelope, left by the stranger before he disappeared into the night, contain? Was it, as he'd claimed, a statement written to Inspector LeCrane, providing an honest account of the event now twenty years in the past? Or were the folded sheets of paper blank, except perhaps for one on which were scrawled a few words such as: 'Fooled You!'.

Threading through these thoughts was the question as to what Florence would think when he told her the story? And when should he do so? On any other day the answer would be as soon as possible, but there had to be taken into account that appointment with the vicar at two o'clock in the afternoon to set their wedding date. Wasn't it far more important she get to enjoy that special event without distraction? They'd agreed he would collect her from Mullings at noon, so they could go for a drive and discuss plans for their rapidly approaching life as husband and wife. As yet undecided was whether to live in the upper rooms of the pub while continuing to look for a house to buy or temporarily move into a leased place.

It wasn't until four a.m. that George sank into a deep sleep.

Surprisingly he woke refreshed with the clarity morning sometimes brings. His concern that the stranger had set out to make a fool of him was gone. There had been too much anguish in the telling of his sister's death and his parents' grief to be anything but the truth. George did not have any illusions that he was a clever man, but in his time behind the bar he'd listened to a lot of verbal outpourings and if he couldn't tell a tall tale when he heard it, then it was time to take to the rocking chair.

He wouldn't say anything on the matter to Florence until their visit to the vicar was over. That decision was easy; he shouldn't have wasted a moment's thought on it. When it came to the envelope with its contents he couldn't pass it on to LeCrane at this time, without violating the trust bestowed on him by the stranger that he would withhold doing so until events dictated the moment. George liked and respected LeCrane; he hoped he was not risking what he'd come to regard as something close to friendship, but there was nothing to be done about that. The stranger had for one evening been a customer of the Dog and Whistle and, even had his revelations not been so tragic, that's where his loyalty lay.

Not one to skimp on breakfast and being a competent cook he speedily produced a platter of sausage, bacon, eggs, fried bread and tomatoes which he polished off with enjoyment. His mind already moving to the day ahead. He had arranged with Dick Saunders, the butcher's younger son to take over at the pub while he was gone. Dick, who said growing up with the never-ending sight and smell of bloody carcasses had made him a devout vegetarian, was always more than ready to help out behind the bar. George had talked to Dick about working more frequently once he and Florence were married. He had the right temperament, easy-going but capable of dealing with and diffusing a contentious situation.

Having completed his early morning routine, he wrote a note to Dick explaining he might not be back by the arranged time of eleven, then put on his hat and coat, took a bottle of brandy off a shelf, went out the side door and was soon heading down the street. Dick had a key. He had let himself in before when tapping had brought no response from inside.

This was not a time to be idle. His mind would settle back on the stranger and what was in store when his sister's remains were discovered as he had predicted would soon be the case. How big a disruption it would make in the life of Dovecote Hatch was questionable, but it would certainly create a stir.

He could not know he was a couple hours ahead of Florence's departure on the same mission to discover how Agnes Younger was faring that morning. They both had a special feeling for her, founded on the memory of their first meeting outside the church. As far as they knew the person who visited her most often was Miss Gillybud, who'd had some years back given her a kitten when her cat had had a litter. Otherwise she lived the lonely life of her choice.

As George was passing Hobbs' Haberdashery he almost collided with Una Newsome who worked there. Her surname might now be Smith but for many she would be Una Newsome for years to come and those who thought poorly of her husband, especially since his questionable departure, would make an acid point of it.

George apologized, although Una had veered in front of him. Her response was the blank-eyed stare of a sleepwalker.

'Are you all right? he asked gently. 'You look pale.'

'Why do people keep asking me that?' She roused to anger. She was a tall woman, with plaited corn-coloured hair wound around her head, light eyelashes and pale blue eyes. Appearing plain because her face had always lacked vivacity, but in her present agitation George caught a glimpse of denied beauty. 'Nobody really cares, it's just nosiness, the spiteful kind; wanting to poke and prod, find out what's really going on with Bill and me, whether he's coming back. So stupid when all he's done is go care for his ill mother.'

'What you, in particular, would expect him to do, your own mother being a nurse.'

'Never takes anyone long to bring her up. The sainted Nurse Newsome, I've spent my life listening to her praises being sung, being at her beck and call, helping out with the patients, staying up with them nights when she needed her rest. Never mind me being on my feet all day at the cash register ringing up hand-kerchiefs and garters and that was going to be my life until I met Bill. I knew she wouldn't take to him, but I didn't care even with her going on about how my father was a chiseller. I'm thirty-five. It was my turn and I took it. And no regrets.' With that she darted away into the shop.

We are what we think we are when it comes to looks, mused

George as he continued down the steep street. Take for instance Lenore Quigley wife of St Peter's churchwarden. George had heard her story discussed from time to time in the Dog and Whistle. She'd been the daughter of an antiquarian bookseller in Large Middlington, spoiled child, of extraordinary beauty: 'That rare and radiant maiden that the angels named Lenore'.

At about the age of fourteen, so he'd heard, she began to be troubled by, as was common upon nearing womanhood, blemishes on her face. At first the occasional spot or pimple, but this worsened to pockets of infection and boils. As a result she was left with a pitted complexion. No longer a perfect face. It wasn't enough that her hair, eyes and bone structure still drew admiration. She closed herself off from the outside world, seeing only, on occasion, those who came to the house. One such was Mr Quigley who shared her father's passion for rare books. It was mouthed about that he'd married her to get his hands on the collection she had inherited when her parents died. Whether or not that was the case she'd arrived in Dovecote Hatch as much as twenty-five years ago, and settled into the role of recluse. Rarely seen outdoors in daylight hours and never without a veil, although she was known to roam Coldwind Common of a night.

George wondered, as he continued down the street, if Lenore Quigley might be jolted, even momentarily, out of her self-pity if she were to set out on Graham Lieland's disfigurement, or cast a thought to Agnes Younger's inability to leave her home without the risky assistance of two sticks.

He had never previously spent much thought on the Quigleys. However, as he neared the church, he decided to walk round to their house. He remembered how last evening, in the lull between the exodus of patrons and the arrival of the stranger, his thought that the early Bible, gifted by Lord Asprey during the war, might be used during the wedding ceremony. What he didn't want was to raise Florence's hopes and then meet with refusal. Mr Quigley with his interest in the Bible, seeing it was appropriately stored when Reverend Pimcrisp had failed to do so, was just the person to ask if it had been previously used for weddings or other ceremonies.

He was at the churchyard, about to cross the lane to the houses facing him, when he gave thought to the bottle of brandy in his hand and whether it might not decrease his opportunity of a cordial reception from Mr Quigley. He had never set foot in the Dog and Whistle, but whether this was because he was loath to abandon his beloved books without sound reason, or because he adhered to Reverend Pimcrisp's on what counted as licentious living was beyond his knowledge of the man. Perhaps it might be wise to deposit the brandy inside the gate.

He got no further in his thinking, because someone came running through the one he'd been looking at, knowing it opened on to the Quigley's house.

'Oh, Mr Bird,' exclaimed a female voice, 'what a sight for sore eyes you are after what've I been through in there! If you wasn't about to be a married man I'd hug you! She's mad! Of course that's not saying nothing everyone doesn't already know. But to go off on me like that, screaming and yelling at me to shut my mouth or she'd do it for me, that took the cake it did!'

The enraged was Sally Barton. She'd been in the Dog and Whistle the previous evening with her brothers, one of whom was celebrating his birthday. George knew little about her. He took her elbow and gently propelled her away from the house. When they were nearing the end of the lane he stopped and looked at her. She was in her early twenties and pretty in a dimpled snub-nosed way.

'Feeling a little better?'

'I could do with a nip of what you've got in that bottle.' She giggled, letting him know she was joking.

'Why were you there?'

'I do for them five mornings a week, the washing, ironing, cooking as well everything else, she never lifts a finger. If she drops her handkerchief, Muggins picks it up.'

'What happened?'

'To set her off, you mean? You're wondering if I deserved it, I suppose.'

'Did you?'

'Being impertinent, you mean?'

'Provoked beyond resistance.'

Sally gave another impish giggle. 'I suppose you could call it cheek saying a blinking word dusting the room while she sits all day staring into space. Most of the time that door's shut and

I don't set eyes on her, the same with Mr Quigley in his study.
It's like being in a house nobody's lived in for a hundred years.
Like I've told my mum, it's enough to give the soundest head
the creeps. But Saturdays is always when I do her room, and
after five minutes the silence gets to me and something or other
hops out of my mouth.'

'What was it this time?' George could not resist a smile. He
had the feeling Sally had that effect on a lot of people; with
the obvious exception of the Quigleys.

'Miss Younger. She's on more minds than mine these days,
dying like she is. You know how it is in the village. Births and
death. And death a favourite because it opens up all sorts of
possibilities, like who'll do well out of the will, or what will
be the carry on if there isn't one. I started out with what I'd
been thinking about – who will move into her house when she's
gone, and how I hoped it'd be nice people and it would be a
happy home again after being an invalid so long. Nurse
Newsome said she never complained, did as much about the
house as she could manage . . .'

'Maybe Mrs Quigley took that as a dig at her idleness.'

'I wouldn't think so. She's the sort to believe that piece in
the Bible about neither toiling nor spinning. Her being a lily
of the field. And she is still beautiful in her dark *Arabian Night*
sort of way, which makes her behaviour stupid. Her complexion
isn't all that bad. There's plenty enough other women far worse
walking around. Some you'd think'd had smallpox and not
seeming to care a whit; too much else in their lives for fretting.
It was when I brought up Nurse Newsome she went off the
deep end.'

'What about Nurse Newsome?'

'Only how lucky we are to have her in the village. There's
not many who haven't needed her care at one time or other,
that she and her husband had needed her on occasion, when that
wicked flu was going around a few years back for instance.
And I had first-hand reason to bless her for the hours she spent
at my mother's bedside when she had rheumatic fever and was
off her head some of the time talking all sorts of nonsense, that
she would've been embarrassed to death about it if she'd been
in her right mind. I didn't see any harm in bringing that up.'

'There are some people,' said George as they continued walking, 'who resent hearing about the good qualities of others; maybe because – though they wouldn't admit it to themselves – doing so pokes at their own inadequacies, or emptiness in Mrs Quigley's case.'

'I could see that if I'd been talking about someone that's good looking or had all the men running after her, she's still capable of being jealous in that way. I remember once mentioning what a beauty Mercy Tenneson is and how it wasn't any wonder how Lord Stodmarsh is smitten with her. She practically spat at me. But today I think she must just have been out of temper, more than usual, that is. Because there really wasn't anything I said to set her off.'

'Let's hope she's forgotten all about it when you next go back to work.' They had reached the bend in the lane where George would continue on to Agnes Younger's house.

'That won't happen.' Sally tossed her head. 'She told me to get out and never come back.'

'She may rethink.'

'I won't. Enough's enough. It's not just her, it's him too, scowling if I says so much as good morning and warning me for the hundred and fiftieth time not to go in his study, as if I'd want to risk my head off to get a look at his dreary old books. Course any normal man could turn difficult stuck with her. I told her I wouldn't see her for dust and there'll be a lot of that without me doing the donkey work. I think I'll go round to the vicarage and try my luck. They've got old Mrs Stubbins, but she was telling me the other day she's ready to retire and take things easy. Her knees have got to bothering her something cruel.'

'I wish you the best,' said George.

'Good of you listening to my tale of woe.' Sally grinned, and went off in the opposite direction to Orchard House.

It wasn't until he reached Miss Younger's house that he gave thought to his aborted visit to Mr Quigley. Not a propitious time to have bearded him in his study, for surely, even with its door closed, he had to be aware of his wife's hysterics. Another time, or perhaps he, George, could on another day have a conversation with Mr North, the verger, about the possibility of celebrating the wedding with Lord Asprey's bible.

He paused before walking up to Agnes Younger's door to look around him at what had been a flourishing orchard. The house was close to two hundred years old and the forebears of these fruit trees had been planted by the first occupant from whom Agnes was descended. Even in their gnarled, unpruned state they still, on this gray March morning, offered not only seclusion but the impression of an enchanted wood. Florence admired Orchard House. She'd said recently that if she could live anywhere she chose it would be here, and then stopped herself. Knowing her as he did, he knew she thought such talk, of what might be possible once Agnes was gone, was heartless.

Nurse Newsome opened the door before George reached it and invited him into the square hall side with a smile. A tired smile. And small wonder considering how little sleep she could have got over the past week or more.

'How good of you to stop by, Mr Bird.' She led him into the sitting room with its whitewashed walls, beamed ceiling, and stone fireplace.

'Not at all, I'd like to be of some small help if I can. Perhaps there are errands I could handle for you.' He handed her the bottle of brandy. She thanked him for it and his offer, but it was clear she wasn't giving him her full attention. Anxiety as well as fatigue was written in sharp lines on her face.

He took back the bottle and set it on a sideboard. 'Is Miss Younger worse this morning?'

'No, perhaps a little more alert today than she was yesterday. Dr Chester was here half an hour ago and will be back tonight. He'll come sooner of course if needed. Devoted to all his patients, but I think he has an extra place in his heart for Miss Younger, having seen her through the initial result of her accidents and its repercussions down through the years.'

'Dovecote Hatch is lucky to have him.' George wondered if the doctor had urged Nurse Newsome to get some rest herself. Very probable, but equally likely she wouldn't do so unless someone – her daughter came to mind – would pitch in for her. She had to be closing in on sixty, although till now he'd thought she looked younger. She was a woman of medium height and build, with softly waving grey hair. She didn't wear a hospital style uniform, but her navy blue skirt and cardigan over a neat collared white blouse gave her the appearance of being dressed for her job.

For a moment she stood silent, before speaking in a strained voice. 'I try not to bring my personal problems to work with me, Mr Bird, but today I started out feeling rather overwhelmed, and now it's got too much to hold in.' Tears came to her eyes; the more pitiable because he suspected she was rarely one to let her guard down.

He got her on to an easy chair, one of two in front of the fireplace, drew a handkerchief out of his coat pocket and handed it to her. 'My mother used to tell me never to leave home without a clean one. So make good use of it. I'll bob off and make you a nice strong cup of tea.'

With that he was out the room as fast as a man of his height and girth could move. Having hung his coat on the hall tree standing against the staircase, he made for the door at the end of the hall as the most likely to be that of the kitchen. It was very much of the farmhouse style, with brick floors, a scrubbed wood table, deep sink, potted plants on the windowsill and a blackened stove of the sort upon which James Watt might have watched his mother's kettle billow out steam. He filled the one to hand and set it down to do its job.

There was a Welsh dresser along one wall from which he took down two cups and saucers, spotted the tea caddy, strainer, milk jug and sugar bowl, and was reaching into a drawer for spoons when he heard footsteps on the stairs. Nurse Newsome going up to look in on her patient. By the time he'd filled the brown earthenware teapot and was setting it on a wooden tray he heard her come down again. On returning to the sitting room he found her about to sit down in the chair where he'd left her.

'How is she?' he asked.

'Much the same. I'll take her up some beef tea in a little while. Mrs Saunders brought it round yesterday, being a butcher's wife she makes it so well.'

'All in good time.' George set the tray on a table within hand's reach of her chair, and asked if she took milk and sugar.

'Just milk.'

He handed her a filled cup, poured one for himself, with three teaspoons of sugar, and settled himself opposite her.

'You're very kind, Mr Bird.'

'Nothing of the sort. Have you eaten this morning? I could fetch you something, perhaps some bread and butter, that always goes down well with tea.'

'I had some earlier, but thank you.'

'Another cup?'

'Not for the moment.'

'I'm sorry to see you so low. You indicated the cause was a personal matter. If it would help to talk about it, I'll listen without offering advice that you don't want or can't use.'

She was speaking before the last few words were out of his mouth.

'It's Una. My daughter. You'll have heard about her husband taking off. Everyone's been talking about it, probably because she went around looking so anguished. It was bound to strike people as way too much, if he'd gone to care for his ill mother. People here, at least those with any feelings, respect a sense of family obligation. It might even have made them like him better.' She paused. 'It might have made me like him better.'

'You didn't take to him.' George had learned from his years behind the bar that stating an obvious fact helped the confidant along, more effectively than questioning.

'I'm afraid not.' Another pause. 'You see, Mr Bird, Una told me very little about him, only that she'd met an attractive man when she was staying with an old school friend at Worthing last June. I was pleased for her and wanted to know more about him, but she wouldn't say a word beyond the bare minimum, even when she went up to London a few times to meet him.'

'I see.'

'Then one day in late October she walked in, with him alongside, the first time I'd ever laid eyes on him and said they were getting married. There was his luggage and practically the next words out of her mouth were that they'd live with me, because it was silly for me to be alone, in a house set apart on the far side of the common from this. She was anxious of course about how I'd take it. She's been a good daughter and we've always been close, especially so I suppose because of her father dying when she was young.'

'And yet she'd kept mostly quiet about this man until that day.'

Nurse Newsome closed her eyes for a moment. 'I've wondered if I was to blame for that. I've depended on her a good deal to sit with patients, especially at night, when Dr Chester couldn't get anyone to relieve me, which has been the case these past days with Miss Younger. Una may have thought I'd resent her no longer being as accessible.'

George said nothing, remembering his early conversation with Una. There so often was some truth on both sides.

'One hates to think one has been that sort of mother, the kind that forgets their children are entitled once grown to lives of their own. I always hoped she'd marry, without saying so in case she got the idea she was dwindling into an old maid. And perhaps I'm wrong about the helping out because she offered do so with Miss Hobbs when she was laid up recently, as everyone here about knows, or I wouldn't mention it.'

'My understanding is she's very devout, very connected to the church and had a breakdown when Reverend Pimcrisp retired.'

Nurse Younger nodded.

George wondered if she thought Miss Hobbs one of those maiden ladies of the sort read about in novels who develop a hopeless, romantic passion for their parish priest. It was hard to see Pimcrisp arousing such emotions even in his younger days, or to imagine him, other than horrified at being the object of a woman's lust, but what did he know of Miss Hobbs – beyond what was said of her from time to time in the pub. That she never missed church on a Sunday, attending both morning and evening services, was a good businesswoman, and that she had been the prettier of Hobbs' two daughters, disappointed in love when a Mr Kaye ceased paying her his attentions and married her sister. Both were now deceased and she and her nephew had inherited the shop jointly. Young Mr Kaye was known to have an antipathy for her. Known because he acted as if she did not exist when they were serving customers together. Most likely resented her assumption of being in charge.

'Did your daughter's husband object to her assisting you with Miss Hobbs?'

'No, Mr Kaye gave her some time off from the shop. Bill could be charming, I could see that from the start. He set about assuring me of his love for Una, and I didn't disbelieve him; I would catch a look in his eyes when she came into the room, but the words were far too flowery. I pushed that aside, the idea that he was too smooth, too plausible. Una was so head over heels about him, convinced he was destined to be way more than a commercial traveller, which I suppose could be true if he were to come into money from his mother. And I have to think she has sufficient to make it worth his while to take off on her behalf and stay away all these weeks.'

George hesitated. 'Unless he's not with his mother at all. That he's gone back to the woman he was with before he met Una.'

'Oh, Mr Bird! It's a relief to have it said out loud, instead of the thought always lurking at the back of my mind. It has to be what she fears.'

'And yet you believe, or did believe, that he was in love with her.'

'But this other woman could have a pull. There could be a child.'

'Does he write?'

'Yes, once a week at least, but that doesn't seem to reassure her. Of course, I understand she misses him dreadfully, but there's something more weighing on her. Something that's twisting her up inside. I've tried to get her to confide in me, but she won't. There's something very wrong.' Nurse Newsome shifted in her chair, clasping her hands. 'I shouldn't be telling you any of this, Mr Bird, but I've reached the point of not knowing which way to turn.'

'We've all been in that place at one time or another,' George replied soothingly. 'Talking it out can sometimes make things a little less bleak.'

'As for that letter, the one everyone knows about, that he said he got from his mother on the Saturday morning, I can't say whether that's true or not, I was in and out all day and never saw any post. Una may only have his word for it. He could have claimed not to wish to show it to her, perhaps saying there was something unpleasant about her in it. Or perhaps they had a row that night, while I was with Miss Hobbs. He had a temper; it didn't flare up often, but I saw him kick a chair once.

All I know for sure about his leaving is this, he came begrudgingly to morning service the next day; I'd been rather insistent about that because it was the new vicar's first Sunday. We were a little late and had to sit right at the back and Mr Fielding had barely begun to introduce himself, when Bill got up and walked out. When Una and I followed him he went into a rattling speech about how being in church had brought him round to realizing he must do his duty by his mother. That's when I first heard about the letter.'

The words 'if there was one' were left unspoken but they rang in George's ears. Newsome might have done better to allow husband and wife privacy on that occasion, but he could well understand bewilderment clouding better judgement.

'It was that display that set tongues wagging. Mrs North, the verger's wife, was sitting right across from us. She's not unkind. She'd have assumed he'd been taken ill and seen no harm in mentioning it. And there'd be others, not well intentioned to quicken the flames. People hadn't taken to Bill. Mr Kaye told me to my face that my new son-in-law looked like a comic-book villain.'

George had heard this description passed around in the pub.

'To be an object of pity is abhorrent to Una.' Nurse Newsome continued in an ever lowering voice. 'It makes the trouble, whatever it is, unbearable.'

'My heart goes out to your daughter, but more immediately to you because something has brought the situation to a head, in a way you weren't prepared for, or didn't expect.' George got up and poured her another cup of tea and watched her drink some before sitting back down. 'What happened this morning?'

'Nothing earthshattering, but sometimes it only takes the straw, doesn't it?'

'Quite right.'

'Yesterday Miss Younger had a couple of requests of me, she has moments of being quite clear about what she wants done. One thing she asked was that I should take a taxi into Large Middlington this afternoon to meet someone – I won't say whom, off the three twenty-seven train. I told Una about it last night and she agreed to stay here while I was gone. She works a half-day twice a month on Saturdays and this was to be the case today. But this morning she came home to say she'd forgotten that she agreed to work a full day instead, that there was no getting out of it and if there was she wouldn't, because she was sick and tired of everyone else's problems, with mine top of the list.'

Remembering his encounter with Una, he hoped her mother had not tried to reason with her.

'I told her I was sorry. That I'd been thoughtless, and I hoped she could put this behind her and have the best day possible. She went off without a word.'

George was thinking. His and Florence's appointment with the vicar was at two o'clock, if they were to return here by a quarter to three that would allow Nurse Newsome sufficient time to get to Large Middlington and meet the train. He explained this.

'Florence and I will be more than happy to take over while you are gone.'

'That's more than kind, Mr Bird' – the smile warmed her face – 'but Alf Thatcher knocked when he brought the post to see if there was anything he could do and I asked him to go round to Miss Gillybud's and asked if she could fill in for me and he came to say that she would.'

'Then please let me at least do this for you, stay a while longer so you can at least get an hour's rest. I'll sit with Miss Younger.' He was helping her to her feet as he spoke and she nodded as she leaned for a moment against him. On reaching the top of the stairs she opened a door to her left, went over to the bed where her patient lay sleeping, smoothed the coverlet and went away. George heard a door down the hall close, but he and Miss Younger were not alone, a large ginger cat was curled up on a cushioned chair by the window. They'd had fifteen minutes to get to know each when he heard the rap of the front-door knocker and tiptoed down the stairs. Every creak sounding as though it would weaken the dead, let alone his two sleepers.

TEN

Florence stared at George filling the doorway of Orchard House; filling it as he had done the empty spaces in her life almost since their first meeting.

Last night's dream and the shadow it had cast, leaving her questioning whether she loved him enough, as deeply as she'd loved Robert, faded. In a rush of joy she knew she was bound to this man in ways she couldn't have imagined when she was young. At the heart of which was liking, friendship, and beyond that, passion. Mellowed, ripe for this season in her life. She knew she could have told him about the dream; that he would have listened to her doubts and fears, letting her talk through them without disrupting the flow with his interpretation, or voicing his emotional response. If she had told him she didn't feel she could marry him he would have held and comforted her. But there was no need to mention it. It wasn't important.

Without a word he took the basket she was carrying, stepped aside for her to enter, pressed a finger to his lips and led the way into the kitchen.

'I was sitting in Miss Younger's bedroom with a large ginger cat on my lap wondering what my life would have been like if she hadn't been the good fairy that brought us together. As it is I can't bear the thought of a day without you.'

She took back the basket, placed it on the table, put her arms around her and kissed him in a way not usually best suited to kitchens.

Several minutes later he said, 'Wouldn't it be nice if we were already married?'

'Mr Bird,' she replied, 'Reverend Pimcrisp would have deemed that a lewd remark.'

'So he would' – George held her tighter – 'how unfortunate for the good of my soul that we won't be seeing him this afternoon. The new bloke mayn't deliver a stern enough lecture to keep my thoughts strictly on the wedding ceremony.'

'It may help if we turn our thoughts to ordinary matters.' Florence began unloading the provisions she had brought from Mullings. 'I gather you've been keeping an eye on Miss Younger, either because Nurse Newsome had to leave for a while, or is taking a rest.'

'She's worn out, poor woman.'

'Of course she is.'

'And not just bodily.' George was putting the kettle on.

'Dealing with her daughter's unhappiness, knowing all the speculation that's going on about the missing husband. It was the discussion at Mullings this morning and the same yesterday. Mrs MacDonald, forewarned by her gift of the sight, knew the marriage was doomed from the start. Her idea is that Bill Smith is on the run from the law. And farfetched as that sounds, it could explain his bolting so abruptly. Perhaps he caught someone staring suspiciously in church.'

'Miss Heron, one of the altar ladies, through her pince-nez.'

'She does have the gimlet eye. Yes, she might pass as someone sent by Scotland Yard to pry him out.'

'She caught that five-year-old pinching a sweet.'

'Did Nurse Newsome confide in you?' Florence looked round and smiled at him. 'Of course she did.'

'She was primed to let her guard down. Something happened today – the straw as she put it that broke the camel's back.'

'I want to hear, but keep back anything you should.'

'There's not much you won't know already, except for the straw.' He looked around for the teapot and remembered he'd left it in the sitting room. As a result he went and fetched it and Florence went upstairs to peek in on Miss Younger. She stayed only to check her breathing, which was even, if shallow. The ginger cat sat up and yawned, prowled towards her, then jumped to the foot of the bed. When she came back down she informed George all was well for the time being, giving them time to talk.

'I stayed down here for fear my thudding footsteps would wake Nurse Newsome. I expect she usually sleeps with one eye open.'

'Did you tell her how long you could stay?'

'Until shortly before noon, because of having to fetch you

from Mullings. I was going to walk back to the Dog and get the car.' His hands stayed momentarily as he was putting the cosy on the teapot. The stranger! He'd forgotten him over the past hour or so, along with the need to keep silent about him during the drive he and Florence had planned on taking before going to the vicarage.

'George?'

'Yes, dear?'

'You looked as though you'd suddenly recalled something important.'

'Nothing to do with Nurse Newsome or her daughter. Something that happened last night at the pub. Someone who came in after everyone had left because of the fog. It's a rather a long story, that doesn't impact on anyone we know, so there's nothing to worry about there. Do you mind if I hold off on telling you till we've had our talk with the vicar?'

'Of course.' Florence knew it was important; had it been otherwise he'd have given her a brief sketch, to be fleshed out later. She directed her mind back to Nurse Newsome and her daughter. They had finished the pot of tea by the time he'd given her a full account of his conversation with Nurse Newsome, along with his having spoken with Una outside Hobbs' Haberdashery.

'Oh, dear! What a horrible situation for both of them, George. Daughter knows mother doesn't like the husband, turning any proffered sympathy into a slap on the face. If he is a rotter Una may know it deep down, and either make all sorts of excuses for him, or not care. I have to say I can understand her agreeing to work a full day. Grabbing the opportunity to get away from her mother's searching eyes. But that doesn't make me any less sympathetic to Nurse Newsome.'

'She loves her daughter.' George set down his empty cup. 'She may, or may not be a possessive mother; it wouldn't be surprising of a widow with one child and Una implied as much, but somehow I don't think so.'

'I agree. I've never heard such a thing suggested, and I think if true it would have been because of her being so well respected.'

'Yes, there are always those who can't stand hearing another's praises sung. There may even be some of that in the current tongue wagging. A means of poking at her through Una.'

Florence reflected. 'Also she's a busy woman, working at what is obviously for her a fulfilling job; I doubt she'd have the time or desire to run anyone's life but her own. And let's not forget we're not talking about a young girl. She's in her mid to late thirties, if she is still tied to her mother's apron strings that's because she's been unwilling to untie them. She chose to move her husband into her childhood home and if she saw that was not going down well, they could have moved somewhere else.'

'Go on,' encouraged George, 'and don't say you've got a nasty mind.'

'You do take the words out of my mouth.' Florence smiled into his eyes.

'Well then! My suspicion is that living on the cheap off his mother-in-law may have suited Bill Smith down to the ground. Unless they have a real flare for it I don't suppose these salesmen make much of a living. The flashy type could probably go through what there was in next to no time on the road and end up in a hole, hounded by people he'd scrounged off.'

'Worse if he'd got in with the loan sharks.'

'And he spotted one of their enforcers lurking behind the font?'

'They have a long reach if what you see in the films is close.'

They both laughed.

'There could be lots of reasons he went,' said Florence. 'The one you and Nurse Newsome came up with – the former lover with a child, or the story as told; the letter came on Saturday. Is it so unlikely he would have been loath at first to leave his new bride and wasn't brought to a sense of duty until he was in church? Now what are you thinking about?'

'Back to Nurse Newsome and people disliking hearing others talk well about her.'

'Who?'

'In Mrs Quigley's case the reaction would seem to be wildly out of proportion.' George went on to describe his conversation with Sally Barton.

'Deranged. To sack the girl because she was grateful to the person who had nursed her mother through a feverish delirium.

If that's all there was to it of course. Is Sally's word to be relied on?'

'I'd say so, although I don't know her. She was in the pub last evening with two of her brothers and she may have been in once or twice before. They're a decent, close family. Hardworking. She struck me as a bit pert, but in an appealing, spirited way. A cheerful girl I'd think in general. Not a liar.'

'I've found as a rule they're the cowering sort.' Florence was thinking of some of the Mullings' kitchen maids who'd come and gone over the years. 'But Sally could have dramatized the hysteria. Embroidered the truth as Mrs MacDonald would say. That might fit her personality, but against that is Mrs Quigley.'

'Agreed. I don't think it judgmental to acknowledge she's an odd one.'

'No, George, that – according to Betty Thatcher – is Mr Quigley with his head in clouds of books. On occasion addressing people on the street in Latin or Greek. But no one could fault his diligence when it comes to his role as church-warden. Maybe it's the history of St Peter's, with its Norman origins, that's a special draw for him. There's that story of how the vicar in residence at the time of Cromwell saved the church from being vandalized by the Roundheads, by convincing them people were dying. Perhaps he's writing a book about it. Mrs Quigley is beyond being odd, peculiar, or anything of the sort that can be rather endearing. I had an aunt who thought she was the reincarnation of Queen Elizabeth.'

'An urge to send people to the Tower and have them hung drawn and quartered.'

Florence laid her hand on his. 'Nothing that malevolent; no need to live in fear I'll turn bloodthirsty if you don't bring me breakfast in bed. She wore a red wig, plucked out her eyebrows, wore lace collars that resembled ruffs and named her dog Sir Walter Raleigh, because that's what he'd come back as.'

'It's a wonder he didn't bite her head off.'

'He was a biter. But most of us have someone in the family who is more or less eccentric and yet still retain a grasp on daily life. Mrs Quigley is in a different category. To have shut herself away for what has to be close on thirty years, existing in semi-darkness in the day time, because the curtains of the room she occupies are tightly drawn, that would have made my batty aunt's eyebrows rise.'

'If she'd had any.'

'True.' Florence thought through her next words. 'And now we have Sally Barton's account of what transpired this morning. People lose their tempers, often for what don't call for bursts of anger, but this was beyond anger, it was unbridled rage. Malevolence, fed by the shadows she's wrapped herself in like a rotting shroud. Yet better perhaps that she remain locked in a prison of her own making, because if she were to venture beyond it I fear she could make for a deadly enemy. Oh, I know I'm sounding melodramatic! Even so, I'm glad her husband has his books and can escape to the church and I'm relieved Sally won't be going back there.'

'I hope they take her on at the vicarage. For her sake and because it sounds as though Mrs Stubbins is getting past working there given her age and rheumatism. We tend to think of rheumatism as something that comes with old age and so is to be born without much complaint or sympathy. But it can be cruel. I remember when I was young coming upon Mrs Rudge, wife of the sexton before Fred Shilling, and her hands were so knotted and twisted that I could have cried for her. Which is why it's thought particularly heartless . . .'

She didn't get to finish what she was saying because they heard footsteps descending the stairs and went out to meet Nurse Newsome's bemused, questioning gaze lingering longest on Florence. They explained the sequence of events following her going up to rest and how they had decided to let her sleep as long as possible. It was now but a quarter to one, giving them abundant time to keep their appointment at the vicarage. She expressed her gratitude but did not attempt to keep them.

Florence took George's arm as they walked out on to the lane. 'I'm glad,' she said, 'that Agnes Younger will get to die so well-tended, but it saddens me that she doesn't have one relative at her bedside, or to mourn for her later. This will sound fanciful, but I think the house was her friend, her dear companion, even her confidant and that such has been the case with others who have lived there over the past couple of hundred years. Wishful thinking, dear.'

'No.' He leaned down and kissed her cheek. 'There is something very special about Orchard House, a nurturing quality – as if it's learned all there is to know of life's up and downs, and stood the stronger for it.'

They decided there was time for them to go to the Spinning Wheel. This was a teashop that served lunch from noon until two. It usually did a brisk trade on Saturdays. Today, however, they were able to choose between a few free tables and within moments of having settled themselves a waitress appeared with menus. George recognized her as the wife of one of Sally Barton's brothers. She hadn't been in the Dog and Whistle the previous evening, but she'd been there on a number of occasions, sticking always to lemonade or ginger beer. He introduced her to Florence.

'Pleased to meet you, Mrs Norris, everybody speaks so highly of you.'

'Thank you.'

'Lovely it is you and Mr Bird getting married. There'll be a right crowd outside church the day you wed.'

'I'll look for you.' Florence was touched by the beaming smile

'There'll be drinks all round, Tilly, on the house that evening,' said George, adding a question. 'New job for you this?'

'Started here last week. Lucky for me a girl left 'cos of having a baby. It's not easy finding a job round here. What makes it so rotten Sally getting the push from hers this morning, like you know all about, Mr Bird. She said you was ever so kind when she told you about it.'

'Do you know if she'd any luck at the vicarage?'

Tilly pulled a face. 'The vicar's sister sent her off with a flea in the ear, said she was shocked Sally would try pushing her way in there after she'd been shown one door already because of impertinence. That's what you get for honesty! I told Sally it probably wouldn't have come out, that I couldn't see Mr Quigley bothering to mention it to the vicar and that witch never sees anyone, leastways not as I've heard.'

And, thought George, would Quigley, as churchwarden, wish to draw attention one moment sooner than necessary to his being married to, putting it mildly, a very strange woman.

Florence read his mind sufficiently well, that it seemed best to turn the conversation away from the Quigleys. 'I'll look into taking Sally on at Mullings, if you think she'd like that.'

'Oh, she would!' Tilly exclaimed. 'I know she'd be thrilled to bits.'

'Don't say anything to her yet. I'll have to work out how much time I'm able to give her. Elsie Trout has been helping out in the kitchen for a while now and I recently promised her another half day, but spring cleaning's coming up and any extra pair of hands is always needed to get us through that and we'll see how things go from there.'

'Thank you, Mrs Norris. And I promise to keep mum.' Tilly realized the eyes of the proprietress were on her and, by a twitch of her apron, conveyed this fact to Florence. Taking down their order with a brisk wiggle of pencil on notepad she departed.

'That was good of you,' said George, 'I hope you didn't feel . . .'

'That I twisted your arm? Of course not. I like the sound of Sally.'

'We haven't left ourselves much time to eat.' The clock on the wall pointed to quarter past one, but Tilly did not leave them to fidget, she returned speedily with the bowls of tomato soup, slices of pork pie and the plate of crusty bread they had requested.

'Again thanks ever so.' Beaming, she placed the bill on the table so they wouldn't have to wait for it and left them to what both, being hungry, seemed a feast. Not something to be swallowed down because it was quick.

They were polishing off the last crumbs of pork pie, when they spotted Mrs North and Miss Heron seating themselves a couple of tables away from theirs. Talking all the while they did so in apparently agitated fashion and continuing with heads close together. At one point they bumped foreheads and Miss Heron's hat got knocked sideways. What was more she either didn't notice, or couldn't be bothered to adjust it.

'This,' murmured George to Florence, 'given that she's a fastidiously neat woman is of the deepest interest.'

'Possibly,' Florence whispered back, 'they have got wind the Bank of England has closed its doors because it can't withstand a run on the pound, or it could be the sweetshop is out of mint imperials. But let's not try and work it out. I think we've done enough talking about our neighbours for one and may have been wrong about most of what we came up with. Let's go to the vicarage.'

And so they did.

ELEVEN

Neither Florence nor George had ever been inside the vicarage. If not as much a recluse as Mrs Quigley, the Reverend Pimcrisp had kept as many of his fellow men at bay as possible and for years the only woman to darken the premises was his housekeeper, now retired, after which had come Mrs Stubbins. She claimed he had never uttered a word to her, conveying any instructions by notes left in her absence on the kitchen table. The bishop and high clerics could not be left to batter on a closed door. Presumably they were invited into the drawing room, or his study, and offered the hospitality of refreshment. Perhaps even a light repast, but if partial to what Mrs Stubbins referred to as a glass of 'Oh, be joyful' they would have been disappointed. Reverend Pimcrisp, so Mr North had once confided to George, was the sort to secretly wish Jesus had turned the water into lemonade. Events that would commonly be held in a vicarage, such as the Mother's Union, and planning committees for the Christmas bazaar and so on were held in the church, even in winter with only a small brazier in the aisle to combat the icy chill. And this was thought odd by some of his most ardent admirers, including those who like Miss Hobbs viewed him as a saint, because the exterior of the house had a welcoming aspect.

It was Georgian, with the long well-spaced windows of that period and its buff stone walls which had a mellowed glow, even when the sun wasn't shining. Florence and George arrived a few minutes before the appointed time. The knocker had rusted, one of several signs of neglect; it fell with a heavy thud despite what George had considered a polite tap.

'I hope that hasn't jolted the pictures off the wall. Don't want to start off on the wrong foot,' George was saying when the door opened with a displeased sounding creak and a woman who had to be the vicar's sister surveyed them. She resembled him quite closely, the same thick brown hair, square face and sturdy build.

That being so, they said together, 'Miss Fielding?'

'Of course.' She stood aside to let – allow – them to enter a large square hall with a handsome staircase, marred by depressing wallpaper. 'I don't win any prizes for knowing you're Mr Bird and Mrs Norris, come to discuss your upcoming wedding with my brother. He's not here, but you are early.'

Two minutes – three at the most – but they, sensing that Miss Fielding would always have the last word, smiled and nodded and waited for her to tell them what to do next.

'We'll go into the drawing room and wait for him.'

'Thank you.'

On reaching this apartment, possessed of a tomb-like quality undiminished by a fire burning briskly in the grate and an attempt made to liven things up by a scattering of cushions on a sofa and armchairs, but wreaths would have done as good, if not a better job of achieving this end.

'Hideous, isn't it?' said Miss Fielding surprisingly. 'I'm itching to get started redecorating it, my brother is happy to leave decisions of that sort to me. I've kept house for him for years, ever since his first curate days. Our parents didn't want him to go into the church, but you will know about that.'

George and Florence looked at each other. 'We didn't,' he said, and Florence didn't counter with what she'd heard mentioned.

'That's a wonder. This is a nattering place, isn't it? Why don't you sit down.' This was spoken in admonishment – as if they were the ones who should have suggested doing so. 'I really can't think what has delayed Aiden. He's never late for any of his many, many obligations.'

'Don't worry about us.' Florence joined George on a very hard sofa.

'I'm not. He left at around eleven to meet with the vicar of Small Middlington, to discuss working together and taking over services for each other when the need arises. What can be keeping him; all I can think is this other man had a problem he needed to discuss at length. A crisis of faith perhaps.' She was interrupted by the ringing of a telephone. 'That'll be my brother now.'

She was gone for a least five minutes, during which Florence and George sat in almost complete silence. The room put a crimp on the sort of conversation that may arise in such situations: 'That's a charming table' or 'I wonder who the man in that portrait is' or 'I like that lamp'. To have said the wallpaper was the colour of mildew, though true, would have been ruder by a mile than either was capable, but they both wondered if it had started out that way, or had been abetted by damp. Florence was thinking that what she had perceived as a sideboard, largely covered by a dusty cloth, was in fact a piano, when Miss Fielding returned to the room. George stood and Florence did likewise, the expression on her face informing them they would not be much longer.

'Bad news?' They spoke as one voice.

'Indeed. That dreadful road!'

They knew which one. Referred to locally as the Middlington Road, because it was the most straightforward route to Small and Large Middlington, it ran parallel to the village street at its start on the far side of the green. There were a few houses at the top, including Major Wainwright's, but then it descended rapidly, dropping off sharply in places above the valley. The locals knew its ways, and in the main drove it with the necessary caution.

'An accident.' George did not put it as a question.

'My poor brother! Out serving his flock. Thank goodness we had the telephone installed. Reverend Pimcrisp wouldn't have one; it must have made the bishop very cross.'

A dreadful silence. During which the piano became for Florence a coffin on a pedestal.

Miss Fielding roused, not to a torrent of anguish but to outrage. 'That stupid, stupid woman!'

'The driver of the other car?' George voiced the natural supposition of himself and Florence.

'There was no other car. It was a bicycle ridden by the village nurse's daughter.'

Una, who'd claimed to be working a full day at Hobbs' Haberdashery.

'He was coming up that nasty bit of the hill when she swerved towards him.'

'Her mind must have been somewhere else entirely,' said Florence, that morning's conversation about her troubles flooding back.

'Forcing him,' Miss Fielding plowed on, 'to spin the wheel so hard he ended up on the other side of the road with the car dangling on the cliff edge.'

Cliff was an exaggeration, but the severest critic could not have faulted Miss Fielding over a particularity. There was a sheer drop of ten or more feet if the place Florence and George were thinking about, was the one where Mr Fielding had been in danger of life and limb.

'Her mind elsewhere, you say! A nursemaid might as well use that excuse after dropping the baby out an upstairs window! And all she got was bruised knees when she came off the bike. I'd like to think she's kneeling on them now, begging not only for God's forgiveness but even more importantly my brother's. But needless to say she became – made herself – the focus of attention and sympathy. Mr North drove up on the scene, on his way back from wherever he'd been, assisted Aiden in getting his car back on the road and between them got the woman to her feet. Sounds as if she was a dead weight one moment and a bundle of hysterics the next.'

This cleared up what Mrs North and Miss Heron had been twittering about in the Spinning Wheel. Mr North would have delivered the news to his wife when he got home and, as no one had died or been seriously injured, it had provided a tantalizing topic of discussion for the women, especially in light of Una Newsome's already intriguing situation.

Florence and George had each attempted to get a question, or comment in edgewise, only to be forestalled; understandably so given Miss Fielding's heightened emotions. 'Aiden got her into his car and Mr North managed to stow the bicycle in the boot. And he not a young man. But she won't have given a thought to that! She's with her mother now, with that busy woman fussing over her.'

'Are they at Miss Younger's house?' Florence managed to squeeze this in.

'That's where Aiden had to take her. He said she clearly was in no fit state to be left alone. Oh, yes, I'm sure she made that very clear. And there he still remains. He asked me to offer you his apologies, and will arrange to see you on another day convenient to you.'

Florence and George made the right sort of responses, cut short by Miss Fielding's surging them into the hall and out the door.

'In her place, George' – they were walking arm in arm – 'I'd be desperate to sit down with a cup of tea.'

'Or something stronger, if her brother does not hold Pimcrisp's views on strong drink.'

'He and Una might both have been killed. You don't think . . .?'

'That was her hope?'

'Precisely.'

'That she'd planned it?'

'When telling her mother she had to work until evening? No, that doesn't make sense.'

'You're right. She could have left Hobbs' at the usual time, gone home to collect her bike, and crucially there was no counting on a vehicle coming towards her on reaching that point of the road.'

'Silly of me.' Florence drew closer to him.

'You're worried about her and with good reason. So am I; it could be that she attempted the collision in an impulse of despair. That's bound to cross her mother's mind, but it could be she desperately needed some time alone and hoped that being out in the fresh air, riding nowhere in particular, would give her time to think.'

'Or she could have had a fixed destination. Perhaps she was on her way to see a friend in either Small or Large Middlington. A woman whose shoulder she could cry on, have a few drinks with, get tidily, or . . .'

'Meet up with her husband.'

Florence nodded. 'Coming in by train to Large Middlington, so they could discuss their situation. That would certainly explain her riding along in a complete daze.'

George squeezed her hand. 'Do you realize how much of the day we've spent speculating on other people's lives?'

'Whilst the story of last evening's stranger remains untold.

I know it has to be concerning, otherwise you wouldn't have decided to hold back on it, until we'd been to the vicarage. I think we should go back to the pub rather than Mullings because we'll have it to ourselves until opening time.'

This was the case because Dick Saunders would have left shortly after closing up at three and it was now twenty past that hour, but as they came up to the Dog and Whistle they saw Lord Stodmarsh and Mercy Tenneson coming towards them, both with set faces, suggesting to Florence that they had been quarrelling, as they had appeared to be doing when she had glimpsed them across the green that morning.

Oh, dear, she thought, they really deserve shaking. This has been going on for a while and if they had the sense they were born with they'd know they were meant for each other. His Lordship brightened instantly on seeing his beloved Florrie and George. And Mercy, despite her temper being up, couldn't withhold a smile. She had grown close to them and was eager to know all details of the upcoming wedding.

'How grim! I shall punish him by not going to church tomorrow.' She stamped her foot on hearing how for reasons beyond the vicar's control they had been unable to meet with him. Another stamp. It should have made her look ridiculously childlike, but every one of Mercy's movements had an element of grace, that heightened the untamed quality of her beauty.

His Lordship shrugged. 'I doubt he'll notice your absence.'

Florence wanted to say, 'Really Ned, be the one to act like a grown-up.' She held her tongue. She was fairly confident he wasn't the one creating the friction between them. Did Mercy enjoy wielding her power over him? Or was she fearful of not keeping his interest, and so tested the limits of what he might feel for her, hoping it was love. So foolish, but she was barely nineteen, without family, living in a cottage with an old lady who'd been kind to her as a child. And he was an earl.

He declined the invitation for them to come inside. Probably too eager to continue bickering, George thought with a smile, then reconsidered. Ned would know he and Florence wanted time alone to talk about the future and their disappointment at not being able to firm up the wedding date.

'It's interesting,' he said as they went by way of the side

door, 'that this new vicar is referred to as Mr Fielding, whereas no one would have dreamed of calling his predecessor anything but Reverend Pimcrisp.'

'Times change even in hidebound places such as this.'

They hung their coats on the pegs in the alcove. The fire in George's office had burned down, but the embers still glowed red and he tossed on a log.

'We should soon have a nice little blaze.'

'You're stalling,' said Florence. 'Now the time has come to begin, you're finding it hard, which tells me it was a troublesome story, even tragic.'

'He walked in and told me that twenty years ago that day he had buried his sister. Perfectly understandable he should state this abruptly.' George moved his desk chair and angled it next to the one she had taken. 'People often blurt out, before I can say good evening, what they've been carrying around in their heads all day. But there was something decidedly odd about him. Eerie. He stood for minutes at a time, saying nothing, staring blank-eyed from a shuttered face. And I began to think there might be more to it than his being consumed by sad memories. That he was mad, possibly dangerously so, and I was trapped as audience of one, waiting for the curtain to rise on a chilling melodrama.'

'That he'd not only buried his sister; he'd murdered her.'

'I pictured the scene, a sky of threatening cloud, wind and shuddering trees, the spade in his hand. He said it had been done at night, but I didn't get round to how he had killed her, I suppose my mind baulked at raising that image.'

'Which wasn't the case' – Florence remained sitting very still – 'otherwise today would have been entirely different. You'd have spent most, if not all, of it talking with the police. Continue dear, and I won't interrupt unless I have a burning question.'

Indeed she said barely anything at all as he went detail by detail through the stranger's story. George wasn't much of a reader, the morning and evening papers were enough for him in that line, but conversations, even of the everyday sort, rarely failed to interest him and if necessary he could have repeated them almost word for word. Last evening's conversation had been well outside the everyday and from the start Florence came to feel she'd been present, seated in a shadowy corner, absorbing every revelation and George's reactions to them.

Silence, except for the crackling of the fire, held them both when he finished. Then she said, 'Heartbreaking, with evil behind it. So many questions to be answered, first and foremost being the identity of the author of the anonymous letter. Of lesser importance, but of interest, is whether Graham Lieland's appearance on the scene was purely for the sake of fetching Major Wainwright's forgotten pipe, or if he's the one who's been keeping the stranger up to date on what's happening in the area.'

George nodded. 'They could have planned to meet at a certain time; the fog delayed things, so he took a walk hoping to spot him, telling the major he was going after the pipe.'

'But there are some things we can guess.'

'Such as where the stranger was headed.'

'Yes.'

'He loved his parents and sister dearly, and he's devoted to his wife and children. He faced, as his character required, two obligations. The first to reveal to the police, by way of the letter to Inspector LeCrane, the cause of her death and hasty burial. That would prevent an innocent person from being suspected of murdering her. His other objective was to get his family out of England so they wouldn't have to deal with seeing the investigation – there'll have to be one – blazed across every newspaper in the country.'

'You said he mentioned his wife's brother had moved to Canada. He won't need to be hunted down over there, George, the address where he can be located will be included in what he's written to LeCrane. You believe and so do I that he's a good man. I understand why you fretted about holding on to the letter for now, but it's the right thing to do. You may get some tut-tutting and a couple of wags of the finger, before we have to tell what we think.'

'And what's that?' George looked at her with tender amusement, touched with pride.

'Where she's buried.'

'And that is?'

'In the churchyard. What safer, more available, place to

bury a body? Added to which we have the stranger's fear of imminent discovery at a time when there is a person in the village expected to die at any minute.'

'Agnes Younger.'

'Meaning the grave where her brother was laid to rest will shortly be re-opened. A brother who, if I remember correctly, died twenty years ago.'

'What else comes to mind?'

'That it seems more likely than not the girl's family lived near the churchyard, otherwise why not take her to a wooded area? And who do we have living in absolutely the right spot, but a man who more than any other was up to the task he took upon himself that night. The grave digger. The one before Fred Shilling. A man named Jeremiah Rudge.'

'That's something of a leap, Florence.'

'Yes. But I'm going on a couple of things that I've remembered. I only knew Mrs. Rudge by sight, but I was struck by how painful her hands looked, they were so terribly twisted and knotted by rheumatism. She and my mother-in-law had been friends when they were young, then lost touch over the years. When she died, Mamma asked me to go with her to the funeral. And what I recall of that event was the talk of how shameful it was that the daughter, who had once seemed so devoted, had not picked up a left home without a moment's notice hadn't bothered to come back for her mother's funeral. Of course, I may be barking up the wrong tree.'

'But it has to be followed up. What's our next move?'

'To talk to Sally Barton and hopefully her mother.'

TWELVE

Sophie took the train to Liverpool Street Station. There she sat on a bench and wrote the two letters, one to the Euwings, the other to Mary Thomas and felt a small sense of accomplishment upon posting them. That's what she must do, focus on positives, such as having parted on reasonably good terms with Mrs Blount, the sandwiches and Thermos of tea had been kind. She must not think of herself as being cast out upon the world, but as having come to another fork in the road, which might well open on to wonderful opportunities she would've otherwise have missed. For the moment, however, it was best not to think about the future. It was filled with too many imminent hurdles not to bring misgivings. She drank the tea, ate the sandwiches, noticed a man who bore sufficient resemblance to Mr Crawley to set her heart pounding and had to keep telling herself over and over again he wasn't some arch villain in a book, with the power to track her down however cleverly she disguised herself or changed her name.

Even so, she looked over her shoulder before passing through the barrier on to the platform and was grateful she had to change trains twice before completing her journey. A man traveling with two children lifted her suitcases into the carriage and on to the rack, replied pleasantly when she thanked him and retired behind his newspaper. The children opened story books. Any other day Sophie might have thought them a nice family – wondered whether the mother was enjoying some relaxation, or preparing a meal for their return. Now she saw the security of normality.

For quite a while she gazed out the windows at buildings and elbow-to-elbow houses, back gardens with the occasional tree drifting past. And she was somewhat fuzzily back in the sitting room of the house in Oglesby. She was eleven, maybe twelve. Uncle Henry sat across from her reading a book. She was doing the same. Hers had a girl and a horse on its bright cover. She raised her head and saw him looking at her.

'Your parents would be proud of you, Sophie. I'm proud of you; now get back to whatever you're reading.'

Had he really said that? She was still in her old home, in the same room, but the man seated across from her was not Uncle Henry, but one considerably younger with brown hair and beard and kind eyes. And she was happy, as if a lamp had been lit inside her. It wasn't right to feel that glow. Uncle Henry was dying. She should be with him upstairs in his bedroom, reading to him – it wouldn't matter if it was that book of long ago, about the girl who went to gymkhanas, Uncle Henry was no longer able to follow the words, but their flow soothed him. And yet she stayed . . .

Sophie startled awake. How silly, how very silly! He would be married by now, with a child, maybe two. He might well always have been married, by always she meant in the brief time she'd known him. She had made the assumption he was a bachelor, because his sister kept house for him, but that was far from conclusive; his wife might be the shy retiring sort who preferred leaving parochial business to someone she deemed more capable. She really knew next to nothing about him. He'd come into her life when she needed comfort, of the common kindness, listening sort, and he'd provided that, most importantly on the evening of Uncle Henry's death. That's why she hadn't forgotten him. People, reasonable people, remembered who was with them at such times.

The man and two children had got off the train at some point and the carriage was now quite full. She must have done more than doze. Her watch confirmed this and she realized she must be within five minutes of the station where she had to change, which as it turned out, meant stepping down on to the platform and crossing to the other side where her next train waited. Her final transfer was just as easy. She had half an hour before arrival at her destination. She had blocked her mind from all but the vaguest thoughts of what awaited there, but setting cowardice aside, she put first things first – locating an inn, or guest house, settling herself in and finding somewhere to eat, if meals weren't offered where she was staying. She'd been making a mountain out of a molehill. She'd write to her relative. Be straightforward in explaining she'd left her job, was drawn to doing domestic work in a stately home, remembered her mother speaking of the one in the district and hoped if someone from the district recommended her, the chance of being taken on would be increased.

As the train was pulling into the station doubts crowded back in, cloaked in words such as presumptuous and encroaching, but she pulled herself together. She had made a hurried, panic-driven decision in coming here. There was time to think it over, consider other options; there were places in England she had always wanted to see and she had sufficient money, if managed carefully, to hold her for a while. She was the only person in that carriage to get off the train, others descended up and down the platform, to weave their way between the small crowd waiting on the platform. There were exclamations of greetings: 'Oh, there you are, Martha, so good to see you' and 'Hello, old chap, must be donkey's years we last got together.' And then she heard her name, 'Miss Dawson', hailed by a male voice. It was a moment to set her reeling and so it did because she knew that voice and it wasn't Mr Crawley's; it belonged to the man she'd dreamed about just a few hours ago. She set down her suitcases and turned very slowly – very slowly for fearing of jerking herself awake. This couldn't be real, she must still be sleeping.

'It's good to see you again. I'm sorry . . . I've startled you.'

The clerical collar. He was there, looking at her with concerned brown eyes. Very much in the flesh. But how?

'Understandably. You were expecting a Nurse Newsome to meet you.'

'I wasn't.' She heard her voice as from a distance. 'I wasn't expecting anyone. There was no one with reason to suppose I was coming here.'

'You didn't get the letter?'

'Letter?'

'The one letting you know your cousin Miss Younger is dying and very much wants to see you. It should have arrived this morning.'

'No.' And then she remembered the post scattered on the floor as a result of the Crawley children's antics. If in the picking up Mrs Blount had seen an envelope addressed to her, she would have told her. It must have slipped out of sight. 'Is Miss Younger – Agnes – in a lot of pain?'

'Little, if any, she sleeps most of the time; the result of a stroke. The letter was written down for her by the village nurse and sent to the address your cousin had in her address book; but perhaps you've moved.'

'No, but there . . . was an upset this morning at my lodgings and it . . . the letter must have been misplaced. I didn't know she was ill; we haven't corresponded in a long time.'

'Then it's chance' – he stood looking at her with a deepening gaze – 'otherwise known as providence that brings you?'

'Yes.'

'Steered by circumstances?'

'I've left my job.'

'I'm sorry you arrive to such sad news; I haven't even shaken hands with you.' He did so before picking up her cases. 'We'll have time to talk in the car, it's right outside. Or, if you'd prefer, you can sleep. It's about a forty-minute drive from here to Dovecote Hatch.'

He guided her out of the station to a car parked outside and opened the front passenger seat. There was a man leaning against the wall a few strides down from them and she saw Mr Fielding glance his way. I mustn't do this, she thought – notice the smallest thing he does, as if I've come home to him from a long journey and feel that his every breath is partly mine. My thoughts should only be of Cousin Agnes.

When he returned from stowing her luggage in the boot and sat down beside her, he said, 'I thought I recognized that man, from years ago, but he headed off before I could get a second look. He won't be someone I saw more than a few times, or I would remember, so it must have been the circumstances under which we met.'

'You have a good memory for faces?'

He turned on the ignition. 'I remembered yours.'

She responded cheerfully. 'Thank goodness! Or you would have had trouble picking me out from every other female on the platform. Please tell me all you can about what has happened to Aunt Agnes.'

'And how I enter the situation?' He eased the car into the flow of traffic.

'That too; is she a friend of yours? Had you come to say a final farewell?'

'I only recently became vicar of St Peter's parish in Dovecote Hatch, but I'd met her years ago, at the end of my school days, when I was for six weeks or so on a visit to the village, staying with the then incumbent, Mr Pimcrisp. My father was against my studying to enter the church. He and a friend of his hit on a plan to put me right off the idea.'

'Which was?'

'The friend was Lord Asprey, a cousin of Pimcrisp, and he assured my father that being cloistered for a duration with Old Sour Face, as he called him, would have me begging to be allowed to become a soldier.'

'Your father's choice for you.'

'A line of them in his family, stretching back, according to him, to a noble warrior fighting alongside Harold at the Battle of Hastings.'

'But the plan didn't succeed.' How foolish she must sound stating the obvious.

'Ah, but I was cunning in those days.' He tilted his face towards her and smiled with the mischievous delight of a schoolboy. 'I insisted I would only do as ordered if I could take my closest friend along and my father was only too happy to agree because Kip was all set on flying aeroplanes for God and country. He had a very serious side to him, but never failed to find enjoyment wherever it was lurking. We had the best winter of our lives. We both fell in love, or believed we had.'

'Kip?' It was all she could come up with that didn't sound prying.

'The name we gave him at school. Short for Kipling; he was so keen on *The Jungle Book* he could practically recite all the stories by heart. I remember your uncle telling me you were a bookworm.'

'So was he.' She drew a breath. 'Tell me about Cousin Agnes, I know nothing of her life, beyond what my mother told me, and she died when I was very young. I got a Christmas card from her every year. That's how I had her address.'

'She was kind, kind to me and Kip that summer, inviting us into her home when she saw us out and about. Made marvellous apple tarts. She kept house for her brother, and helped him in the orchard and with getting the fruit to market. The brother died while we were there, some sort of fever that took him between one day and the next; Kip and I went to the funeral. We hoped her sorrow would be eased by her having recently become engaged to a neigbouring farmer; they'd known each other since they were children.'

Sophie turned swiftly to face him. 'But she didn't marry!'

'I discovered that, and the reason, when I returned all these years later and went to see her. She had an accident within a month of the wedding date; the banns had been read, but she refused to go through with it because her legs had been so badly damaged.'

'How did it happen?'

'She was standing close to a tree when it fell.'

'Did the farmer still want to marry her?'

'Oh, yes! I've heard from people who knew him that he was broken-hearted; remained a bachelor until his death a few years ago.'

'How sad, but I can understand her unwillingness to be a burden on him.' Sophie stared out the window without seeing much. She had from the time she went to live with Uncle Henry been determined not to be one on him. She had heard the murmurings following the deaths of her parents. 'It's not an easy thing taking on someone else's child . . . Let's hope she shows a grateful spirit . . . It's one thing sacrificing for your own.'

'Are you thinking,' Mr Fielding asked with the interest which had meant so much to her three years ago, 'that after a while he might have come to feel he'd bitten off more than he could chew?'

'It could have turned out that way. That's the saddest part of all, the never knowing. Thank you for telling me. I now understand why she replied the way she did to the letter I wrote to her before leaving Oglesby.'

'Want to tell me about that?' He eased the car on to the verge and turned off the motor.

And so she did, with the ease of thinking aloud, letting it seep through that she had been hurt, but felt she shouldn't be, had written a polite response, so polite that it must have revealed the fullness of her disappointment. 'And now I discover why she brushed me off.'

'She was afraid, Miss Dawson, that if you came for a visit you might be the sort of young woman who'd be moved by sympathy to offer to remain and take care of her, or if dissuaded from that, spend every summer holiday and Christmas with her. She wouldn't have wanted to put you, or herself, through that. Unless, as she wrote, you have reached a point of great need.'

'I thought . . .' There was a catch in Sophie's voice.

'That she felt compelled to say something of the sort, in order to ease her conscience?'

'Yes.'

'But today that need arose.' His voice was gently encouraging. 'You mentioned an occurrence at your lodgings and that you'd left your job. Were the two events linked?'

She sat, not wanting to burden him to sound as though she expected pity. But it would be such a relief to tell him. Tell him how the day had begun in an ordinary way . . . and then the doorbell ringing and Mrs Blount pounding up the stairs . . . Mrs Crawley outside with the children, Em'ly in the push-chair, the boy chalking the pavement . . . all of them. Sam glowering.

He didn't break the silence. It smoothed into a softness of the most comforting sort.

'It's Sam I mind about most,' she said, 'his pain and the thought of him carrying it with him through life. He was the eldest. So fierce, so much the grown-up, taking charge of his brothers and sisters and he so very young himself. Of course the way he expressed himself was dreadful. What Uncle Henry would have called strong language, I suppose. I'd never heard anything like it. I imagine you would have been thoroughly shocked, Mr Fielding.'

A smile touched his mouth. 'I don't shock easily, Miss

Dawson; my sister encourages me to work on this failing, but there's a lot of back sliding.'

'Oh, that is good to hear! Knowing you won't judge me out of hand the way Mrs Blount did; although she warmed up later and even told me about the man who got it into his head she had designs on him. Which I'd discovered was the idea that Mr Crawley had seized on about me, or rather, that I returned his feelings for me, causing his wife to get so upset she brought their children round to my lodging. Her parting words were that if I wanted him I could take what went with him.'

'Highly unpleasant for you and deeply disturbing for the children.'

'Mr Fielding, please don't think I don't pity her, although not enough at that moment.'

'I'd be surprised if you managed a clear thought for hours afterwards. I don't need to ask whether she was mistaken in regard to you.'

'No?' The gratitude she felt warmed her all through.

'Any more than I'd believe you'd robbed a bank, or joined a witches' coven.'

'I could've changed since you last saw me.'

'You haven't.' He fumbled in his coat pockets, then shook his head. 'I don't have them – pipe or matches. Anyway I don't smoke in the car. Continue, Miss Dawson, just as I'm not easily shocked, I'm not readily bored, particularly when listening to an account of harrowing, life-changing matters.'

And so Sophie went through it all, from beginning to end. When she'd boarded the train from Ilford. Only leaving out the fear that had gripped her that she was not fully done with Mr Crawley, that somehow or other he'd find a way to discover where she'd gone. She didn't want to bother Mr Fielding with such foolishness, which in any case was fading and, with him at her side, would likely vanish by the time she reached Cousin Agnes's home.

'I hope you don't feel responsible for any of this,' he said.

'It's hard not to.'

'For you it would be. Others would be angry, or shrug it off.'

They left it there. He didn't urge her to say more. His thoughts must have returned as hers were doing to the dying woman; he already had the car back on the road, one that a short way on began to climb steeply and he told her they were now but ten minutes from Dovecote Hatch. And she remembered something.

'You said at the railway station that I was supposed to have been met by a nurse, the one taking care of Cousin Agnes. How did it happen that you came instead?'

'Ah, that leads to the one harrowing moment of my day. I was returning from Small Middlington by way of this road, sometime between noon and one when I had a near collision with a woman on a bicycle. Nurse Newsome's daughter.' He gestured with his hand. 'It happened right here. As you see, a particularly nasty place to happen.'

Sophie did. She saw the nasty drop off on the other side of the road. 'Was she badly hurt?'

'Fortunately not. Bruised legs and scraped hands when she came off the bike.'

'But it could have ended terribly, she could have gone over the side, or your car could have plunged down into that valley with you inside.'

'But here I am safe and sound. I took Una Smith to her mother at Miss Younger's house, rather than the one where they live together, although that was what she wanted. I didn't, however, think she should be left alone after suffering such a shock.'

'Una, as in St George and the dragon, I loved that story; we read it at school when I was about eight. I hope her mother helped her get over her fright.'

'Nurse Newsome is very well regarded in the village, a widow and I understand close to her daughter.'

'Is Una Smith also widowed?'

'No, she is only recenty married. She and her husband are living with Nurse Newsome. At the moment he's visiting his ailing mother. They met in Worthing. Nurse Newsome mentioned that to me because, as you know, it's close to Brighton and I told her that's the nearest town to Oglesby.'

'I hope his mother recovers quickly, it must be hard for a newlywed couple to be parted.'

The car had rounded the green and was passing the Dog and

Whistle. 'I'm afraid there's been gossip as to why he really left. I only mention it because you're bound to catch wind of it. It's the same here as it was in Oglesby and I imagine a lot of villages. Someone decides something odd's going on, someone else agrees and it goes from there. I remember your Uncle Henry telling me that was one of the reasons he steered clear of churches, people praying out loud and gossiping under their breath.'

'He had lots of reasons. The main being it was a lot of rigmarole, but he did detest gossip, he said it went under the virtuous guise of being interested in your neighbours.'

'I liked him.'

'I'm glad. I often hear his voice in my head.'

'Some people are chattier in the next world than in this one.' Mr Fielding turned to smile at her; it made his face incredibly attractive and she found herself laughing in return. They'd wended their way through a series of lanes and now halted outside a stone-walled house surrounded by trees.

Orchard House, Cousin Agnes's house. She felt a wave of shame on getting out of the car. She hadn't been able or willing to keep her thoughts on the dying woman for more than several minutes at a time during the drive, she'd been wrapped up in the happiness and comfort of being, miraculously, with Mr Fielding. Spilling out her woes regarding Mr Crawley, encouraging him to talk of himself. And she hadn't come here out of regard for this woman, but for the help she hoped to gain.

Mr Fielding knocked lightly on the door and it was quickly opened by a middle-aged woman with a spreading figure and a pleasant, still pretty face. Sophie assumed this was Nurse Newsome, but once inside it soon became clear she was Mrs Chester, the doctor's wife. After greeting them and saying how glad she was that Miss Younger's wish was fulfilled and she would get to see her dear cousin's daughter before the end, she led the way into the sitting room.

'So kind of you, Mr Fielding, to collect Miss Dawson from Large Middlington, when Nurse Newsome needed to be with Una. Don't worry. My husband looked her over when he arrived about an hour ago, found her injuries minimal, and took her to Miss Gillybud's house, knowing she would be well taken care of there, and it would allow Nurse to concentrate on her patient. Then he fetched me and drove them both home. He's upstairs now and I'll take you up, Miss Dawson, and you too if you wish, vicar.'

Sophie looked at him.

'I think you and she should have some private time together. I'll return to the vicarage, but I'll be back before you notice I've gone.'

'Thank you for all you've done.' She held out her hand and smiled as he shook it.

'Chin up, Miss Dawson,' he said. And when the front door closed behind him she followed Mrs Chester up the stairs into the bedroom where death waited.

THIRTEEN

M rs Chester touched her gently on the shoulder. 'I'll leave you now, my dear. My husband will have a talk with you and then join me downstairs.'

The doctor turned as she entered, shook her hand in a pleasantly brisk manner, much as Mr Fielding had done, and stepped aside providing a view of the patient's face. It was a gaunt, but not emaciated one, framed by grey hair hanging in a plait over her right shoulder. She looked peaceful.

'She's not as deeply asleep as she appears, every so often she will rouse, and when she does she asks for you. She knows' – he lowered his voice to a murmur – 'the end is near . . . a day, two at most, perhaps sooner.'

Sophie whispered back, 'I'm not afraid to be alone with her.'

'Good girl.' He drew a chair close to the bed. 'If anything about her breathing worries you, or for other reasons you think she is worse, come to the top of the stairs and call down. My wife was a nurse before our marriage. That's a lot of years ago but she hasn't forgotten the hang of it. She says it's like riding a bicycle.'

'I'm grateful.'

'No need to be; she'll be up in a little while with a pot of tea. The fire will last for a while. I have to go and see other patients, but I'll be back.'

Mr Fielding had made the same promise; but that mightn't be until he was required and summoned. He wouldn't wish to get under the doctor's feet, or oblige Mrs Chester to produce refreshment for him. She had just sat down and was leaning towards Cousin Agnes, when a large ginger cat jumped on to her lap and began kneading at her with its paws.

'My goodness! Where did you did you spring from?'

'Probably from behind the curtain,' rasped Cousin Agnes without opening her eyes. 'Who're you?'

'Sophie . . . Sophie Dawson; I've just arrived.'

'Have you now, well, let me get a look at Elizabeth's daughter.' Her eyelids parted sufficiently to reveal a sliver of faded blue. 'We saw a lot of each other when we were children and remained fond of each other through the years.'

'Mother told me so. She said you both loved walking in the woods, especially at bluebell time. And the sound of the cuckoo.'

'I should have helped you, it was selfish of me, wicked.' Cousin Agnes stirred restlessly and her voice slurred. 'That nice boy . . . grown up now . . . says it wasn't, but I know . . . I let pride get in the way as I did before. You know the one I sent away, never married.'

'I had heard that. Would you like to tell me about him?'

But she was once more asleep. Sophie sat with the cat on her lap, listening for every breath from those pale lips. I wish I'd known her, she thought, or at least remembered more of what my mother told me about her. I'm so grateful today brought me to her bedside. I wonder what Uncle Henry would have made of it all. I wonder if there was ever a woman he loved and couldn't marry for one reason or another, and life, rather than choice, made him a confirmed bachelor. He'd never have told her, never have shared anything of a personal nature with her. Would he have done so with Dr Maitland or Mr Kent? She didn't think so; he'd told her on more than one occasion he'd no time for blather. This usually meant questions such as what he would like for lunch or dinner, or if he needed help finding his glasses when he was irritably hunting for them. Had he left this earth without revealing the joys or sorrow of his life to anyone? Or had he found in those final weeks a confidant in Mr Fielding? It should have seemed unlikely and yet . . . it didn't.

Cousin Agnes still slept, but the large orange cat stirred, stretched and looked up as if to enquire who she was and what she was doing there.

'I'm Sophie Dawson. Your mistress doesn't mind me being here; she asked me to come. What's your name?'

'Marmalade.'

Sophie, after a long day, was sufficiently startled to think the cat had spoken, but a woman came into view. Not Mrs Chester, but one similarly middle-aged, even elderly, with wispy mousy hair and twinkling eyes.

'Hello,' she said, 'I'm Miss Gillybud, a friend of Miss Younger. No, don't get up, or Marmalade will think you haven't taken to him and you'll never get on his right side. How are you? You should have been named Rose, you look like one. That pink and cream summer rose, I don't remember the name, something Latin, of course, but Greek was my subject, I taught it for years. But you won't want to hear about that.' The breathless rush ended with a finger pressed to the lips.

'Oh, but I would,' said Sophie. Miss Gillybud hadn't lowered her voice and now she forgot to do so. 'It's wonderful to meet someone close to Cousin Agnes.'

They looked over at the still figure on the bed. 'We won't wake her, Summer Rose, she'll open her eyes or start talking in her own good time; she never allowed anything or anyone to force her to do what she didn't want. You need to know that about her.'

Sophie couldn't be sure whether Miss Gillybud was lacing her words with meaning, or scattering the words like bird seed, but what she did know was that she liked her.

'Agnes is a good woman and a dear friend of nearly over twenty years. I gave her Marmalade, which I take as a right to be bossy about him. As I was with you just now. She and her brother had always had outdoor cats for the mousing, but it took the length of the *Odyssey* for her to agree to take one of my kittens. My two toms are Bovril and Marmite and I never know which is the father of which litter, or if it's both of them. Tammie, my female, has never said, nor would I ask her. My females, only one at a time because I don't believe in harems of the sort to pleasure sultans, are always named Tammie. It's short for Tamiera, the name of a heroine in a book I read and wished I'd been named that instead of Doris.'

'I think Doris is a pretty name. Has Cousin Agnes grown very fond of . . .?' Sophie caught herself in time. Marmalade might be hurt by the question. He certainly looked capable of understanding every word said. Perhaps it was best this conversation was cut short by Mrs Chester coming through the door with a tea tray, which she deposited on a chest of drawers.

'I left you two to get to know each other,' she said, before joining them at the bedside and taking the patient's pulse. 'My husband is downstairs talking to Mr Fielding, but he'll be up shortly.'

'How interesting it is, that no one speaks of him as Reverend Fielding as was the case with Pimcrisp. I imagine he would've insisted on your being cast in hell if you addressed or referred to him as a mere mister. Of course he and I never spoke at all, he would look right through me if we passed. No running after lost sheep for him.'

'Miss Gillybud is an atheist,' Mrs Chester said as matter of factly as if letting Sophie know that she was a poet or a tennis player.

'So was the uncle who brought me up. I'm not sure whether I believe in God, or if I wish I could.'

'That's what church should be for, to help you to decide, not frighten people with the idea of a bogey man up in the sky eager to scare you out of your wits. This dear woman' – Mrs Chester smoothed the pillow – 'told me she refused to let Pimcrisp send her scrambling out of church for fear of hitting him over the head with her stick and sending him to whichever was God's intended place for him.'

She straightened up. 'Miss Dawson, we will leave you to help yourself to the tea and sandwiches.'

Taking Miss Gillybud's elbow, she propelled her to the doorway. 'Come Doris, dear, you can tell me about that extremely long book you are reading that I feel I should be interested in, though I know I could never wade through, but if you give me enough of an idea of what it's about I can pretend I have. And look and sound reasonably intelligent when others are discussing its brilliance.'

Their voices faded as they descended the stairs. Sophie poured herself a cup of tea and put some of the sandwiches on a plate. There were cheese and mustard and cress ones, along with salmon and cucumber. She doubted she would be able to taste them. Fatigue, the effects of the day, had taken hold and she wasn't hungry. But she must keep herself going. She was determined to stay awake as long as she could through the night. She had finished the sandwiches and a second cup of tea and was adjusting Marmalade on her lap when Cousin Agnes opened her eyes.

'You're still here?'

'And I'm not going anywhere.'

Marmalade leaped on to the foot of the bed, his emerald eyes fixed on his mistress.

'There are some of the letters your mother wrote to me in the drawer of that bureau under the window. Would you mind reading them to me?'

'I'd like to.' She fetched them, a dozen or so, still in their envelopes. She sat back down and opened the one on the top, saw that forgotten handwriting, with both a pang and a lightening of heart.

> My dear Agnes,
>
> I thought of you this morning when I was making plum jam, and remembered how your mother taught us how to get it to set one summer, the one when we spent the entire holidays at Orchard House. My parents had gone out to visit my paternal grandfather who was due to retire from the Indian Civil Service. I'd expected to miss them dreadfully, but being with you made that impossible . . .

'It all comes back, those lovely golden days. We had a swing . . . it may still be there. Lost amongst the trees.'

'We can look for it.'

'When spring comes.'

'And the bluebells are out.'

'Read me some more.'

Sophie did so, even after Cousin Agnes fell asleep. She had returned five of the letters – windows opening on to her mother's life – and returned them to their envelopes, when Cousin Agnes spoke again.

'Have you come to the one when she'd fallen in love with your father, but wasn't sure he returned her feelings?'

'Not yet.'

'I told her not to be afraid of revealing her heart.'

'That would take courage.'

'Read the one she wrote when you were born.'

Her eyes closed. Marmalade moved further up the bed to nestle against the outline of her feet and Dr Chester entered the bedroom, acknowledged Sophie, and bent over Cousin Agnes. On lifting his head he beckoned her out on to the landing.

'She seems much the same, but something – call it experience or instinct – tells me the end is drawing very near. I think you should rest while you have the opportunity.'

'If you don't mind I'd rather stay with her.'

'I understand, but you need to husband your strength. I'll send my wife up to show you where you can sleep and then she'll make Miss Younger comfortable without disturbing her. She's a woman I admire and like' – he smiled – 'not always possible to do both. I believe she held on until you got here and now is free to go in peace.'

'The vicar?'

'Is here and intends to stay throughout the night. And so is Miss Gillybud whom I understand you've met. Delightful person – a bit of a willow the wisp, as is often the case with brilliant women, but a better neighbour or truer friend isn't to be found.'

Sophie still had her mother's letters to Cousin Agnes in her hand when Mrs Chester showed her into a bedroom at the other end of the landing where her suitcases had been placed on the window seat. She was sure she wouldn't be able to even doze, and meant to read the ones she hadn't opened. But having found the toilet, taken her sponge bag along to the bathroom and removed her shoes and suit jacket, not willing to risk getting further undressed, she got under the eiderdown. Realized someone, presumably Mrs Chester, had put a hot water bottle into the bed and did not waken until a tap sounded at the door. A glance at her watch as she went to open it showed it was four in the morning.

Mrs Chester was outside. 'I'm sorry, dear, my husband said it was time to wake you. Better put on your jacket, or you'll be frozen even with the fire going well.'

Sophie did as advised, but did not bother with her shoes. She asked no questions, stood silent on entering Cousin Agnes's bedroom. It seemed to her blurred gaze full of people, but other than herself and Mrs Chester, there was only Dr Chester on one side of the bed, Mr Fielding on the other and Miss Gillybud at the foot with Marmalade in her arms. Sophie thought, I'm a stranger in their midst, a stranger to Cousin Agnes.

Mr Fielding looked up and smiled at her and beckoned for her to join him. When she had done so, he began the Lord's Prayer. Sophie added hers to the other voices, including Miss Gillybud's sweet treble. Mr Fielding added a blessing and at its ending, Dr Chester held up a hand.

'She's gone.'

Sophie slipped out on to the landing and made her way down to the sitting room; hearing footsteps behind her, she turned to face Mr Fielding.

'You need a good cry, Miss Dawson.' His expression was unreadable.

'I can't; I haven't really since I was a child.'

'All the more reason. Would holding a handkerchief' – he held out a snowy white one – 'help bring them on?'

She took it, but shook her head.

'What you also need' – his voice deepened – 'are a pair of arms around you, but for obvious reasons they can't be mine.'

'Against church policy.'

'Utterly precluded, but this isn't.' He took her hands in his, handkerchief included.

It was enough. More than enough. She knew his urge to hold her sprang from the wish to provide comfort as a relative would have done. And he knew she had none left. She loved him which meant she could not remain in Dovecote Hatch. To be near him would be too hard. But he was giving her the memory of his touch to take with her when she left, as soon as possible after the funeral. It would be a secret happiness taken into whatever the future offered.

FOURTEEN

For the first time in weeks there was little talk of Una Smith during the early morning kitchen bustle at Mullings. Winnie, one of the kitchen maids, did mention hearing the poor lady had fallen off her bicycle yesterday on that spiteful bit of road at the top of the hill. She was immediately reproved by Mrs MacDonald.

'Happens to people every day of the week. Why you should be bothering me and Mrs Norris with it, that kettle knows better than I do! You know, Miss Big Ears, that what Mrs Norris and I have on our minds ever since the newspaper boy brought word of it, is Miss Younger at Orchard House dying in.'

'And very sad, but wasn't like it come as a shock. My gran's got her best 'at all brushed and ready. Bought herself a new hanky at Hobbs'. She don't get out much and bin looking forward to the funeral.'

'I'm sure she has,' said Florence, before Mrs MacDonald could open her mouth. 'A lot of older people prefer funerals to weddings, they get to imagine their own send-off and all the nice things that'll be said about them.'

'And be glad it's not them, least till next time.'

'That could be so.'

'There's more I knows about, an' it do be about Miss Younger.'

'And that is?' Winnie needed squelching, but Florence gave Mrs MacDonald a warning glance. The time might come, and soon, when information gathered by way of the staff might be useful.

'Seems a young lady come yesterday, vicar brung her from train station. She's a niece or whatever. Wouldn't wonder if she was hoping to get something for her trouble. A nice little parting present to remember the old girl by.'

'That's enough, Winnie. I happen to know Miss Younger sent for her. Now go and do what Mrs Grumidge needs done in the scullery and please put your back into it; she's a bit off colour this morning.'

'She'll be round the corner sticking her tongue out,' Mrs MacDonald grumbled when Winnie had left with something close to a flounce. 'I don't know what girls are coming to these days. Really I don't, Florence. They don't know to keep their thoughts to themselves and, better yet, not have any when it comes to their betters. She'll have got her information from her follower, one of the undergardeners, no doubt.'

'Probably. She's only fifteen.'

'You were younger when you came here and you knew on walking through the door not to open it unless someone did it for you.'

'We can't turn back the clock. Sally Barton is looking for work.'

'The one with all those brothers?'

'That's her. And she has to be twenty. George says they're a good family. She was with Mr and Mrs Quigley, but there's been a parting of the ways.'

'Well, that doesn't speak ill of her.'

Florence poured their tea. 'My thinking.'

'Difficult to put up with on any level.' Mrs MacDonald added two spoonfuls of sugar to her cup and stirred vigorously. 'A funny couple if ever there was one. Her shutting herself away like Miss Havisham and him creeping into the church at dead of night, or so is said and when it comes to tittle tattle there's usually more than a few grains of truth.'

'I'll go and see Sally this morning. I think I could start her out as a chamber maid and see where to go from there, if she does well.'

'Not all that much of a rush, is there?'

'Actually there is, I need to talk to her about something else.'

'And you're not going to tell me what it is.'

'You'll soon find out.' Florence suppressed a smile. When that time came Mrs MacDonald would have experienced a feeling of foreboding, a sense of brooding horror that would increase in particulars, when acquainted with the facts as established in the real world. She'd already claimed to have woken with a shiver and a prickling of the spine informing her, well ahead of the paperboy, that Agnes Younger was gone. That had covered a good deal of the subsequent conversation, causing Winnie to interrupt out of boredom. Florence was dearly fond of Mrs MacDonald, but she'd been eager to say after fifteen minutes, that it was all very interesting, but she needed to telephone George.

She said it now.

'Of course you do, after the disappointment of not getting to talk to the vicar about fixing the wedding date, and all because Una Newsome, as was, fell off her bicycle. I tell you, Florence, I'm getting rather tired of her and all this business of her supposed troubles. Needs to forget that sorry husband of hers and give a thought to her poor, overworked mother. Good thing Mrs Chester took over for her last night.' The paperboy had been a fount of information.

George answered at the first ring. 'I've already tried to reach LeCrane,' he said after little preamble. 'Unfortunately he's on holiday and not due back until Wednesday. I left word for him to contact us as soon as he gets in. How soon can you be ready for me to fetch you, so we can pick up last evening's conversation where we left off?'

'I only have to put on my coat and hat.'

'I'm out the door.'

Ten minutes later they were in his office at the Dog and Whistle. On the way he'd asked if she'd eaten breakfast. She hadn't, but wasn't hungry; there was too much to think about. To this he'd answered that today of all days she needed at least a boiled egg and toast and was to sit down while he got them for her.

'And,' he said now, 'no talking till they're inside you. I'll let Dick Saunders know I need him to open up for me again at eleven thirty.'

Florence promised. It was lovely to be looked after, to have this little quiet time to sit and sift through what actions on their part to suggest to him. Twenty minutes later having consumed every morsel set before her, along with two cups of tea, strong the way she liked it, he spoke the words uppermost in her mind.

'We can't wait for LeCrane without making a move in the meantime, can we?'

'No. It may result in his giving us a good ticking off, but we know this village in a way he doesn't and never can. It's actually a relief he's unavailable for a few days. It gives us time to pave the way before the police descend in force. That means putting Constable Trout in the picture and letting the vicar know what awaits in his churchyard, well ahead of Fred Shilling sticking his spade unwittingly into that grave.'

'Where to first?'

'To the Bartons. I want to tell Sally she can come and work at Mullings if she wishes, but more importantly, I'm hoping her mother can help us with my guess as to the identity of the stranger's sister. Let me know if I'm more likely to be right than wrong. Maybe' – she squeezed his wrist – 'it's vanity – the idea of getting in ahead of Inspector LeCrane.'

'I'd say that poor girl is tugging at your heartstrings and won't let go until you feel she can finally rest in peace.'

'Which can't happen unless the identity of the anonymous writer is discovered. That, the wicked ugly part, is what's going to be the hardest for the village to deal with. Some may find it rather thrilling having a long buried body – a skeleton found where it shouldn't be; but the letters are different. They're sly, creeping, cruel things. Making the mind behind them spine-chilling. A figure who, if still here, moved amongst them, perhaps known only by sight or casually, but what if it were someone respected, even admired, a trusted friend, or worse yet deeply loved?'

'Who,' said George, 'after the lapse of time may get to carry on his or her life just as they are doing now. Hiding in plain sight. And it'll be the never knowing that'll likely sour attitudes one to another. Time to be off? It's after ten, meaning that if Sally and her mother have gone to church they'll be well back when we get there.'

The Bartons lived on a byway, at the bottom of the village street, about a five-minute walk from St Peter's. A small house that must once have overflowed with children, but now only Sally lived there with her parents. Mrs Barton opened the door before they reached it.

'Mr Bird and Mrs Norris. I saw you from the front room window and thought isn't this nice, they've come to see how Sally's got over that nastiness from Mrs Quigley. Come in do, and I'll tell you what's happened about that.' She was an older version of her daughter, same dimples, same snub nose, and that suggestion of a giggle that came into Sally's voice when she was enjoying herself. 'Getting close to your wedding, lovely for you both. My husband will be sorry to've missed you. He's gone off to his allotment.' She continued talking as she took them into the front room with its inviting feel of organized muddle. 'Loves his lotty. Has a nice little shed where he can sit down when he feels like a cup from his Thermos of tea. And a ginger nut. He always keeps a tin of them out there. Last vicar told him working of a Sunday was as wicked as you could get.'

'He said the same to me.' George laughed.

'And a lot more I'd think, about your working hand in glove with the Demon of Drink.' Mrs Barton giggled. 'But back to our Sally and that nasty Mrs Quigley. It's all come out right. Miss Gillybud had heard about it from Jane what does for her and she came round bout an hour ago and asked if she'd be willing to help out at Orchard House at least for a while, and stay over nights, so's the young lady that's staying there won't be alone. Never nice with a coffin in the house. Seems vicar was also concerned. Course you'll have heard all about Miss Younger being taken in the night.'

'Yes,' said Florence. She and George expressed how sorry they were and so on.

Then she got down to why they were there, before Mrs Barton could take off again. 'One of the reasons we're here is that I wanted to offer her work at Mullings and she can still come if she doesn't want to stay on longer than needed at Orchard House.'

'Oh, Mrs Norris, she'll be ever so thrilled. Wait till I tell her . . .'

George nipped in. 'But we also wanted to talk to you. About something else.'

'Well, I never! What can that be?'

'Something Sally mentioned when she was in the pub, Friday night, before the fog drove everyone out. It may be completely unimportant, but there's a reason, one I'm afraid we can't tell you now, that we'd like to ask you about it.'

'Then we'd best sit down. Where've my manners bin? I should've offered sooner.'

They made the right responses and settled themselves, along with Mrs Barton in sagging, but comfortable armchairs.

'I hope Sally didn't say anything wrong,' she said worriedly.

'Not at all,' George reassured her, 'just a casual remark that got Florence and me thinking. It was how she remembered you mentioning that years ago a young girl that had run off to go on the stage. At her age Sally probably thinks differently about time than we do. To us years ago could mean a hundred, to her twenty-five. Does this bring anything, or anyone, to mind?'

Mrs Barton nodded. 'It does, though I never believed that talk about the stage. I must have told Sally that's what was spread around at the time. Because no one could take in that she'd abandon her parents and brother.'

'What if she'd got into trouble?'

'I wouldn't think that likely either, she wasn't that sort of girl.'

'I don't know if there is a sort,' said Florence gently.

'Could be you're right, Mrs Norris, perhaps we just tell ourselves that so's we worry less about our own daughters. But if it'd happened to Anne, I don't see her deciding to run away. Her mother would've helped her, worked out what was best to be done, maybe sent her to stay with her aunt – in Yorkshire, I think it was, gone with her if need be. And I see her father coming down on her like the hand of wrath. He was one of those silent, stern looking types, but I'd bet my Post Office book, that Jeremiah Rudge – as was sexton before Fred Shilling – wouldn't never raise his voice to that girl, let alone touch a hair on her head. He loved her and the boy, Timothy. A few years younger he was.'

'Was there a lad in the picture?' asked George.

'None she was courting as such; but there was two young gentlemen, as had just finished their schooldays, that'd bin staying up at the vicarage with old Pimcrisp through the winter. That's easy called to mind because such a thing'd never happened before nor after. I've heard since he's come to take over at St Peter's that Mr Fielding was one of those two boys, for that's all they was really. But it was the other one I'd sometimes see talking to Anne in the church yard or outside the sexton's cottage and looked to me like they'd taken a fancy to each other, but couldn't have come to nothing with the difference in their stations. She'd have known that, she was a sensible girl.'

'And her disappearance would have been how many years ago?'

'Must've bin twenty if I'm doing my sums right. Mrs Rudge died three, or four years after. A blessing that was because by then she was bent almost double from her rheumatism. She'd had it terrible in her hands for years. That's why Anne left off working at Hobbs after only a short time of being there. She was needed to do what her mum couldn't no longer in the home, it'd become so's she couldn't peg a handkerchief on the washing line. A nice girl was Anne, never a frown on her face, always spoke up friendly when met. Many's the time she carried my shopping basket for me, and I've seen her do same for Miss Gillybud and others. That's not the sort of thing you forget. She'd never of been heartless enough to leave her family in the lurch.'

That had been the thought Florence had voiced to George the previous day when he'd told her the stranger said it had been dreadful seeing his mother wring her poor rheumatic hands on looking at her daughter lying dead in the bloody water of the tin bath. And she remembered how she had felt for Mrs Rudge when she talked of the pain her hands gave her.

'What did you think became of Anne?' Florence said, again in that gentle voice.

Mrs Barton stared at her with distressed eyes. 'Well, nothing terrible – I mean that she could be dead and that's why she never came back even for her mother's funeral! But it's what you and Mr Bird are thinking, isn't it?'

'George met someone a little while ago who told him a story and we're trying to piece it together. And we're grateful to you for helping us do this.'

'Her parents and Timothy must have known, or at least suspected something bad had happened to her wherever she'd gone. What came to mind for me and the husband was a city, so's to get a job, in a factory perhaps, or a big shop where they'd pay double at least what she'd been making at Hobbs. That maybe the doctor bills had built up; the ones for Mrs Rudge's rheumatism. Dr Chester would've been good about it, but they'd think it was as good as stealing to keep him waiting on what was owed. And nobody would've known if they was in a pickle. To their way of thinking telling anyone they was short of money was asking to be helped out. They was a proud couple, Mr and Mrs Rudge. Oh, I can't get my head around the idea of Anne being dead, but looking back I should have known something had happened to her.'

'Sorry to have distressed you, Mrs Barton,' said George.

'I take it as a compliment you both coming to ask me what I remember of that time, I do really. I liked Anne, I liked the family a lot.' She pulled out a handkerchief and wiped her teary eyes.

Florence waited until Mrs Barton looked as though she could go on. 'Do you recall how the rumour that she'd run off to go on the stage got started?'

'From Miss Hobbs. She told someone . . . I think it was Mrs Saunders, though I could be wrong about that, maybe Mrs North, both very nice women like you'll know. Anyhow Miss Hobbs told someone that when she interviewed Anne for the job at the haberdashery, she asked what she'd wanted, when she was little, to do when she grew up. Miss Hobbs expected her to say it'd bin to go into service, not aiming so high as to work in such a nice shop. The answer she got was: "Be a bally dancer". And to that Miss Hobbs said there'd be no dancing in the shop and no airs and graces neither, but when the girl vanished all of a sudden and the parents were so silent about it, she told whoever that she'd given in to the wicked lure of the stage. As we all know, Miss Hobbs is very strict in her views. Nice to be religious, of course.'

George agreed it was. 'But why did that idea catch hold, at least for a short while?'

'Because, like Miss Gillybud said to me, that Anne always moved so lovely, like her feet barely touched the ground, that you could picture her in one of those ballys by that Russian bloke with the name that sounds like you're sneezing.'

'Tchaikovsky.'

'That's him. Feel like I should offer you my hanky.' Mrs Barton managed a weak giggle. 'One about swans, isn't there?'

'Yes, it's breathtaking. And you've been splendid, Mrs Barton,' said Florence. 'We've dragged you back into the past and you haven't raised one objection.'

'Will Anne's death be a police matter?'

'Yes.' They owed her that and more.

She nodded. 'I won't say a word. Times are when I can talk out of turn, but not when I've given my promise.'

FIFTEEN

The vicarage door was opened for them, not by Miss Fielding as had been the case yesterday, but by the vicar, who ushered them into the gloomy hall, looking – for a man who'd not previously struck them as the least bit vague and dithery – as if he couldn't fathom where they had sprung from, or for what earthly, or unearthly reason they had done so. And yet he knew their names. Used them in an extended hand greeting, said how sorry he was he'd been unable to keep the appointment to discuss their wedding plans. Looked as though he was reaching deep for something else to say, when his voice petered out.

'Glad you were able to pick up Miss Younger's young relation.' In trying to sound as though he wasn't noticing anything odd about the man's manner, George came across sounding as overly hearty as Major Wainwright tended to do in uncomfortable situations.

Florence noticed, and fearing George might throw in a 'Jolly good show, old boy!' hastened to say they'd come about another matter entirely, one they felt it important to put before him. And now she thought, ruefully, I must sound like some tattle-tattling woman with nothing better to do than believe it was her moral obligation to inform him that one of the altar ladies wasn't pulling her weight, or one of the choir boys had been singing out of tune.

Mr Fielding startled her and George by replying he knew what it was about and appreciated their coming to discuss it with him. His air of befuddlement had vanished, to be replaced by a keen focus. The opposite was now their lot. Seeing this he assured them he was not a mind reader, let alone blessed with the gift of prophecy.

'A friend of mine, one I haven't seen in many years and did not previously realize lives in Dovecote Hatch, came round an hour or so ago. What brought him was learning of Agnes

Younger's death. He has been, you see, in the confidence' – Mr
Fielding looked from Florence to George – 'of the man who
came into the pub on Friday night and left a letter to pass on
to a particular member of the police.'

'We've been thinking of him as the stranger,' said George,
'but now we know his name is Timothy Rudge.'

'My friend didn't think it would take you long to make that
discovery, along with a good deal else. Your discerning reputa-
tions go before you.'

'Thank you.' Florence smiled faintly. 'Others might consider
us interfering. Are you able to reveal the name of your friend?'

'You know him as Graham Lieland, but he'll tell you about
himself. About three minutes before you knocked on the door
he telephoned you, Mr Bird, at the pub, to ask if you could
come here to meet with him and myself at whatever time possible
this afternoon. He was told you were out and left a message.
For a moment it seemed incredible that here you were.'

'As if summoned by some irresistible force.'

'Something of the sort, Mrs Norris. I'd been rather knocked
off balance when Kip, as he was called in our schooldays, told
me about Anne's death and the tragedy behind it. We'd both
known her years ago.'

'When,' supplied George, 'you both stayed here one winter.'

'Simplifies matters, your knowing so much already.' Mr
Fielding took their coats and hats, hung them on a monstrous
Victorian coat rack, explaining as he did so that his sister had
gone to call upon Agnes Younger's cousin Miss Sophie Dawson
to offer to spend the night with her. 'I was curate of the parish
where she lived with an uncle until his death. I knew both of
them briefly. She's a very decent young woman.'

'What a sad arrival for her,' said Florence.

'A harrowing day.'

There was something in his voice. A determined briskness
perhaps? Understandable, since he wouldn't want to distract
from what lay immediately ahead – the conversation with
Graham Lieland – but that couldn't be entirely it, thought
Florence.

Mr Fielding continued. 'I imagine you wish me to warn her
that she is about to be enveloped in an unpleasantness that has

its roots in a time when she was a very small child. One that involved Agnes Younger only by chance.'

'We hoped you would do so,' said George.

Mr Fielding nodded. 'It's important the news be broken to her before word spreads in the village. Such would be the case for anyone in her position, but she's very much alone in the world. Agnes was her last living relative, the final link with her parents, and she's not had a real home in several years. Now,' he said quickly, 'I'll take you along to the study where Kip must be wondering what's kept me. He was surprised I recognized him instantly, before he spoke.'

Florence and George followed him to a door at the far end of the hall. Opening it, he leaned in, said, 'The very people we were hoping for, Kip,' and ushered them into a room even gloomier than the hall.

It was cast of blackish green shadows, causing Graham Lieland, standing at an angle to the window, to appear insubstantial for a few seconds until their eyes adjusted. Did he in general, wondered Florence, expect people to grab at a reprieve, however short, from looking further at his face once they had glimpsed it? Was it the pity he minded most? Mr Fielding would know the answer; as he would have known Mr Lieland anywhere, even on a crowded street. From the little she had seen of him before today she'd thought him a sensible, even-keeled man. But there was more, a lot more to him. He'd be the right person to have in one's corner when calm as much as courage was required. Greetings and handshakes were absorbed into these reflections, as was a brief reprise, by Mr Fielding, of what had brought her and George to the vicarage.

'I told them, Kip,' he was saying now, 'they would know you as Graham Lieland. Why don't we all sit down – regrettably there's not a comfortable chair to offer and you can tell them what I meant by that.'

'Thanks, Aiden.' A grimace was turned by a gleam of the eyes into a smile. 'You always did know where to get started on a tale, whereas I'd wander around in circles before landing on the wrong spot.'

'That was because your head was always in the one you were reading at the time. I told someone recently that a friend of

mine could recite *The Jungle Book* beginning to end by heart.
But now I'm getting you off track. I'm keeping Mrs Norris and
Mr Bird waiting.'

'Ah, yes. The name business. Graham and Lieland were
mine from birth, but in reverse order. When one has a Christian
name that sounds like a surname, and a surname that sounds
a Christian name' – the lips twisted and jerked at the corners
– 'it makes more sense than using entirely different ones,
that'll bring you up with a jerk or have you fail to respond
when addressed. The question of course is why?'

'We'd like to hear about it. Should we continue to call you
Mr Lieland, at least for the time being?' George leaned slightly
forward in his chair, which was every bit as uncomfortable as
Mr Fielding had promised.

'Easier. I'll begin with how I came to reinvent myself to
a small extent. After extended periods in hospital I returned
to my parents' home, with the intention of hiding myself
away there permanently. They devoted themselves to me, my
mother in anguished pity, my father with bracing encourage-
ment – walks around the grounds, chess in the evenings, he
got me a dog that much preferred him to me. Their social
life dwindled to nothing. They neglected my married brother
and sister and their families, whom I preferred didn't visit.
Suffice to say I was bloody minded and wallowing in self-
pity, tearing up unopened letters from those I'd known in that
previous world.'

Here he looked at Mr Fielding who did not interpose and
continued to remain silent, along with Florence and George, as
his recounting continued. 'And then one day my sister arrived
without husband or children, but with the flourish that always
distinguished her, bearded me in my shuttered nook, threw a
cushion at my head, ordered me to pull myself together, stop
behaving like a complete beast and killing our parents. It really
was quite a treat listening to her. I hadn't realized how fright-
fully bored I'd become. She told me I'd never been good
company and what I needed was a job. When I said I'd think
about it, she handed me a newspaper cutting. It was an advertisement from *The Times*; Major Wainwright was seeking a
secretary to assist in sorting out material for his memoirs. She

reminded me that I'd had contact with him during the war and that he was an acquaintance of our father.'

Mr Lieland dug into his jacket pocket, fumbled open a packet of cigarettes, reached for the box of matches on the desk and upon lighting up eyed Florence and George. 'You'd think I wouldn't smoke! Back to Wainwright. I answered his advertisement, with my round the right way signature. We met up for a chat at his London club. He was jolly decent about the face as I knew he would be and we had everything agreeably settled when he mentioned he was now living in a small village named Dovecote Hatch. That gave me pause. I'd known for a while from Tim that Anne was dead and what had driven her to take her own life. Returning here meant facing up to my part – as I saw it – and the terrible regrets that brought. But it needed to be done and Tim had long wished for an ear to the ground. What I wasn't up to, unlikely as it might seem, was someone remembering my name, along with my having been here very shortly before she supposedly ran off for whatever reason had been concocted by people in the aftermath. The change solved that problem. Lieland, my mother's maiden name, would ring no bells and Graham would pass unnoticed.'

He stubbed out his cigarette and immediately lit another.

'How did you reconnect with Timothy Rudge?' Florence asked.

'It came about shortly after the end of the war. I was in hospital, one converted from a manor house in Kent, all bandaged up following another operation. The nurses would wheel us into the grounds so we could enjoy the fresh air. I didn't give a damn about fresh air, or the shade of a lovely elm, but one morning as I was stuck there, one of the head gardener's lads appeared. He asked how I was getting along and if he could position my chair so I'd get a better view of the cricket match some of the patients had got up on a flat stretch of lawn. Before I could close my eyes, I recognized him and exclaimed, "Timothy Rudge!" He said, "I know that voice!" So I told him who I was and we talked for about ten minutes, until he caught the eye of another of the gardener's lads who needed help with something or other. He told me he had left Dovecote Hatch following the death of his mother and his father's urging that he make a new start. Had found work at the manor before its temporary conversion into a hospital for the wounded. He said his aim was to have his own market garden. As for Anne, when I asked after her, he said – after obvious hesitation – that she was a long way off.'

'I know this isn't easy for you, Kip,' said Mr Fielding, 'but you're almost through and you're helping Tim enormously in helping corroborate what he will have written in the letter he left with Mr Bird, at least to the extent he gave you the same account many years ago.'

'When he had no need to do so.' Florence spoke encouraging. 'Inspector LeCrane is a fair and clever man, but any background you can supply to bolster Mr Rudge's credibility will go a long way, George and I hope, to allay ideas that there is something more sinister lurking for him to explore. It's the reason, in addition to asking Mr Fielding to help ease things for Miss Younger's young cousin, that we came here today.'

'And why I suggested to Aiden that we meet with you and Mr Bird and tried to reach him on the telephone just before you arrived.'

'How long was it before Mr Rudge told you what had happened to Anne?' George inserted.

'About a week later. It rained for the next two or three days, so I didn't go out into the grounds. That afforded me time to gather my courage and determine that I needed to pursue a fuller account of how her life had turned out. I had failed her at a crucial time, and this made even more despicable because I hadn't merely liked her – thought her a nice girl – I'd been transported, considered myself head over heels in love with her. And believed she felt the same way, until shortly before Aiden and I were due to return to our homes, when she seemed to withdraw into herself. I thought at first it was sadness at the prospect of parting, although I had promised to write and find a way to see her again before too long.'

'She'd begun to receive the anonymous letters,' said George.

'One afternoon when I had gone to her home and had time alone with her she told me about them, how she couldn't believe that someone saw her as a temptress, one causing a good man to lust after her and risk losing his soul, that she deserved to be punished and her family publicly shamed along with her.'

'Man, not men,' mused Mr Fielding, before asking Florence if she would mind if he smoked his pipe.

'Please do. It's the specific that to my mind makes it all the more threatening, as well as horrible.'

'Go on, Kip, tell Mrs Norris and Mr Bird how the letters were delivered to Anne.'

'In the peg basket that was always left in the shed after she'd taken in the wash. The person who wrote them had to know she was the only person who touched it, since her mother could no longer hang anything on the line. After receiving the first letter she thought of taking in the basket, but knew that if there were to be more, another means of reaching her would be found. And she was terrified of her parents or Tim seeing them and learning what was in the mind of someone in the village. She had agonized about turning to me for help. Help that I failed to give her. She'd realized, as was clearly the writer's intent – the letters becoming increasingly vile – that she had to get away. She asked if I would lend her travel money, take her with me and talk to my parents about taking her on as a maid. That's when I became the complete coward. Suddenly I saw the reality of what I had deemed a love equal to that of Romeo and Juliet. My parents would be appalled at my showing up with a girl from the lower classes, they wouldn't believe a word of my claims of wishing to help out a fellow human being in distress. They would most certainly not have given her a job or encouraged any of their acquaintances to do so. At the time I accepted that as reasonable. I told her she should confide in her parents, have them go to the police, they'd find this person and put an end to the kind of spite that probably happened, more often than was known to decent girls and women in villages throughout the country.'

'You were a boy.' George eyed him with sympathy.

'A callow one; another might have possessed the guts and compassion to understand how hard it must have been for her to bring them into the open. It was clear she felt shame, feared she had done something, however unwittingly, to deserve them.'

'Did she show you the letters?' Florence wanted this to be over for him, whilst hoping his revelations would bring further healing.

'She offered, but I said there wasn't any need. The truth is I didn't want to read them, I suppose for fear they'd force me to reconsider taking her home with me. She was so strong; she didn't weep, or plead with me. She said she'd think about confiding in her parents. I saw her once or twice after that when out walking, but either Tim was with her, or I was with you, Aiden. And now to return to Tim and my second meeting with him at the hospital.'

He lit another cigarette, Mr Fielding smoked his pipe and Florence and George sat without any undue movement, waiting for him to continue.

'I was sharing a room with another fellow, one morning he was wheeled away for an operation. His eyes, a hope of restoring some sight to one of them. It worked, thank God. When a nurse came in shortly afterwards I asked her if she could have Tim stop by so we could have a chat, said I'd known him and his family before the war and it would cheer me up. She went right off to fetch him and he came and he didn't shy away from my questions about Anne and told me how she died. He said he'd needed to talk about it for a very long time. And I told him of the part I'd played and how I could have prevented her death. He never uttered a word of blame. He said that his father made up his mind quickly where they should bury her. In the recently dug grave of Miss Younger's brother. His funeral had been only a couple of weeks before.'

'As Agnes was engaged to be married,' said Florence, 'it must have seemed a safe, as well as convenient place to lay Anne, but then came the accident and the broken engagement, which made it almost certain that one day the sister would be buried in the brother's grave. That thought must have increasingly haunted Mr Rudge.'

'It did. Tim and I kept in touch after I left the hospital and he went on to another job in a market garden, married and had children. His were the only letters I didn't tear up, but replied to promptly. When I told him about the possibility of my working for Major Wainwright, he asked if I'd let him know if Miss

Younger's health began to fail, because at that point he would have to let the facts be known to the authorities.'

'Thank you, Mr Lieland, for helping put so much in place for us before we hand Mr Rudge's letter to Inspector LeCrane. He may not be pleased if Mr Rudge has taken his family to Canada, but I think George and I can get him to see that a wish to keep one's family removed as far as possible from unpleasant publicity is a very human reaction.'

'How did you figure out that's what he planned?'

'He mentioned that his wife's brother had emigrated to Canada and had a market garden business,' said George, 'and Florence picked up on that when I gave her all I could remember of the conversation. And now you've told us what he did for work after he left the place where you met him again. By the way what brought you to the Dog and Whistle Friday night? Was it only to collect Major Wainwright's forgotten pipe?'

'I knew he was going to tell you as much of the story as he could, without stating where Anne was buried, and ask for your help with LeCrane. We'd arranged to meet afterwards. The plan was for his parish priest to telephone me when they arrived in the village, which he did; he told me he had parked around the corner and I went and sat in the car with him to wait, but as time passed Father O'Neil grew anxious that all wasn't going well, so to ease his mind I came in to see you and said I'd come for Major Wainwright's pipe. Tim nipped off for fear one of us would inadvertently give the game away that we knew each other.'

Florence was about to ask when Tim Rudge had been set to take off for Canada, when the study door opened and Miss Fielding came in, making it clear by the frown on her face she was none too pleased at finding her brother's morning intruded upon. Therefore, she and George said their goodbyes and, accompanied by Mr Fielding, made their way down the hall.

'Thank you,' he said, 'as you won't be enlightening the inspector until Wednesday, I'll give it a couple of days before explaining matters to Miss Dawson. She'll need a respite after what's she's just been through. Tim will have hoped he'd have until the funeral, probably about a week until the balloon went up. He couldn't have anticipated anyone that close to Miss

Younger being affected, requiring things to be sped up. I have to say I'm glad Fred Shilling isn't in for a shock when he starts digging, although from the little I know of him he'd have taken it in his stride.'

Their visits to Mrs Barton and the vicarage behind them, Florence and George made their way to Constable Trout's home, the front space of which served as the police station. He was a solidly reliable man, with no sense of his own importance, as willing to climb trees to rescue cats as plod the beat without hope of encountering nefarious activity, beyond youthful horseplay. Yet when murder had breathed its evil on Dovecote Hatch he had retained the easy assurance of it being all in a day's work and had supported Inspector LeCrane's every decision without a sucked-in breath or twitch of an eyebrow. He heard Florence and George out today in the same easy manner, only asking at the conclusion if it would be all right to tell his wife, at the moment out on a walk with their son Rupert and his dog, about the situation. They assured him, knowing that she would keep it to herself, that he could do so.

They did not expect anything more from warning the constable what was in store for him and the village than his full cooperation following the arrival of the inspector. But on the following morning when Elsie Trout arrived at Mullings to begin work in the kitchen with Mrs MacDonald, she asked to speak to Florence in private and gave her a piece of information relating to the anonymous letters. Which if proved true would send shock waves through the village, more specifically St Peter's parish.

SIXTEEN

Sophie had been roused from sleep by a barking dog at half past seven that Sunday morning. She hadn't gone to bed until five, but she didn't open her eyes and lie wondering where she was, or how she'd got there. The occurrences of the night were too vivid to bear any likeness to a dream. Agnes was laid out in the bedroom at the other end of the landing, the precious legacy – the letters from her mother to her cousin – were on the bedside table. That Agnes had kept them and passed them on to her created a bond between them that would help make up for time lost and she would be forever grateful that fate had brought them together for those few hours. She had no second thoughts about leaving Dovecote Hatch once the funeral was over, firmly squashing the hope that Aiden Fielding might come and see her today. What had faded to the semblance of a dream was the arrival of Mrs Crawley and the children yesterday morning and her fear that Mr Crawley would somehow manage to track her down. Life in Ilford seemed further in the past than her years in Oglesby.

Sophie tried to go back to sleep, but wasn't tired and something nudged at her mind. It was Marmalade the cat. Miss Gillybud had offered to take him home with her, but she'd said she would be glad of his company. She hadn't said she needed him because that might have caused Miss Gillybud to again repeat her offer to spend the rest of the night with her and she hadn't wanted her to do so, because Mr Fielding had left and she had longed to be alone. But a cat was different, he wouldn't require her to think or talk. She had left her bedroom door ajar, so he could come in if he wished, but he hadn't taken advantage of the invitation.

She didn't have anything black to wear; Uncle Henry had said that if she put on mourning for him he would haunt her for the rest of her days, so she had worn navy blue to his funeral. This dress she still had and took from her suitcase and because the day was chill added a matching cardigan. Before going downstairs she went hesitantly to look at Agnes. She was concerned she wouldn't look peaceful, but she did. And younger than she'd appeared in life. What the room needed was flowers, but with the shops being closed for Sunday that would have to wait until tomorrow.

Feeling like a trespasser in the kitchen she made herself a pot of tea and pouring herself a cup thought about how to fill her day in a productive fashion. Marmalade then emerged out of nowhere to stand at the back door meowing a request to go out. In the few minutes before she let him back in she had found a covered bowl of cat food in the pantry and filled the dish she spotted under the sink and poured a saucer of milk. He went straight to his breakfast. No eye contact. When he had finished she made no attempt to touch him let alone pick him up.

'I'm sorry for your loss. I only met your mistress yesterday, but I believe I'd have grown very fond of her. It's different for you, Marmalade, the two of you were long time companions and, according to your friend Miss Gillybud, loved each other deeply. If there's anything I can do to help you through this hard time, please let me know.'

Uncle Henry would have told her to take a couple of aspirin and go to bed, but Marmalade eyed her as if assimilating this overture, before drifting out into the hall. He would go and live with Miss Gillybud when she left, unless . . . unless she found a job where she could take him with her. She pictured an old lady taking her on as companion and errand girl, offering to let her bring her cat if she agreed to accept a reduced wage. On the whole it was a fairly pleasant prospect. The old lady might be querulous and exacting, but she wouldn't find that daunting.

She knew from her previous search for a job that such posts were frequently advertised and decided to set about looking into what might be presently offered the next morning. She remembered her promise to let Mrs Blount know that she had obtained a roof over her head and was settled at least for the time being.

On returning upstairs, she made her bed, emptied her suitcase and installed her clothes and shoes in the wardrobe and sat down at the dressing table to write her letter making no mention of her cousin's death. Marmalade wandered in as she was stamping the envelope, prowled around and departed. She was tempted to sit and read her mother's letters, but decided they would be especially comforting if read at night when the house closed in upon her. In one she'd read to Agnes her mother had mentioned how she had that morning made a sieved vegetable soup, using up all the potatoes, onions, carrots and whatever else she had on hand, adding the cream from the top of the milk before serving. 'For some reason,' she had written, 'putting on a pot of soup always makes me feel I'm coping, however upside down life is.'

'Oh, thanks for the suggestion, dear Mother, I seem to remember now watching you make soup when I was little, and I've always enjoyed it,' said Sophie out loud to herself. Back in the kitchen, she explored the pantry and found a good supply of vegetables including celery and a couple of parsnips. Her mother had used a marrow bone stock, this lacking she spotted a jar labelled beef tea, which someone must have kindly made for Agnes. She had just added this to the large saucepan on the cooker in which she had sautéed the vegetables in butter and seasoned with salt and pepper, when she heard a knock at the door. It wouldn't be Mr Fielding, of course it wouldn't.

It was Miss Gillybud and a young woman. Sophie stepped back and they were in the hall. 'We'd have gone away if you hadn't answered at the first knock,' said the former with her bright look and fluttery gesture of hands. 'But somehow I thought you'd be up even after so few hours rest, Summer Rose, the mind is so on the jump after a death, or so I've found. And human nature's much of a muchness.'

'I woke and couldn't go back to sleep.'

'Something smells good,' remarked the young woman.

'Soup.' Sophie wondered who she was. Perhaps a niece of Miss Gillybud. 'It's very good of you to come.'

'This is Sally Barton,' explained that lady, 'I've brought her along with the hope you'll welcome a hand with the housework. Poor Agnes could never do much in that way after her accident; I know it bothered her but she didn't want someone in all the time. When I saw it really was needed I'd send Jane, who does for me, helps me out, to give this place a go through and Nurse Newsome had done what she could over the past few weeks.'

'It's very good of you both,' said Sophie. To say she didn't need the help, that she was eager to occupy herself over the coming days, setting the house to rights, would be a rebuff. Also having someone about the house would help keep her from dwelling on herself.

They were now in the sitting room. Clearly sensing uncertainty Miss Gillybud played her high card. 'Sally needs the work. She's just left people she been with for a few years. A husband and wife both difficult in their own ways. I wonder she didn't walk out sooner.'

Sally met Sophie's eyes. 'She, the wife, give me the sack. Went into a fit for what I call a silly reason – saying some nice things about Nurse Newsome. Yelled she couldn't take my stupid chattering.'

Miss Gillybud twinkled at her. 'I'd have given myself the sack ages ago. But I'm sure if you had kowtowed Mrs Quigley would have kept you on. What do you say, Summer Rose?'

'I'll be glad to have you, Sally.'

'Miss Gillybud thinks I should live in, but it's up to you, miss.'

'Only sensible to have another person around at night when there's no telephone; not that we have break-ins, or that sort of thing, but a creaking branch when in a strange house can set the nerves on end, and you're going to need a really good sleep tonight and afterwards with the funeral coming up.'

'Left my suitcase by the doorstep,' said Sally. 'Mind if I fetch it?'

'Oh, please do!'

When they were briefly alone, Miss Gillybud said, 'Sally's a nice girl. You may think her a bit pert, Summer Rose; but to my mind that comes from having spirit and intelligence. You don't have to keep her on permanently, if you don't suit each other.'

'I won't be here permanently,' said Sophie as they heard Sally come back into the hall.

'I'll come back this evening and we can have a little discussion about that and whatever else you'd like to talk about.' Miss Gillybud looked around the room. 'Ah, there's Marmalade curled up on Agnes's chair.'

'It's strange how he's not there and then he is.'

'He'll begin to make his presence felt the more he gets to know you. He was rarely out of Agnes's sight, unlike my Tammie, who requires hours alone to meditate on the follies of mankind. I adore her and I don't think she even likes me.'

'Is that disappointing?'

Miss Gillybud laughed. 'On the contrary; I find it particularly endearing.'

With that she made her departure and as Sophie shut the front door Sally came down the stairs. 'I put my case on the landing. Where do you want me to sleep, miss? I dunno if in the old days Miss Younger and the family 'ad a maid's room. Could be it were in the attic.'

'I haven't seen any steps leading up to it; we can explore and find out, but I wouldn't want you up there anyway. It'll be much nicer having you close.'

'If you say so, miss.'

Sophie wondered if she'd put a foot wrong. 'I do hope, Sally, I haven't offended you, by asking you to be more companionable than you wish.'

Sally stood with her head tilted to one side, then her dimples appeared and she giggled. 'Ooh, miss, you are unexpected, in a nice way, I mean. I'll admit I was a bit on me high horse on account of Miss Gillybud thinking I'd be pleased as Punch to be plucked up and marched over here on a Sunday when I'd been looking forward to Mum's roast beef and Yorkshire, but I think I'll enjoy meself no end, having a bit of a getaway. Not that I won't work hard mind.'

'But not today. You'll need to get settled in and so will I, I've still got a suitcase to unpack, and of course Sunday being a day of rest it wouldn't be right anyway. Not that I'm particularly religious myself, but you may be.'

'Well, I believe in Jesus and all the stories, but I only go to church because Mum still drags me there like she did with the lot of us when we were kiddies. Though I've got to say it's different now we've got the new vicar, seems opposite of

Reverend Pimcrisp, sermons more like chats really, but the worm can turn.'

'Oh, I don't think that'll happen.' Sophie felt herself blush. 'He was the curate in the village where I lived until three years ago. He was well thought of, and very kind to my dying uncle when he visited.'

'That's nice to know. He's good looking for all he's practically middle-aged, I'll say that for him, miss. Let's hope getting to be a proper vicar won't go to his head. I wouldn't want him going after Miss Gillybud, because she doesn't believe in what's written in the Bible. She can butt in like she did today and set your back up, but more often than not turns out she done a good turn.'

Sophie could still feel the blush and hoped Sally hadn't noticed. Better not to prolong this conversation by saying that her uncle had been a non-believer and Mr Fielding had not spoken to him of hell fire and brimstone or otherwise endeavour to lead him to the path of righteousness.

'Well, miss,' said Sally, 'what now?'

'We'll find you a bedroom. We had a housekeeper who'd have told my uncle to install himself along with the trunks and discards, if he'd even hinted she might like to sleep in ours. But I am curious to discover if this house has one or just a loft with a pulldown ladder. There's a door in a nook I haven't opened.'

Once upstairs, Sally picked up her case and Sophie pointed out Agnes's room.

'I hope you don't find it scary being in a house where someone's lying dead.'

'Maybe would if I was on me own, but not with you here, miss.' Sally stopped short in the middle of the landing. 'Goodness! Me mum would give it to me good an' proper if she were here, I mean about not offering you me condolences right off.'

'Thank you, but I'm so glad I got to be with her during her final hours. She was my mother's cousin and we hadn't met before. Miss Gillybud said the undertakers will bring the coffin tomorrow.' Sophie opened the door between Agnes's room and the one she was occupying. It was the smallest of the three, but pleasantly furnished with a washed pine wardrobe, dressing table and headboard for the twin bed, a braided rug and floral curtains at the good-sized window.

'We'll have to find where the bed linen and blankets are stored and hopefully an eiderdown,' she said, looking at the stripped-down bed. 'There was what looked to be an airing cupboard in the bathroom, that's across from the bedroom where I slept last night, let me show you.'

They didn't have any luck finding bedding in the airing cupboard, but behind the door Sophie hadn't previously opened they found a box room, one wall of which was lined with cupboards all containing either bedding, towels or table linen. There was also another door leading to a narrow flight of steps wending their way upward.

'So there is an attic,' said Sophie, 'we'll have to explore it and take Marmalade the cat with us for there are bound to be mice. Although that's silly really, idle curiosity because I'll only be here until after the funeral.'

She was showing Sally the bedroom she was using, when they heard a sharp knock on the front door. 'I'll get it if you like, miss,' offered Sally, 'might as well start making meself useful.'

'Thank you.' Sophie hoped she didn't sound as breathless as she felt. If it were Mr Fielding on the doorstep it wouldn't do to make a display of eagerness at seeing him. Twisting her ankle hurrying down the stairs would be highly embarrassing. He'd think she'd done it on purpose, so he'd have to lift her in his arms and carry her over to the sofa.

She stood in the open doorway trying to pull herself together, without much success, because she counted every one of Sally's descending steps, breathed in the momentary silence, and waited for the sound of voices. She couldn't decipher what was said, or get a sense of the one engaging with Sally. They were going into the sitting room, no longer possible to hear anything, and then footsteps mounting the stairs.

'Pardon me, miss,' said Sally, with assumed primness, as Sophie came out on to the landing, 'it's Miss Fielding, the vicar's sister, come to call. I said I'd see if you was up to seeing her.'

'Please tell her,' answered Sophie as if she too were playing a part in a play, 'that I will be down in a few minutes.'

'Certainly, miss.'

His sister. Had he suggested she call? Very likely, and completely meaningless. It was his obligation to tend to his flock and for the time being she was one of his sheep. She must make it clear to Miss Fielding that she was not in need of special attention and stress that she would not remain much longer in Dovecote Hatch. On entering the sitting room she was instantly intimidated by Miss Fielding's stare. She was seated on the chair to the left of the fire and shifted a few inches upward as Sophie came towards her.

'How very kind of you to call, Miss Fielding.' She took the chair opposite.

'My brother asked me to enquire how you are doing today.'

'Well, thank you. Had you got to know Miss Younger?'

'I came a couple of times, but she was either sleeping or, according to Nurse Newsome, not up to seeing anyone. She was by all accounts a God-fearing woman in life.'

Sophie was tempted to say Agnes had been in life until early this morning, but she agreed this was so.

'I understand from my brother, Miss Dawson, that you once lived in Oglesby, but did not attend church services.'

'Which makes his visiting my uncle in his last days particularly kind.'

'That's what the clergy do.'

'Is it?' Sophie asked enquiringly. 'Please don't think I expect any special attention from Mr Fielding because I had a brief contact with him in Oglesby.'

'He's never neglectful' – Miss Fielding's bobbed brown hair seemed to bristle – 'but being as busy as he is he welcomes my assistance where his presence isn't necessary.'

She's telling me, thought Sophie, such is the case with me. Is she always like this? She must be because there's no reason she'd dislike me on sight. 'You may not remember, Miss Fielding,' she said, 'that when I was in Oglesby an acquaintance of mine spoke to you about lending me a typewriter. Which you very kindly did. I bought a book and learned to type on it, which enabled me to get a job when I moved away.'

'Lent? I don't recall getting it back.'

'Didn't you? Oh, dear I thought I asked my uncle's house-keeper to return it.'

'Then she let you and me down.'

Was this the reason she was being really quite unpleasant? 'She was always very reliable,' said Sophie, 'so I must have been at fault. I do thank you and I'll be glad to get you a new one.'

'Don't be silly, Miss Dawson.'

Sophie's temper, rarely provoked, had been simmering and now flared. Fortunately, before she could respond, there came an interruption.

'Excuse me, miss.' Sally was standing a few feet into the room. 'Would you like me to bring in tea and biscuits?'

Miss Fielding was the one to answer. 'I won't be staying long enough for that.'

'Very good, madam.' Sally, snub nose elevated, dipped a curtsy and departed.

'Impertinent girl!'

'She sees herself as a maid in an earlier age.'

'I've no patience with playacting. You do know she got the sack from her last employers? Instead of being ashamed she then came round to the vicarage and asked me if I'd hire her on. Made no secret of being let go for cheek.'

'I find such frankness admirable.' Sophie had a revelation. She heartily disliked Miss Fielding and wished she'd take herself off.

'If that's your opinion, Miss Dawson, I hope you enjoy dealing with her until you return to your job.'

How spiteful she sounded. It really was unaccountable, unless the typewriter that hadn't been returned was a treasured family heirloom, which seemed unlikely. Equally unlikely was Sophie's response.

'I don't have a job. I gave it up recently – very recently; it was time for a change. I'm going to stay in Dovecote Hatch.'

Miss Fielding's frown took over her whole face. 'Stay?'

'My mother was Agnes Younger's first cousin; she spent a good deal of time here when she was a child and into her early married life. There's so much I've forgotten, because she died when I was six, but I do remember her telling me about a stately home called Mullings. The name stayed with me because when I went to live with my uncle I had a piano teacher called Mr Mullings. I'm going to apply there for work.'

'As what? A maid?'

'Why not, Miss Fielding? I like housework. Our housekeeper believed that every woman, whatever her state in life, should know how to scrub a floor.'

'As well you're not aiming for the position of companion to Mrs Tressler, Lord Stodmarsh's maternal grandmother who resides with him at Mullings. That is the role, unofficially, of a young woman named Mercy Tenneson and it may well be she will one day hold an even more pleasant one, that of granddaughter-in-law. Romance, so I've heard, is definitely in the air.'

'How very nice.'

'I happened to meet Lord Stodmarsh and Miss Tenneson on my way here. They were out for a walk with his dog and really she is a strikingly beautiful girl, not merely pretty, or verging on it, which is a case of two a penny.' Miss Fielding scrutinized Sophie's every feature. 'I do hope you won't give yourself airs if you are taken on at Mullings, that sort of thing doesn't go down well.'

'I'm sure it doesn't.'

Miss Fielding rose. 'Good day to you, Miss Dawson, I'll tell my brother you appear to have recovered well from your bereavement.'

Sophie saw her to the door, hopefully without undue haste, being left in a state between a closeness to tears and a desire to laugh. One positive of the encounter was that for the past half hour she only thought of Mr Fielding with sympathy. Having such a sister under the same roof would be like having to wear a hair shirt day and night.

She went into the kitchen where she found Sally stirring the soup and thanked her for doing so.

'I'd forgotten all about it.'

'I'm not surprised, miss, with your mind being taken off it.' Sally, as was appropriate, made no further comment relating to Miss Fielding, but added that she doubted there wouldn't be other callers throughout the day. In this she was correct. Mrs Chester arrived an hour later as Sophie was arranging sheets and pillow-cases on the clothes horse in front of the fire. She explained that they needed a good airing before being put on Sally's bed, going on to say that Miss Gillybud had brought Sally along to help out.

'And very sensible too,' said Mrs Chester. 'You shouldn't be alone in a strange house in unfamiliar surroundings, espe-cially one without a telephone. Agnes was adamant about not having one. I talked with Nurse Newsome and she wanted to come and see you, but I encouraged her to have a rest today, spend it with her daughter and she said to tell you she'll be by tomorrow.'

'I look forward to meeting her and thanking her for all she did for Agnes.'

'Such a devoted nurse. My husband thinks the world of her. My dear is there anything I can do for you? Have you enough food and milk?'

'You're very kind. We have everything we need for the next couple of days. Sally found a pork pie in the pantry, cheese, oats for porridge and some bottled plums that she's used to make a crumble. She's also just taken some scones out of the oven.'

Mrs Chester accepted Sophie's invitation to stay and sample these, and was altogether pleasant and encouraging.

Shortly after her departure, Mrs Saunders arrived, explained to Sophie she was the butcher's wife and handed over two packages. One she said contained sausages and the other neck of lamb. 'Lovely with plenty of onions, carrots and barley,' she said and stayed to chat for ten minutes about village life; without asking any inquisitive questions, and apologized 'for not being able to stay longer because she had to get the Sunday roast in the oven'.

'What a pleasant woman,' Sophie said to Sally after telling her what was in the two packages and putting them on the marble shelf in the pantry.

'Well liked is her and Mr Saunders. Open handed, rather go over the pound than under. Gives us girls the eye he does, but no harm in him. Told me once when I was in the shop as how

I were a picture and I said, "Who of? Your Grandma?". Me and Mrs Saunders had a good giggle. Says he's all talk and no do. Run for his life he would if any of us took him serious.'

'She knows him,' said Sophie.

'Don't worry, miss! He won't be silly with you.'

'No?'

'Not with you being a stranger and a lady at that.'

This was a relief. Mr Crawley had crept back into her mind, but she got rid of him and she and Sally had their midday meal of soup, pork pie, bread and cheese and plum crumble. Sally hadn't thought it right to sit down at the kitchen table with her, but had been persuaded that doing so made sense under the circumstance that the dining room needed dusting and today was no time to make extra work.

She had gone upstairs to make up her bed with the aired bedlinen when again a knock sounded at the door, and when Sophie opened it, she found a middle-aged woman on the step who introduced herself as Mrs North the verger's wife. She sat for half an hour in the sitting room, expressing her regret at Miss Younger's death and talking about the fellowship to be found at St Peter's Church, how her husband rejoiced at having a more approachable vicar and expressed the hope of seeing Miss Dawson in church next Sunday.

Sophie stopped herself from saying this would only be possible if the funeral wasn't until next week, but she was on the verge of falling asleep, and indeed lay down on the sofa within moments of seeing Mrs North out the door, and slept deeply into the middle of the afternoon. When she woke, she found Sally in the kitchen, taking a bacon and egg pie out of the oven.

'Oh, that does smell good,' she said.

'Sundays at home we have what Mum calls high tea and she sometimes makes one of these. There's not a lot in the pantry to go with it, but I found a jar of beetroot and another of pickled cauliflower.'

'Oh, thank you, Sally.' She looked round and saw Marmalade engrossed in his food bowl and a lovely feeling of home brought happiness to her face. 'I'd welcome some fresh air and I've a letter to post. Will you come with me to show me around?'

'Course I will, miss. Better bundle up, it's chilly. I'll let the cat out and get me coat.'

They were gone for nearly an hour. Sophie, relieved at sending off the letter to Mrs Blount, enjoyed the walk through the surrounding lanes and across Coldwind Common and around to the village street which they climbed with Sally remarking on what the shops offered or lacked. On pointing out the Dog and Whistle she said the owner, George Bird was as nice as they come and soon to be married to Mrs Norris, housekeeper at Mullings.

'Them iron gates,' she said when they reached the top of the hill, 'open on to a pathway to the estate. The house is beautiful, Georgian with older bits. I expect you'll be invited for tea, or somethin', miss.'

'I wouldn't think so.'

'Oh, but they're not a bit puffed up, like you'd think. Lord Stodmarsh, that's not much older than me, is ever so down to earth and his gran, Mrs Tressler, is just the same. They'll pay you a call that's certain. They never let a week go by without going to see Miss Younger after she begun to fail. Promise to tell me all about Mullings, when you go, miss?'

'Would you like to work there?'

'Course I would, but not till you find out how long you'll be here.'

'Not much above a week, Sally.'

They returned to Orchard House to find Miss Gillybud waiting for them. 'I guessed you'd gone for a walk when I knocked and got no answer. I was dithering as to whether to go home and come back later, but here you come. Can't make a world tour out of wandering around Dovercote Hatch. Let's get inside. Sally, be the sweet girl you are and make a pot of tea. Off with our coats and hats, Summer Rose – that's it and now into the sitting room so we can sit down and talk.'

This accomplished, Sophie – assuming the conversation was to be about Sally and how the situation was working out – said how appreciative she was of having her help and company.

'I was sure you would be.' Miss Gillybud's hair was every which way and she made a twitch or two at getting it to behave. 'But my reason for coming is about something else.'

'It is?'

'Agnes said that if you did come to Dovecote Hatch, she wanted me to tell you, ahead of her solicitor getting in touch, that she left you this house and hopes you won't have the cherry tree outside her bedroom window cut down.'

SEVENTEEN

At seven thirty on Monday morning Florence was in the housekeeper's room reviewing her list of matters to be discussed with Mrs Tressler when they had their weekly meeting at ten o'clock. This was held in the drawing room, tea and biscuits were brought in by Grumidge, and after a discussion of such details as the meals for the week, the necessary replenishment of utility items and the rooms requiring special attention was gone over and approved, it was their habit to settle into a pleasant chat. Florence's upcoming marriage being these days a particular topic of interest to Mrs Tressler, who despite never have considered remarrying after a relatively early widowhood, thought it very pleasant when other people did so. Too kind to say so, she believed romance was reserved for the young and made no secret of her hope that her grandson and Mercy Tenneson would come to their senses and get engaged. Florence who shared this sentiment was always more than pleased to turn the conversation in their direction. Usually she enjoyed the time spent with Mrs Tressler, but today there would be discomfort in holding back from her the return on Wednesday of Inspector LeCrane.

A tap at the door came when Florence was closing up her notebook and Elsie Trout entered the room. She was a comfortably built woman with dark eyes and curly brown hair. Since starting work at Mullings several months previously, she had proved a great asset. Reliable – never taking a day off unless her twelve-year-old son Rupert was ill – diligent and thorough. She had started out in the kitchen, heartily welcomed by Mrs MacDonald, who said having a woman of sense at her right hand was a gift from God, and it was to be hoped Winnie would learn a thing or two from her. Before long her duties were expanded to ironing the table linen, polishing silver for Grumidge in the butler's pantry and doing whatever Molly requested of her, which had happened more frequently since Molly hadn't been feeling herself.

Florence liked her, believed that if circumstances allowed, which they would soon when she left Mullings shortly before the wedding, they could be friends. Today she was instantly concerned. Elsie was trembling. Her voice barely above a whisper.

'If I could please have a word with you, Mrs Norris.'

Florence already on her feet went towards her. 'Of course you can, but first I want you to sit down, your legs don't look as though they can hold you.'

Without protest, Elsie allowed herself to be settled in a chair facing the desk as a sob broke through and she pressed the handkerchief she had in her clenched hand to her face.

'You'll tell me what has you so upset,' said Florence soothingly, 'but first you're going to have a swallow of brandy to help steady you.' Reaching into a cupboard she produced a bottle, reserved for such occasions, and half-filled a small round glass.

Elsie took one uncertain sip after another. About a minute passed until her voice broke out in a jerky rush. 'You're always so kind, Mrs Norris, and I'm undeserving, horribly so.'

'No, you're not. But go on, get whatever it is off your chest, you'll feel so much better.'

'Maybe . . .' Elsie set the empty glass down on the small table beside her chair. 'It's been hard holding it in since yesterday. Oh, Mrs Norris! I did a terrible thing twenty years ago and who knows what damage I did by not telling Len what Miss Gillybud told me when Len wasn't home. Maybe Anne Rudge would be alive today if I'd not got to worrying about how he'd be stirring up a hornet's nest if he went round asking questions, trying to find out if she could be right about what she'd seen, or said she had. He'd only been constable in Dovecote Hatch a year or two then. It didn't seem likely there'd be many standing up for him and he'd be booted out. I was selfish, wickedly selfish.'

'No, you weren't,' said Florence with outward calm, but racing interest. 'We all find ourselves in situations where we're torn as to what to do. Sometimes the decision we make turns out to be the right one, sometimes not; but it's so understandable to think first of those we love.'

'It was cowardly,' Elsie repeated and returned the handkerchief to her pocket.

'I've been a coward,' said Florence, thinking of when she had put off marrying George for fear of upsetting Ned who at that time hadn't been ready for her to leave Mullings. 'When Mr Bird and I went to talk to Constable Trout yesterday, we told him he could tell you why we had done so. Obviously he did.'

'He could tell I'd taken it bad, but thought it was because I'd known Anne and liked her. I couldn't bring myself to . . . to tell him the rest. I'll have to get up the courage to do it, but I turn funny inside at the thought. He won't be angry; he never is unless he catches boys tormenting cats, but I'll know what he's thinking and it'll near kill me.'

'Tell me and see how you feel after that. Your remembering the conversation with Miss Gillybud could be of tremendous help in uncovering who contributed to Anne's death.'

'It's very clear in my mind, Mrs Norris, perhaps because I hid it deep so long and all of a sudden it's like it just happened. It was around this time of year. I know that because she said she'd about given up on spring being just around the corner when it should be here already. She always had that fluttery way with her; so when she talked on about this, that and nothing longer than I wanted to listen, I thought that was just her, being Miss Gillybud. It wasn't till after that I realized she'd had trouble getting to the point.'

'Which was?' Florence waited in suspense.

'That she'd seen Reverend Pimcrisp standing on a bench peering into the Rudge's kitchen window. It was a Friday night, between nine and ten, she couldn't be exact, but she knew that was around the time when Anne had her bath.'

'I understand why you had trouble passing this on to your husband.' Florence who could take much in her stride was shocked. The idea of the former vicar being a peeping Tom appalled. The ramifications for the village and in particular St Peter's Church if this were now brought to light would be shattering. She reminded herself that as yet they only had Miss Gillybud's word to impugn him. The Reverend Pimcrisp had had his enthusiasts in the parish, which he'd served for what had to be close on forty years, and was now living in what would seem to be well-earned retirement. And, given that he'd seemed to be growing increasingly addled, what was the chance of Inspector LeCrane getting anything useful out of him?

'How well known was it that Anne had a bath on a Friday night?'

'If Miss Gillybud did, there'd be others. It's a small neighbourhood.' Elsie hadn't exactly brightened, but she sounded steadier.

'Did she say why she was out that night?'

'Looking for one of her cats. She'd gone round the lanes thereabouts and then out on to Coldwind Common. And from there, with the back gardens on Silkwood facing it, she could see the light in the Rudge's kitchen and who was standing on the bench under it.'

'It would have been dark.'

'She had a torch.'

'Of course, for searching out the cat. But weren't there trees at least partially obscuring her view?'

'I think so, and if it's true about Reverend Pimcrisp, he'd have counted on them to help keep him from being spotted, but she said the torch beam picked him out clear as could be.'

Florence sat thinking. 'Or maybe she saw the back of a man's head and along with height and build thought it was him. Elsie, I think this is very much up in the air. I want you to stop worrying as best you can and I'll go see Miss Gillybud after my meeting with Mrs Tressler and find out what she has to say about it now. If she sticks to her story, I'm sure you won't be in hot water with Inspector LeCrane; he may even send you flowers in gratitude for saving him a lot of legwork. I know for you it's about your husband's feelings and you won't feel halfway right until you've talked to him. So go home at once and put it right.'

'It would be a weight off my mind.'

'Away with you.' Florence got up and pressed her hand. 'I'll explain to Mrs MacDonald you need to take the day off because of things to do at home, she'll understand and not ask any questions.'

'Thank you, Mrs Norris. Will you let me know what Miss Gillybud has to say?'

Florence assured her she would and once more alone decided it would be best to wait until she'd spoken to Miss Gillybud to discuss Elsie's disclosure with George. No point in alarming him about Reverend Pimcrisp before she knew if there was meat on the bone.

Her meeting with Mrs Tressler was shorter than usual because Grumidge entered the drawing room after fifteen minutes to announce that Dr Chester had called and was waiting in the hall.

'I'm so sorry, Mrs Norris, not to able to sit over tea long, but I telephoned earlier and asked him to come round to take a look at my eye. I think I have a stye coming and I always like to get ahead of them.'

Florence expressed her sympathy, said she'd have a new curtain rod put in the blue bedroom, and after a minimum of conversation with Mrs MacDonald, put on her coat, hat and gloves and set off for Miss Gillybud's house.

The exterior was charming in the cottage style with latticed windows and a green front door, its knocker being a brass fish. Within seconds of her applying it, Miss Gillybud was ushering her inside, saying what an unexpected pleasure this was and asking if she could take her outdoor things. These she tossed on to a chest, already piled with hats, scarves and gloves, along with a wellington boot lying on its side. Two, no three, cats wandered down the stairs, eyeing Florence as if she were something mistakenly delivered by the post.

'Some of my toms.' Miss Gillybud waved a hand catching Florence on the arm. 'You'll have to forgive me, Mrs Norris, I'm always clumsy – elbowing pictures crooked on the wall and sending lampshades spinning. You'll wish you hadn't come. Why did you?' Abrupt, but twinkling eyes and impish smile put Florence at ease.

'There's something I'd like to talk to you about.'

'How interesting! The boys may not be delighted to see you' – Miss Gillybud looked towards the stairs, keeping her arms at her sides – 'but I've wanted to meet you for a long time. You've had adventures, not pleasant ones with the murder at Mullings and the other one. But adventures none the less. My life has been of the tranquil sort and I've sometimes wished for it to be more eventful and exciting.'

Florence made note of this remark before being whisked towards a fireside chair in a room piled everywhere with books and hung with a great many pictures, of all shapes and sizes, begging to be knocked askew. She tried not to stare at the charcoal female nude, focusing instead on two that appealed – a watercolour of a Chinese bowl and one of an African woman standing in a market place with a tall basket on her head.

'Lovely to be in a state of suspense!' Miss Gillybud sat down herself in the chair across from Florence, who was thinking how to begin.

'You probably know that Elsie Trout has been working at Mullings for a while now.'

'Of course! Nice woman. Such pretty curly hair.'

'Very. This morning she told me something that happened about twenty years ago. It involved you and I felt I had to come and ask if you remember it.'

'I'm all agog.' She listened attentively and when Florence was finished nodded. 'I do indeed recall going to the police station in hope of talking to Constable Trout about what I'd witnessed. Something of that sort is seared in the memory. Unless I'd made it up. There are people who do that sort of thing, so don't think you've offended me.'

'Thank you for being understanding.'

'He wasn't there, off on patrol, or helping children across the road. A nice man, Constable Trout. I can't count the times he's rescued one of the cats when they got stuck in a tree. That day I must have needed to get home without delay, because I couldn't wait for his return.' Her eyes widened. 'It comes back to me. My dear Tammie had a litter of newborn kittens. All my females are named Tammie, but she was extra special. What a mind she had of her own! Mrs Trout is correct in saying I asked her to pass along to her husband what I'd told her about Pimcrisp and I was confident she would do so.'

Florence wasn't going to enlighten her. 'You're convinced it was him.'

'Absolutely. I may be a dithering creature, hunting for my spectacles when they're on my head, or going into the pantry for something and then having no idea why I was there, but I know who it is I see in front of me. He turned his face sideways as I beamed the torch towards the house.'

'Mrs Trout said you were out looking for one of your cats.'

'That's right. Tammie hadn't come back in after I'd let her out earlier in the evening. That mind of her own! I was particularly anxious because she was due to have those kittens any day. On reaching the rear of the Rudge's back garden, I stopped and was about to call out to her when I spotted Pimcrisp and realized what he was about. To say I was sickened doesn't nearly describe it, Mrs Norris. Anne was a lovely girl with a particularly innocent way about her.'

Florence felt a wave of sorrow, suffused with anger. 'Perhaps that's why he chose her.'

'I thought of that – the desire to feast his eyes on the pure and untouched.' One of the cats had climbed the back of Miss Gillybud's chair and landed on her lap. She sat stroking him. Neither she nor Florence spoke for a while.

It was Miss Gillybud who broke the silence. 'Something has happened. It must have for Mrs Trout to bring this up after all these years. That it was you she went to tells me the something is of a nature requiring investigation, of the sort you're good at after your experience with murder.'

'It isn't murder, but it does involve a death.'

'Anne's.' It wasn't a question.

'Yes.'

'I should have known . . . the way her parents and brother were after she was gone, steadfastly saying nothing. How did it happen?'

'She took her own life.'

'Oh, that poor dear girl.'

'She's been at rest a long time, but the story has to come out and thanks to you we have a vital piece of the puzzle. In a couple of days the village will be set by the ears, but it will survive.'

'No one will get a preview from me.'

'I know that I, or I should say Anne, can rely on you.' Florence sighed and got up. She asked how Agnes Younger's young cousin was doing, said it was good of Miss Gillybud to arrange for Sally to live in, and that she'd call at Orchard House the next day. They parted with a sense of mutual liking.

Much achieved because twenty years ago a woman had not walked by on the other side. So much learned, but there remained the question of who had written the anonymous letters. On reaching the village street she saw Constable Trout pedal his bicycle around a corner. Good, Elsie would be on her own at the police station. They could have a talk and afterwards she would go to the Dog and Whistle. With George's arms around her, the ugliness would recede and the world would seem a cleaner, as well as better, place.

EIGHTEEN

When Miss Gillybud informed Sophie on Sunday night that Agnes had left her the house she was stunned. She hadn't thought about who would inherit it, but if she had she'd have assumed it would go to a long-time friend, such as Miss Gillybud herself, or Nurse Newsome perhaps. Someone whose life had over the years been woven into hers, someone who'd been good to her, someone with whom she shared memories. All those things were true of her mother and Agnes; but she was a stranger to Agnes, or was until those final hours.

'I can't accept it,' she said when she got her breath back. 'The only reason she would have done it, is because I wrote to her after my uncle died – hoping she'd invite me for a visit, but her answer made it clear she didn't want that. Now I know about her accident and how it left her I understand why, but she must have felt uncomfortable about being unwelcoming and that's why she did it.'

'Not so, Summer Rose,' said Miss Gillybud. 'Agnes rewrote her will after your mother died. She told me years ago that it would have gone to her, but she trusted you'd have enough of her in you that there'd be much to love, and you have the chance of living here if you choose. If not she hoped you would only sell it to someone who felt at home the moment they walked through the door.'

Miss Gillybud left after advising Sophie to go to bed early and not begin thinking of what to do until the morning. Words of wisdom, but only the strongest minded person could have adhered to them. She went, followed by Marmalade, into the kitchen where Sally was scrubbing the draining board.

'Could you leave that, please, I want to talk to you,' Sophie said.

Sally set down her brush and looked at her uncertainly. 'What is it, miss? Not going to give me the push, are you?'

'Oh, no! Just the opposite. I should have said I'd like to confide in you.'

'Course you can, miss.' Sally's face lit up.

'I'm going to be here longer than I expected and I'd love it if you stayed on; unless you'd rather go somewhere else.'

'No fear of that. I've enjoyed today no end. I can't wait to get mending some of that stock of bed linen in the box room. I took a look and some of it's only good for rags, but the rest could be brought back good as new. Any chance' – her voice held a wistful note – 'of you staying on permanent, miss?'

'Miss Gillybud came to tell me Miss Younger left me this house. I'll have to decide whether to live here or sell it.'

'Ooh, I do hope you stay.'

'There are reasons, Sally, why that might not be best for me, but either way there's a lot to do, lots of spring cleaning rolled into one, we'll get it done together. I can sew, in the sense of fixing hems, but I'm sure you're far more proficient.'

'Learned it from me mum. A great needlewoman she is. When me oldest brother got engaged Dad got 'er a machine and she made the wedding dress and the bridesmaids' ones and done the same when the rest of me brothers got married.'

'Please ask her to come over whenever you like; I'll enjoy meeting her.'

'She'll be glad to, miss!'

'We'll work as a team. Now I'm going to act on Miss Gillybud's suggestion and have an early night.'

'How 'bout I make you a cup of cocoa to help you sleep?'

'Oh, thank you, Sally, that sounds wonderful. Half an hour will be perfect.'

'I'll bring it up, miss.'

When Sophie went up to her room the stairs had a different feel and look to them. They were now her stairs and if she decided to remain they would get to know her tread, add it to footsteps of the many other inhabitants who had gone endlessly up and down from hall to landing over the years. She would become a part of the house and it of her, lean out the windows, prowl the attic, explore the orchards and with luck find that old swing which had been part of her mother's childhood on her many visits here.

Her preparations for bed were lengthened by her thoughts going one way, then another. How could she turn away from this gift? Surely she owed it to Agnes to give living here a try. She wanted to, wanted to give way to the wonder of having her own home, but she must, she decided – shedding her dressing gown before getting into bed – stick to her resolution to get as far away from Mr Fielding's distracting presence as possible. Sally brought up the cocoa and they wished each other goodnight. Difficult to believe they hadn't met before today. There was the beginning of friendship between them and then there was Miss Gillybud who already seemed an anchor as well as a delight. And what about Marmalade? He'd come out from behind the wardrobe and settled on the dressing table bench. Was she prepared to abandon him as though he was a piece of furniture? She sipped the cocoa, set it down on the bedside table, picked it up and sipped again. To sacrifice a settled life because of a man who'd had no interest in her as a woman was folly.

'Cowardly!' Uncle Henry's voice rumbled as she turned off the lamp.

Waking the next morning she realized she must have fallen asleep the moment her head touched the pillow. She sat up feeling thoroughly awake and clear headed. She was going to live at Orchard House and get to know and enjoy Dovecote Hatch. To do otherwise, to run away to some random place, would be miserably weak. Conquering her feelings for Aiden – Mr Fielding – would be hard, but if Agnes had got on with her life after feeling obliged to give up the man she loved, there was no excuse for her not snapping rapidly to her senses.

Having a lot to do, staying busy, would keep her mind where it needed to be. She opened the bedroom window, inhaled the fragrantly cool air and went along to the bathroom where she washed and brushed her teeth vigorously.

On reaching the bottom of the stairs she saw the dining room was open and on looking in saw Sally polishing the table.

'You're an early bird,' she said.

'Morning, miss. Thought I'd best get started in here. The undertaker's men will be along with the coffin sometime this morning and this is where they'll think to put her when they bring her down, unless that's not what you want.'

'Thank you for thinking of this.' Sophie stepped into the good-sized, square room with its simple pine furniture in keeping with that of the sitting room. 'Of course, you're right. My uncle's coffin was placed on our dining room table till the day. We'll find vases and fill them with flowers. And draw the curtains in here. Then leave the rest as they are until the day of the funeral.'

Over breakfast Sophie broke the news to Sally that she planned on giving it a go of making her home at Orchard House.

'Ooh, miss. In't that marvellous. I'm pleased as Punch for you.' Sally fiddled with a slice of toast. 'Will you be wanting to keep me on?'

'Is that what you'd like?'

'More than anything, miss.'

'I'll have to get a job to cover the expenses. When I came here I had it in mind to apply for work at Mullings. I remember my mother speaking of it. And being little, I thought it was something out of a fairy tale. It's one of the few things I can remember her talking about. Mostly it's like watching a silent movie, with my mother and father moving across the screen.'

'I'm sorry, miss. I can't imagine what it'd be like to lose you mum and dad. But what was it you thought of doing at Mullings? Typing letters for Mrs Tressler as a companion like?'

'No. I've had enough of doing that for a while.' Thoughts of the estate agency and Mr Crawley encroached. 'I'd much rather do housework and learn about the origins of the house and the history of the furniture. I've always wanted to know more about antiques.'

'You mean' – Sally stared at her – 'you'd go as a maid.'

'What's wrong with being a maid?'

'Nothing, miss. But you're a lady.'

'I'm nothing of the sort. I'm a working woman. The same as you, and you're not going to be my maid. You're my companion.'

'Ooh, miss. That's a big thing to take in. I'm so happy I feel sort of floaty.'

'Have another cup tea.' Sophie poured it for her.

'After that nasty business with Mrs Quigley, I made up me mind to try for a place at Mullings. Mrs Norris, the house-keeper is ever so nice. She won't be there much longer seeing she's soon going to marry Mr Bird that has the pub – the Dog and Whistle. He'd have put in a word for me, so I think me chances would've been good. But now I'd a hundred times rather be with you.'

'I've also been thinking I might enquire at the library whether they could use an extra pair of hands, sorting the books, or stamping them as they go in and out. I'd enjoy being surrounded by shelves and shelves of books.'

They set about making a list of what needed to be done that day, beginning with Sally going to the florist for flowers while Sophie searched the cupboards for vases, or otherwise suitable containers. They were interrupted by a knock on the door and in came Miss Gillybud with an armload of hyacinth, daffodils and roses.

'These are amongst the flowers Agnes loved.'

Sophie thanked her, adding that Sally had been about to go and get some, but it was much appreciated that Miss Gillybud had done so. 'By the way, Miss Gillybud' – she smiled warmly – 'I've decided to stay.'

Miss Gillybud beamed back at her. 'And here comes Marmalade to let me know he's pleased. Agnes talked to me about what she wanted for the service – no sermon, just a reading from the gospel and a couple of hymns that she liked. Would you like me to see the vicar about it?'

'I'd be so grateful.' Sophie meant it more than Miss Gillybud could know. What a reprieve.

'However I can be of help, Summer Rose, it's going to be splendid having you as a neighbour and friend.' A kiss on the cheek.

She did not stay long. Sophie was standing in the scullery reaching up onto a high shelf for vases, having failed to find any in the dining room's china cabinet, and Sally was filling the sink to wash them when there was another knock on the door.

'I'll get it, miss.' A murmur of voices and Sally returned to say the undertaker's men were in the hall. She left what they were carrying unspoken. 'I told them where she is – what bedroom it is and where you want her put.'

Lumbering footsteps going up. Heavier ones coming down.

'Did we leave the dining room door open?'

'Yes, miss.'

Sophie steadily counted to sixty before going in there. The coffin, a very plain one, took up all but a few inches of table at either end. The two men standing off to the side, ducked their heads, said the lady was all nice and comfy and when she asked what else was required of her one of them replied nothing but to let the boss know when she'd be setting off, making it sound as if it would be on her holidays. He handed her a card, said if she was thinking about payment that had been seen to ahead of time.

'If I was them,' said Sally after they left, 'I'd head straight for the Dog and Whistle and have a glass of "oh be joyful". Not a fun job, is it? No disrespect.'

'Not everyone's cup of tea.'

'And of course we've to be grateful for them that does it.'

Sophie agreed, placed her hand on the coffin and wondered where Agnes, the real Agnes, was now, if anywhere. This brought her too close to thinking about Mr Fielding, so she hurried back into the kitchen and went up the stepladder again in search of vases.

She and Sally shared the remnants of pork pie for lunch, decided to have sausages and mash for supper and set about working through their list of jobs to do. The kitchen floor had been scrubbed, the insides of the sitting room windows cleaned, all the downstairs furniture dusted and the stairs swept when the afternoon post plopped through the letter box. One letter, from Wendell, Wardle & Wendell. It informed her that Mr Horace Wendell would call upon her tomorrow, at eleven a.m., unless inconvenient, to discuss Miss Younger's final wishes with her.

She informed Sally of this development and went up to her bedroom to write a reply, stating that tomorrow morning would suit her very well. She then put on her coat, called out to Sally that she was off to the post box and welcomed the five minutes of brisk fresh air. Going round to the back door, which they kept unlocked during the day, she heard voices coming from the sitting room ahead of Sally meeting her in the kitchen.

'It's Lord Stodmarsh and Mercy Tenneson come to call, miss.'

'Miss Tenneson?' Sophie queried.

'She's a young lady, a bit younger than me, that used to live at a big house called Bogmire till her guardian got murdered.'

'How dreadful!'

'Horrid. But I don't want you thinking, miss, as how everybody gets knocked off sooner or later in Dovecote Hatch. It's only been the twice, the first being at Mullings. I suppose it makes for a bond between her and His Lordship. They're seen a lot together and his grandmother, Mrs Tressler, has taken her up. Took her on holiday to Scotland a short time back. For now she's living with old Mrs Weedy.'

The 'for now' sounded to Sophie as though romance was in the air between Miss Tenneson and Lord Stodmarsh, with the possibility of a wedding around the corner. And on entering the sitting room she was convinced of this. His Lordship was a slight young man, of medium height and reddish brown hair, attractive because of his engaging smile, but to Sophie's eyes Mercy Tenneson was extraordinarily beautiful. She was twilight, with her dusky grey eyes, the dark hair flowing down her back and the sheen of moonlight on her skin.

Greetings were exchanged, condolences offered; His Lordship making it all so easy. He might have been a next-door neighbour dropping in as if by habit. When they were seated he began a leisurely conversation in which his affection for his housekeeper Florence Norris featured. He told her how she'd filled the role of a mother for him, had Sophie telling him about growing up in Oglesby and Uncle Henry, his love of books and how he'd been keen on her learning to play the piano. At this his eyes lit up. He said how much he enjoyed listening to music. By the time Sally brought in tea and scones they were discussing her love of Chopin and Liszt, and his for Mendelson.

All the while Mercy Tenneson had said next to nothing. When His Lordship tried to draw her into the conversation, she responded at the minimum and when Sophie attempted an overture it was the same. A couple of times she was met with a shrug. The lovely grey eyes had turned sullen. And watchful. She dislikes me, thought Sophie, which makes no sense because she doesn't know me, and I have no looks to compare with hers. What does it say about me that I already have Miss Fielding objecting to my presence on the scene?

By the time Miss Tenneson and His Lordship left a cloud was cast on what had been a surprisingly happy day. She hoped, ungratefully, there would be no more callers that day, but a half hour later, Nurse Newsome arrived. She was very kind, talked with admiration and liking of Agnes. Sophie instantly warmed to her, could see why she was regarded as such a treasure by Miss Gillybud, along with Dr and Mrs Chester, but saw that she was struggling to maintain a hold on some trouble verging on distress.

She brought this up with Sally when they were by themselves once more.

'It'll be 'cos of her daughter, Una, Mrs Smith as she is now, more's the pity if you go by what half the village says.' Sally imparted a detailed telling of Una's wedded woes, leaving Sophie, holding judgement on whether or not Bill Smith had been torn from his wife's side to care for his ailing mother, or as Sally tended to believe, had taken the chance to hop it.

'And now she's had that bicycle accident,' said Sophie, 'I thought Nurse Newsome would mention it. That would have seemed a little odd considering it had led to a change of plans in picking me up from the station, if the poor woman has to be at her wit's end dealing with what she already has on her plate.'

'Wonder how many callers there'll be tomorrow, besides the solicitor that is, miss.'

'And Mrs Norris, His Lordship's housekeeper. He mentioned she planned on coming.'

'Now that does seem strange, her not being round today. She's always so thoughtful, but then she'll be all caught up in making wedding plans. I'm sure Mr Fielding will make the service lovely for them.'

'Yes, he will.'

'I wonder if he'll show up tomorrow.'

Sophie felt suddenly tired and irritable. She would wash her hair that evening, though not because Mr Fielding might trouble himself to show up. The person for whom she should make herself presentable was Mr Wendell of Wendell, Wardle & Wendell. Perhaps he would stay to lunch and tongues would start wagging about her instead of poor Una Smith. She was instantly heartily ashamed of herself.

NINETEEN

Mr Horace Wendell, of Wendell, Wardle & Wendell arrived as promised at eleven a.m. Sophie had pictured him in the mould of solicitors commonly depicted in books: thin, elderly, bespectacled and fussily intent on explaining every detail of the document presented to her down to each semicolon. He was nothing of the sort. He was a tall, stout man of under forty with his coat buttoned in a couple of the wrong places, which when removed revealed a rumpled suit. He was pleasant, said all the right things, but it was clear he was in a rush from the moment he set his foot over the threshold, followed her into the sitting room, and politely declined her offer of a chair.

'You, however, Miss Dawson, may wish to sit down. I don't know if the news I bring will come as a surprise, I trust you will be pleased, but a change in circumstances is always a jolt to the system.'

'Her friend Miss Gillybud told me about the house.'

'That's not the whole of it. As the executor of Miss Younger's estate I am in the position to inform you she left everything of which she was possessed to you. This in addition to the house, includes her investments, which amount to above six thousand pounds, and of course whatever she currently has in her bank account.'

Sophie couldn't answer. Her mind had gone blank.

'You'll need to come to our office in Large Middlington to sign the documents. Let us say Monday of next week, if that suits you, Miss Dawson.'

'Of course.'

'Then, with my apologies, I must be off. My wife is in hospital about to have a baby and I need to be in reach of my telephone. I've been through this four times before, but I'm always' – Marmalade sat looking at him – 'jumpy as a cat.'

'I do hope all goes well,' she said as she saw him out the

door. She hadn't moved when the knocker thumped again. He must have forgotten to tell me something, or realized he'd been talking about the wrong will, she thought, and reopened the door.

It was Mr Fielding on the step. Her mind went blank again.

'May I come in, Miss Dawson?'

'Please do.'

He eyed her quizzically. 'You look only half awake. Late night?'

'Do people have late nights in Dovecote Hatch?'

'Touchy, Miss Dawson! I was not referring to the sort of late night that involves dancing to loud music in a room so thick with smoke you'd think you were trapped in a fog. What I thought likely was that you stayed up beyond midnight, putting this house to rights. I smell polish.'

Sophie's heart skipped several beats. He was smiling at her irresistibly. All her good intentions of treating him with cool politeness went out the window. 'I'm sorry, I didn't mean to be rude.' They were now in the sitting room. 'Please sit down. I was up late, I'd been arranging the personal items I brought with me about the bedroom I'm using, when Sally brought up the cocoa. I'm sure you know she's staying here.'

'Miss Gillybud told me she arranged it.'

'She noticed the stack of books I'd put on a chair, in particular the ones about girls at boarding schools and said she still loved reading them and could she borrow some. We sat talking until after twelve, about what made them fun. But that's not why I'm in a bit of a daze. It's nothing unpleasant, quite the reverse.'

She was on the sofa, he had taken a chair across from her.

'Would you like to tell me about it?'

'Very much.' She was happy. Surprisingly at ease with him. She finished telling him about inheriting the house and the investments and he expressed pleasure at the news. But his expression was thoughtful – disturbed.

'Will you stay on here?'

'Yes.' Her heart was sinking.

'I hope I can get you to change your mind.'

Her face burned. 'Because your sister took an instant dislike to me?'

'Pardon me, miss,' came Sally's welcome voice from the doorway, 'will you and the vicar be wanting tea and maybe some plum cake still warm from the oven?'

'No thank you, Mr Fielding is just about to leave.'

'Very good, miss.' Sally vanished.

'I am not making my departure, Sophie.'

'You most certainly are.' She got to her feet. He couldn't soften her by using her Christian name for the first time, not after . . .

'My sister has nothing do with my wishing you away from here.' He came over to her, took her hand, drew her back down onto the sofa and seated himself at an appropriate distance from her. 'Maud doesn't like any woman, unless elderly, that I like. And, Sophie I do like and admire you; I did in Oglesby and when I picked you up at the station and we talked in the car about what happened with Crawley I knew why I hadn't forgotten you. My mistake was telling Maude about you.'

She couldn't think about this now, tantalizing as it was. 'Then why don't you want me to stay here?'

'Because something very disturbing has happened that impacts on Miss Younger's burial.'

'Why?' Apprehension grew.

'It's a long story, dating back twenty years, but I'll begin with a stranger coming into the Dog and Whistle this past Friday evening and laying it in the lap of the proprietor, George Bird, before making a request of him – that he pass on a letter to an Inspector LeCrane, when the time to do so became apparent. George talked to Florence Norris, they're soon to be married, and between them they quickly figured out what had to occur before he did as asked.'

Sophie drew in a sharp breath. 'Agnes's death.'

'You're quick.'

'What else could it be if her funeral has to be delayed?' She twisted her hands, looking at him with beseeching eyes. 'Please don't tell me, there's a body that shouldn't be there, in that grave?'

His silence was the answer. She did not say much during the hour it took for him to provide her with the information he'd gained from Florence, George and Graham Lieland. He'd explained about the switch of his friend's Christian and surnames. She was left feeling unbelievably wretched, the anguish, and the horror of what Anne Rudge had suffered before her death enveloped her like a wet, heavy coat.

'What will happen to the brother?' she asked. 'He risked so much. Do you think the police will drag him back from Canada?'

'They could, but Florence and George believe he'll return of his own will.'

'What a remarkable couple. Sally told me they've done this before, solved murders.'

'This isn't that sort of case.'

'Of course it is. Anne was murdered by the anonymous letter writer.'

'Florence and George hope it will be possible to track him, or her, down; difficult after this length of time, but yesterday Mrs Norris came round to tell me she'd learned something which may make for a starting point.'

'You look worried.'

'The village is in for some shocking revelations.'

'One in particular? The one Mrs Norris told you about yesterday.'

'I can't say any more, Sophie.'

'No, of course you can't, I shouldn't have probed, but . . .' The words were out before she could stop them. 'I don't want you to get worn down. You're the one, Mr Fielding, who will have to uplift not only your parish, but the village as a whole. Mrs Norris knows that. It has to be one of the reasons she's taken you so fully into her confidence.'

'Thank you, Sophie.'

She could no longer read his face. 'I shouldn't interfere.'

His eyes were alight with amusement . . . and something else that made her heart beat faster. 'I take your concern as the highest compliment.' His voice and face sobered. 'Allow me to be the one to interfere. I again urge you to leave before matters are placed in the hands of the police, as early as tomorrow, when Inspector LeCrane returns from his holiday.'

'I can't.'

'You'll have reporters at the door, hounding you morning,

noon and night. Telling them to go will keep bringing them back.'

'I shan't say anything to them. I'll sob, cry, piteous tears and turn faint. I'll have Sally call out that she's fetching the doctor.'

'You would?' He was smiling again. 'There must be a side to you I haven't seen.'

'It hasn't been there before. My world keeps shifting. What would it say to people around here if I took myself off till the worst was over, and then came nipping back expecting to be absorbed into village life, invited out for tea or piano recitals? And who would arrange where Agnes is to be buried if her brother's grave is off limits for the foreseeable future? Do I just leave her coffin on the dining room table?'

'I'll take care of that today, request that she be taken to the undertaker's chapel of rest.'

'Thank you,' Sophie said. 'But this isn't only about now. Anne's parents didn't cut and run. They stayed, stoically withstanding the barrage of gossip swirling around her supposed leave-taking.' She paused. 'I wonder why they didn't make up a story. Said she'd gone to stay with her aunt, or to find a good paying job to help support the family. They could have made it convincing, pretended to receive letters, no postman worth his job would have contradicted them.'

'They were the type known as the salt of the earth, incapable of lying. Tim is the same. I haven't seen him in years, but I know that every word in that letter to LeCrane will be the truth.'

Sophie sat in silence.

'You feel a bond with Anne.'

'You mean because of Mr Crawley? It's not the same. I wasn't dealing with hate coming from someone I couldn't see. But, yes, I do feel a connection to her. I want her to be at peace and for her brother to one day soon return and give her a proper funeral, with flowers on her coffin and see her buried alongside their parents.'

'That will happen.'

'And there's your friend, Kip. I hope he'll be comforted in knowing he helped bring out the truth and he can look forward in a new way.'

'There's a woman he's fond of. I suspect more than fond.

She nursed him during the war and has seen him when he hardly had a face at all. She's now a sister at Guy's hospital and they meet in London from time to time.'

'Happiness waiting perhaps.'

Mr Fielding stood up and drew her to her feet. 'I wonder,' he said, 'if you have any idea of how rare you are, and how any person of sense should know that on meeting you for the first time.'

She took too long to answer. Sally was in the doorway.

'Mrs Norris is here, miss. Shall I show her in?'

Sophie stepped away from Mr Fielding. She hadn't heard the doorbell, either because she was preoccupied, or because it had thumped so often over the past couple of days the sound had become as negligible as a creaking floorboard.

'She told me she would come to see how the news had affected you,' Mr Fielding murmured.

'Please show in Mrs Norris. The vicar realized he could stay longer than he'd thought.'

'And very nice too, miss.'

So it was, but Sophie wished she could have been alone a little while longer with him in case he wished to add something, anything at all, to what he'd been saying.

TWENTY

It was ten o'clock on Wednesday morning. Florence was in the housekeeper's room hoping the telephone would ring again. George had called a half hour before to let her know he'd tried to contact Inspector LeCrane to find out if he was back at work. He had been told that the inspector was back at work but had gone out again. Nothing to be done, but leave another message. Florence didn't often get on edge, but for all her insistence to George, and herself, over the past few days that they wouldn't land on the inspector's wrong side because of so vigorously taking affairs into their own hands while he, the cat, was away, she was preparing for his annoyance. This was different from the past when he'd sought her assistance.

A tap on the door brought Elsie Trout, with her own reason for being on edge. Her husband had told her not to fuss; she'd been of more help than hindrance, but at the moment his words rang hollow. Florence assured her she would not let Inspector LeCrane chew her up and spit her out.

'All his anger, if he is angry, will be directed at me and to a lesser degree at George.'

'It shouldn't be, as you and Mr Bird have done half his work for him.'

'I'm not counting on him being appreciative. I don't regret finding out what we could and neither does George, so we'll take what comes. Why don't you ask His Lordship if you can take his dog for a good walk. He'll be more than glad to have you do so; he had a cup of tea with me at what for him is the middle of the night, six thirty this morning, and lamented that he would be spending all day on the accounts for the home farm and that Rouser would think the world had ended if he didn't get his usual exercise.'

Ned hadn't contained himself to that subject alone. He'd asked her what she thought of the new occupant of Orchard House when she'd gone there yesterday.

'I took to her right away,' she'd said. 'There's character behind that pretty face.'

'I agree. We had a great chat. Some man will be lucky to marry her. I hoped she and Mercy might strike up a friendship. But that was clearly not in the cards.'

This came as no surprise to Florence. Elsie had not been gone three minutes when Mercy came gliding into the room. It wasn't big enough for prowling, but Mercy made a good attempt, before picking up items on the desk and moving them about with her long graceful fingers.

Florence didn't need this distraction when the telephone obstinately refused to ring. No point in wasting further time. 'Is this about Sophie Dawson?'

'Has His high and mighty Lordship been telling you how smitten he was with her?'

'The only girl he's smitten with is you, Mercy.'

'You wouldn't have thought so had you been there. It was pitiful the way he hung on her every word, eyes gazing into hers, as if she were some radiant being from another world. Oh, I'll admit she's pretty in an insipid, milkmaid way, the sort that never have a brain in their heads.'

Florence strove for patience. 'Mercy,' she said, 'I'm very fond of you, Mrs Tressler even more so, but if you wish Ned to direct his attentions elsewhere you're doing a very good job of it.'

'It wouldn't bother me if he did.'

'If that's how you really feel, leave him alone. My opinion is you're behaving like a child who should be put in the corner.'

The telephone finally lived up to its obligations. 'That will be George,' she said. Mercy took herself off and she picked up the receiver.

'He's here, Florence.'

'Without warning?'

'Said he wasn't going to waste time letting me know he was on his way.'

'That sounds like him. What's happening?'

'I gave him the letter, explained briefly how I came by it and left him to read it.'

'Offer him breakfast, it'll be harder for him to fume while he's eating?'

'I made the suggestion and he requested an egg boiled three and a half minutes, bread and butter, thinly sliced and coffee as strong as I can make it. While he's nibbling and sipping I'll come and get you.'

'Don't. Stay with him to soothe any ruffled feathers. I'll arrange what I have to say to him on the walk over. You can do the same while you're boiling that egg.'

The morning had brought warm sunshine for the first time in several days. When she came through the Mullings' iron gates on to the top of the street, she spotted Elsie on the green walking Rouser. He turned and barked hopefully at her, causing Elsie also to look her way. She waved and took the few steps needed to reach the Dog and Whistle. She entered by the side door, removed her hat and coat, but before she could hang them up George appeared in the passage, and took them from her and reached for a hook.

'How are things?' Florence asked.

'Mellow. His response to reading the letter was to hand it to me, suggest I take a look at it and asked if there was anything there that surprised me. I said it was all very much as you and I had anticipated, including that Timothy Rudge had taken his family to Canada. He laughed, said he'd be much surprised if we hadn't by now have come by a great deal of information and that he is entirely at our disposal. He swivelled my desk chair around, put his feet on a foot stool and said he'd take forty winks until you turned up to enlarge his view of the case.'

'I hope he enjoyed his holiday.'

'He said he'd spent it with an aunt, who insisted on their riding out every day for the joy of watching him coming off at every fence.'

'I don't believe he ever fell off a horse in his life.'

'I don't believe in the aunt.' George kissed her and they went into the office where a third chair had been added. Inspector LeCrane rose to his feet. He was a man in his early forties, tall, lean and elegant with aquiline features. Florence thought, as she had done on previous occasions, that his tailor was worthy of a knighthood. He eyed her with sardonic amusement.

'Good morning, Mrs Norris. You've been at it again – gathering information before I have a finger in the pie. Some instinct should have warned me not to absent myself, not leave the building to have my hair cut, let alone take off on the first holiday I've had in two years.'

'I'm sorry if you're upset, but Timothy Rudge handed George so many clues on Friday night as to where his sister was buried, that when Agnes Younger died it seemed imperative to provide some warning to what lay ahead to her young relative staying at the house. That required a couple of conversations beforehand to fill in the picture.'

'I'm not the least upset, Mrs Norris. As usual I'm grateful for your inter—'

'Interference?

'Intervention.' He was now openly smiling. 'As I've said to you in the past, you know the workings of this village and how to get people to open up better than I could if I moved in for six months. May we sit down and go over what Mr Bird has told me thus far?'

'Let's make ourselves comfortable.' George moved a chair a shade nearer to Florence and suggested the inspector take the one behind the desk. 'I can only stay for fifteen minutes or so because I have to get ready to open up.'

'Then let us go over everything you have uncovered thus far. As of now I know you've spoken with a Mrs Barton, Mr Fielding, Mr Lieland and Miss Dawson. Who else if anyone?'

'Mrs Barton's daughter, Sally,' said Florence. 'She's gone to Orchard House as a live-in maid. When I went there yesterday to explain matters to Miss Dawson I suggested we talk to Sally, so she'll also be prepared for all the attention that will be directed at them. It was clear to me that she has quickly become attached to Miss Dawson and will be of great support to her in the days ahead.'

'Very well; is that it?'

'There's Elsie Trout, Constable Trout's wife, and because of what she told me I went to see a Miss Gillybud.'

Inspector LeCrane shot her an alert look. 'This sounds important.'

'It is. The most crucial piece of information we've acquired yet.'

'Please go on.'

'On Sunday we went to the police station to tell Constable Trout to expect your arrival and the reason why. It seemed only fair to do so.'

'Indeed.' The inspector's lips twitched. 'Ever conscientious, Mrs Norris.'

'The next morning, Elsie, who now works at Mullings, asked me if she could have a word; she was very upset. She said that twenty years ago Miss Gillybud came to the police station and asked her to give a message to her husband, who wasn't present, that one night she'd seen a man standing on a bench peering in through the Rudge's kitchen window. It was on a Friday, when Anne took her bath.'

'Am I to infer that Mrs Trout did not pass along this message to her husband?'

'She was afraid it would cause the most frightful stir in the village and he would be blamed, perhaps lose his job, if it couldn't be proved true.'

'There must have been the occasional peeping Toms in the past.'

'Perhaps. But not a vicar, of St Peter's parish.'

'I see the difficulty.' Inspector LeCrane opened his silver cigarette case and studied the contents, before making a selection and applying his matching lighter. 'His name?'

'Pimcrisp,' said George, 'if I ever knew his Christian name I've forgotten it.'

'Well liked? Revered?'

'By those who shared his puritanical views, disliked by others.'

'He was a fanatic.'

'In my opinion, and others', yes.'

'You have spoken with Miss . . .?' The inspector flicked a glance at his notebook. 'Gillybud?'

'I did,' said Florence. 'She confirmed what Elsie had said, remembered that visit to the police station clearly, was not surprised when Constable Trout didn't get in touch with her, assuming he wanted to steer clear of a nasty business. When

Anne Rudge supposedly took off, a few weeks later, she thought she knew who'd driven her away.'

'Could Miss Gillybud have a grudge again Pimcrisp?'

'It might be thought she had by those who disapprove of her. She's a nonbeliever; her credibility was part of Elsie's concern.'

George excused himself and departed to prepare for his customers.

Inspector LeCrane lit another cigarette. 'A small matter, Mrs Norris. How would Pimcrisp have known that Anne always had her bath on a Friday night?'

'It wouldn't have been uncommon. An easy guess, or he could have spied on her, watched her regular habit of taking the tin bath from the shed into the house, but I also think it likely that, being obsessed with her, he questioned people about her under the guise of concern for her soul. He might have pretended to have heard she spent Friday or Saturday nights at dances where drinking and smoking went on.'

'And being a fanatic, no one would find this strange.'

'You might ask Mr Fielding and Mr Lieland if they remember anything of the sort.'

Inspector LeCrane made some jottings in his notebook. 'The question, which you will already have considered, is whether Pimcrisp, with his twisted mind, was also the anonymous letter writer. I showed Mr Bird the ones Timothy Rudge enclosed and they were filled with ravings about fallen women in the Bible and the horrors awaiting them for eternity. In the letter Anne wrote and left for him she said the anonymous ones were placed in the peg bag in the shed where only she would come upon them, her mother no longer being able to hang the washing out. Pimcrisp could have known it would suit his purposes, but he wouldn't be alone in that knowledge.'

'That suggests,' said Florence, 'that if someone else decided to save him from Anne's temptations, by frightening her away, he or she would most likely live in the neighbourhood of her home. That's Silkwood Way. It has only a few houses on it, and some have changed hands over the years, so only long-time residents would be of interest.'

'I agree that if Pimcrisp wasn't the writer that's where we

should look for whatever can be revealed after twenty years. To be frank with you, Mrs Norris, I'm not optimistic.'

'May George and I have a try at what we can ferret out?'

'By all means. I would terrify the guilt free into silence.'

'I think, however, I'll wait a few days or a week until the furore begins to ebb.'

'I'll send one of our men to see what he can get out of Pimcrisp. Where is he now?'

'On his cousin Lord Asprey's estate in Northumbria. Lord Stodmarsh can let you know where it's located, his grandfather was a good friend of his and Mr Fielding's father was, or is acquainted with him.'

Inspector LeCrane's mouth quirked. 'Thank you, Mrs Norris, but we're not talking about someone named Smith.'

'No,' she said, 'that has . . . would have its difficulties.'

'I'll also have a chat with this new vicar and his boyhood friend about what they remember from their stay at the vicarage. There's also the possibility that one or other of them wrote those letters because Anne had lost interest in their attentions. The young can take rejection hard, beyond all proportion.'

'I thought of that,' said Florence.

'But dismissed the idea?'

'After speaking with them, yes, but I could be proved wrong.'

The inspector got to his feet. 'Many thanks, Mrs Norris, I'll be back in touch. Now for a talk with Constable Trout, before bringing in the necessary people for the disinterment. What an ugly word that is, Mrs Norris. I'm tempted to linger over a pint of Mr Bird's excellent ale, but best to get on with it. Please tell Elsie she's in my good books, not the reverse.'

Something to be glad about, thought Florence when she returned to Mullings to seek out Ned and Mrs Tressler to let them know the past was about to shake up the present and life in Dovecote Hatch would not be itself for the foreseeable future. She wondered if Frank Shilling would mind having his job as grave digger taken over by others. Policemen, or whatever, who mightn't be Church of England. Or even christened. His rousing singing voice would be absent, leaving room for an unearthly silence.

TWENTY-ONE

That morning the undertakers returned to remove Agnes's coffin to the Chapel of Rest. Sophie asked if they would take the flowers if she emptied the water from the vases, was told it would be easier if she wrapped them in newspaper instead. There'd be plenty of containers at the chapel. She thanked them and went into the kitchen where Sally was doing the breakfast washing up.

'Newspapers, Miss? There's some in the scullery, I've been using them to clean the windows; I'll get some. Want me to take care of the flowers?'

'Let's do it together.'

Sophie wondered frequently over the next couple of days how she could have got through them without Sally. She'd listened thoughtfully yesterday to Mrs Norris's account of Anne Rudge's death and her burial in the grave where Agnes was to have been laid to rest with her brother. At intervals her eyes blurred with tears, but they did not fall.

Mrs Norris had concluded with the Reverend Pimcrisp's activities, omitting the source of this information. And Sally had spoken up stoutly. 'It was a horrible wickedness all round. I'm not surprised he turned out to be a dirty old man.'

'Remember we only have one witness to his behaviour, who will need to be questioned further. But there's point in my hushing it up because questions will have to be asked to see if anyone else can provide corroboration.'

'Well, I'll bet it's true. And I hope whoever wrote them letters is shaking in their boots at the thought of being found out and punished. And they will be, till they pleads for mercy, Mrs Norris, 'cos there's no one better at getting to the truth than you. As for Miss Younger's funeral being put off, she'd want right to be done and no fuss made. No need to worry about miss. I'll get rid of anyone showing up just to be nosy. And I pity the newspaper man who thinks he can charm a word out of me beyond good riddance.'

After Mrs Norris left Sally had made a pot of tea and as Uncle Henry would've said, talked sense to Sophie.

'Now, miss, if it doesn't rain it pours. Mrs Younger dies before you had a proper time with her and now this terrible business. Your heart goes out to Anne Rudge and her family, mine does too, but you've got a particularly big heart, but like my mum says, take time being upset, but then find a way to cheer yourself up. Why not sit quiet a while and read a book.'

Sophie had agreed meekly, gone up to her bedroom and decided escape was to be found in one of the boarding-school books of which Sally had now borrowed three and said they whisked her away to a world a girl of her upbringing could never have known. Sophie, who had been a day pupil at a boarding school, did not enlighten her that midnight feasts, secret societies holding meetings in crypts, or teachers engaged in espionage, were not the norm. She, herself, could still believe they did happen on opening up *New Girl at Maryville*.

She closed it on page thirty-seven, at the point where Carole, our heroine, has discovered her hockey stick was missing immediately prior to the start of a match between Maryville and their chief rival. Reading had also had the benefit of keeping thoughts at bay of Mr Fielding and what, if anything, he might have said if Mrs Norris had not arrived when she did.

She found Sally in the sitting room mending a tablecloth.

'Oh, don't get up,' she said and sat down. 'Your advice was exactly right, I'm back to myself again. I've been reading about this girl who'd broken her leg badly and had been in a cast for months and didn't think she'd ever be able to play hockey well, but when she started at a new school she kept improving until she was better than the captain of the team. In one of my mother's letters to Agnes she mentioned how Mrs Younger had taken them out to buy hockey sticks for when they started at their secondary school. I think you'll like this one.'

'Thanks ever so, miss. I'm just finishing up *For the Sake of the School* by Angela Brazil. *The Fortunes of Philippa* was the first one I read by her when I was about twelve. That's why I was excited when I saw you had those books.'

'This one isn't by her, but I'll hand it over when I'm done. Now I want to tell you what Mr Wendell came to talk to me about.' She explained about Agnes's investments and the income they would provide and had the overdue talk with her about wages and days off.

'Sally, how does three pounds a week sound?'

'For what, miss?'

'Your earnings?'

'But, I couldn't, it's far . . . far too much.'

'I've looked it up' – this wasn't true – 'and it's on the low side for a companion.'

'I don't want it.'

'Well, that's a pity. If you continue to argue I will have hysterics like Mrs Quigley.'

'Oh, miss, you'll make me laugh and I'll splutter me tea.'

'How about one and a half days off a week?'

'One'd be lovely.'

'All right. And you can take two when something comes up.'

'However can me thank you, miss. This'll mean I can help the family out, get the extras they wouldn't spend money on. Mum's been wanting one of Miss Milligan's boxer pups forever, but there's the price and then the feeding of it.'

The rest of Wednesday passed quietly; there wasn't much housework needing immediate attention, and knowing that the inspector was expected to make his appearance, it was not one for leaving the house. Sophie suggested they explore the attics. This, with its trove of belongings from past lives, proved enthralling. They were particularly enchanted with their discovery in the far corner of an inner room of a cradle, a doll's house with its tiny furniture and family dressed in mid Victorian clothes, a rocking horse and a box containing all that was required for a little girl's play kitchen.

'I wonder who she was, miss, I picture gold ringlets and big blue eyes, but she could've been quite different and dark and sallow, the kind that makes up a world of her own and grows up, remembering what it's like to be a child, and writes books for them and gets to be famous even though she doesn't care about that.'

'I'm glad you love it,' said Sophie. 'Maybe she was Agnes's mother. But she could have written books, boarding school ones, under an assumed name.'

Sally giggled. 'You are fun, miss.'

'If I am it's because you bring it out in me.'

They spent the next half hour or so looking over the attics, lifting coverings from pieces of furniture that could be brought downstairs if there was a need or a place for them. They were about to leave when they spotted a spinning wheel and could not resist it and between the two of them carried it downstairs.

They were in the hall, getting their breaths back, when the door knocker fell. It was Mr Fielding and Sophie hoped her flushed face and unsteady voice would be explained by exertion. But before she had time to respond to whatever he was saying about why he was there, the knocker went again. This time it was Miss Gillybud, whose mind went instantly to the question of what was a spinning wheel doing in the hall.

'Do you spin, Summer Rose, oh, please tell me you do? I'll come and watch you; it's the sort of thing everyone should see at least once, like glass blowing.'

'I don't, but now you talk of it I think I'd like to learn. Sally and I found it in the attic.'

'And do you plan on keeping it in the hall?' Mr Fielding asked, his smile making Sophie's heart turn over.

'No, in the sitting room, maybe, possibly, under the window.'

'Then let's try it there.' He'd already picked up the spinning wheel and now carried it through, set it down and asked Sophie what she thought.

'If you would angle it slightly.' She was about to say it now looked perfect, when Sally, who had discreetly vanished when the callers arrived, now came into the room.

'Pardon me.' Her eyes took in Miss Gillybud and Mr Fielding as well as Sophie before searching the room. 'Any sign of Marmalade? He was on one of the kitchen chairs when we went upstairs; he's not there now, nor in the scullery, the pantry and the dining room neither and the bedroom and other doors is shut like always, so I thought I'd find out if he was here before going back to the attics in case he followed us there and now's shut in. Could be meowing his head off and we wouldn't hear none.'

'Oh, dear. You're quite right, Sally.' Miss Gillybud flapped her hands, 'I've been up there with Agnes and I remember thinking someone could be getting murdered down here, screaming their lungs out and we'd be none the wiser. I'll come with you, he knows my voice and always comes when I say fish paste sandwiches.'

'Who would come into this house to get themselves murdered?' Mr Fielding asked wryly.

'I don't know, but it could happen, dreadful things abound. I was, however, making the point that if Sally had not been so observant that poor boy could be languishing in isolation for hours.'

Sophie said she should go. She had grown much attached to Marmalade. He was now her cat and she was concerned; there was also the added factor that she was fluttery at the thought of being alone with Aiden . . . Mr Fielding. It wouldn't do to appear too friendly and being detached could be a mistake.

In the end they all went and, sure enough, when they entered the box room they heard Marmalade meowing irritably from above. When rescued he put on a display of indifference that convinced nobody but himself.

Miss Gillybud and Mr Fielding did not stay long. They explained that they had come to let Sophie know that the activity in the churchyard with its police presence and that of Dr Chester was over. What remained of Anne Rudge had been taken away for examination. The coffin containing Agnes's brother remained where it was. At least for the time being and the still open grave roped off.

As he was leaving Mr Fielding said, 'Be strong, Sophie; you have more courage than you realize. If you need me send Sally and I'll be right over.'

'Thank you.' She again felt that lovely warmth on sensing tenderness from him. 'I'm not going to hole up here as if unwilling to face people's questions. Tomorrow I'll go to the shops and if I'm stopped along the way say I'm saddened by what has happened, but am doing very well.'

'Splendid!'

Sophie told Sally of this plan over their evening meal of mince and potatoes and apple crumble.

'You want me to come with you, miss?'

'Of course. We should have quite a bit to buy and when we're thoroughly exhausted we can go into that teashop you pointed out to me the other day.'

'You'll get to meet my sister-in-law, she started working there. Ever so nice she is.'

A list was compiled of necessary purchases and at ten o'clock the next morning they set off, shopping baskets in hand. There had been no newspaper reporters thronging around the door to detain them. Their first stop was the grocer's which was abuzz with the expected. They caught some of the scraps – 'terrible!' . . . 'who'd have thought?' . . . 'in the churchyard all this time' – before silence fell. Sally dealt with the awkward moment by breezily introducing Sophie to the shop at large and then chatting away about how fast you could go through sugar and what a nuisance it was to find yourself out of baking powder.

Normality restored. The focus was now on welcoming Sophie to Dovecote Hatch. Condolences were offered for the loss of her cousin and the hope extended that she would enjoy life in the village if she stayed on. She said that was her plan, that her home had been a small village, so she expected to be very happy here.

They went next to the butcher's where they were the only customers and received a warm welcome from Mrs Saunders. She said she was sorry about this new trouble, patted Sophie's hand and introduced her to her son, Dick, who looked bashfully at her and dreamily at Sally, until elbowed aside by his beaming father.

'He admires you,' said Sophie when they left with their rashers of bacon and a veal and ham pie.

'Mr Saunders? He likes to look, but there's no harm in him.'

'No, the son.'

'Yes, well, he's asked me to walk out with him and I wouldn't mind if he didn't take it serious. I'm not ready to think wedding bells and babies, especially now you've taken me on.'

They went on to the fishmonger where again Sally success-fully steered a conversation into generalities with others waiting to be served. And then, finally to Hobbs' Haberdashery because Sally needed some reels of cotton. There the only customer present was Miss Gillybud. She was asking the woman behind the counter if she might possibly have left behind the dressing gown cord she had bought the previous morning.

'I thought I put it in my coat pocket, Miss Hobbs, you may remember I said I didn't want a bag, and it's entirely possible that on the way home I reached in for my handkerchief or door key and it dropped out. I know my purse was in my other pocket, at least I think it was. Yesterday was difficult for all of us – with a body that shouldn't be there being dug up in the churchyard and my mind does tend to wander at the best of times.'

Miss Hobbs cut in briskly. She was a middle-aged woman, wearing rimless glasses and blessed with abundant still fair hair. 'You didn't leave it here, Miss Gillybud, I remember you putting it in your pocket, and thinking you should have let me put it in a paper bag.'

'So foolish of me.'

'With God's grace someone may find it and bring it back here. I will say a prayer. Yesterday was difficult, but one also for reflection on how to avoid straying from the path of right-eousness. Anne Rudge worked here briefly, she was a diligent worker; it's a shame she died as she did and is denied the glory of heaven.'

'There is that passage about glass houses and throwing stones,' said Miss Gillybud vaguely.

Miss Hobbs' eyes flashed behind her spectacles. 'Exactly what are you implying?'

'Nothing personal.' Turning, Miss Gillybud saw Sophie and Sally behind her, beamed at them and made muddled introduc-tions. Miss Hobbs said she hoped to see Miss Dawson in church. Sophie said that would be nice. And Miss Gillybud asked if this was Una Smith's day off.

'She phoned to say her leg, the one she hurt falling off her bicycle, is bothering her again. I may have to let her go if this keeps up. When my nephew returns from his buying trip, I'll insist either he puts his foot down or I will.'

'Such an attractive young man, so very like his mother,' murmured Miss Gillybud. 'It must comfort you knowing your dear sister is looking down from above seeing how the two of you get along.'

Sally remembered her reel of cotton. And out the shop they went.

'Ooh, Miss Gillybud,' Sally giggled. 'You said that last bit to irritate her; everyone knows Mr Kaye can't stick her and she's tried to buy him out of the business.'

'Yes. For the moment I couldn't help myself. Childish. But I should remember to make allowances for her. She had that recent breakdown when Pimcrisp retired, and I imagine is always on the verge of one. I'll have to go back and buy another dressing gown cord if the one I've lost doesn't turn up. Such a particularly attractive colour! Royal blue with threads of green, I don't suppose I dropped it in your hall yesterday, Summer Rose?'

'I'll look under the hall rack and bring it round if it's there.'

'It isn't, miss,' said Sally after they separated from Miss Gillybud outside the greengrocer's. 'I give the hall a good go round with the mop this morning and I'd've spotted it, same in the sitting room.'

'If she hasn't found it when we see her next, I'll go and buy her another. Hopefully they'll have one in the same colour.'

Coming towards them was a woman walking a boxer dog.

'That's Miss Milligan,' said Sally.

The woman drew level with them and ordered the dog to sit. 'Ah, Sally!' she rumbled. 'And this lady with you must be Miss Dawson, now of Orchard House. Nasty start for you. Don't mean about Agnes. Told me the last time I saw her she was ready to go, but no, this other business. Hope they find the blighter who drove her to it. Won't say more. Think about getting one of my pups. New litter on the way. Come, Horatio!'

Sally giggled. 'Never can get a word in edgewise with her. I didn't get to ask her about a puppy for Mum, but she's a good sort.'

They reached the Spinning Wheel Tea Shop, where several curious looks came their way. They were greeted pleasantly by the owner, who listened with interest to Sally's account of the spinning wheel found in the attic. Sally's sister-in-law wasn't due to come in until the afternoon shift, but they spent a pleasant half hour over Chelsea buns and tea, nodding and smiling and occasionally chatting with other customers.

Back at Orchard House, they put away their shopping, attended to a few tasks, had a latish lunch and settled in for a quiet afternoon. It began raining around four, in a softly pattering way and Sally replenished the fire, making the sitting room feel especially cosy. Their evening meal was fish with parsley sauce, new potatoes and peas. Sophie insisted on doing the washing up.

Sally had mentioned earlier that she would love to go back up in the attics and see what else of interest she could discover.

'Go on,' she said, 'I've Marmalade for company and I'll curl up by the fire and finish *The New Girl at Maryville*.'

'Are you sure, miss? It's your stuff up there.'

'And you're doing me a favour going through it.'

Sally nodded at Marmalade who was sitting, as forbidden, on the kitchen table. 'I'll shut the box room door, so he don't get up to tricks like yesterday.'

Sophie went and sat down by the fire, but she didn't pick up her book. She closed her eyes and thought of Aiden. Was she misreading his feelings for her? When he was nearby, she believed he experienced the same pull; that he wanted to take her into his arms as much as she longed to be there. But what experience did she have of being found desirable?

The knocker sounded. It was him. She was sure of it and on opening the door she stepped back to let him get quickly out of the rain. But the man who entered the hall wasn't Aiden; it was Mr Crawley.

TWENTY-TWO

It took the flicker of a second for her to recognize him. He was wearing a black wig and a false black moustache, but the eyes . . . those pale, opaque eyes were unmistakable. He was closing the door behind him, leaning against it.

'My sweet Sophie, don't be shy and pretend you didn't know I'd find you. I don't blame you for running away. You were afraid of my wife. I understand. She made you think you were in the wrong, when what could be more right than our being together for always.' He took off his hat, walked over to the hall rack, hung it up. She edged towards the door.

'Don't.' It was a command. He removed the wig, peeled off the moustache and stuffed it in his raincoat pocket. 'Don't annoy me, Sophie.'

The meek pathetic man was no more; here was one enjoying his power to subjugate her, frighten her. He could smell her fear, would play with it, until the rage burning just below the surface erupted. He did blame her for disappearing. Saw it as a betrayal of his right to determine their future. She must appease him, play for time, hope and pray, she could think of a way out.

'I was making sure the door was closed properly as the rain could blow it open.'

'There's no wind.'

She didn't risk another word.

'Is there anyone else here?'

'No.' She couldn't risk him going up to the attic and finding Sally.

'Where's the cousin?'

'Dead. She died the night I got here.' What was the point in pretending otherwise? He'd have no fear of an elderly woman, easily dealt with, suddenly appearing.

'Do you want to know how clever I was in discovering your whereabouts?'

'You must have got it out of Mrs Blount; only she knew about my cousin.'

'I admit I impressed myself. I've spent so long being over-looked, underrated, and ignored. It eats away at you until either you're nothing but a shell, or one day you lash out at life, until it's beaten down to your terms. It's how I wormed my way into your landlady's good graces that was genius.'

'I want to hear.'

'Have you noticed this new raincoat?'

'It's of excellent quality.'

'And the shoes. The salesman at Clark's said they were top tree. The hat's second-hand but looks like it's from Bond Street. Remind you of anyone?'

'A well-dressed man about town?'

'Mr Euwing.'

'Oh.' Her mind had stopped working.

'I added the moustache and wig, in case you'd ever described him to her. It was also easy; I knocked on her door, said I was him and went on for a bit about how worried I was by your leaving so abruptly, especially as you had wages owing. She invited me in as pleasant as could be, told me you'd gone to stay with a cousin and that just that morning she'd received a letter from you. And if I waited just a minute, she'd write down the address for me.'

She had stopped listening to him halfway through. What would happen if Sally came down the stairs? Would he return to his craven self and get out fast? Or would her appearance on the scene increase his rage to the point that he turned it on her. Sophie had lied to him about being alone in the house. That would be enough for him to turn violent. He was on the edge of some-thing far darker than talk. She closed her mind to how bad, unbearable, it would be if she didn't find a way to outwit him.

'I wore the wig and the moustache here because I thought you'd be amused as well as proud of my ingenuity. But it means nothing to you at all.' His eyes narrowed to colourless slits. 'I thought you would rush into my arms, that everything you'd felt for me would be released. But there you stand like a block of ice. You led me on, Sophie, playing the sweet innocent. You offered, you little bitch, and I'm taking what was promised.'

He made a grab for her, but she jerked free. If she could get to the kitchen and out the back door he might be afraid to follow her even though it was dark. She shoved at the coatrack and it swayed towards him. He stayed it with a lunge, wrenched at her arm and dragged her through the open sitting room door.

'I pawned my mother's gold locket, wedding and engagement rings for those clothes, my dear, dear mother who I thought you resembled. She warned me what to expect from women. She was right! She was always right. My wife has kept me back from all I could have achieved in life and you . . .' He was panting heavily as she struggled against him. 'You had better enjoy this.'

He was thrusting her on to the sofa, forcing her head back. She screamed. Screamed without hope. Miss Gillybud's voice drifted in her head saying that murder could be committed down here and no one in the attics would be any the wiser. And Sally had said she would shut the box-room door behind her sealing off any pitiful chance of any sound getting through. He was lying on top of her, his hands over her mouth. Hands hurting. She was drowning . . . She had to be drowning because her life was beginning to flash before her. Her parents were dead, she was arriving at Uncle Henry's. So stern, she was going to be frightened of him, but she hadn't been . . . what she hadn't known, never realized until he was gone, was that he loved her. She must tell Aiden. Must live to see Aiden again. She was coming up for air, had a moment of free breath. She heard a meow, followed by a sharp yelp, the weight lifted, a scrambling on the floor as of someone crawling to their feet. Her weakened gaze saw the figure straighten up, saw someone, something else move up behind him with a long object held aloft before bringing it cracking down on his head.

Sophie saw Sally bending over her. 'It's all right now, miss. You're safe, he's knocked out cold. Pity I didn't kill him. Do you think you can sit up? Let me help you, that's it. And take hold of this.' It was a hockey stick. 'Give him a hard whack if he so much as stirs. Do you understand?'

'Yes, my mind's clearing. You saved me, Sally.'

'Marmalade got to him first; scratched him. I hope he gets blood poisoning.'

'What brought you down? I thought you'd be up in the attics for hours.'

'I'll tell you about that later. I don't like leaving you a minute, but I have to run to Miss Gillybud's and use her telephone to fetch Constable Trout.'

'But I don't want anyone to know. It's bad enough that it happened. I can't face having to talk about it . . . answer questions.'

'I understand, miss, but he can't stay on the floor till he wakes up.'

'No, no, of course not. I'll do what you say, hit him with the hockey stick if he twitches a muscle.'

'Do you know who he is, miss?'

'Mr Crawley. The bookkeeper at the estate agency where I worked. He'd got ideas in his head . . . that there's something between us. There was an incident. I told Mr Fielding about it, but I'd stopped being afraid he'd find me.'

'I'll be quick.'

Sophie should have been frightened on being left alone with Mr Crawley however lifeless he appeared, but all she felt was exhaustion. It seemed an age before Sally returned although it couldn't have been more than five minutes. Behind her came Miss Gillybud, issuing soothing noises and soon after Aiden Fielding was in the room. He dragged Mr Crawley out into the hall and returned with the information that Constable Trout had arrived. 'He's going to stand guard in the dining room; the fellow's coming round, but reinforcements are coming from Large Middlington and he'll be out of here soon.' He turned to Sally. 'Please fill a hot water bottle and fetch a blanket or two. We have to keep her warm.' He came towards Sophie, looking down at her with his hand clenched at his sides.

'You aren't going to be asked to talk about it tonight. I've informed Constable Trout who Crawley is and that you were concerned he might find a means to track you down. Sally has already told him she heard you scream, what she saw on entering the room and the action she took.'

Sophie stared at him.

'Would you like Miss Gillybud to sit down beside you?'

'That would be nice, but could it be you?'

'That's my girl,' said Miss Gillybud, 'I'll go and ask Sally how I can make myself useful.'

Mr Fielding joined Sophie on the sofa. 'I cannot,' he said softly, 'find words to express both the sorrow and anger I feel.'

'Could you move closer,' she whispered.

'Of course. And may I take your hand?'

'Yes, please.' They sat in silence, until she found her voice again. 'I just want him gone. I was terrified that he would . . .'

'I understand.'

'But it didn't get that far, because of Sally. I felt his fingers digging into my sides, but he didn't touch me where . . . it would have mattered. I don't want to press charges against him, have to relive it, have to go to court. He said I'd led him on, that I was getting what I wanted. How can I prove I didn't?'

'You don't have go through that, Sophie. I'll tell Trout what you've said. He'll need to talk to you for form's sake, but tomorrow, not tonight. He'll have Sally's statement of what she saw and the action she took. He's a kind man.'

'Could you be there when he does come to see me?'

'Of course. I'll let him know that's your wish.'

Sophie longed to lay her head on his shoulder, instead she clung to his hand.

'How did Crawley find you?'

She explained about the letter to Mrs Blount, about the disguise and passing himself off as Mr Euwing. 'He was wearing the wig and false moustache when I opened the door to him. He wanted to show me how clever he'd been.'

'Did you notice what he did with them when he took them off?'

'He put them in his coat pocket. It's on the hall tree. I think he hung it up to make clear he wasn't going to leave until he chose.'

'I told him Agnes was dead because I didn't want him going upstairs, not with Sally in the attic. He might have heard something, an object being moved, especially if he'd gone into the box room. I couldn't risk it; he was in a mood to go after anyone he came upon. I tried to knock the hall tree over on him, but it didn't work.'

'Sophie, I wish I could have spared . . .' He began, but Miss Gillybud was suddenly there.

'Time for you to be tucked into bed, Summer Rose. Sally has put in the hot water bottles, so let me take you up.'

'I am tired. But where is . . .?'

'In the dining room, but only for a tiny while longer. He'll be taken away and meanwhile Constable Trout has his truncheon.'

Even so Sophie avoided looking at the door holding Crawley at bay. Mr Fielding went with her and Miss Gillybud to the foot of the stairs. Sally was waiting in her bedroom. And within fifteen minutes had her tucked under the covers.

'You're the best friend anyone could have, Sally.'

'No one will ever lay a finger on you again, miss, while I'm around. And I plan on that being until I'm a hundred and two.'

After that time seemed to float. Miss Gillybud who had left them returned with a cup of tea. Her voice bracing. 'Strong and sweet, just the way you need it.'

Sophie sipped dutifully.

Then Mrs Chester bustled in, saying her husband was downstairs, but there was no need for him to come up unless Miss Dawson wished it; but he did want her to take a couple of tablets to help her sleep through the night. She stayed only a short time, talking comfortingly in a non-specific way about respecting her privacy.

Sophie looked doubtful when Sally handed her the tablets.

'It's all right, miss. They won't make you feel funny, or turn you like Mrs Quigley that was always sending me back to the chemist for more until Dr Chester put a stop to it.'

'That's not it; I'm afraid of falling asleep until I know . . . he's gone.'

Fortunately, Miss Gillybud reappeared at that moment to report a car had arrived from Large Middlington with two policemen and the menace had been removed. The relief was enormous and with it came a wave of gratitude that she had survived and would not have to endure the aftermath alone. Sally was by the bed holding her hand, and Aiden and Miss Gillybud would remain downstairs throughout the night. She did not need to be told this. She knew. Her last waking thought was of Anne Rudge who'd had no one with whom to share the fear that stalked her.

Sophie slept dreamlessly until almost eleven o'clock the next morning. On opening her eyes she saw Sally standing by the bed and Marmalade curled up on a chair. I should feel much worse – panicky, she thought – in the aftermath of something so awful, but I feel almost normal. I suppose it's some form of shock. A numbing affect.

'Ready for breakfast, miss?'

'But you're not going to bring it up' – she was getting out of bed – 'I'm coming down. But first I want to know why you brought that hockey stick down from the attic?'

'Because of what you told me about Miss Younger and your mother being bought hockey sticks the summer before they went on to secondary school. When I spotted one stuck in a corner I just had to come and show you.'

'Sally . . .' Sophie looked at her soberly. 'If you hadn't been interested in what I talked about, you wouldn't have remembered the hockey sticks.'

'You listened to me too, miss. And I love our chats.'

'Another thing; here you've been taking care of me when you've also been through a nightmarish experience.'

'I wasn't afraid of him. From what Constable Trout said he turned into a snivelling coward, babbling on about wanting his mum.'

'Yes, he would.' Sophie experienced the faintest of shivers. 'But, Sally, I do hope you got some sleep.'

'Wouldn't't've dared not to with Miss Gillybud saying she'd stand over me till she heard me snore. Mr Fielding sent her home after a while and had her telephone his sister to come and join him here. They left a little after six, right after I got up.'

'Oh!' Sophie couldn't imagine Miss Fielding had welcomed the late-night summons.

The rest of that day was relatively uneventful. Mr Fielding, as promised, accompanied Constable Trout for what turned out to be a brief, and not disquieting, interview. He asked Sophie how she was feeling today, said wasn't this a wicked world, produced a notepad, flipped it open, and tapped it with a stubby pencil. Expressed his belief that he had all the facts, added that

the person in question had been dispatched to the area where
he lived, following a lengthy interrogation, followed by a
warning that proceedings would be undertaking if he didn't give
Dovecote Hatch, and indeed the whole county a wide berth in
future.

'I don't think you'll have any more trouble with him, Miss
Dawson.'

Sophie was comforted, but saw Aiden looking at her ques-
tioningly. As he was leaving in the constable's wake, he said,
'Sally has asked Dick Saunders to watch the house tonight.
Don't argue with her about this, Sophie.'

'I won't,' she promised.

Later Sally brought up the matter. 'I told Dick we'd had an
intruder, probably a poor old tramp scrounging around for
something to eat, 'cos we couldn't find anything else missing,
but having a big strong man outside would let us sleep easier,
women being as all the world knows of sensitive dispositions.
I'd read something like it in a book and it must've sounded
good because he looked ready to run off and put on his suit of
armour.'

Sophie woke the following morning to the thought that this
was Saturday, she had been here less than a week and her life
had entirely changed. Was it because so much had happened in
such a short time that the impact of Mr Crawley's attack had
been lessened. Not that she didn't think about it, she was seized
by flashes of fright, but her life hadn't gone to pieces.

Over breakfast Sally assured her Dick had reported cheerfully
that he hadn't spotted any prowlers, but it'd been good practice
for the next time he was needed to protect the village from
no-gooders.

'Do you think he'd like to be a policeman?'

'Nothing regular like that. What he would like is for Mr Bird
to take him on full time at the pub.'

Sophie had been in the sitting room for an hour with her
knitting when the door knocker tapped smartly. Neither she,
nor Sally, any longer opened the door without first looking out
one of the front windows to see who was there. Sally now called
out to her from the dining room.

'It's Mr Fielding, I'll let him in.'

Sophie set the knitting aside and rose expectantly. This as far as she could remember was the first time he'd called on his own.

'Good morning,' he said coming towards her. 'I hope I'm not disturbing you.'

'Not at all, just whiling away the time on a cardigan I was making for work.'

He nodded. 'Navy blue; a sensible colour, but now you can allow yourself more choice. A softer blue, or green; I think you would look very nice in green.'

Sophie felt her face flush.

'Shall I bring in tea, miss?' Sally asked from the doorway.

'Perhaps later . . .?' Mr Fielding looked inquiringly at Sophie. 'After we've had time to talk?'

'Of course. I'll come and fetch you, Sally.'

'Right you are, miss. I'll be in the kitchen.'

When the two of them were alone he asked if they might sit down. 'I wish I'd brought my pipe,' he said taking a chair across from her. 'It helps me organize my mind.'

'You said something of the sort in the car on our return from Large Millington.'

'Did I?' He smiled. 'Well, it didn't seem appropriate to bring it on this occasion. But you may wish I had if I start pacing. Sophie, I've come to ask you to marry me.'

She waited without breathing.

'I've already told you I like and admire you; I now add that I have become deeply fond of you.' The words were matter of fact, but something in his voice told her he was having difficulty with them. 'I don't think you realize how endearing you are. Sally is devoted to you and Miss Gillybud is fast becoming so. Because of my increasing affection for you I have the wish to help keep you safe. I don't like the idea of your living here, with only Sally for protection.'

'Dick Saunders has said he'll continue to keep watch at night.'

'But he can't do that forever.'

'No.'

'I'm not suggesting that Crawley is likely to return, but I don't want you going around in fear that he might and find you unprotected.'

'You can't marry me out of kindness or sympathy.' She couldn't keep the edge out of her voice.

'I'd be doing nothing of the sort. If you accept me I will look forward with pleasure to a life with you. The question is could you do likewise?'

'Yes.' That it wasn't the proposal of any girl's dreams couldn't override the truth.

'I wish I had my pipe.'

'You should have brought it.'

'Do you like me, Sophie?'

'Very much.'

'But you haven't thought beyond that,' he said softly and was silent for several moments. 'Let me then put my own feelings more clearly. Poets write of love in high flown terms. An ordinary man may speak of coming home on a cold winter's night to the warmth and glow, not only of a fire in the hearth, but to that of their wife's smile.' He looked at her with the touch of a smile. 'I'm not good at speaking in verse, Sophie. But I do know I find happiness in the thought of coming home to you at the end of each day.' Her heart leapt, but uncertainty crept back when he didn't leave it there. 'Friendship, trust and respect make for a strong foundation.'

'I'm sure that's true.' She wished she didn't sound so stilted.

'I think starting out you should have your own bedroom and I will never urge physical intimacy upon you until you decide you are ready. In a sense it would be an engagement period. Is that acceptable?'

'Yes, Aiden. I do appreciate your being so thoughtful.'

'I'll get a special license, we can be married without delay. Would Saturday week give you enough time to get ready?'

'There won't be that much to do. But I do have two conditions. I must bring Sally and Marmalade.'

'You may bring a whole battalion of companions and cats.' He got to his feet and came towards her, hands extended. His kiss touched the edge of her mouth. She might wonder when he was gone if she was making the mistake of her life, but at that moment she had hope for their future.

TWENTY-THREE

On the following Monday morning Mrs MacDonald laid no claim to having foreseen Mr Fielding's announcement of his upcoming wedding to Sophie Dawson at yesterday's morning service. She might remember to do in the near future, but as of now the thrill of romance outweighed the opportunity to preen.

'What a lovely thing to happen,' she said for the third, or possibly fourth, time, as she sat with Florence over cups of tea. 'There was the poor lass, losing her only living relation and then all that horror of Anne Rudge and the grave being dug up, and Miss Younger's funeral being delayed, it's as though fate had it in for her. And then along comes the handsome vicar to sweep her off her feet.'

'They've known each other in the past,' said Florence.

''Course' – Mrs MacDonald's eyes turned dreamy – 'it would be better if he got to carry her off to his castle instead of that grim old vicarage.'

'Clergymen don't have castles.'

'I understand why the wedding's to be so quick. He can't have had a moment's peace, knowing she's alone, but for Sally Barton, of a night at Orchard House. Not right for a young girl at the best of times, but now with the police digging up dirt in every sense of the word, even if it's from twenty years gone, it's no surprise the wedding's to be this Saturday.'

'And it's worse than you've said,' piped in Winnie who was supposed to be in the scullery, not the kitchen, 'about how some horrible old tramp broke in Thursday evening an' tried to rob the place blind.'

'It's a wicked world,' said Mrs MacDonald in the lofty tone of having invented the phrase. 'Someone reads in the papers about the death of a middle-aged spinster and expects to find the house empty.'

'If it was me I'd tell the vicar he'd better marry me right this minute, 'cos I wouldn't be sitting round till Sat'day waiting for the rest of the world to fall in.'

'That's enough, Winnie,' snapped Mrs MacDonald. 'Go stick your nose where it's wanted, which isn't here.' When the girl had departed with an injured air, she shook her head. 'Truth is she's the sort that'll push her way up and do better than the hard working sort. It's the way the world is going now. But there'll always be the comfort of births and weddings. Like yours coming up and now Miss Dawson and the vicar.'

Florence agreed. She had listened affectionately to Mrs MacDonald's enthusiasm for this latest village news, had even been faintly amused that Una Newsome was no longer the prominent topic of early morning conversations. But she could not sit idle much longer; she was eager to set out for the village.

On Saturday afternoon she had been with George at the Dog and Whistle when Constable Trout had telephoned to say that Inspector LeCrane was with him and would it be convenient for Mr Bird and Mrs Norris to come along to the police station to hear where things now stood in regard to the inquiry. They'd set off immediately and found LeCrane in a brisk mood, due to being required elsewhere on another case. What they learned in the half hour he had to give them was that the detectives who'd been sent to speak to Pimcrisp had found him so deep into senility they got nothing of sense out of him let alone any reaction when they brought up the name Anne Rudge. They'd also spoken with Lord Asprey who assured them his cousin's response to their questioning was not assumed; that he now required round-the-clock care and the doctor did not think he was long for this world. For form's sake they met with this medic, who offered confirmation, adding that His Lordship should be up for sainthood, considering his long-time generosity to a man he heartily disliked.

Additionally, LeCrane had informed them that Tim Rudge had telephoned him from Canada, while he was still considering what to do about him. He'd provided the address of the house where he and his family were staying in Ottawa with his brother-in-law and having seen them settled was willing to return and deal with the consequences.

'His brother-in-law has done well for himself setting up a

market garden business, which Rudge is to join, and will loan him the money. I told him there might be no need for him to come back.' LeCrane had opened his silver case and selected a cigarette. 'There'll be a coroner's inquest, probably in the next week or so, and very likely, his letter to me, along with the anonymous letters he provided will suffice. This all happened such a long time ago and he was a boy at the time of his sister's death, and under the guidance of his parents. The chief constable will be only too glad to be done with it. He'll insist he has bigger fish to fry.'

LeCrane had stubbed out his cigarette and eased into his coat. 'Miss Dawson will be notified that her cousin can now be buried as intended in the grave where her brother lies, or in another of her choosing.'

'Her marriage to Mr Fielding is set for Saturday,' said Constable Trout. 'Not an easy choice for them, sir, wedding or funeral first.'

'And before too long Anne Rudge can be properly laid to rest,' the inspector had mused. 'I imagine her brother will wish to return for that. In the meantime, I'm sure you two' – he was looking at Florence and George – 'will stay busy. Let's not forget your own wedding plans.'

With that he was gone. Florence knew he hadn't forgotten her agreement to talk with those living closest to the scene of past events who just might possibly have some information to provide regarding the activities of the anonymous letter writer and, or, Pimcrisp. There might be something, perhaps they'd barely noticed at the time, but now nudged its way to the surface. On the way back to the Dog she and George decided she would pay calls on certain people on Monday morning. And now here she sat over tea with Mrs MacDonald and she still had a few instructions to give Molly and Elsie Trout before she could put on her coat and hat.

'So, what do you think?' said Mrs MacDonald.

Apart from the occasional disconnected word Florence had missed what she'd been saying for the past few minutes. So, she tried something that had worked before at such times. 'You have a wiser head than I do.'

Mrs MacDonald beamed. 'You wouldn't have thought of it?'

'I'm afraid not.'

'But you agree Miss Dawson is likely to be pleased?'

'Delighted.'

'Then will you get in touch and let her know I'll be pleased to make the wedding cake. The rush won't bother me like it'd do an ordinary person and the ones from shops are a disgrace.'

'I'll go and see her this morning.'

As she spoke an idea came to Florence that she turned over in her mind as she walked towards Orchard House. The door was opened for her by Sally, wearing a smart navy blue dress and matching cardigan. Nothing about it to indicate a maid's uniform. She welcomed Florence inside, with a bright smile, saying Miss Sophie was in the sitting room and she'd take her through because that's how they were doing things these days, rather a lot of popping in and out. Of course, if it's someone Miss doesn't know and could have come just to be nosy that'd be different.

'This has to be a very busy time for Miss Dawson and you.'

'Yes, but lovely too.'

Sophie came to the doorway and when she and Florence were settled in the sitting room, Sally having whisked away, thanked her warmly for coming.

She is like a rose, the Summer Rose as Miss Gillybud called her, thought Florence as she offered best wishes on her engagement. There was no ring on her left hand, but there hadn't been time for that. She spoke of her happiness, of how she had come to like and admire Aiden Fielding when she had known him in the past and how those feelings had been rekindled when they met again. Some might have been surprised she hadn't gone into raptures, but Florence heard something in her voice, that suggested she was being deliberately constrained. She might feel the circumstances required that, or there might be personal reasons. It was none of Florence's business, but she was intrigued, more so because she saw in Sophie something of herself as a young woman, uncertainly, but determinedly treading new paths.

She told her about Mrs MacDonald's offer to make the wedding cake and here delight appeared.

'How kind of her. That would be wonderful; do please thank

her very much. I hadn't thought about a cake, but there should be one. After announcing in church that we're to be married, he invited the congregation to a reception at the vicarage following the ceremony. And Miss Gillybud is writing notes to others in the village, whom she thinks might wish to come. I do hope you and Mr Bird will do so.'

'With pleasure.'

'Mrs Norris' – Sophie looked at her shyly – 'I hope you don't think it's presumptuous of me but I feel a closeness to you, because of how you've striven to find out who drove Anne Rudge to her death. That's partly because Aiden knew and liked her and for what his friend Kip – Graham Lieland – has suffered in guilt. Then there's the connection with Cousin Agnes. But, it's more than that. From the beginning I had a sense of a strong thread pulling us together, as if she needed something from me, and I from her. And over the past several days that feeling has grown.'

'Would you like to tell me about it?' asked Florence.

'Yes.' Sophie was hesitant on getting started, but after a few stammered words she told her about Mr Crawley, from the Saturday morning when his wife showed up with the children till his arrival last Thursday evening. She spoke more of Sally's courage than she did of her terror.

Florence sat still and quiet throughout, not allowing any of her anger and sorrow to show through. Sophie needed to speak as if to the calm of an empty room.

'Miss Gillybud and Mrs Chester were a comfort and Constable Trout was very sensitive in his questions. But it was Aiden . . . his strength and compassion that got me through that night. And I am doing much better than I ever would have expected. I have not had horrible dreams, but sometimes I dream of Anne.'

The hasty wedding was explained. Mr Fielding might, or might not, have been swept off his feet by a grand passion as Mrs MacDonald believed, but Sophie meant sufficient to him that he would not leave her unprotected at Orchard House a day longer than necessary. Her feelings, though veiled, were visible. She loved him enough to take what was given.

'I am grateful you felt you could confide in me. I think you very brave, Miss Dawson, to have picked up the pieces of your life as best you can. And I understand why Anne matters to you so much. You have known fear, as she did, but she was unable to turn to anyone for help, out of fear for her parents paying a price. As it happens, I didn't only come to tell you about the wedding cake, I wanted to ask your help in trying to find out if anyone living close to the Rudges remembers anything from that time that might be of help. As Sally's mother did. As you know she was of enormous help.'

'She's a lovely woman. She and her husband came for tea yesterday afternoon and I was able to tell them what a gift she has been. Yes, of course, I will help you in any way you ask. Tell me what I can do.'

'I'd like you to come with me when I go and speak with the Quigleys and Mr Kaye. They are the only ones who were living on Silkwood Way twenty years ago, the few other homes have since changed hands. I'd also like to talk to Nurse Newsome who'd frequently have crossed from the far side of Coldwind Common, when she had a patient in this part of the village, giving her a rear view of the houses. It's possible she might remember seeing someone slipping into the Rudge's shed at an odd hour, maybe more than once and thought there was something furtive in his, or her, manner. Of course, this is all grasping at straws. The person who put those letters in the peg bag, might have lived further away.'

'I think you're right. It makes sense that it was someone living very close to Anne and her family. And that might well place them on Silkwood Way.' Sophie paused. 'That includes Miss Gillybud. I'd never believe in a thousand years it was her. But people might start suspecting her, maybe are doing so already, whispering to each other that she wrote them and then went to the police station with a made-up story of having seen Reverend Pimcrisp peering in that kitchen window when he knew Anne would be taking her bath.'

'The thinking would be that as an atheist she was striking a blow at religion.'

'But she doesn't care what other people believe, as long as it makes them happy. Mrs Norris, when do you want to go and have these talks?'

'Would it be possible for you this morning?'

'Yes. Aiden is driving me to Large Middlington this afternoon to discuss with Agnes's solicitor the details of her estate, but the appointment isn't until four. But how can I be of help to you on your mission?'

'By giving me an excuse for showing up and doing some probing. I'll say you've asked me to introduce you to your future husband's parishioners so you can express your sympathy for what the village is going through. This being particularly close to your heart because Agnes was unwittingly brought into it.'

'But what about Mr Kaye? Won't he be at the shop?'

'We may have to tackle him later. Unless he comes home for lunch.'

'I'll ask Sally.' Sophie went to fetch her.

She provided the answer. 'He does sometimes, Mrs Norris, and others not. But Mondays he don't go into Hobbs, liking to do the book work at home. For the peace of it, I suppose.'

'Thank you. Mrs Norris and I are going out for a bit.' Sophie went upstairs to get her coat and hat.

Sally stood smiling at Florence. 'I'm more than obliged that you told Mum you have given me a place at Mullings. It was my dream, but this is where I'm meant to be. I never in a million years would've thought I could love the person I worked for, but I do. It's not even like work. We pitch in together so to speak.'

'I'm so happy for you, Sally.'

'She said if I put on a maid's outfit, she'd give it to the rag and bone man. So, Mum made me this dress and brought it yesterday, and Miss give me the cardigan she's just finished knitting because it goes so well with it.'

'I've always thought this a house with a lovely feeling to it, and your happiness adds to it.' Florence looked a little wistfully around the room. 'So many lives lived within these walls, lived and embraced.'

She was about to ask Sally if she would mind leaving it for the vicarage, but Sophie had come in and it was time to set out.

'Where first, Mrs Norris?'

'The Quigleys. As you know Mrs Quigley does not leave the house during day time hours, but I've heard she sometimes walks on Coldwind Common at night and her husband is in and out of the church at all hours. Either of them might have seen something that struck them as odd and could prove useful. If they remember it, which admittedly is doubtful.'

'Is Mr Quigley so deeply religious?'

'I don't know. He is the churchwarden; but his passion is antiquities and he may want to spend time absorbing the twelfth-century atmosphere. He takes pride in preserving the early bible that was the gift of his cousin Lord Asprey.'

'Aiden hasn't mentioned it, but there hasn't been time.'

They had arrived at the Quigley's house. The exterior would have been as charming as the others on Silkwood Way, but paint was peeling and the garden weed-ridden. And it had a shuttered look on account of all the closed curtains. There was a doorbell that Florence pressed. After a wait she pressed again. Another wait.

'Maybe they don't answer,' said Sophie, 'before they had Sally to do it.'

At that moment the door opened and a man's querulous face peered out at them.

'Yes?'

'Good morning, Mr Quigley. So sorry if we have disturbed you.' Florence introduced herself and Sophie. 'Miss Dawson is to marry the vicar on Saturday and would like to meet some of his parishioners beforehand.'

Mr Quigley merely looked perplexed, but he stepped back allowing them to enter. Florence had always thought he looked as though he'd stepped out of an oil painting from a century ago, to which he would return when others weren't present. He had a crop of tightly curled white hair and side whiskers and instead of a tie he wore a cravat, tucked into a velvet smoking jacket.

'I've heard you take splendid care of the early Bible that was gifted to the church,' said Sophie.

His eyes bored into hers. 'Did Mr Fielding tell you to come and talk to me about it? Persuade me it would be better off in his keeping. It wouldn't! Such volumes require specialized care.'

Poor Sophie, thought Florence, he looks as though he's about to bite her. Eventually, he said, 'I suppose I should take you through to my wife. She doesn't see people in the general way, but neither of us would wish to offend the vicar.'

As I hoped, thought Florence.

He opened the first door on the wall across from the staircase and they followed him into a dim room in which only two small lamps provided illumination. They made out an armchair in front of the curtained windows and the shadowy form of a woman.

'Lenore,' said Mr Quigley, 'the young woman engaged to the vicar has come to call and brought with her Mrs Norris from Mullings.'

'Haven't they been told I see no one?'

'I'm sure, but this must be an exception. I am the churchwarden.'

'As if you don't remind me often enough. But if they are here, so be it. Let me take a look at the bride to be.'

A hand beckoned from the chair and Sophie stepped forward.

Florence's eyes were adjusting to the lack of light and she saw a woman of extraordinary beauty, of the dark exotic type – magnificent eyes, perfect facial structure and a full, rich mouth. She could not define the pitted skin, but even had it been visible she could not imagine it would be the first thing anyone noticed, or would be much taken into account.

'You're moderately pretty,' she heard Mrs Quigley say to Sophie, 'in the way so many girls are when young and which fades as they grow older. If you were burdened with my affliction, it could not matter much. You have not near enough to lose.'

Oh, dear! Florence thought she is quite dreadful and heard Sophie's calm reply.

'You are quite right, Mrs Quigley, no one expects the looks of a vicar's wife to be anything out of the ordinary and I am so very sorry for your suffering.'

'You can have no idea of what my life is, forced to shut myself away from cruel eyes, every day another to be endured. And now since that girl, Sally, left, there is the added burden of fending more or less for ourselves. We have an elderly woman from Small Middlington who comes in most days, but she's as good as useless. Practically deaf so she doesn't hear the doorbell as now, and I either have to listen to it peel, or hope my husband will stir himself from his books to answer it.'

'I do,' inserted Mr Quigley, 'even when I'm in the midst of cataloguing my newest acquisitions. And always I'm interrupted for some trivial purpose. Gypsies with wax flowers on top of sticks, the fishmonger's boy coming to the wrong house, or that woman who wouldn't leave until I took what she was foisting on me.'

'I hear you have taken Sally on.' Mrs Quigley didn't give Sophie room to reply. 'Well good luck to you. I suppose she's telling a pack of lies about why I let her go. She'll be saying I lost my temper because she was praising Nurse Newsome. As though I have anything against the woman. It was the mindless chatter that caused me to lose my temper. The subject was immaterial. But I suppose it doesn't bother you.'

'It doesn't, but I don't have the need for quiet you do.'

'Indeed, your life must be very hard,' said Florence. 'Do you never leave the house?'

'Sometimes at night I veil myself and walk on Coldwind Common and there find a measure of freedom.'

'Have you done so for many years?'

'Now we come to the real reason you have come.' The beautiful eyes fixed on Florence. 'I know all about your involvement in solving past crimes. And you want to know if my husband or I remember anything useful related to the anonymous letters and the girl who's been dug up.'

'You're right, but it's also true that Mr Fielding and Sophie are concerned about how this is impacting the village.'

'That is good of them,' said Mr Quigley. Neither he nor his wife had invited them to sit down and he remained standing behind them, eager no doubt to flee back to his beloved collection of books.

'I really can't understand what all the fuss is about. A girl chose to end her life, though why in such a messy fashion I can't understand. All that unnecessary blood, as if she wanted to make a martyr of herself. If I were to end my life in the bath, I'd enough sleeping powders to ensure I'd sink peacefully into oblivion.'

'Lenore, don't.'

'I'm saying that is the way a woman of sense and breeding would have conducted herself.'

'I don't suppose,' said Sophie, 'that Anne Rudge had any sleeping powders handy.'

'No, because people of her sort, peasant stock, don't. If you care to know what I think about the whole situation, I'll tell you.'

'Please do.' Florence thought how well Sophie was maintaining her calm and kept a tight grip on her own emotions.

'Very likely the girl was never right in the head and wrote those letters herself and left them behind to punish her parents for some sense of ill-usage. Or they were written, as is common in cases I have read about, by a repressed spinster. And you don't have to look far around here to find them.'

'I've never understood,' said Florence, 'why we don't talk about repressed bachelors, surely they exist.'

'Mrs Norris, what world do you live in? Men's behaviour is never subject to scrutiny unless they take up with someone out of their class. I never had any great desire to marry, the running of a home or having children did not interest me. But I knew what my fate would be, given my disfigurement, if it looked as though I couldn't find a man to marry me. My husband was a frequent visitor at our house. My father was also a rare book collector. I brought to the marriage his library and in return I got live-in sanctuary with a companion who shares my desire for quiet. And now I grow weary and must request you leave.'

On showing them into the hall Mr Quigley entered into a muddled expression of gratitude – for what it wasn't quite clear.

'Mr Quigley,' said Florence, 'I know it's been twenty years, but do you remember noticing anything around the time of Anne Rudge's death that might shed a light on who wrote those letters. Might you, perhaps, have seen someone, looking furtive, entering her family's back garden?'

'I have no memory of anything of the sort. I'm frequently oblivious to what is around and if I had seen such an action, it would have been meaningless to me.'

Once outside Florence said, 'That is a horrible woman.'

'Perhaps she can't help it. Sally describes her as batty.'

'Well expressed. Did you think her face anywhere close to disfigured?'

'No. A few pitted areas, not enough to be bothered about. I wonder if you are brought up to believe your beauty is the most, only, worthwhile quality, you feel when a small part of it is taken away, that you have nothing left of value.'

'Sophie, you have the kindest heart.'

'Did you glean anything helpful from them? I couldn't see it, although Mr Quigley in his own way is extraordinarily peculiar. His reaction to my mentioning the Bible was rather alarming. Like a dog snarling at someone who might snatch away his bone.'

'I'm not sure what was worth gleaning and what was not,' returned Florence. 'I'll have to think. And now for Mr Kaye.'

TWENTY-FOUR

Gervaise Kaye was frequently spoken of as Young Mr Kaye, because his father had made himself a presence in Dovecote Hatch and he was thought by some to have an important career that nobody knew much about. Perhaps an author writing under an assumed name. He had that literary air to him, it was said. Others thought he lived off his wife's income from the shop and after her death what he could scrape out of Miss Hobbs until his son entered the business. He had now been dead for a decade and he'd been rarely mentioned since.

Florence and Sophie did not wait on the doorstep more than a few moments before being admitted graciously. Mr Kaye was of medium height, slim and dark-haired with an impish, boyish face. 'What a pleasure,' he said when they had introduced themselves, 'you have saved me from myself. I was getting bored. Eating lunch alone is always boring and thinking about the washing up is even worse.'

'Don't you have any help in the house?' Sophie smiled at him.

'Don't want it. I'm fussy to a crazy fault. Can't stand my stuff being touched. Even the dust is my dust and I wouldn't want to hurt some poor woman's feelings by telling her to keep her hands off it.'

'I can understand that,' said Florence.

'Music to my ears. My father thought I should be in Bedlam.' He invited them to shed their coats, but they said they wouldn't be staying long and followed him into a room that was similar in size to the Quigley's. Its window also faced the front garden and the lane alongside. In every other sense it was a world apart, both inviting and elegant. The wallpaper, with its gold-and-silver sheen on a dark background and much of the furniture was fashionably modern, but there were a few old and beautiful pieces to provide added interest. Florence wasn't sure what the splodges of paint that comprised the painting above the fireplace were but she liked the colours. She also liked the small charcoal etching of a water spaniel on a brass easel set next to a crystal vase of daffodils on the bookcase.

'Approve?' Mr Kaye asked her.

'Very much.'

'I am a weak male. I bask in admiration.'

Sophie was looking at some blue knitting cast down on the tea table in front of the sofa. Mr Kaye's eyes followed hers. 'No, Miss Dawson, I don't have a lady friend hidden upstairs. My mother taught me to knit when I was five or six.'

'How special. I learned at school which is not at all the same. What is this going to be?'

'A shawl for an aunt on my father's side. She feels the cold and likes something pretty. But do let us be seated and Mrs Norris can get down to business.'

'You're direct, Mr Kaye.' Florence smiled at him as she took her seat. 'I thought it would take a little while to get down to what we wanted to speak with you about.'

'Mrs Norris, I am not the most acute of men, but there is no need to tell me why you are here and brought Miss Dawson to pave the way with very reasonable explanations that you wished to introduce her to the village. I have been expecting either you, or a police inspector, to appear on my doorstep, asking if I have any knowledge of events leading up to the discovery of Anne Rudge. It's the obvious course of action to look first to those living closest to her. I expect you've already been to Miss Gillybud and the Quigleys.'

'Yes, Miss Gillybud a little while back and the Quigleys just now.'

'Never fear, I won't ask if you learned anything from them. You wouldn't tell me. And rightly so. I imagine your first question to be what, if anything, do I remember of that time twenty years ago. I was after all only twelve years old.'

'It does seem like looking for a needle in a haystack.'

'Not so. I remember vividly that March when Anne Rudge was supposed to have taken off. My mother was dying at that time and every distraction brought some small relief. I knew

Tim Rudge; he was only a couple of years older than I. One afternoon I found him crying in the churchyard and I sat down on a bench and talked to him. I thought his sister may come back and my mother wouldn't, but we're both miserable now. It was a bond. It only helped a little, but it helped.'

'I can see that,' said Florence. 'Did he say anything . . .?'

'Not that I can offer you as a clue to who wrote the letters. What I have to tell relates to my aunt.'

'The one you're knitting the cardigan for?' Sophie asked.

'My aunt Victoria Hobbs. My mother was devoted to her and wanted her near in her final days and came to stay here for the whole of March. What my mother didn't know was that Victoria and my father had been having an affair for several years. But I knew and hated her. You cannot imagine my revulsion at being in the same room with her. I recall thinking if I were a grown-up, I'd kill her.'

'I'm so sorry.' Florence looking at him could clearly picture that twelve-year-old boy.

'I loathed my father too, of course. But her betrayal seemed worse.'

'When did you find out about them?'

'A couple of years before. It was early closing day at the shop, but in the afternoon my mother remembered something about an order she wanted Victoria reminded about and asked me to go and tell her. She gave me her key because Victoria wouldn't hear me knock or ring the bell because she'd be upstairs in her living quarters. I went up and tapped on the door to her sitting room and getting no answer went in. I heard noises from the bedroom – groans rising into screams. I thought someone had broken in and she was being attacked, so I cracked open the door and looked in. I don't need to tell you what I saw.'

Mr Kaye sat silent, staring into space. Neither Florence nor Sophie spoke.

Finally, he did. 'You must be wondering what this has to do with Anne Rudge. Possibly nothing. Victoria had always been insistent that I not go into her rooms unless she was there. She didn't want anyone up there unless she was present. She made a big point of that. And after what I had witnessed, it offered the possibility of a small, but very satisfying revenge. At half term my mother would take me with her to the shop and set me some small tasks. I'd wait until she and Victoria were busy and sneak up the stairs and poke around, usually just touching everything in sight. Because, even at that age, I didn't like my stuff touched. I dislike knowing we have anything in common, but there it is. Then I began opening drawers. Usually there was nothing of interest in them, but one day I discovered, after some poking and twiddling, a secret drawer in her bureau. Inside was a red leather notebook. It was a diary, page after page about the sins of the fallen woman, that could not be forgiven by God without constant reflection on the Reverend Pimcrisp's dire warnings that we all stand on the brink of hell fire and only the most saintly have a chance of not toppling into it. There were loads of biblical references, or Pimcrisp's interpretation of them, with the names Delilah, Lott's wife and Salome under-scored. I didn't read it all at once. I went back several times. A few times I found the diary left out on her bedside table. Either she had forgotten to put it away or had been interrupted before she could do so.'

'Did she mention your father?' Florence asked.

'Not by name, but she wrote in the third person of a man who was a betrayer, a liar, a beast, whose sins would one day be brought to light and he would pay the full price if he did not publicly confess and accept his banishment from the community. Of course, my father went to the grave having done nothing of the sort.'

'Did you ever tell her you knew?'

Mr Kaye's lip curled. 'What would have been the point? I've never told anyone before today. And I'm not sure if I'm doing so out of a need for revenge, or because I feel obliged to do so. Probably a blend of both. I only knew Anne Rudge slightly, but I liked just seeing her pass by, she was like a woodland nymph and I was at an age to believe such creatures existed and be charmed into fairy tales. And, as I've said, I liked Tim and want things set right for him.'

'Thank you for that.'

'I don't know that Victoria wrote those letters, let alone she why she would have done so, but I believe it possible. For my mother's sake I hope she didn't. I've been preparing myself to be questioned because it makes sense that whoever did this awful thing lived close to the Rudge family. I'm glad it was you who came, rather than Constable Trout. And' – he smiled at Sophie – 'brought Miss Dawson with you to make it more pleasant. Mrs Norris, I'm not going to put you in the difficult position of in a sense reporting on Victoria. I'll go down to the police station this afternoon and talk with the constable and let him know I'm willing to speak with the inspector. For all I know Victoria may not have kept the diary and they won't be able to go on my word. Everyone knows we don't get along, so I could be taking the chance to injure her.'

'I can't thank you enough for easing the way for me.' Florence got to her feet as did Sophie, and on walking them to the front door he said that if Miss Dawson, when Mrs Fielding, decided to start a knitting group he would be the first to join.

'Oh, what a good idea,' exclaimed Sophie, 'I will do it.'

She and Florence walked away from the house and did not speak until they rounded the corner of Silkwood Way and reached Coldwind Common. 'I liked him, Mrs Norris, but do you think we've found the person we're looking for in Miss Hobbs?'

'She seems a strong possibility.'

'Do you think he was lying about that diary?'

'No, I don't. And I should be feeling better about what we've uncovered, but I have the feeling that whoever caused Anne's death will get away with it for lack of evidence. It'll take a confession.'

'The police might get one out of Miss Hobbs if the diary still exists.'

'What comfort and strength you'll be to this village, Miss Dawson.'

'That's kind, but I wish you'd call me Sophie.'

'Gladly, if you'll call me Florence.'

'Oh, I'd love to. It would feel like friends.'

'I sensed we would be when I first met you.'

They smiled at each other. They were now three quarters of the way across the common on their way to pay their last call, the final one of the morning, on Nurse Newsome, when they saw Mrs Chester coming towards them. Greetings over she told them she guessed where they were going.

'My dears,' she said, 'I've just come from Nurse Newsome and she is in a low state of mind. Exhaustion is the ready explanation, but I don't think it's the real problem, although of cause fatigue always make everything seem worse than perhaps it is. I think she's worried, terribly worried about something. Most likely Una. Who for once in her life should be thinking of someone other than herself. I get so irritated when I get word of her telling people how put upon, she is, having to be at her mother's beck and call when extra help is needed with patients. I know for a fact she doesn't do it for free and that despite never contributing a penny for her keep over the years. How do I know? Because she brags about it.'

'I don't suppose she earns a lot,' said Sophie.

'And whose fault is that?' Mrs Chester replied. 'Her mother made sure she went to a private school, which must have taken some scrimping as she wasn't well placed after her husband's death. Una could have gone in for nursing herself, or become a teacher or a librarian. But the studying would have taken more effort than she was prepared to put in. Forgive me, you must think me dreadful. I shouldn't be talking out of school. My husband and Nurse Newsome never would. Models of discretion. But I'm not in a professional position where she's concerned. I view her as my friend. Despite being liked and admired, she doesn't have many.'

'I can understand why you're upset,' Florence assured her, 'I would feel the same in your place. You don't think we should try and see her?'

'I only stayed ten minutes and knew she was aching for me to be gone. I told her my husband would bring round a bottle of tonic. She said she didn't need it, all she required was rest. And I assured her I would take on any nursing cases as they come up.'

The three of them turned to walk back across the common, saying very little, and parted on getting back to Silkwood Way, Sophie and Mrs Chester to make their ways home and Florence to the Dog and Whistle. She wouldn't be able to digest what the morning had brought to light or what still lurked in the shadows until she talked to George. He wouldn't be surprised by what Mrs Chester had said about Una. He'd come to the conclusion, after his conversation with her outside Hobbs' Haberdashery, that she had a spiteful side. At least when it came to her mother.

TWENTY-FIVE

In the days before her wedding Sophie had moments of wondrous happiness and even when she accepted the realization that Aiden might not love her as she did him, at no point did she regret agreeing to marry him. He wouldn't have asked her to be his wife if he didn't believe they could have a good marriage, even if different, at least at the beginning, from other unions. She had gone to church on the Sunday and sat in a daze when he announced from the pulpit that they were to be married on the coming Saturday. Still feeling it was unreal she had stood with him on going outside after the service and received the well wishes of all who offered them. Faces were a blur and the voices dimmed by the beating of her heart.

Her biggest concern was whether Sally would wish to leave Orchard House, of which she had grown fond, for the vicarage, but this was something quickly laid to rest.

'Goodness, miss, I'd go with you to Timbuctoo. I'm happy as a lark for you and Mr Fielding. I thought there was something in the works, the way he come so often. It'll be a rush to get everything done by Saturday. But we'll manage. You just make a list of what needs doing and I'll be on it.'

Sophie made the list, crossing out anything but the essentials. Sent written invitations to those who deserved special acknowledgement. Discussed with Aiden's sister Maude what should be provided at the wedding breakfast. Asked if she would like someone to come in and help Mrs Stubbins give the house some extra cleaning. Perhaps there needn't be a wedding cake. But thanks to Mrs MacDonald that could be put out of mind.

As for the rest, all had been soon settled. Maude had arrived early afternoon on the Sunday. Her best wishes had been chilly and, therefore, her brief stay uncomfortable. She said she saw no reason to provide more than cups of tea and biscuits to people showing up after the service. If Sophie thought differently, she should arrange it. She thought Mrs Stubbins could exert herself for once with the housework, but again Sophie should do as she wished in this matter.

The way cleared, Sally said her mum would be tickled pink to handle the refreshments. And that she herself would go all day Friday and help poor old Mrs Stubbins get the rooms people would wander into looking their best. Miss Gillybud, popping in, had offered to write and send off the invitations. Having Mr and Mrs Barton for tea, following Maude's departure, had been heart-warming. Sophie immediately took to them. Sausage rolls, cheese straws, Scotch eggs and dainty sandwiches, along with other offers of help were cheerfully discussed.

On Monday afternoon there was the meeting with the solicitor with Aiden only putting in a few words here and there. Agreeing with the advice given that she leave the money inherited invested as it now was until she'd had time to decide what she wanted to do with it. At the edge of her mind was what to do about Orchard House – whether to sell or let it, but she preferred to let that alone until she and Aiden could discuss the pros and cons at length. On the ride back from Large Middlington she'd told him about going with Mrs Norris to talk with the Quigleys and Mr Kaye, also the meeting with Mrs Chester and her concern for Nurse Newsome. He'd said little about the first two, only that if anyone could get to the bottom of things it would be Mrs Norris. His focus was on Nurse Newsome.

'I'll go to her home this evening and hope she will agree to see me.' They had then talked about themselves. She hadn't known his parents were deceased and that Maude was his only sibling, until she'd asked him if his family would be upset by the quick wedding. He had an uncle still living and several cousins, none of whom would be put out by not being invited to the wedding. She now asked him about them and he'd chatted away, filling in what might have been gaps in their conversation, because of the shyness that she now felt with him at times, something she had never felt before.

Tuesday morning brought the purchase of a wedding outfit. Sally and Miss Gillybud had decried her idea of wearing the dress she had worn five years before for a school friend's wedding. Miss Gillybud said she would drive her into Great

Middlington where there was a rather nice dress shop. Sophie insisted Sally go with them.

'I want to buy you a dress. It will be much too simple a wedding for a bridesmaid, but if I had one it would be you. And in a way you can be. I'll hand my flowers to you.'

'Oh, miss! You've no idea how much that means.'

It suddenly occurred to Sophie that Aiden might not remember to get her a bouquet, so she'd buy herself a spray of flowers to have on hand. That went on the list. The shopping expedition turned out well. She found a simple, but elegant silk dress with matching three-quarter-length jacket in a lovely shade of periwinkle, and a charming hat of a deeper shade with a cluster of satin leaves to one side. Sally was delighted by a deep rose dress in crêpe de Chine, also with a jacket and a hat that was clearly meant to complement it. Miss Gillybud said cheerfully that she was hopeless with clothes so would proffer no advice. But admiration she could and did provide and after Sophie had purchased shoes and stockings she took them out for a splendid lunch. Wedding outfit crossed off the list.

When Aiden came in the evening, she told him about the shopping trip and how afterwards she and Sally had begun packing up what they would bring with them. For Sally it would only be a couple of suitcases and for herself if would be much the same, because she would need some weeks to go over carefully what she would like to bring from the house.

It all met with his agreement. He said she could bring the house if she wanted. 'I want you to grow to feel the vicarage is home, Sophie, and likely to be so for many long years, as I have no ambition to be anything other than a country clergyman. If you wish to refurnish the entire house, or choose to buy new, that is entirely your domain. My parents left me comfortably placed financially, as is also the case with Maude. I at no time want you to feel the need to dip into your inheritance to contribute to our income.'

He then turned the conversation to Agnes's funeral which was set for ten a.m. this Thursday. 'She left a note with Miss Gillybud stating that she wanted only an "ashes to ashes" graveside service, with no reception following.'

'That sounds like Agnes.' Sophie smiled.

'Would you feel up to coming back to the vicarage afterwards and exploring the house? Of course, bring Sally with you as she will be the one helping you bring some new life to the place. It's a dreadfully gloomy old house.'

'Of course, I will ask your sister's opinion on what we do. I don't want to her feel pushed aside.'

'She's not going to make things easy for you. Come to me if she becomes too difficult. And I'll take care of it.'

But how? Sophie thought. Tell Maude she had to go because his wife couldn't put up with her? The sister who had run his household for years? She who had the means to live wherever she chose, but had sacrificed the other choices life offered her for him.

No, she must do all in her power to bring about a harmonious relationship with her new sister-in-law.

As Aiden was leaving, she remembered to tell him she'd told Sally about having gone with Florence Norris to see the Quigleys and Mr Kaye, and had explained to her that she couldn't repeat the conversation with the latter because it would fall in the line of gossip. Neither had she repeated what Mrs Chester had said about Nurse Newsome's state of mind. 'You may wonder,' she had added, 'why I confide in Sally, but I have never had a friend like her before. I'd trust her with my life.'

'I understand completely,' he said. 'Will you trust me as such a friend?'

'Always.'

He'd kissed her cheek and was gone, knowing the house was protected at night. Two of Sally's brothers had taken over the watch from Dick Saunders, taking turns sleeping on the sofa or staying awake in a chair.

Agnes's well attended funeral came and went. Sophie laid a spray of flowers on the coffin, her eyes dry, but her heart full. Miss Gillybud stood beside her, handkerchief bunched for frequent dabbing. Sally and her family grouped around them. Afterward a number of people came forward to offer their condolences, amongst them Mrs Tressler and Lord Stodmarsh. Also, Mr Kaye. She noticed Mr Quigley standing alone off to the side. Then it was time for her and Sally to walk with Aiden to the vicarage. Shortly before reaching it, Maude joined them and was the one to open the door for them to enter the hall. Sophie thought it every bit as depressing as Florence and George had done, but as she went from room to room, she had the sense that the rooms were calling out to her as their potential rescuer. Behind the drawing room and study was the dining room – the darkest of all. To the left of the staircase wall was the hopelessly outdated and dingy kitchen. Behind it was a darkly panelled corridor, its first door opening on to a sitting room with French doors offering a view of a mangled garden. But here, thought Sophie, is the first sign of something approaching cosiness. The second door opened onto an entirely empty space, the size of the drawing room.

'Mr North told me,' said Aiden, 'that it used to be a library but woodworm got into the bookshelves and they had to be taken down. I've no thoughts about what to do with it. But I'm sure you'll come up with something.'

'A meeting room for the Mother's Union and other groups. Mr Kaye suggested I start a knitting one.'

'There' – he clasped her hand – 'you'll breathe new life into this house and send the grim packing.'

They were on their own. Maude had remained in the drawing room and Sally had said she'd like to explore the second floor. She'd already told Sophie that's where she would prefer to sleep.

'I'm sorry Maude isn't mellowing as fast as I'd hoped.'

'Oh, please, you mustn't let it cause a breach between you, I would hate for her to feel unwanted. It will get better. I'm sure of it.'

'If it doesn't, I'll handle it. Shall we go up, so I can show you the bedrooms and so on . . .?'

'Yes, please.'

Her shyness increased as they mounted the stairs and entered an L-shaped corridor lined with doors. He opened the first to their right. Her initial impression was that what she'd thought horrible wallpaper elsewhere was nothing to this dark floral horror. But the wardrobe and dressing table were all right. She gave the most cursory of glances at the double bed. A moment later he opened a door on the right.

'This is the dressing room where I'll be sleeping, if that is all right with you. There is a key you can turn if you wish, although I promise to keep to the agreement we made not to intrude on you privacy until you decide you are ready for the intimate side of marriage.'

'I wouldn't dream of turning the key,' she responded quite fiercely. 'Maybe years ago, some wife who'd already had twelve children thought it a good idea and who could blame her. Well, maybe her husband.'

He laughed. 'Whatever life holds in store for us I promise not to burden you with such a number.'

Immediately she felt happier. He did think that one day, perhaps in the near future, he would share the bedroom with her. William Morris wallpaper and properly aired sheets. And then he raised her hopes even further.

'Neither this house nor I am deserving of one as lovely in every way as you, Sophie, but I want to be. Your happiness means more to me than I can express.'

'Thank you, Aiden,' was all she could manage for the lump in her throat.

They took a quick glance at the other rooms at the far end of the corridor.

They found Sally in the hall when they went down and she asked if she might have the bedroom opening off the nursery. They assured her she could and the nursery could become her sitting room. She beamed at them.

'Ooh! Thanks ever so, I was hoping I could.'

Sophie's heart did sink when they went into the dining room and saw that Maude had laid the table for only three. But Aiden addressed the situation. Drawing out a chair for Sally, he smiled at his sister.

'Maude, you've been so occupied getting the meal on the table you forgot plates and cutlery for yourself.'

In an expressionless manner she fetched these from the sideboard, then planted herself with a thud in a chair. The meal comprised of shepherd's pie, the meat dry and the potatoes lumpy, followed by prunes and custard, also lumpy. All served cold.

'This is very nice,' Sophie managed.

'I shall continue doing the cooking.' It was clear Maude was brooking no argument. 'I must have something to do to keep myself from falling completely useless. You, Miss Dawson – Sophie, can do as you wish running the house. I tried to make the drawing room a little better by setting a couple of cushions on the couch, but you can dispose of them.'

'I thought they looked perfect,' Sophie replied, regrettably – reprehensibly she had failed to notice them.

When they rose at the end of the meal, Aiden smiled at Sally. 'We are going to enjoy having you here, and it's my hope you'll share meals with us as often as you wish.'

'Thank you, Mr Fielding.' Sally beamed at him and shortly afterwards he drove them back to Orchard House.

'I'm sorry Miss Fielding was unpleasant to you,' said Sophie when she and Sally were alone, 'and will likely make difficulties for you.' She didn't add the obvious that she, herself, would have to deal with even fiercer hostility from Maude.

'Don't you worry about me, miss! If you don't mind me saying so she seemed to me a sad old stick, trembling to the knees at the thought of having to take a back seat to you from now on. You'll bring her around in no time.'

Sophie wasn't so sure of this. But time was now racing by. As Sally said Saturday would be here in the wink of an eye.

'Not being sure what's in the china and glass cabinets over there, Mum asked around and between this person and that she thinks she's she got enough plates and glasses and whatnots for the reception.'

'You have the best of mothers. I'm so grateful for her kindness.'

As had been arranged, Aiden arrived at eight o'clock the following morning and drove Sally to the vicarage to ready it for the reception. On the way there they stopped at her home and collected what Mrs Barton had gathered together. Only stopping to chat for a brief while. After thanking her warmly for all she had done, he got the boxes into the boot of the car, waved goodbye to where she stood in the doorway and was off.

Meanwhile, Sophie occupied herself sorting out the pantry, deciding what could be left there for the time being and boxing up what should be taken to the vicarage. Aiden had said he'd collect it when he brought Sally back, which would not be later than two clock, because by then she should take a well-earned rest.

At around eleven Sophie walked to the florist shop and bought a small bunch of violets and primroses and had them tied with white ribbon. In case Aiden forgot to send her flowers. He'd been so busy. She was smiled at and offered best wishes from the woman at the counter, and by others on her way there and her return. She had come to love Orchard House. She again thought about what to with it. Sally had said that if she decided to sell, she knew Mrs Norris and Mr Bird would take it in a twinkling.

'She's got a feel for it, miss, that's quite special.'

Sophie had sensed this too, and now decided what she would like to do. Of course, she would discuss it with Aiden. Tomorrow they would be husband and wife. The horror of the past few weeks would be safely behind her, and if the only dragon she had to face was Maude, she would survive again.

TWENTY-SIX

Sophie woke around six on the following morning. She didn't remember dreaming, but felt she was in one now. The wardrobe, the dressing table, the window and the door all seemed to have taken different shapes and sizes. She sat up to hear Uncle Henry's voice in her ear. Something that hadn't happened often in the past couple of weeks. 'No flutterings and foolish fancies. You're a sensible woman. Of course, you are. You were a sensible child. Get that piano in the vicarage drawing room tuned, play it for me, and anyone else who cares to listen.'

Her last thought before falling asleep last night was that the piano must need tuning. Oh, Uncle Henry! How she wished he could drive beside her to St Peter's and walk her down the aisle. But Aiden had settled her concerns about her arrival. He'd told her he'd collect her in the car at quarter to ten and they would enter the church together. It had also been arranged that Miss Gillybud would drive Sally and her parents. Dear Miss Gillybud. Yesterday evening she had taken Marmalade to her house, to be returned to Sophie on Monday when things had settled back down.

At seven thirty Sally brought her breakfast in bed, for tradition's sake she'd explained. Toast, a boiled egg and a cup of tea. Sophie was surprised that her head was uncluttered enough that she could enjoy it. At eight o'clock a delivery arrived from the florists. A bouquet of yellow tea roses for Sophie and a spray of the mixed spring flowers for Sally.

'Oh, miss! Yours are beautiful. And I can't tell you how touched I am he thought of me. When I was little, I wanted to marry a prince and you've found one.'

'Sally, I'd like you to give the bunch of flowers I bought yesterday to your mother, for thanks for all she has done and is doing.'

They were ready with a half hour to spare when Aiden arrived for them. Sophie had washed her hair the night before and laid out everything she was to wear. The last thing she put on were the pearls Uncle Henry had given her on her eighteenth birthday. Something old, something blue, something borrowed and something new. She had all but the borrowed, and this was achieved by Sally lending her a bottle of scent.

'Just a dab behind the ears, and on the wrists, miss.'

When she heard the sound of the car on the drive, she picked up her bouquet and Sally opened the door for her to step outside. It was a warm, sunny day under clear blue skies. Aiden strode swiftly towards her. 'You look lovely, I like the dress and the hat, but nothing is equal to the serenity of your face. I remembered that look. I used to watch for it at your home with Uncle Henry.'

'Thank you for mentioning him. I never knew how much he'd loved me until he was gone.'

'He knew.'

As they drove off, they saw Miss Gillybud nearing the drive. Then, suddenly, they were at the church with good wishers, including children, waving to them. And then everything seemed to drift by. It was like being on a bus or train, gazing out the window and seeing everything beyond it pass before you could grasp at the memory. She couldn't have said what music was played, or hymns sung. The vicar of Small Middlington, Mr Hawthorn, celebrated the service. She and Aiden made their vows. His voice was firm and steady, hers clear and calm. Then they were in the vestry, signing the registry. With Kip and Miss Gillybud as witnesses. And then they were outside again, being greeted and cheerfully shaken by the hand.

They saw no sign of Maude, who'd been driven to the church by the Norths, and who intended to bring her home, but when approached they hadn't seen her since she walked out just ahead of them.

'Perhaps she decided to walk home,' said Aiden. And after looking around some more to no avail, he tucked Sophie's hand in his arm and made for the car.

Maude was not in evidence on their return to the vicarage and it wasn't because the hall and downstairs rooms were milling with guests, because they weren't due to arrive for another half hour. The dining room table was laid end to end with the wedding breakfast produced by Mrs Barton. She was obviously a marvellous cook. The sausage rolls and cheese straws glistened a golden brown and all was attractively arranged.

'I don't know how we can ever thank her,' said Sophie, 'or Mrs MacDonald for the beautiful wedding cake.' It stood resplendent on the sideboard, surrounded by little plates.

'And there's George Bird who provided the hock and other potables, for those who prefer them to fruit punch.' He reached for her hand. 'We'll find a way to show our appreciation.'

They found Sally and her mother in the kitchen setting out another platter of Scotch eggs. 'Just to make sure it don't look like we've run short.' Mrs Barton looked up and beamed at them.

'She's always like this.' Sally flapped her hands. 'Afraid everyone's going to starve, if she do double what's needed.'

Sophie had known they were going on ahead to make sure all was ready, but expected this to be a cursory peek, nothing requiring putting on aprons and trotting to and fro.

'Pease,' she appealed to them, 'you've both been so wonderful, but from this second on I want you to relax and enjoy yourselves. By the way, where's Mr Barton?'

'Out on the back step smoking his pipe,' replied his wife apologetically.

'Well, tell him to come inside and smoke it,' said Aiden. 'If there's a free moment I'll have one with him.'

'I will,' Mrs Barton beamed. 'And thanks ever so for the pretty flowers.'

Sophie didn't catch up with Sally until about half an hour later, because within minutes the hall flooded with guests, and she stood at Aiden's side welcoming them, the ones she recognized and those she didn't. After a while they all merged together. There was no feeling shy or letting her smile slip. But all the time she was wondering what had become of Maude. It wasn't until George Bird asked Aiden if there was another bottle opener, so Dick Saunders could help him with opening the hock, that she was able to slip away and find Sally to ask if she'd seen Miss Fielding.

'She got back before you and Mr Fielding did, I saw her in the hall, miss . . . ma'am.'

'Then where is she?'

'Now, don't you go upsetting yourself. Said she was going upstairs for a lie down. Perhaps she had a headache coming on, could be the excitement of a good time did it and a half hour on her bed with the curtains drawn have her right as rain again. My gran was just the same anytime there was lots of people about and she got to really enjoying herself.'

Sophie didn't think Maude had been enjoying herself at any point of the morning and she was sure Sally didn't either. If Maude had come down with a headache, rather than merely wishing to make her absence felt, it would more likely have been brought on from lagging spirits. And despite how difficult she'd been, something had to be done about it.

She found Aiden, explained the situation, and he said he'd go upstairs and rout his sister out.

While he was gone, she found herself talking with Mrs Tressler, who couldn't have been nicer and completely unpretentious. 'I do hope you and your husband and sister-in-law will dine with us at Mullings before too long. But you'll be wanting a few weeks to get settled into your new life.'

Lord Stodmarsh appeared at that moment and chatted easily for several minutes. Afterwards came Florence and George Bird, bringing with them the feeling of friendship. On her own for a moment, glancing around in the hope of seeing Aiden with Maude beside him, she saw Mercy Tenneson join His Lordship, noticed a woman who fitted the description she'd been given of Nurse Newsome's daughter, but had yet to spot Nurse Newsome. Neither had she seen Miss Hobbs. And Mr Kaye, with whom she had spent several minutes discussing her decision to start the knitting group, of which he'd asserted he intended to be a founding member, did not mention whether his aunt was there or not. She had just finished a warm talk with Mr and Mrs Saunders and was about to go over and spend a little more time with Dr and Mrs Chester, hoping to learn how Nurse Newsome was doing, when Aiden reappeared, but without Maude.

'She says she still has a headache. I tried to persuade her

she might feel better for having something to eat, but without success. She told me to make her apologies to the guests.'

But not to me, thought Sophie sadly. If Aiden felt the omission, he couldn't say so. It would only have made the situation worse.

'I rarely have headaches,' she said, 'but I know how miserable and depleting they can be.'

His eyes searched hers before he spoke. 'You're not only the loveliest bride I've ever seen. You're also quite the nicest person I've ever known.'

Everything in her came to life. Not the most propitious moment for Mr and Mrs North to come to them, to say how much they appreciated sharing this day with them, but were about to leave. And their departure was swiftly followed by others, until the drawing and dining rooms emptied out but for a few lingerers. Including Major Wainwright who collared Aiden to talk about his memoirs, which he could never have done such a good job of them without Kip, or, as he referred to him that great chap, Lieland.

Sophie left them to it. She hadn't seen Sally for a while and went in search of her and found her in the kitchen with her parents, Mrs Barton at the sink busy with the washing up, her father doing the drying up and a woman with a barking voice that Sally introduced to her as Miss Milligan.

'We've just been talking about me getting Mum one of her boxer pups. They won't be ready to go to their new homes for a few weeks more. But it's exciting. You're pleased, aren't you, Dad.'

Dad agreed he was. Miss Milligan gave a woofing sound. 'You should think about taking one, Mrs Fielding. No charge. My wedding present to you and the vicar.'

Sophie was instantly tempted, sufficiently so she forgot the problem of Maude. A dog to play with and take for walks. Oh, yes! She would love that. But would Marmalade accept a puppy. She would ask Miss Gillybud.

'Thank you,' she said, 'it's a lovely offer. May I talk to Aiden and let you know?'

'Only dogs to have, boxers! Loving, loyal and protective.'

Sophie requested that the Bartons stop working and have a

cup of tea. She was going upstairs to change out of her wedding clothes and would come back to do whatever else was needed done. She couldn't find Aiden to tell him this. Perhaps he was outside saying goodbye to Major Wainwright, Kip, or others. He might also be seeing how Maude was now doing.

She went into her bedroom, where Sally had hung up some clothing and put others in drawers, besides setting out her personal possessions. She had replaced her wedding finery with a skirt, blouse and cardigan, and was about to pick up the comb on the dressing table when she noticed an envelope tucked under her hand mirror. And smiled because she was sure Aiden had left it there for her. The writing, however, was odd – printed in pencil in what looked to be a child's hand, or maybe that of an elderly person. And Aiden would not play that kind of joke, on anyone, let alone herself.

Now, she was curious, nothing more. She sat down on the bed, opened the envelope and took out a single sheet of note-paper, the lined kind that you might buy at Woolworths. And as she read – every word leaped up at her.

How could you have been taken in by him? He doesn't love you. He's a lustful beast, any other woman would have done for his purposes. He wrote those letters to Anne Rudge.

She felt sick. Who would have done this to her? Who could hate that much? Who would wish to threaten her marriage before it had even begun? The house had been full of people. Anyone could have mounted the stairs unnoticed and entered her bedroom. She told herself whoever it was must be the anonymous letter writer from all those years ago. But why? What was to be gained by frightening her? She had gone with Florence to talk with the Quigleys and Mr Kaye, and they had known that it wasn't just a social call. Florence would have passed on the information regarding Miss Hobbs' diary to Constable Trout and Inspector LeCrane. Had that aroused panic? Possibly, but how would scaring her stop Florence and George continuing to unofficially investigate? It wouldn't. It might well make them push harder to identify the culprit.

So where did that leave her? The answer stared her in the face. Maude! Maude who resented and disliked her. Who'd gone openly upstairs to nurse her headache. She got up and paced the room, before replacing the letter – if it could be called that – in the envelope, and tucking it under the mattress. She couldn't say anything to Aiden, that was all she could decide right now. But how to face him, act as though nothing was wrong? He'd know she was withholding something from him and likely assume she was having second thoughts about marrying him. If only she could talk to Sally. But she couldn't. Not about this.

When she came downstairs, Aiden met her in the hall and asked if she'd like to go for a walk. That proved the easiest part of the rest of the day. After setting off, he said he hoped Maude's absence from the reception had not upset her. He did not mention the headache. She thought it probable he hadn't believed in it either. Her quick response that she'd understood and had not been the least offended, sounded overly bright, but he'd know it was rather awkward. She then told him of Miss Milligan's offer of a puppy and asked what he thought about it.

'Would you like a dog, Sophie?' he asked as they wandered on to Coldwind Common.

'Yes, but only if you'd want one too. And it may seem a bit much a cat and a dog all at once.'

'You're concerned that Maude will object, but don't allow that to weigh with you. I'm fond of her. We've lived quite comfortably together in the past, but she has to accept now she must adjust to the new way of things. As far as I'm concerned you may have ten dogs and twelve cats.'

She mustn't let the conversation return to Maude, so she immediately shifted to what she had been thinking in regard to Orchard House.

'Sally says Florence Norris has a special feeling for it and I've seen that for myself. She and George Bird need a place to live when they get married and, if you agree, I'd like to offer it to them. But on a lifetime lease, not an outright sale, because for sentimental reasons I'd like to hold on to the idea of it one day coming back to us.'

'I think that's a splendid idea. Talk to them and see what they think. By the way, I'm going to telephone and set up a time for them to come in and discuss what they want for their wedding service. I feel I've let them down on that.'

'So much has happened between their original appointment and now, but I do agree it should be as soon as possible. I like them both so much.'

'Why don't I suggest Friday evening, and ask them to stay on for dinner?'

'Oh, yes do.'

He took her hand and they walked back to the vicarage like happy newlyweds, but once there the reality that she had an enemy, eager to destroy her peace of mind, sank back in. This, she thought, was worse than what she'd gone through with Mr Crawley. Here she couldn't be completely sure from whence the threat came. What if it weren't Maude and she was wickedly misjudging her. Mercy Tenneson had been at the reception. She'd been rude to her when she'd accompanied Lord Stodmarsh to Orchard House, but even if she'd got some silly, jealous idea into her head because he'd been so pleasant, that was now put to rest.

Maud had reappeared and produced dinner whilst they were gone. Fortunately just ham sandwiches and tinned soup.

'No need for pudding after all that wedding cake,' she said.

When asked about her headache, she'd compressed her lips and asked if Sally intended to keep the mustard pot entirely to herself. As soon as the meal was over, she departed, presumably to her bedroom. Afternoon had turned into evening when she reappeared in her coat and hat and said she was off to the church to sit and reflect in peace and quiet. And when Aiden said that if Sophie didn't mind, he would go to his study and take a final look at tomorrow's sermon, she assured him she could keep herself occupied, planning with Sally what furniture they could bring from Orchard House to furnish the small sitting room.

Once there, Sally turned to her excitedly and announced she'd made a discovery.

'Over in that corner, miss . . . ma'am. The door that looks like it'd be to a cupboard. But it opens on to a staircase that goes up to the nursery. I suppose it was so the nanny could bring the children down that way instead of them using the main one and getting underfoot when company was around and if they wanted, they could go out through those French windows into the garden.'

Sophie, glad to be distracted, went up with her to explore.

'This is perfect,' she said. 'As we said before, you can use the nursery as your sitting room. We could block up the fireplace and install a gas one. And if you want you can furnish it with pieces you'd like sent over from Orchard House.'

Sally was thrilled and they discussed ideas before going down the hall staircase because Sophie wanted to collect her knitting bag so she could get started on a jumper in a tawny brown wool which she had thought would go well with a tweed skirt she had. She could forget for moments at a time the horrible message, or at least keep it at bay, but it always kept creeping back.

It was a relief in a way to Sophie that Maude followed Aiden into the drawing room a while later; it enabled her to avoid meeting his eyes, as they talked. The knitting provided the excuse to keep looking down. But she did see him look over at the piano. He said he'd arranged to have it tuned on Tuesday, so she could have the pleasure of playing again. She managed to put life into her voice when she thanked him, but he had to feel the distance she was putting between them.

At ten o'clock she put the knitting aside and said she was going up to bed. Maude, staring into space, bade her goodnight. Aiden opened the door for her saying that he would be up in half an hour. It would have been awkward even if nothing else had changed. Once in her bedroom, she battled the urge to reach under the mattress for the envelope and reread the contents. She lay still in the bed when she heard Aiden enter the dressing room from the corridor. What was he thinking? What did he imagine her thoughts to be?

She spent a wretched night and woke feeling groggy at seven, which gave her scant time to get ready for church at eight. She found Aiden in the kitchen, standing drinking a cup of tea and eating toast. He greeted her with a kiss on the cheek, which might have been for appearances sake, given Maude's presence.

'I'm not going with you,' she announced. 'It's another

pleasant day and I will take a deckchair on to the lawn and rest.'

'That sounds very sensible.' Sophie smiled into the frigid face.

In the hall she met up with Sally, dressed to leave. 'I'll think I'll walk, ma'am.'

'Whatever you'd like; will you do me favour though? I'm sure you normally sit with your family, but today would you mind coming with me? It's silly but I really don't want to sit in that front pew alone.'

''Course I will. I won't be moments behind you.'

It should have been pleasant to be greeted on all sides by numbers of parishioners outside the church when Aiden went ahead of her into the vestry. Many of whom she remembered from the reception, but she was glad to reach the pew and have Sally soon join her. She heard nothing of Aiden's sermon, but his voice moved over and into her. Most of the time she kept her eyes closed, except when standing for the hymns. And then she failed to pick up her hymn book, until she saw out the corner of her eye Sally pick up hers and give a start. She didn't wonder what this was about, because she was struggling to pray. Pray for courage to do what was right for Aiden and, yes, Maude.

Once outside, the struggled to say what sounded right and normal to those mingling around her. At last, she spotted Florence and George and quickly wove her way towards them. A moment later Aiden joined them, and they issued the invitation for Friday evening, which was readily accepted. And then she brought up the matter of Orchard House.

'I know you'll want to think about it.'

Florence looked at George and he nodded. 'We accept gladly,' they responded in unison.

'I'll be going to Orchard House each morning, to make an inventory of what's there and start boxing things up.' The thought had just come to her. In the quiet there she'd be able to think. 'So do come and have a look round. There may be some things you'd like to stay. And time is short for you.'

'I'm glad they're pleased,' Aiden said as they got into the car.

Sally came up as they did so, saying she was going to walk.

But she wasn't long behind them, because Sophie had barely taken off her coat and hat and hung them in the bedroom wardrobe, when Sally tapped on the door, called out and came in. She stood there, hesitantly, gazing down at the envelope she was holding.

'I think I sat in what was meant to be your seat in the pew, because when I opened the hymnbook in front of me this was inside.' She handed it over and Sophie dropped down on the bed. 'Oh, miss . . . ma'am! What is it, you're white as a ghost. I thought there was something funny about it, from it being printed sort of peculiar.'

'I got one written the same yesterday. It was under my hand mirror when I came in to change out of my wedding clothes. Oh, Sally, it was beastly and unsigned. It's under the mattress.'

'Do you want me to open this one for you? Your hands are shaking!'

'Please.'

Sally sat down on the bed beside her. The contents were very much the same as the first.

> All women are fools and you the most stupid of all to fall
> for his smooth talk and the pretense of love. He wrote those
> letters to Anne Rudge. And you will pay along with him.

Sophie hadn't realized she'd read it aloud. Until Sally put an arm round her and spoke through tears. 'Cruel . . . evil, and all a pack of lies. Who could do this to you? And why? Why? Did you tell Mr Fielding about the other one?'

'I couldn't, I daren't! What if it's Maude? She was upstairs throughout the reception. And yesterday afternoon she went over to the church; she could have put it in the hymnbook then. I'll get the other one out from under the mattress.' She did so and handed it to Sally.

'If it is her, ma'am, and it does seem the most likely, it'll be her way of putting a wedge between you and Mr Fielding, knowing you'll keep quiet because you won't want to start your married life with trouble between him and his sister. And if you was to go to him about it, she'd deny it and call you liar.'

'And then he'd have to take it to the police and they'd have to look into the possibility that what was said about him was true. I can't bear that for him. What if his bishop decided there was no smoke without fire and ousted him from the parish?'

'The question is, if it's not her, who else could have it in for you, ma'am?'

'Oh, Sally, please, do something for me.'

'Anything.'

'Then call me Sophie! You're not a servant, a maid, you're my dear, dear friend and I need to hold on to that every minute of the day.'

'Then, course I will. Won't bother me if Her Nastiness thinks I'm uppish, or anyone else neither. We're in this business together and will see it through to the end. What needs doing is standing up to her, not letting her go on ruling the roost. She's bullying you and getting away with it. You don't have to be unpleasant, just firm.'

'Part of me feels sorry for her; she's afraid of being cast out to sea.'

'Time she got her own boat and set off in it.'

Incredibly, Sophie found herself laughing. She put both envelopes back under the mattress and found the rest of the day less unbearable than might have been expected. She and Aiden took another walk in the afternoon. She talked about Miss Gillybud bringing Marmalade back tomorrow morning and hoping he would settle down in his new home.

When they got back, she went and found Maude and said she'd enjoy preparing afternoon tea.

'I've already told you I wish the preparation of meals left to me.'

Was this the moment to do battle? The coward in Sophie had the upper voice. She retreated to her knitting and Aiden picked up a book.

During the following week, however, she gathered strength a small bit at a time. She asked Aiden if he would like to have Uncle Henry's desk clock in his study and he told her it would mean a lot him. When Maude saw her taking it in there, she said it wasn't needed, Aiden already had a clock she had given to him years ago.

'Well, now he'll have two,' said Sophie. 'It means a great deal to me that my husband' – emphasis on the word – 'and Uncle knew and liked each other.'

Even so, she told herself, Rome wasn't built in a day. The strain had lifted briefly during Gillybud's return of Marmalade, who once released from her arms, stalked off to claim the nearest chair.

'Oh, and here's the key Agnes gave me to Orchard House, so she wouldn't have to let me in when she was having a particularly hard time getting around. Apologies, Summer Rose for not returning it sooner, but first I forgot, and then I couldn't find it. Nurse Newsome had the other. If she hasn't given it to you yet, she will. I went and tried to see her the other day, but Una said she was resting. I do worry about her, always energized and steadfast until now.'

On an impulse, she was so glad of Miss Gillybud's company she invited her to the Friday night dinner, with Florence and George. The numbers would be uneven, with Maude and Sally, but that didn't matter. Miss Gillybud said she'd be delighted. And when Sophie went to tell Aiden, he said it was a splendid idea and he'd be delighted to have her with them.

Shortly afterward she asked Sally if she wanted to go with her to Orchard House. Sally said that if in her shoes she'd need time alone, so off with her. When she went to tell Aiden where she was going he said he no longer needed to worry about her being there on her own.

'Constable Trout, just this minute, telephoned to say he's learned that Mr Crawley's behavior on his return was so alarming to his wife, that he was placed in a secured ward of a mental hospital.'

'I'll pray for him.'

'Of course, you will, and so will I. Everything else all right, Sophie?'

'Oh, yes. Thank you, Aiden.'

She felt like an actress in a play, not yet mastering her part. Up until Thursday she spent every morning at Orchard House. On the Wednesday Florence came by and she suggested she explore the rooms on her own and that if she thought there was anything she and George might want from the contents, that was not going to the vicarage, they could keep them. They had an enjoyable chat. On leaving, Florence mentioned that Inspector LeCrane had got in touch to say that he had spoken with Miss Hobbs regarding what she remembered about the time Anne Rudge went missing, and inquired if she might possibly have kept a diary that might jog an idea. And she had without too much fuss handed it over. It was still being gone through to discover what if anything could link it to the anonymous letters.

Sophie fought down the urge to tell Florence about the ones she had received. She had to face up to what life had landed her, pull herself together. Make a plan to take an active part in dealing in what was, for now, her problem. She would face down Maude about the Friday night dinner. Insist on having the right to cook a meal for her husband and guests. On Thursday afternoon she did the shopping and when she got home she told Sally that a row was in the making.

'Tomorrow morning why don't you go to Orchard House and decide what you'd like for your sitting room. No point in both of us getting embroiled.'

'Are you sure, Sophie?'

She had to be.

That evening she played Chopin on the newly tuned piano and was swept towards a place of loveliness awaiting to be discovered, if nothing even more terrible intervened.

TWENTY-SEVEN

That Friday when Florence was having her early morning cup of tea with Mrs MacDonald, she mentioned how much better Molly was looking this past week or so. Whereupon Winnie popped out of nowhere with one of her uninvited pronouncements.

'Well, that's how it is, in't it?'

'How what is, Miss Busybody?' snapped Mrs MacDonald.

Winnie didn't roll her eyes, but the effect was there. 'When you're in the family way and get past the morning sickness part.'

Florence expected her to add everyone knows that! But she must have had sufficient sense to realize that would've been too smug by half. She'd had her moment of triumph and departed for the scullery before Florence or Mrs MacDonald could order her thither.

'Picturing us left to gulp,' said Florence. 'It never crossed my mind that Molly might be expecting.'

'Nor mine.' Mrs MacDonald sat down with a thud at the kitchen table. 'That girl must think us a pair of idiots and be laughing her head off.' Florence sipped at her lukewarm tea.

And here am I, she thought, flattering myself I've the knack of detection and I've missed what was right under my nose. So, what else that should be obvious have I not spotted in my efforts to assist Inspector LeCrane discover the identity of the anonymous letter writer? What else could I have gone back over with George that might have nudged neglected thoughts and observations to the surface of our minds? The excuse was there. So much had happened to occupy them since the stranger came into the Dog and Whistle that foggy night. One thing adding on top of another. The dream she'd had of being in the church about to marry George, came flooding back to her, with all its vivid uncertainty that perhaps she didn't or couldn't love as deeply as she had Robert. Then that moment when he opened the door of Orchard House for her and every doubt vanished. And love encircled them. She hadn't told George about the dream; it had been forgotten. Until now something nudged it back. What had it really been trying to tell her? The answer was there, just below the surface of her mind. But something else was clear.

'At one time this piece of news might have led me to post-pone the wedding,' she told Mrs MacDonald. 'If Molly is going to have a baby, she may decide taking over as housekeeper is no longer what she wants, or can manage. But I won't let that stand in my way.'

'And neither it should,' her friend responded stoutly. 'It'll have to work itself out. You know how much I'll miss you, but it won't be like you've gone to the moon.'

'I think Elsie Trout might be interested. She's intelligent, capable and I think would have a better knack of dealing with Winnie than either of us. Also, she's ambitious for young Rupert's future and could appreciate the extra money. But the decision will be Mrs Tressler's.'

Her spirits rose at the prospect of discussing the wedding plans that evening with Mr Fielding and having dinner after-wards with him and Sophie. Later in the morning she went for a walk around the grounds. It was a cooler day than those earlier in the week and the scent of rain was in the air, but she enjoyed the freshness. She'd only been out there for a few minutes when Mercy emerged from the pathway that led to the village.

'Hello!' she called out, quickening her step. 'Behold me returning from a mission of penance, only to be foiled in the attempt.'

'Tell me.' Florence smiled at her.

'You know how beastly I can be, and I was to Sophie Dawson – now Fielding – when Ned and I went to see them that afternoon. It was all my silly insecurity; he was so nice to her that . . .'

'You were convinced he'd give way to the instant attraction of a pretty face and forget all about you on the spot.'

'I know how that must come across, but I love him so much and I have this fear he'll realize that what he feels for me isn't enough . . . that I'm not at all suited to be his wife and the mistress of Mullings. Yes, Florence, he has asked me. I pretend not to take him seriously and go on about being too young. And then I deliberately start quarrels.'

'To test whether you can push him away?'

'Yes.'

'Stop it. You suffered a terrible loss when your guardian was murdered, but don't let that tragedy have you thinking all happiness is at risk of being stripped away. Mrs Tressler is very fond of you and she'll offer you all the guidance necessary and I will always be glad to tell you what I've learned from working here. Now tell me about your foiled attempt at penance.'

They had walked as they spoke and continued to do so. 'I'd heard that Sophie, Mrs Fielding, has been going to Orchard House every morning, I suppose there must still be lots to do there. It was Mrs North who told me. You know how it is in the village, there's always somebody who knows something. I wanted to apologize to her. But when I got there, it was Sally Barton who opened the door. And Florence, she looked quite strange, as though she'd had a shock. She said Mrs Fielding was at the vicarage, as she had lots to do there, and then she as good as shut the door in my face.'

'I wonder what that could be about.'

'I thought about going to the vicarage, but decided to wait for another time.'

'George and I are going there this evening and Sally will be at dinner with us.'

This, however, proved not to be the case. When George collected her in the car at shortly after six that evening, he said that Alf Thatcher, the postman and his good friend, had taken over at the Dog and Whistle in his absence.

'It was going to be Dick Saunders, but he came round late morning to say he had to call off. Didn't give a reason and I didn't ask. He was clearly worked up about something. And he's always such a steady lad.'

'Perhaps it has something to do with Sally,' Florence said. 'I don't know if they're courting, but I think that may be the way the wind is blowing.' She then told him what Mercy had said about her call at Orchard House.

They learned something more when they arrived at the

vicarage. Sophie welcomed them into the hall and as they shed their outerwear mentioned that Sally would not be with them for dinner.

'She's gone to spend the evening with her parents. She asked me if that would be all right when she got back from Orchard House this morning. And of course, it was. She's refused to take any time off until now. I'm afraid she's been overdoing things, she looked pale and not quite herself.'

Florence thought Sophie didn't look blooming herself. Was the cause Miss Fielding, or something more serious?

'We so appreciate the invitation,' she said.

'Miss Gillybud's here already. She was out for a walk and spotted Marmalade on the drive and brought him in. I asked if she'd stay and keep Maude company while I did some last things with the meal. They're in the drawing room now. But let me take you to Aiden so you can finally discuss what you want for your wedding.'

She opened the study door, announced them with a smile and disappeared. Aiden Fielding greeted them with obvious pleasure and saw that they were seated before returning to his chair. After a few minutes of light conversation, he said he was ready if they were to talk over their wishes for the wedding. They selected a Saturday morning five weeks ahead, and had listed their choice of hymns and a few other preferences, when George suddenly mentioned the early Bible, asking if it was possible for it to be used during the ceremony.

Turning to Florence, he said, 'I know what an interest the late Lord Stodmarsh took in it, giving it a special meaning for you. In fact, on the day we were originally due to come in for this purpose, I had the idea of surprising you with the idea. But that part doesn't seem important now. That's how I came to talk to Sally outside the Quigleys' house. I'd decided to walk round and talk to him before going on to Orchard House, but decided what with the upset it was the wrong time. And then I forgot all about it.'

Just as she had forgotten the dream. 'I'm really touched you thought of it.' She resisted the urge to take George's hand. 'And he would know if the Bible is too fragile to be opened or even handled without the greatest care. He has such a reverence for it.'

'I hope, Mr Fielding,' said George, 'you aren't offended that I thought him the one to ask first.'

'Of course not. Very sensible. I know very little about the Bible other than it is kept in a drawer in the vestry and Quigley has a bee in his bonnet about it. He became quite worked up when I merely asked how old it was. Demanded to know if I was thinking of moving it – perhaps to the vicarage. I can understand his becoming somewhat possessive of it over the years, but he was like a dog with a bone.'

Florence remembered that Sophie had said the same thing following their visit to the Quigleys.

'He'll claim, I'm sure, that it would be a travesty to put it to any kind of use, but I'll ask a friend of mine, who also knows about old, rare books, for his opinion. And if it can be used for your wedding I will be delighted.'

Their wedding. So close, so real at last. The reading of the banns. *If there is anyone present who knows of any impediment why these two should not be joined together in holy matrimony let them speak now or forever after hold your peace.* The dream was rising, breaking through the surface revealing all it hadn't been about . . . and what it had been trying to show her.

'Bigamy!'

George and Mr Fielding had to be looking at her oddly, but all she could see was that word. Attached to the name of Una and Bill Smith.

'I'll explain,' she said, 'and you may decide I'm letting my imagination run away with me and that may certainly be the case.' She told them about the dream, of what she'd thought it was about at the time.

'You were afraid with the wedding drawing close your love for me might not be enough compared to what you'd known with Robert.' George looked at her with so much understanding and it was he who now reached for her hand. It was the most natural thing in the world.

'But it wasn't about us at all. For the previous week the early morning conversations had revolved around Una Smith and the absconding husband. How before their marriage she'd been so secretive about him, even with her mother, keeping back the details of how she'd come to meet him. How it was fishy that if he'd received word on Saturday that his mother was seriously ill and needed him, that he'd waited until the next day to make his abrupt departure. Leaping up in the pew and racing out of the church within minutes of coming in. It could be said God spoke to him, told him his place was with his mother. But what if he acted out of panic? If when he saw you, Mr Fielding, he recognized you as the clergyman who presided over a past marriage to a woman other than Una. A woman who is still living. And he couldn't risk your spotting him and revealing him as a bigamist.'

'Seems to me as likely,' said George, 'as the other villainies people came up with after deciding he was a bad lot.'

Aiden had been listening with marked concentration. 'I remember a bridegroom named Smith. It would have been about five years ago. I recall it with special clarity, because he was a rather flashy type of around thirty and his bride had to be well in her sixties. She was an occasional attendee at the church, had a guesthouse on the coast and they'd come to know each other when he stayed there from time to time. He was a commercial traveller.'

'As is Una's husband,' put in George.

'And here's something else. The Saturday you were meant to be here, but I went instead to pick Sophie up in Large Middlington, I noticed a man outside the station that I was sure I'd met, or at least seen somewhere before. I couldn't place him, but now I'm sure he was Smith.'

'He was waiting for Una,' said Florence, 'but she didn't turn up because of running her bicycle into your car. Maybe that wasn't an accident. Let us suppose you were the obstacle to her happiness. Did the impulse seize her to ride directly towards your car – crossing into your lane, with the hope you'd swerve right to avoid her and go over the drop off. Either being killed or so seriously injured you wouldn't be able to continue your duties here. It seems extreme, but if we view Una as a woman obsessed by an overpowering passion, with an unpleasant nature to begin with, it's a possibility.' She paused. 'You may think I'm wicked to say such things, Mr Fielding.'

'No, I don't, and do please call me Aiden. We've shared too much for formalities and Sophie is very fond of you both.'

'And we of her,' said George. 'The trouble is there are so many William Smiths. But at least we know this one lives, or did, in Oglesby.'

'But he isn't a William Smith, that was another oddity that comes back to me. His Christian name wasn't William. It was Bill, he told me so, and signed the registry that way.'

The three of them looked at each other.

'Why don't we take a look at the one in the church,' said George, 'and see if he did the same when it came to marrying Una.'

'I'll go and let Sophie know we're going over there for a few minutes. I'll tell her I'll explain later.' Florence and George followed Aiden into the hall and he was back with them directly. They found what they hoped for in the registry. The signature of a Bill Smith, bachelor, wedded to Una Newsome, spinster. On the way back to the vestry they discussed their responsibilities in this matter and agreed to pass on the information to Inspector LeCrane, but there was a feeling of distress. If Nurse Newsome didn't know, or at least guess, she would be heartbroken. There was also pity for Una and the hope that she wouldn't face harsh consequences.

'We can all be victims of folly,' said George, 'I learned that listening to the stories of customers in the pub, the ones telling me of how they went astray.'

It was seven thirty when they returned to the vicarage. Dinner had been planned for eight. They found Sophie, Maude and Miss Gillybud in the drawing room, the latter looking the most comfortable with Marmalade in her lap as she discoursed on Greek mythology. 'Hector was such a hero to me when I was a schoolgirl, not as Greeks view the word, of course, more like dear Harold at Hastings, if you understand me.'

'We don't know for certain if there was a Troy,' flashed Maude before noting the entrance of her brother, Florence and George and a flurry of general conversation began. Aiden offered sherry which was accepted by everyone except Miss Gillybud who said it gave her hiccups, but she wouldn't mind a small brandy.

'Before dinner?' Maude raised an eyebrow.

'As good a time as any,' said Aiden and handed Miss Gillybud her glass. Florence noted his look of concern at Sophie. This, though a low-key affair, was the first dinner party she was hosting as his wife and here was his sister creating an atmosphere that could be cut with a knife. And a time when he had been landed with a very difficult situation. And not the first. There remained the likelyhood that his predecessor had been a peeping Tom. At some point he would have to notify his bishop that St Peter's was liable to be caught up in a scandal.

Sophie produced a simple but delicious meal. Cream of spinach soup, Lancashire hot pot, apple tart with custard, followed by cheese and biscuits. Miss Gillybud helped her bring in the courses while Maude sat put. Aiden served a very pleasant wine and everyone, except Maude, did their utmost, with a fair success, to keep the conversation going, despite the thoughts of at least three of those present being elsewhere.

Sophie was saying that she and Aiden had talked about using the library when restored as a place where they could bring their children in the morning and leave in the hands of volunteers.

'Mothers need a little time to themselves, when they're busy or have to go out and prefer not to take the little ones along, or just need quiet time to think.'

'We hope you'll be involved, Maude,' said Aiden.

'I shan't be here. Your marriage has altered everything.'

Florence sat up with a jolt, but not because of this outburst. Her mind had been drifting and then circling around the word obsession. 'I know,' she said, 'I know who wrote those letters. But I don't know how we'll be able to prove . . .' Her voice was cut by a pounding on the front door. Heavy urgent fists. They all rose as one, even Maude, and headed into the hall.

'Whatever can it be?' exclaimed Miss Gillybud.

'Who?' whispered Sophie.

Aiden had the door open and Sally, incomprehensibly wearing Sophie's coat and hat, came first, followed by Dick Saunders holding up Una as he heaved and spluttered. 'Have to get her somewhere to lie down, she's about to faint. Explain then.'

George took her from him, carried her into the drawing room and lowered her on to the sofa.

'I'll get the brandy,' said Aiden.

'Smelling salts.' Maude's martyred air was gone. It was as though she put on another, kinder face. 'I've got some in my room.'

'I'd leave her be for the moment,' advised Dick, 'she's out cold and that's for the best. Her mother's dead, strangled with a dressing-gown cord halfway across Coldwind Common. We fetched Constable Trout and he's with her waiting for reinforcements.'

'Oh, no! How horrible,' cried Miss Gillybud. 'Dear Nurse Newsome!'

'There's more to tell you,' said Sally calmly, 'and it's best we do it before she' – pointing at the sofa – 'comes round. This morning when I went to Orchard House to see if there was something I'd like for my rooms I saw an envelope on the mantelpiece written in the same hand as the other nasty two you got, Miss Sophie.'

'Oh, Sally!' cried Sophie.

Aiden looked as though he was about to speak, instead tightened his lips.

'Could be said it were a cheek for me to open this one, but I'm not sorry. It said if you didn't want your disgusting husband, writer of the anonymous letters, exposed, you was to be close to the big oak that's midway on the common at nine tonight to talk things through. So, I made up me mind to go in your place.'

'Sally!'

''Course I wasn't stupid enough to go on me own. I went and told Dick all about it and we set up how we'd go about it. I came back here; said I'd like to spend the evening with Mum and Dad. Left at a little after six, or acted like I was, because I nipped back round to the French windows the morning room has and up that little staircase as is there. I got your hat and coat and then waited, part time in my room till it was time to set off.'

'I went on to the common around half eight,' put in Dick. 'It was already darkish and I didn't want to go to near the time Sally set off. There's a cluster of trees, I could crouch down behind, close enough to the big oak so's I could see what was going on and get to her if need be.'

'And that's what he did – came rushing out with his torch

when I let out a yelp, when I felt her come up behind me and turned to see a rock above my head. She's so much taller than me. I didn't know it was her, then she had, a scarf wrapped around her face. As soon as she saw Dick she raced away to the far side of the common. And then we heard this piercing scream. When we caught up with her, she was on her knees beside her mother's body. Dick got her up and we more or less dragged her to Constable Trout. We only told him that Nurse Newsome had been murdered, nothing about Una. It seemed best to bring her here.'

'How incredibly brave of you both.' Maude sounded and looked stunned by this realization. 'And here am I being petty and nasty for selfish wounded feelings. I've never been more ashamed in my life.'

'Oh, please don't be.' Sophie went and put an arm around her. 'We all have to hold close together through this. And we will.'

'Sophie' – Aiden drew her back to him – 'why didn't you tell me you'd received those letters?'

'Because she thought I'd written them,' said Maude. 'And I completely understand why she would, and she was afraid of creating a rift between you and me.'

Miss Gillybud, who'd been keeping watch over Una looked across at them. 'I don't understand any of this – what her motive could be. Unless she was the original anonymous letter writer, and that doesn't make sense, because why call attention to herself when it could stay in the past.'

George, Florence and Aiden explained between them what they had just that evening discovered about Una's marriage to Bill Smith.

'Yes, I see. There is something that's bothering me personally. I'm thinking of that dressing gown cord I lost a couple of weeks ago. Silly to think about it, but what if it's the one the killer used, after having found it and picked it up. It will depend on how long Nurse Newsome has been dead as to whether, or not, I'm a suspect.'

Before anyone could respond to her Una stirred and with Florence's help managed to sit up. Aiden handed her the glass of brandy.

'Could you use my smelling salts?' Maude asked her as if the faint had been of an ordinary sort. Una sipped the brandy, staring straight ahead.

'Do you remember what happened?' said George.

'I didn't murder my mother. You may all think I'm wicked enough to have done it, but I had no reason to wish her out of the way. She had the house and agreed to Bill living with us. She didn't like him, but she probably wouldn't have been thrilled by anyone I chose. She was a rather boring person, decent of course, but I don't think she had a clue what it's like to be desperately, blindingly in love. In the course of time, she'd have died anyway and I'd inherit what savings she had along with the house.'

'That sounds rather cold-blooded, my dear.' Miss Gillybud took the empty brandy glass from her.

'I'm sorry for what's happened her. It was a shock finding her that way, but I'm not cut to pieces.'

'That's obvious,' replied Florence, 'but I don't believe you killed her.'

'The only person on earth who matters to me is Bill. I met him a couple of years ago when I went to spend a week with a school friend who lives in Eastbourne. Her children came down with the mumps, so I looked for somewhere else to stay and heard of the guesthouse in Oglesby that was nearby. He was married to this old woman, for the money, of course. That didn't bother me. Why shouldn't he look out for himself? It was instant attraction. We started meeting every chance we could get away. It was easy with his being a commercial traveller. And we continued after I left. I'd go to him at some hotel, but it got to be it wasn't enough.'

'You don't need to tell us, you're not legally married to Bill Smith, that the relationship is bigamous.' Aiden looked at her dispassionately. Turning he briefly explained this revelation to those not already privy to it.

'As soon as he saw you in church that day, he realized you might remember him and that he had to clear out. I wish I had forced you off the road and down the incline that day. I thought that was it – that we were stuck with you, but then you married her.' Una pointed, with vivid spite, at Sophie. 'Those anonymous letters everyone's been talking about gave me the idea that if I frightened her enough, she might persuade you to leave, request another parish. I'd read Victoria Hobbs' diary, when she had her recent breakdown and Mother had me sit with her at the time. I took passages from it – all about her vile seducer – and fitted them into the ones I wrote.'

'You really are a rather nasty woman,' said Miss Gillybud.

Una shrugged.

'I couldn't agree with you more.' Maude eyed Miss Gillybud in friendly fashion. 'Although I have to believe in the promise of redemption.'

'We'll talk about that some time when you come for tea and get to know my cats.'

'One needs something to brighten the future.'

Una was talking again. 'I don't care if I have to go to prison and Bill won't mind for himself. They can't keep us there forever. When we get out nothing will ever keep us apart again. And now I'd like be alone and try to sleep until Constable Trout turns up.'

'I'll take you up to a bedroom,' Maude told her. 'Sorry about it, but I'll have to lock you in.'

It was past eleven when the constable arrived, and he had more news to impart. Mr Quigley had telephoned the police station to say that he had found his wife drowned in the bath.

'So that's the end of it,' he said. 'She must have strangled Nurse Newsome and in a fit of remorse, or fear of being found out, decided to end it all.'

'No, it isn't,' said Florence. 'That's how he, her husband, wanted it to look. The difficulty will be proving the truth.'

TWENTY-EIGHT

Constable Trout listened respectfully to Florence's reasoning, said she was a clever woman who'd been of great help to the police in the past, but it would be up to what Inspector LeCrane thought about it. He passed on the information that Dr Chester on arriving at the murder scene had concluded, near as could be, that Nurse Newsome had been dead no more than an hour, possibly less. When he asked to interview Una he was given an account of her attack on Sally and what had led up to it.

'Dear me!' He sighed. 'Who'd a thought she'd grow up so nasty, what with having such a good person as Nurse Newsome for a mother. But, there, you never can tell, rotten parents can have children that ends up right as rain.'

'Very true.' Maude handed him a cup of tea. 'Wish it could be something stronger, but I know you can't, being on duty.'

Constable Trout looked as though he'd be grateful to bend the rules for once. It was well after midnight and he looked worn to the bone. After noting down what Sally and Dick Saunders had to say regarding their involvement, he asked for the letter she had found at Orchard House.

'And I'll need the other two, if you please, Mrs Fielding.'

'I'll go and fetch them' – Sophie stood up – 'they're under my mattress.'

'I'll get them,' said Aiden. His eyes had rarely left hers as the night progressed.

On these being handed over, Constable Trout tucked them into his notebook. 'And now I'd best get down to dealing with Una. Can't call her Smith, can I? There's a car with a couple of officers inside waiting to take her to the police station in Large Middlington. It'll be up to the courts to decide what to do with her and Bill the bigamist. Sometimes it's possible to feel a bit sorry for some criminals, but she's a vicious one.'

All but Aiden remained in the drawing room, door closed,

when Constable Trout brought Una downstairs. Shortly they heard the card drive off. And for the first time in hours there came something of a settling silence. Dick Saunders walked Miss Gillybud to her house, before proceeding home, but Florence and George readily agreed to spend the remainder of the night at the vicarage. Partly because they, like everyone else, were exhausted, but also Constable Trout had said it would be simpler for LeCrane to meet them all there.

On parting with Sally for the night, Sophie hugged her close. 'This is the second time you've stepped in to save me. You're the bravest person I'll ever know. And there's someone else who knows what a prize you are, and that's Dick Saunders. And he's one too.'

'He is dependable, would do anything for me, but he'll have to be patient when it comes to courting. Right now I couldn't be happier where I am. You and I are going to put this house to rights and have fun times doing it.'

Aiden was waiting in the hall when Sophie was about to go up to bed. He touched her hair before cupping her face in his hands. 'This isn't the time to talk about us, but we must soon. I knew something was troubling you, beyond the difficulties with Maude, I should have talked to you about it, but was afraid of increasing the distance between us.'

'I know. I know,' she said. She was already half asleep.

He put his arm around her and she leaned against him as they went upstairs. He saw her into the bedroom. 'Will you let me leave the door from the dressing room open, so you feel closer?' he asked.

'I'd like that,' she said and was aware of little more until morning.

The group reassembled at a little after seven. Sally cooked breakfast, Maude laid the table in the dining room. Nobody said much, not because of sleep deprivation, but because they were intent on their own thoughts. Florence had told them why she believed Mr Quigley had done away with his wife, by way of drowning her in the bath. She'd brought up what Mrs Quigley had said to her and Sophie regarding Anne Rudge's suicide. That if she were to end her own life, it wouldn't be by the messy way of slashing her wrists, but by taking a heavy dose of sleeping tablets and allowing herself to sink obliviously under the water. Mr Quigley had heard her say this, providing him with the ideal way of getting rid of her. Sally had then added that to her knowledge Mrs Quigley had unnecessarily refilled her prescriptions until Dr Chester put a stop to it, and Mr Quigley might well know she still had enough of a supply to overdo the appropriate dosage.

'You're right, Florence,' George had said, 'he'll get away with murdering her and Nurse Newsome, unless we can break him down, so he confesses.'

Sophie had looked at him as if about to speak, but didn't.

Maude kept supplying coffee, until the doorbell rang at a little after eight with the arrival of Inspector LeCrane, looking as elegant as ever, despite likely having had as little sleep as any of them. He took a seat in the drawing room when urged to do so by Aiden and looked around at those assembled.

'I understand, Miss Barton, you were the heroine of the hour yesterday.'

'There was Dick Saunders with me at the ready.'

'He must also be congratulated, but you're still a remarkable young woman. Thanks to you we've got Una Newsome for her crimes of bigamy, and assault. And it seems, due to subsequent events, we can set her aside as to the murder of her mother. Such is even clearer in the case of Miss Hobbs and Mr Kaye. They left Dovecote Hatch after closing their store at noon yesterday, to attend a weekend function of some county haberdasher's association. I understand from Constable Trout's report that Miss Newsome helped herself to passages from Miss Hobbs' diary. No doubt with the hope of implicating her if necessary in the letters written to you, Mrs Fielding.'

'It's heartbreaking what happened to Nurse Newsome,' Sophie said, seated on the sofa next to her husband, 'but it would also have been terrible if she'd lived to find out the sort of person her daughter really was.'

Inspector LeCrane asked if it would all right if he smoked, and being assured it was fine for him to do so, opened up his silver cigarette case, produced his lighter, leaned back and inhaled.

'As on previous occasions, Mrs Norris, you and Mr Bird have helped enormously in bringing matters relating to Anne Rudge's death to light. But now, I understand from Constable Trout, when evidence points strongly to Mrs Quigley as the original anonymous letter writer, you are inserting doubts.'

'I'm not saying you're wrong. Only that I'm far from convinced. It's possible she resented Anne because of her youth and unblemished skin, and coming upon Reverend Pimcrisp up to his antics, thought she'd give the girl a good fright. I can imagine her finding doing so amusing. We also know that she talked about taking sleeping pills and drowning herself without mess in the bath.'

'Yes, you passed that along after going, accompanied by Mrs Fielding to the Quigley's house.'

'I just don't see her rousing from her self-absorption to murder anyone. What I do believe her capable of is going into a fit of rage when she felt her cherished isolation threatened. I'll come back to that later.' She looked at Sally.

'So, you think her husband killed Nurse Newsome and returned home to drown his wife. Why?' LeCrane reached for an ashtray.

'Obsession. It came to me last evening that the two cases, that of Una and her uncontrollable passion for Bill Smith, and the origin of the letters to Anne Rudge were linked by that one word. The difference was that the object of Mr Quigley's desire wasn't a person – a woman. It was a book. The early Bible that he was able to make his own when Lord Asprey, after several delays, gave it to his cousin Reverend Pimcrisp for St Peter's Church.'

Inspector LeCrane was listening intently. As were the rest, who though they were hearing this for the second time, were none the less captivated.

'How do you know there were delays in the bestowing of this Bible, Mrs Norris?'

'My employer, the late Lord Stodmarsh, was a good friend of Lord Asprey, who told him his mother had been a Pimcrisp, that the Bible had been in her family for hundreds of years and that it had been her wish it should be passed to the last of the line, in particular because he was a clergyman. He felt an obligation to honour her wishes. But he disliked his cousin, did not share his strident religious views, but when it came to the point he kept hesitating. I think in the end, he decided to go ahead because St Peter's was in his friend's parish and would remain there long after Pimcrisp was gone.'

'When did Lord Asprey finally make the decision?'

'After the start of the war. I believe it was in fifteen.'

'A couple of years after Anne Rudge's death.'

'My father was also acquainted with Lord Asprey,' said Aiden. 'That's how I came to spend that winter here twenty years ago. I found out later they'd discussed His Lordship's views on Pimcrisp, which put the idea in my father's head that a stay of several months with him would drive the idea of entering the church out of my mind. I recall the story of a family Bible that His Lordship was resistant to handing over. But he was a man with a strong sense of duty. Which has to be the reason his cousin is now living on his estate. A remarkable man.'

Inspector LeCrane lit another cigarette. 'And Quigley would have been aware of the situation?'

'Of course.' Florence and George responded in unison.

'And you're saying that as a collector of rare books, he coveted that Bible above all else?'

'He married for the ones Mrs Quigley brought with her,' said Sophie. 'But he left them, every chance he got, to be with that one in the church that consumed him.'

'I agree wholeheartedly with Florence,' supplied George, 'that Mrs Quigley's motive for murder pales in comparison to his. He must have come upon Pimcrisp up to his antics with Anne Rudge and realized he had to drive her away before anyone else found out what was going on, or he'd never get to hold that Bible in his hands.'

'Very well,' said LeCrane, 'now tell me, why he felt the need to dispose of Nurse Newsome.'

'She nursed him and his wife on different occasions. Once in his case, several years back, when he had a bad case of the flu,' said George. 'It was talked about in the pub at the time and brought up later when people spoke of what a devoted nurse she was. The Quigleys tended to be a topic of interest whenever chance brought them up, because they were viewed as cocooned in secret lives. During that illness, or possibly another, he must have rambled in a delirious state about writing the letters, revealing enough of what was in them to be a problem.'

'His wife knew, must have overheard. Which is why' – Florence looked at Sally – 'she panicked and became enraged when you spoke to her of the likelihood that Nurse Newsome had to be privy to a lot of people's secrets.'

'Tell me about that, Miss Barton.' Inspector LeCrane was now on his third cigarette. After hearing her out, he nodded. 'Interesting.'

'I don't think she cared a jot for her husband, or what became of him,' said Florence, 'but she didn't want her life turned upside down.'

'I'm growing convinced you're on the right track,' responded the inspector. 'Any suggestions how to get him to spill the beans?'

'I have an idea and I want to try it,' said Sophie.

They all looked at her.

'He has to be made to believe he's about to lose that Bible. If Florence tried what I propose, his suspicions would be aroused due to her being known to help the police. And if it were to be Aiden' – she looked at her husband – 'he might be intimidated into taking no action. But he'll see me as a negligible person, dithering and ineffectual, easily dealt with. So this is the plan. I'll go to him, proffering sympathy for his loss and acting upset for him because Aiden, having discovered Reverend Pimcrisp's despicable, unchristian behaviour, has determined the right thing to do is to return the Bible to Lord Asprey. Will in fact be posting it off tomorrow.'

'It could work. Cause him to crack.' LeCrane lit yet another cigarette.

'I don't like it, Sophie.' Aiden put his hand on her shoulder.

'Nor do I,' exclaimed Maude. 'As your sister-in-law I have to speak up. And so would Miss Gillybud if she were here.'

'I think you're right, Sophie,' said Sally. 'I can see it doing the trick and the inspector will make sure you're protected.'

'That means so much coming from you.' Sophie looked at her with grateful affection. 'But I'd like everyone's support, especially yours, Aiden. I know what it's like to be rescued and now I want to do my part to save Anne Rudge from continuing to lie in the dark, buried under that man's evil.'

'I'll tell you what I'll do,' said LeCrane. 'I'll go round and see Quigley now, tell him I'm sure the inquest on his wife will bring a verdict of suicide while the balance of the mind was disturbed. That there'll be no need to delve further into the murder of Nurse Newsome. I'll take Trout with me to take notes. And have him pretend to leave ahead of me, whilst instead hiding himself away. Upstairs if he can do so quietly enough. I'll then telephone from the police station and let you know it's time to move, Mrs Fielding.'

After he was gone Aiden went to the church vestry and brought back the Bible, wrapped in cloth and brown paper. Time passed either too slowly, or too fast, and Sophie was ready in her coat and hat. Maude stood in the hall waiting for the telephone to ring. But when it did so, Aiden picked it up ahead of her. 'Yes,' he said, 'yes. She'll leave now.'

Instantly he and Sophie were alone and she was in his arms. 'I love you,' he said, 'I should have said it before, but I believed you needed time.'

'I love you, too, I did, even at Oglesby.'

'I'm going to follow and be outside the house.' She wasn't able to say anything because he was kissing her. And with courage high, and Bible in hand, she went out the door.

Mr Quigley did not take long to admit her and lead her into his study. Perhaps he thought it was Inspector LeCrane returning with a forgotten question. All went as anticipated. She played her part even better than she'd hoped, stammering out her distress, that in the aftermath of his great loss her husband was intent on returning the Bible to Lord Asprey.

'Oh, Mr Quigley! I'm so sorry because after all you've done to preserve it, this strikes me as unfair to you. The thought of your being caused more pain compelled me to bring it to you, so you can see it one last time.'

It was enough. He went into a frenzy. Screaming out all he'd done to ensure it was his. His! The one thing she learned was that he'd used Miss Gillybud's dressing gown cord to strangle Nurse Newsome.

'Some woman came to the door one day, said she found

it outside our gate. Told her it wasn't ours, but only way I could get rid of her was to take it and say I'd try and find the owner. Automatically I brought it back in here. Set it on the desk and forgot it until Nurse Newsome came last night to tell me she'd worried herself into a state of acute anxiety because she'd remembered me muttering when I was ill with the flu, about writing letters to Anne Rudge and what a relief it'd been when she disappeared. Said she didn't think it right for her to go to the police, the ethics of her job and so on, begged me to confess. She kept picking up that dressing gown cord, twisting in her hands. I told her I'd do what she asked. Knew I couldn't trust her to keep quiet forever, and saw my way out of it. Followed her when she left, came up behind her and shut her up for good. But I had to stop the police from being a nuisance. Came home, lifted my drugged wife out of bed and put an end to her.'

Sophie yelled. Backed away and as Quigley rushed toward her, Constable Trout charged into the room.

'Now, now! None of that!' He might have been admonishing a boy for chasing a cat up a tree, but the effect was remarkable. Quigley crumpled into a shuddering huddle. Inspector LeCrane advanced upon him, and in came Aiden to take her outside and hold her as if he'd never let her go.

'Let's go home, my darling,' he said, but he was not in that much of a hurry because he kissed her lengthily, at first with tender then increasing passion.

'I made it worse for you with Maude,' he at last murmured against her cheek. 'I didn't just tell her, when I got back after collecting you from the train, that I liked and admired you. I said I had fallen desperately in love with you.'

'Oh, dear! That doesn't sound clergyman-like; I can see why she was shocked. And I suspect most of the altar ladies would think her completely in the right. But Aiden, I don't think we need to worry any more about Maude making difficulties. She's already changed, or returned to her real self and Miss Gillybud will take her under her wing. She's a rescuer, not in the way dear Sally is, but a rescuer none-the-less.'

He kissed her again in full view of anyone who happened along Silkwood Way.

'There is one thing that still bothers me,' she told him when she had sufficient breath.

'What's that, my love?'

'The wallpaper in the bedroom is so hideous you'll be afraid to leave the dressing room for it.'

'Let's go home and inspect it. And if necessary, I'll tear it down.'

'I was rather hoping you'd see it that way,' said Sophie. And they walked quickly back to the vicarage.

EPILOGUE

In the subsequent weeks Dovecote Hatch went from the shock and horror that any reasonable community would experience following murder in its midst, to settling back into all the consolations of community that village life offers.

Anne Rudge was laid to rest alongside her parents. No objections being murmured, even by those usually particularly strict in their views on such matters, about her being allowed within the confines of consecrated ground. Her brother Tim wrote to George thanking him for listening to his story and all that he and Mrs Norris had done on Anne's behalf. Adding that he hoped when he returned to visit her grave the three of them could spend some time together.

Maude joined a whist club organized by Mrs North and talked about taking a trip to Greece with an old school friend following frequent discussions with Miss Gillybud on the *Iliad*, which led to their reading *The Odyssey* together and both pitying poor Penelope stuck at home weaving and unweaving day and night. She was interested in buying a house on a lane off Silkwood Way that had become available.

Sophie and Aiden had their bedroom repapered and the library restored. She thought at times about Mrs Crawley and the children, especially Sam, increasing her interest in providing a place where mothers could bring their children for a few hours during the week. Aiden contacted a clergyman in the area where they lived who paid them a visit to look into their welfare and offer help. Their boxer puppy arrived courtesy of Miss Milligan. He and Marmalade at first thought they didn't like each other but quickly changed their minds. Sophie decided to name him Jam.

George asked Dick Saunders if he would like to work at the Dog and Whistle full time, allowing himself more time off in future. The offer was gladly accepted and much discussed with Sally.

And on a fine, sunny morning, George and Florence, following the reception at Mullings, went home to Orchard House, to begin their long awaited and, therefore the more treasured, lives together.